REACH OUT FROM EARTH TO THE STARS!

Crusifixus Etiam—Before he can conquer the planets, man must first discover how to stop breathing. . . .

Four in One—When humans and amoeba meet, who shall prove triumphant, the one cell or the many?

The Nine Billion Names of God—When a computer undertakes a religious mission, will it unlock the secrets of our universe to find our beginnings . . . or our end?

Warm—When a voice called for help from the depths of his mind, how could he do anything but think out a rescue?

ISAAC ASIMOV PRESENTS THE GREAT SF STORIES 15

ISAAC ASIMOV

PRESENTS

THE GREAT SF STORIES

#15

(1953)

EDITED BY ISAAC ASIMOV AND MARTIN H. GREENBERG

DAW BOOKS, INC.

DONALD A. WOLLHEIM, PUBLISHER

1633 Broadway, New York, NY 10019

First DAW Printing, December 1986

1 2 3 4 5 6 7 8 9

PRINTED IN THE U.S.A.

ACKNOWLEDGMENTS

Sturgeon—Copyright 1953 by Galaxy Publishing Corporation; copyright renewed © 1981 by Theodore Sturgeon. Reprinted by permission of Kirby McCauley, Ltd.

Knight—Copyright 1953 by Galaxy Publishing Corporation; copyright renewed © 1981 by Damon Knight. Reprinted by permission of the author.

Leiber—Copyright 1953 by Fantasy House, Inc.; renewed © 1981 by Fritz Leiber. From *The Magazine of Fantasy and Science Fiction*. Reprinted by permission of Richard Curtis Associates, Inc.

Miller—Copyright 1953 by Street & Smith Publications, Inc.; renewed © 1981 by Walter M. Miller, Jr. Reprinted by permission of Don Congdon Associates, Inc.

Tenn—Copyright 1953 by Columbia Publications, Inc.; copyright 1955 by William Tenn; copyright renewed © 1981 by William Tenn. Reprinted by permission of the author and the author's agent, Virginia Kidd.

Moore—Copyright 1953 by Fantasy House, Inc.; copyright renewed © 1981 by Mercury Press, Inc.; reprinted by permission of Virginia Kidd, Literary Agent, on behalf of the Estate of Ward Moore. From *The Magazine of Fantasy and Science Fiction*.

Clarke—Copyright 1953; renewed © 1981 by Arthur C. Clarke. Reprinted by permission of the Scott Meredith Literary Agency, Inc., 845 Third Avenue, New York, NY 10022.

Sheckley—Copyright 1953 by Galaxy Publishing Corporation; renewed © 1981 by Robert Sheckley. Reprinted by permission of Kirby McCauley, Ltd.

Dick—Copyright 1953 by Street & Smith Publications, Inc.; renewed © 1981 by Philip K. Dick. Reprinted by permission of the agents for the author's Estate, the Scott Meredith Literary Agency, Inc., 845 Third Avenue, New York, NY 10022.

Sturgeon—Copyright 1953; renewed © 1981 by Theodore Sturgeon. Reprinted by permission of Kirby McCauley, Ltd.

Contents

INTRODUCTION

In the world outside reality the year got off to a good start with the inauguration of Dwight David Eisenhower as President of the United States. Then, on March 5 Joseph Stalin died, meaning that new leaders were at the head of the two most powerful nations on Earth. A wave of relief swept over the Soviet Union as a power struggle began that would eventually see Nikita Khrushchev emerge supreme in the U.S.S.R., but not until the elimination of the hated chief of the Secret Police, Beria, who was executed by his rivals late in the year. On March 31 Dag Hammarskjold of Sweden was elected Secretary General of the United Nations.

On April 2 Jomo Kenyatta was found guilty of Mau Mau crimes as the African continent seethed with nationalism. Elizabeth became Queen Elizabeth II of Great Britain on June 2, while on the 19th Julius and Ethel Rosenberg were executed for supplying atomic secrets to the Soviets. The Korean War finally came to an end on July 27 with the signing of an armistice agreement at Panmunjom, but an ominous cloud rose as the Soviet Union detonated its first hydrogen bomb on August 29.

During 1953 Ian Fleming published *Casino Royale*, the first of the James Bond series, while J.B. Rhine's *The New World Of The Man* explored parapsychology, a subject that would be too fully explored in the science fiction of the 1950s. Chagall painted his "Eiffel Tower." *Kismet* was a hit musical on Broadway as Lipmann and Krebs won the Noble Prize for Medicine for their research into the nature of living cells. The great Maureen Connolly won the Grand Slam of women's tennis with victories in Australia, the U.S., England, and France. Arthur Miller's *The Crucible* was one of many outstanding dramatic productions in the United States. B.F. Skinner published his influential work on behavioral psychology, *The New World Of The Mind*, while Henry Moore sculpted "King and Queen."

Ben Hogan had a terrific year, winning the Masters, the U.S. Open, and the British Open. Winston S. Churchill won the Nobel Prize for Literature for his writing on World War II, but Martin Heidegger's *Introduction To Metaphysics* was a better book. Outstanding films included *Julius Caesar, The Robe, Roman Holiday, The Living Desert,* and the great *From Here To Eternity.* Leonard Bernstein's *Wonderful Town* was another good Broadway musical. Hillary and his guide Tenzing did the impossible by climbing Mount Everest. The long shot Dark Star upset the heavily favored Native Dancer to win the Kentucky Derby. Saul Bellow wrote *The Adventures of Augie March,* while Simone de Beauvoir's *The Second Sex* caused a sensation. The top songs of the year included "I Believe," "How Much Is That Doggie in the Window," the beautiful "Ebb Tide," "Stranger in Paradise," and "I Love Paris."

The first clear evidence linking lung cancer with cigarette smoking was published in 1953, the year that Kinsey's *Sexual Behavior In The Human Female* made its appearance. Wisconsin lost the Rose Bowl game to Southern Cal by seven points. *Battle Cry* by Leon Uris was a bestseller, but the Dodgers lost the World Series to the Yankees again—revenge was now only two years away.

Death took Dylan Thomas, Hilaire Belloc, Eugene O'Neill, Sergei Prokofiev, tennis great Bill Tilden, Senator Robert A. Taft, and Richard von Mises.

Mel Brooks was no longer Melvin Kaminsky and

hadn't been for many years—sorry about that, Mel.

In the real world it was another outstanding year as the paperback book revolution took hold and a number of outstanding novels, including several that became landmarks in the field, were published, including *The Demolished Man* by Alfred Bester, *More Than Human* by Theodore Sturgeon, *Childhood's End* by Arthur C. Clarke, *Ring Around The Sun* by Clifford D. Simak, *Bring The Jubilee* by Ward Moore, *The Sword of Rhiannon* by Leigh Brackett, and *Children Of The Atom* by Wilmar H. Shiras.

More wondrous things were happening as six important writers made their maiden voyages into reality: James White with "Assisted Passage" in January; John Brunner with "Thou Good and Faithful" in March; and Marion Zimmer Bradley with "For Women Only," Tom Godwin with "The Gulf Between," Arthur Sellings with "The Haunting," and Anne McCaffrey with "Freedom of the Race," all in October (not a bad month).

Two magazines were born and died within the confines of 1953—*Rocket Stories* and *Space Stories*. *Famous Fantastic Mysteries* and *Science Fiction Plus* were the third and fourth fatalities of the year. However, they were replaced by four new ones that made it through the year and in a couple of cases beyond—*Science Fiction Stories*, the latest version of a magazine that had had many incarnations; *Beyond Fantasy Fiction*, a sister publication to *Galaxy; Orbit Science Fiction;* and *Fantastic Universe Science Fiction*, which, under the editorship of Leo Margulies and Sam Merwin, would make its mark on the genre.

The real people gathered for the eleventh time as the World Science Fiction Convention met in Philadelphia. This was a particularly important Worldcon, because it was here that the first Science Fiction Achievement Awards (the Hugos) were given out, an event that is now one of the highlights of any Worldcon. The first winners were: Alfred Bester, Best Novel for *The Demolished Man; Astounding Science Fiction* and *Galaxy Science Fiction*, Best Professional Magazines; Virgil Finlay, Best Interior Illustration; Ed Emshwiller and Hannes Bok, Best Cover Artists; Willy Ley, Excellence in Fact Articles; Philip José Farmer, Best New Author; and Forrest J Ackerman, #1 Fan Personality.

Science fiction movies came hot and heavy during 1953, including *Donovan's Brain*, the underrated *Four-Sided Triangle*, the excellent *Invaders From Mars*, *The War Of The Worlds*, *The Maze*, *The Twonky*, *It Came From Outer Space*, *The Beast From 20,000 Fathoms*, and three unforgettable Masterpieces—*Abbot and Costello Go To Mars*, *Mesa Of Lost Women*, and *Cat-Women Of The Moon*.

Let us travel back to that honored year of 1953 and enjoy the best stories that the real world bequeathed to us.

THE BIG HOLIDAY

FRITZ LEIBER (1910–   )
THE MAGAZINE OF FANTASY AND
SCIENCE FICTION, JANUARY

*Isaac, what do you think is the problem with this won-
derful story? It made some immediate impact, since it
was selected for inclusion in Everett F. Bleiler and Ted
Dikty's* The Best Science Fiction Stories: 1954 *(which
covered 1953), beating out many excellent stories in a
strong year for sf. It then disappeared for some twenty
years, never being anthologized again, and Leiber never
included it in any of the many collections of his stories
published between 1954 and 1974. It does appear in*
The Best of Fritz Leiber *(1974), but hasn't been reprinted since then. I can't understand how a story of
this quality could have been missed or found unworthy
by the many excellent anthologists working in our field.*

*We should mention at this point that Bleiler and
Dikty chose thirteen stories for their book, six of which
(two by Leiber, and one each by Miller, Morrison,
Bester, and Moore) we feel have stood the test of time
and appear in this retrospective anthology. A good
batting average.*

—MHG

*My own theory, Marty, is that "The Big Holiday" is,
to a large extent, a "mood piece," and such a thing
requires a more educated taste than a "simple story"
does.*

At the other end of the spectrum, in place of a story that pulls the emotional strings, there is one that pulls the cerebral strings and that gives us a "think piece."

Sometimes it is conceivable that we can have a story that does both at once.

However, whether you have a mood piece, or a think piece, or a combination, you are in trouble because you may end up just hitting a corner of the audience.

A simple story, that is an "event piece," one in which things happen one after the other, a leading to b leading to c and so on, with a beginning, middle and end, usually hits the audience in the center so that more people enjoy it. The intensity of the enjoyment may not be as great as that experienced by the smaller number who like a well-done mood piece or think piece, but very frequently it is numbers, not intensity, that counts.

I didn't intend to make this headnote a mini-lecture, but you asked me a question, Marty, and where I'm involved that is sometimes a near-fatal mistake. —And, by the way, before anyone writes to inform us of it, I know very well that most of my fiction consists of simple stories. We all do what we can.

—IA

THE WHISTLES BLEW. A thousand hands switched off pocket radios and wall-size television screens, right in the middle of the Martian newscast. Another 500 all around the town locked the motors of sky scooters and ground buggies. A dozen cash registers rang up lucky last sales and were silent, locked. Two thousand throats breathed a sigh of relief. Two thousand hearts began to warm.

The whistles blew. Mrs. Pullen slammed a last batch of cookies into the electronic oven, counted to ten, switched it off, wiped her face, and stood there beaming at the fragrant towers of her handiwork—a gray-haired princess in a cookie castle. Mrs. Goldfarb smiled at her brown and cream-flecked woodpiles of blintzes. Mr. Gianelli, his eyes watering with heat and spices, admired his steaming log-jams of Italian sausage.

Widowed Mr. Tomlinson was contemplating his bowls of hardboiled eggs when a goddess shot him in the back with a silver arrow. He turned around and commented, "That tunic is a bit daring, pet." His daughter, new to grown-up life as a pussy willow, waved her plastic bow and said, "I'm going as Diana." Mr. Tomlinson mused, "Ah, the fleet-footed huntress."

The whistles blew. Mr. Jingles, so called by the children for the silver coins he always carried, emptied his pockets of them, added his green money, put it all away in the top drawer of his dresser. Everywhere else in the town billfolds and purses disappeared. Offices closed. Secretaries sprayed their noses with powder and fluttered into their cloudlike electrosilk coats.

Mr. Debevois tore a May-something 207 date-sheet off his desk calendar, made a paper dart of it, and shot it at his lagging stenographer, who was stooping to return a folder of microfilm to a bottom file drawer. Storekeepers took off their aprons and walked out, leaving doors unlocked. Plump Mr. Wilson pressed a button and a sign appeared on the movie house marquee: NO SHOW TONIGHT. Beardy Mr. Goldfarb shrugged, smiled, put away a sheaf of teleflashed stock reports, unbuttoned a great big drawer and took out a great big parchment scroll. School children tore off across the soft sandy schoolyard and green lawns slippery with sunlight. Down at the little aluminum station the atomic train inched to a stop like a golden caterpillar and the engineer jumped out in his best clothes.

The whistles blew. Mr. Moriarty, the town mortician, with black-clad limbs thin as a spider's and hat tall as Abraham Lincoln's, looked around at the bare gleaming tables and rubbed his hands. He opened a big thick icebox door and looked into two coffins. "They'll keep," he said. He opened another and looked at the empty shelves and nodded. "In case anybody has the bad luck to die the next three days," he said. Then the spiderweb of wrinkles all over his face contracted in a smile. He said softly, "Or maybe that would be the nicest time of year to go."

The whistles stopped. From back of the firehouse, around the lovely new red-vaned fire-copter, twenty pairs of strong hands pushed an old-fashioned automobile, a convertible, black and fat as sin, armored with chromium and sprouting three antennae—for radio, phone, and television. They shoved it across the street with a shout and it jounced to rest in front of the courthouse, its antennae quivering.

While toward the courthouse square, down the leaf-bowered streets silent of traffic, 4,000 big and little feet came pounding.

In the empty schoolhouse, before the mirror in the girls' room, Miss Kidd decided that her inch-long eyelashes were securely attached. She painted her sultry lips, then almost ruined them making anguished faces as she tugged at the girdle borrowed from the museum. Pausing to catch her breath, she leafed with morbid curiosity through the pile of themes her class had turned in. They were all titled "The Big Holiday." The first one began:

By some it is thot that the Big Holiday started with the merrimaking of the Pre-lentin festeval at Reo D. Janero . . .

She hastily turned to the next.

In the olden times of the 20th Century, people didn't injoy holidays very much. They worred too much about making money and buying and selling. They even tried to sell each other, like in the very faroff times of slavery. . . .

(Besides this, Miss Kidd had red-penciled, "*Sell* a person on something. Old idiom. Means to persuade to buy, or convince of worth; has nothing to do with slavery.")

Resisting further temptation, Miss Kidd turned the themes face down and got back to work. She pinned together the plunging neckline of her antique cocktail dress, hesitated, then recklessly unpinned it. She put on a weird picture hat about three feet across, tossed a mink fur around her shoulders. "The fourth grade will have things to say about you," she told her reflection and hobbled out on unfamiliar French heels.

In the barber shop Mr. Felton, the town drunkard, lifted incredulous fingers to his fresh-shaven, lotioned cheeks. He watched the mirror with a beery wonder as they clad him in silk shirt, stiff collar, and a pin-striped suit. He gaped with delight as they draped a huge gold watch-chain across his paunch and speared his tie with a blinding diamond pin. Mr. Kantarian, the barber, stood back, walked around, and curtly nodded his approval.

Mr. Wilson stepped into a money bag with arms and legs, tightened the drawstring around his neck, and put on a golden crown. A thought struck him and he got out his pocketbook. "It isn't breaking a holiday rule," he reassured himself, "if I use the junk as a stage property." And he artistically stuffed twenty or thirty dollar bills into his neckband. Then he walked out of his movie house.

The square was already a-chatter and a-swirl with the town's two thousand. Mr. Wilson, conscious of the dignity of his role, ignored the attention he attracted. At the firehouse corner he was joined by Miss Kidd and Mr. Felton. The drunkard eyed the crowd, then stiffened his back. With ritualistic solemnity the three walked to the fat black convertible. There they were met by Mr. Moriarty, whose spider-webbed face was set in the gloomiest lines. He tipped his stovepipe hat and opened the rear door for Miss Kidd and Mr. Felton, then got in front beside Mr. Wilson, who had taken the wheel.

There was a shot and a puff of smoke. A figure in track pants and shirt emblazoned with golden bolts of lightning took off from across the square. He sped like the wind, the propeller of his beanie making a golden glory over his bent head. A goddess with a plastic bow gave an excited little yip. Mr. Tomlinson lifted a comprehending brow and remarked to her, "Jim Kelly, pet? So that's why you need to be fleet-footed."

"He's awfully shy, too," she told him frankly.

Meanwhile the speedy topic of their conversation had sprung up on the back of the seat behind Mr. Wilson and begun pounding him on his money-green ruff and pointing frantically to the big old alarm clock strapped to his own wrist.

A dark man beat on a drum. Things got quiet. Mr. Goldfarb unrolled his parchment, cleared his throat, directed a severe stare at the occupants of the black car, and recited loudly, "Hear ye! Hear ye! Know all men here present that for the good of our hearts and minds and souls, the following creatures are banished from town.

"First," he said, eyeing Mr. Wilson, "Money! Because he's a tryant, a very Midas who turns the moon to two bits and the green grass to dingy green paper.

"Second," (Mr. Felton beamed as the stern gaze turned his way). "Success! Because he goes around with the wrong sort of people—I mean the gentleman I referred to first and the lady I'm referring to next." He looked at Miss Kidd. "Glamour! Because she's a huzzy who doesn't play fair. We like girls too much to let them be used to help sell soft drinks.

"And finally," he went on, turning to Jim Kelly and Mr. Moriarty, "Hurry and Worry! The one because while he's a good boy on a trip to Mars or the doctor, he's too hard on our hearts. The other—Worry—because he aids and abets all four aforementioned."

Mr. Jingles stepped up and began to tootle the funeral march, while dark Mr. Ambrose rumbled his drums ever so softly.

Mr. Goldfarb concluded, "These five are directed to leave town at once without pause or prayer. If they—or any of their equally guilty accomplices, such as Work, War, and Glory—should venture within the town limits during the next three days, we will violate the Constitution and visit upon them various cruel and unusual punishments."

He rolled up the parchment, folded his arms, stuck out his beard, and said, "Now, get!"

Mr. Wilson stamped on the starter. The exhaust puffed nose-wrinkling blue smoke. The fat black car moved forward ponderously. Ahead the bright-clad people lined up on either side, like rows of flowers.

"Goodby," they called.

They waved at Mr. Wilson. "Goodby, Money." He stared solemnly ahead, intent on steering.

"Goodby, Success," they called to Mr. Felton. Forgetting character, he waved happily back.

"Goodby, Glamour," they called to Miss Kidd. She smiled at them scornfully, threw back her shoulders, looked down her plunging neckline, gathered her courage and held her position.

"Goodby, Hurry. Goodby, Worry," they called to Jim Kelly and Mr. Moriarty. The latter creased his brow and shook his head doomfully. The sprinter wildly pleaded with Wilson for more speed.

The car passed between Mason's Hardware and the town's sole skyscraper, a ten-story glastic skylon. Buckets of black confetti filled the air, snowed on the car, peppered Miss Kidd with beauty spots. Black paper streamers unrolled lazily downward, snagged chromium grills, dragged behind like a black fringe.

Moving majestically always, the car reached the schoolyard with its new-gathered ranks of children. A line of third and fourth grade boys raised cap pistols and solemnly discharged them. "Goodby, Hurry. Goodby, Worry." A few fourth graders called, "Goodby, Miss Kidd!" and some added, "Goodby, themes," but their voices were lost.

One boy, greatly daring, darted in front of the car, planted two suction-cupped black plumes on the hood, and skipped away. They waved like black banderillas in the shoulders of a sluggish black bull.

"Goodby, Money. Goodby, Success. Goodby, Glamour.

"Goodby, goodby, goodby."

A half mile out of town, just beyond the flower-gay

cemetery, Mr. Wilson parked the fat black car. They all got out and took suitcases from the trunk compartment, changed to regular holiday clothes and strolled back to join the fun, half-listening to a bibulous harangue by Mr. Felton on the pros and cons of the Big Holiday.

"Who's your girl friend this time?" Miss Kidd asked Jim Kelly with teacher-like camaraderie, but he blushed and sidled away without answering.

Two blocks off they could hear Mr. Pullen, the banker, sawing on his fiddle. Right in the dappling shade in front of the courthouse, Mr. Jingles was twittering with his flute. Dark Mr. Ambrose was making his drums talk gay. The whole village band was tuning its happiness to sound. Around, streams of women were piling tables high. Suddenly there was a rush to the west side of the square. Up Main Street, swept speckless for dancing, creaked a museum carriage, pulled like a rickshaw by half the eighth grade boys. Out of it jumped Mr. Ferguson, the butcher, dressed in a domino, face red with glee. He lifted down a girl dressed in white like a nymph or a bride. Seeing her in the insurance office, you'd never have guessed that Miss Wolzynski could look so pretty.

"Welcome, Friendship! Welcome, Love!"

Up from the back of the carriage, yawning and armstretching, rose tall Mr. Gutknecht, teacher and town historian, dressed like an oldtime farmer, with hay in his hair.

"Welcome, Laziness!"

Clang! Up popped a magnesium manhole cover and out shot Joe Turner, the town policeman, dressed in motley with a bladder on a stick.

"Welcome, Fun!"

Fun chased Mr. Ferguson, chased Miss Wolzynski, chased Mr. Gutknecht, who wouldn't be chased and only yawned as the bladder bounced off his back.

Buzz-buzz. A silver ambulance-copter droned over the square. Down snowed bushels of flowers. Down came a silken line. And down that, on a flower-decked parachute in a flower-decked dress, came Jenny, waitress at the Skylon Cafe. Her hair was so full of flowers you'd need to have seen her before to know it was corn-colored.

"Welcome, Joy!"

Mr. Goldfarb smiled at everything, wiped his forehead and his neck under his beard, and wrapped comradely fingers around a lapel of Mr. Wilson, who had just got back.

"Say," he said, "did you notice in the last flash that Amalgamated Planetoid shares have climbed to—"

Biff! Fun's bladder dented Mr. Goldfarb's fuzzy homburg and Fun roared triumphantly, "Caught you talking news, Mr. Goldfarb! Next you'll be reading inch-thick newspapers, like the ancients did to pass away holidays. The forfeit is to wear your hat upside down for the next three days."

Mr. Goldfarb shrugged happily, upended the homburg so he looked like an ancient bearded sailor, and headed for the food tables.

Things got livelier. Rotary, Baptist Church, Volunteer Fire Department, and Space Veterans put on acts and skits—just little stuff, the big shows were for tomorrow: the town's own live movies on real stages, the town's own lifesize TV shows without screens, ballets they danced themselves, games they played with their own hands, races they ran with their own feet, poetry they read with their own mouths—not to mention an original epic by Mr. Tomlinson entitled *Roosevelt's Farewell.*

People laughed, people talked, people milled, people mocked, people got it off their chests. It got dark. Small children were herded off to dormitories to be told wonderful stories by parents who baby-sat by turns. The square blossomed with bobbing lanterns. People ate quite a bit and drank quite a little. Space was cleared in the street and the dancing started.

Mr. Felton weaved up to Mr. Wilson, decided that this was the man he'd been arguing with in the dark for a long, long time. "Look," he said with brotherly aggressiveness, "I don't hold with those folk who say

America never had any good holidays and parties until now. Why, America's the home of holidays." His aplomb became professiorial and his tongue began to trip more lightly than any sober man's possibly could. "There's the clambake, the cocktail party, the Sunday school picnic, the convention, the moon-jaunt, the field day, the jam session, the ten-way telephone call, the treasure hunt, the week end, the round-the-world-in-a-day-and-a-half—" He gulped a huge breath and grabbed tight to Mr. Wilson, who showed signs of edging off. "—the pub crawl, the night-to-howl, the barbecue, the wiener roast, the Sunday copter soar, the Kentucky frolic, the county fair, the retreat, the psychodrama, the psychoanalysis, the space-scoot, the blanket party, bundling, the revival, the over-the-top-of-the-world, and the fishing trip!" He waved his arms wildly and proclaimed, "They had Christmas, New Year's, Labor Day, Mother's Day, Father's Day, Sweetest Day—oh, and all sorts of holidays a man might enjoy with pleasure and profit. Only—" (and he hiccuped wisely) "—they got just a little too profitable."

Miss Kidd, dressed like Cleopatra, glided in front of Mr. Wilson. He put his arms around her.

"I've always wanted to know what it was like to kiss a schoolteacher," he said.

"Now you know," she told him three seconds later.

"Yes, I do," he agreed in awed tones, as Mr. Felton swayed off through the dancers.

It got real dark. New lights flamed and flared. The music got faster. Miss Kidd danced with Mr. Gutknecht. Mr. Felton swooped around with Mrs. Goldfarb. Mr. Kantarian danced with Mrs. Ferguson. Mr. Gianelli danced with Mrs. Lovesmith. Mr. Moriarty danced with Jenny and the wrinkles danced right off his face, maybe into his ears or under his collar. Octavia Tomlinson went to ask Jim Kelly to dance with her, but he saw her coming and ran away into the dark. So Diana strung a silver arrow to her plastic bow and went hunting.

Joy spun and flowers sprang from her dress, joined those underfoot. Friendship waltzed with Love, Fun cut didoes, while Laziness smiled and snoozed by turns. Dark shopfronts all around the square reflected a whirling rout of colors. But overhead there was nothing to turn back the happy hues and they shot upward, through air untroubled by radio waves or the roar of jets, to join those from a hundred thousand other towns on Earth and Mars, and flash a gay message to the twinkling, friendly stars.

CRUCIFIXUS·ETIAM

ASTOUNDING SCIENCE FICTION, FEBRUARY
WALTER M. MILLER, JR. (1922–   )

*The roughly forty short stories, novelettes, and novellas
published by Walter M. Miller in an eight or nine year
period are a treasure trove for the anthologist. The
average quality is amazingly high, but I believe that
"Crucifixus Etiam" is his finest short story, a wonderful
moving analysis of what it means to be human, of
alienation, and ultimately, of optimism. Walt Miller has
had only two collections,* Conditionally Human *(1962)
and* The View From the Stars *(1964); (The Best of
Walter M. Miller, Jr., 1980, combines these two volumes), and there remain a goodly number of excellent
stories that are not in either book.*

He, is of course, most famous for A Canticle for
Leibowitz *(1960), justly regarded as the seminal post-
holocaust novel. I had the pleasure of co-editing an
anthology on this theme with him,* Beyond Armageddon:
Twenty-One Sermons to the Dead *(1985).*

—MHG

*I always get worried about a title in a foreign lan-
guage. Since I think of titles as integral parts of a story
and as representing a key to what the writer himself/
herself thinks of the story's meaning, I get upset if I
cannot understand it. I think that "Crucifixus Etiam"
may mean "Crucifixion Again," but I'm not sure.*

A passage in the story reminds me of Horace Gold, who was editing Galaxy in 1953. Every editor may have some mad "idee fixe" ("fixed idea," for those who don't want me to use foreign phrases, either.) Certainly I've talked frequently about some of John Campbell's.

As for Horace, he had one that always struck me as particularly peculiar. He was convinced that the world was heading for a period of wild overproduction and that people would be madly forced to consume, consume, consume.

Fred Pohl, either because he believed it, too; or because he thought the idea would make for good satire; or because he simply wanted to oblige Horace; wrote a couple of excellent stories on this theme, and I catch a whiff of it in "Crucifixus Etiam." That makes me wonder if the story were originally intended for Horace, who may have rejected it, so that Walter was forced to turn to Campbell, perhaps at the cost of a different ending.

This is just a speculation, of course, but I'm so used to speculating—

—IA

MANUE NANTI JOINED the project to make some dough. Five dollars an hour was good pay, even in 2134 A.D., and there was no way to spend it while on the job. Everything would be furnished: housing, chow, clothing, toiletries, medicine, cigarettes, even a daily ration of 180 proof beverage alcohol, locally distilled from fermented Martian mosses as fuel for the project's vehicles. He figured that if he avoided crap games, he could finish his five-year contract with fifty thousand dollars in the bank, return to Earth, and retire at the age of twenty-four. Manue wanted to travel, to see the far corners of the world, the strange cultures, the simple people, the small towns, deserts, mountains, jungles—for until he came to Mars, he had never been farther than a hundred miles from Cerro de Pasco, his birthplace in Peru.

A great wistfulness came over him in the cold Martian night when the frost haze broke, revealing the black, gleam-stung sky, and the blue-green Earth-star of his birth. *El mundo de mi carne, de mi alma,* he thought— yet, he had seen so little of it that many of its places would be more alien to him than the homogeneously ugly vistas of Mars. These he longed to see: the volcanoes of the South Pacific, the monstrous mountains of Tibet, the concrete cyclops of New York, the radioactive craters of Russia, the artificial islands in the China Sea, the Black Forest, the Ganges, the Grand Canyon— but most of all, the works of human art, the pyramids, the Gothic cathedrals of Europe, Notre Dame du Chartres, Saint Peter's, the tile-work wonders of Anacapri. But the dream was still a long labor from realization.

Manue was a big youth, heavy-boned and built for labor, clever in a simple mechanical way, and with a wistful good humor that helped him take a lot of guff from whisky-breathed foremen and sharp-eyed engineers who made ten dollars an hour and figured ways for making more, legitimately or otherwise.

He had been on Mars only a month, and it hurt. Each time he swung the heavy pick into the red-brown sod, his face winced with pain. The plastic aerator valves, surgically stitched in his chest, pulled and twisted and seemed to tear with each lurch of his body. The mechanical oxygenator served as a lung, sucking blood through an artificially grated network of veins and plastic tubing, frothing it with air from a chemical generator, and returning it to his circulatory system. Breathing was unnecessary, except to provide wind for talking, but Manue breathed in desperate gulps of the 4.0 psi Martian air; for he had seen the wasted, atrophied chests of the men who had served four or five years, and he knew that when they returned to Earth—if ever—they would still need the auxiliary oxygenator equipment.

"If you don't stop breathing," the surgeon told him, "you'll be all right. When you go to bed at night, turn the oxy down low—so low you feel like panting. There's a critical point that's just right for sleeping. If you get it too low, you'll wake up screaming, and you'll get claustrophobia. If you get it too high, your reflex mechanisms will go to pot and you won't breathe; your lungs'll dry up after a time. Watch it."

Manue watched it carefully, although the oldsters laughed at him—in their dry wheezing chuckles. Some of them could scarcely speak more than two or three words at a shallow breath.

"Breathe deep, boy," they told him. "Enjoy it while you can. You'll forget how pretty soon. Unless you're an engineer."

The engineers had it soft, he learned. They slept in a pressurized barracks where the air was ten psi and twenty-five per cent oxygen, where they turned their oxies off and slept in peace. Even their oxies were self-regulating, controlling the output according to the carbon dioxide content of the input blood. But the Commission could afford no such luxuries for the labor gangs. The payload of a cargo rocket from Earth was only about two per cent of the ship's total mass, and nothing superfluous could be carried. The ships brought the bare essentials, basic industrial equipment, big reactors, generators, engines, heavy tools.

Small tools, building materials, foods, non-nuclear fuels—these things had to be made on Mars. There was an open pit mine in the belly of the Syrtis Major where a "lake" of nearly pure iron-rust was scooped into a smelter, and processed into various grades of steel for building purposes, tools, and machinery. A quarry in the Flathead Mountains dug up large quantities of cement rock, burned it, and crushed it to make concrete.

It was rumored that Mars was even preparing to grow her own labor force. An old-timer told him that the Commission had brought five hundred married couples to a new underground city in the Mare Erythraeum, supposedly as personnel for a local commission headquarters, but according to the old-timer, they were to be paid a bonus of three thousand dollars for every child born on the red planet. But Manue knew that the old "troffies" had a way of inventing such stories, and he reserved a certain amount of skepticism.

As for his own share in the Project, he knew—and needed to know—very little. The encampment was at the north end of the Mare Cimmerium, surrounded by the bleak brown and green landscape of rock and giant lichens, stretching toward sharply defined horizons except for one mountain range in the distance, and hung over by a blue sky so dark that the Earth-star occasionally became dimly visible during the dim daytime. The encampment consisted of a dozen double-walled stone huts, windowless, and roofed with flat slabs of rock covered over by a tarry resin boiled out of the cactuslike spineplants. The camp was ugly, lonely, and dominated by the gaunt skeleton of a drill rig set up in its midst.

Manue joined the excavating crew in the job of digging a yard-wide, six feet deep foundation trench in a hundred yard square around the drill rig, which day and night was biting deeper through the crust of Mars in a dry cut that necessitated frequent stoppages for changing rotary bits. He learned that the geologists had predicted a subterranean pocket of tritium oxide ice at sixteen thousand feet, and that it was for this that they were drilling. The foundation he was helping to dig would be for a control station of some sort.

He worked too hard to be very curious. Mars was a nightmare, a grim, womanless, frigid, disinterestedly evil world. His digging partner was a sloe-eyed Tibetan nicknamed "Gee" who spoke the Omnalingua clumsily at best. He followed two paces behind Manue with a shovel, scooping up the broken ground, and humming a monotonous chant in his own tongue. Manue seldom heard his own language, and missed it; one of the engineers, a haughty Chilean, spoke the modern Spanish, but not to such as Manue Nanti. Most of the other laborers used either Basic English or the Omnalingua. He spoke both, but longed to hear the tongue of his people. Even when he tried to talk to Gee, the cultural gulf was so wide that satisfying communication was nearly impossible. Peruvian jokes were unfunny to Tibetan ears, although Gee bent double with gales of laughter when Manue nearly crushed his own foot with a clumsy stroke of the pick.

He found no close companions. His foreman was a narrow-eyed, orange-browed Low German named Vögeli, usually half-drunk, and intent upon keeping his lung-power by bellowing at his crew. A meaty, florid man, he stalked slowly along the lip of the excavation, pausing to stare coldly down at each pair of laborers who, if they dared to look up, caught a guttural tongue-lashing for the moment's pause. When he had words for a digger, he called a halt by kicking a small avalanche of dirt back into the trench about the man's feet.

Manue learned about Vögeli's disposition before the end of his first month. The aerator tubes had become nearly unbearable; the skin, in trying to grow fast to the plastic, was beginning to form a tight little neck where the tubes entered his flesh, and the skin stretched and burned and stung with each movement of his trunk. Suddenly he felt sick. He staggered dizzily against the side of the trench, dropped the pick, and swayed heavily, bracing himself against collapse. Shock and nausea rocked him, while Gee stared at him and giggled foolishly.

"Hoy!" Vögeli bellowed from across the pit. "Get back on that pick! Hoy, there! Get with it—"

Manue moved dizzily to recover the tool, saw patches of black swimming before him, sank weakly back to pant in shallow gasps. The nagging sting of the valves was a portable hell that he carried with him always. He fought an impulse to jerk them out of his flesh; if a valve came loose, he would bleed to death in a few minutes.

Vögeli came stamping along the heap of fresh earth and lumbered up to stand over the sagging Manue in the trench. He glared down at him for a moment, then nudged the back of his neck with a heavy boot. "Get to work!"

Manue looked up and moved his lips silently. His forehead glinted with moisture in the faint sun, although the temperature was far below freezing.

"Grab that pick and get started."

"Can't," Manue gasped. "Hoses—hurt."

Vögeli grumbled a curse and vaulted down into the trench beside him. "Unzip that jacket," he ordered.

Weakly, Manue fumbled to obey, but the foreman knocked his hand aside and jerked the zipper down. Roughly he unbuttoned the Peruvian's shirt, laying open the bare brown chest to the icy cold.

"*No!*—not the hoses, *please!*"

Vögeli took one of the thin tubes in his blunt fingers and leaned close to peer at the puffy, callused nodule of irritated skin that formed around it where it entered the flesh. He touched the nodule lightly, causing the digger to whimper.

"No, please!"

"Stop sniveling!"

Vögeli laid his thumbs against the nodule and exerted a sudden pressure. There was a slight popping sound as the skin slid back a fraction of an inch along the tube. Manue yelped and closed his eyes.

"Shut up! I know what I'm doing."

He repeated the process with the other tube. Then he seized both tubes in his hands and wiggled them slightly in and out, as if to insure a proper resetting of the skin. The digger cried weakly and slumped in a dead faint.

When he awoke, he was in bed in the barracks, and a medic was painting the sore spots with a bright yellow solution that chilled his skin.

"Woke up, huh?" the medic grunted cheerfully. "How you feel?"

"*Malo!*" he hissed.

"Stay in bed for the day, son. Keep your oxy up high. Make you feel better."

The medic went away, but Vögeli lingered, smiling at him grimly from the doorway. "Don't try goofing off tomorrow, too."

Manue hated the closed door with silent eyes, and listened intently until Vögeli's footsteps left the building. Then, following the medic's instructions, he turned his oxy to maximum, even though the faster flow of blood made the chestvalves ache. The sickness fled, to be replaced with a weary afterglow. Drowsiness came over him, and he slept.

Sleep was a dread black-robed phantom on Mars. Mars pressed the same incubus upon all newcomers to her soul: a nightmare of falling, falling, falling into bottomless space. It was the faint gravity, they said, that caused it. The body felt buoyed up, and the subconscious mind recalled down-going elevators, and diving airplanes, and a fall from a high cliff. It suggested these things in dreams, or if the dreamer's oxy were set too low, it conjured up a nightmare of sinking slowly deeper, and deeper in cold black water that filled the victim's throat. Newcomers were segregated in a separate barracks so that their nightly screams would not disturb the old-timers who had finally adjusted to Martian conditions.

But now, for the first time since his arrival, Manue slept soundly, airily, and felt borne up by beams of bright light.

When he awoke again, he lay clammy in the horrifying knowledge that he had not been breathing! It was so comfortable not to breathe. His chest stopped hurting because of the stillness of his rib-case. He felt refreshed and alive. Peaceful sleep.

Suddenly he was breathing again in harsh gasps, and cursing himself for the lapse, and praying amid quiet tears as he visualized the wasted chest of a troffie.

"*Heh heh!*" wheezed an oldster who had come in to readjust the furnace in the rookie barracks. "You'll get to be a Martian pretty soon, boy. I been here seven years. Look at *me*."

Manue heard the gasping voice and shuddered; there was no need to look.

"You just as well not fight it. It'll get you. Give in, make it easy on yourself. Go crazy if you don't."

"Stop it! Let me alone!"

"Sure. Just one thing. You wanta go home, you think. I went home. Came back. You will, too. They all do, 'cept engineers. Know why?"

"Shut up!" Manue pulled himself erect on the cot and hissed anger at the old-timer, who was neither old nor young, but only withered by Mars. His head suggested that he might be around thirty-five, but his body was weak and old.

The veteran grinned. "Sorry," he wheezed. "I'll keep my mouth shut." He hesitated, then extended his hand. "I'm Sam Donnell, mech-repairs."

Manue still glowered at him. Donnell shrugged and dropped his hand.

"Just trying to be friends," he muttered and walked away.

The digger started to call after him but only closed his mouth again, tightly. Friends? He needed friends, but not a troffie. He couldn't even bear to look at them, for fear he might be looking into the mirror of his own future.

Manue climbed out of his bunk and donned his fleeceskins. Night had fallen, and the temperature was already twenty below. A soft sift of icedust obscured the stars. He stared about in the darkness. The mess hall was closed, but a light burned in the canteen and another in the foremen's club, where the men were playing cards and drinking. He went to get his alcohol ration, gulped it mixed with a little water, and trudged back to the barracks alone.

The Tibetan was in bed, staring blankly at the ceiling. Manue sat down and gazed at his flat, empty face.

"Why did you come here, Gee?"

"Come where?"

"To Mars."

Gee grinned, revealing large black-streaked teeth. "Make money. Good money on Mars."

"Everybody make money, huh?"

"Sure."

"Where's the money come from?"

Gee rolled his face toward the Peruvian and frowned. "You crazy? Money come from Earth, where all money come from."

"And what does Earth get back from Mars?"

Gee looked puzzled for a moment, then gathered anger because he found no answer. He grunted a mono-syllable in his native tongue, then rolled over and went to sleep.

Manue was not normally given to worrying about such things, but now he found himself asking, "What am I doing here?"—and then, "What is *anybody* doing here?"

The Mars Project had started eighty or ninety years ago, and its end goal was to make Mars habitable for colonists without Earth support, without oxies and insulated suits and the various gadgets a man now had to use to keep himself alive on the fourth planet. But thus far, Earth had planted without reaping. The sky was a bottomless well into which Earth poured her tools, dollars, manpower, and engineering skill. And there appeared to be no hope for the near future.

Manue felt suddenly trapped. He could not return to Earth before the end of his contract. He was trading five years of virtual enslavement for a sum of money which would buy a limited amount of freedom. But what if he lost his lungs, became a servant of a small aerator for the rest of his days? Worst of all: whose ends was he serving? The contractors were getting rich—on government contracts. Some of the engineers and fore-men were getting rich—by various forms of embezzle-ment of government funds. But what were the people back on Earth getting for their money?

Nothing.

He lay awake for a long time, thinking about it. Then he resolved to ask someone tomorrow, someone smarter than himself.

But he found the question brushed aside. He sum-moned enough nerve to ask Vögeli, but the foreman told him harshly to keep working and quit wondering. He asked the structural engineer who supervised the

building, but the man only laughed, and said: "What do
you care? You're making good money."

They were running concrete now, laying the long
strips of Martian steel in the bottom of the trench and
dumping in great slobbering wheelbarrowfuls of gray-
green mix. The drillers were continuing their tedious
dry cut deep into the red world's crust. Twice a day
they brought up a yard-long cylindrical sample of the
rock and gave it to a geologist who weighed it, roasted
it, weighed it again, and tested a sample of the condensed
steam—if any—for tritium content. Daily, he chalked
up the results on a blackboard in front of the engineering hut, and the technical staff crowded around for a
look. Manue always glanced at the figures, but failed to
understand.

Life became an endless routine of pain, fear, hard
work, anger. There were few diversions. Sometimes a
crew of entertainers came out from the Mare Erythraeum,
but the labor gang could not all crowd in the pressurized staff-barracks where the shows were presented,
and when Manue managed to catch a glimpse of one of
the girls walking across the clearing, she was bundled
in fleeceskins and hooded by a parka.

Itinerant rabbis, clergymen, and priests of the world's
major faiths came occasionally to the camp: Buddhist,
Moslem, and the Christian sects. Padre Antonio Selni
made monthly visits to hear confessions and offer Mass.
Most of the gang attended all services as a diversion
from routine, as an escape from nostalgia. Somehow it
gave Manue a strange feeling in the pit of his stomach
to see the sacrifice of the Mass, two thousand years old,
being offered in the same ritual under the strange dark
sky of Mars—with a section of the new foundation
serving as an altar upon which the priest set crucifix,
candles, relicstone, missal, chalice, paten, ciborium,
cruets, and all the rest. In filling the wine-cruet before
the service, Manue saw him spill a little of the wine-
cruet fluid upon the brown soil—wine, Earth-wine from
sunny Sicilian vineyards, trampled from the grapes by

the bare stamping feet of children. Wine, the rich red blood of Earth, soaking slowly into the crust of another planet.

Bowing low at the consecration, the unhappy Peruvian thought of a prayer a rabbi had sung the week before: "Blessed be the Lord our God, King of the Universe, Who makest bread to spring forth out of the Earth."

Earth chalice, Earth blood, Earth God, Earth worshipers—with plastic tubes in their chests and a great sickness in their hearts.

He went away saddened. There was no faith here. Faith needed familiar surroundings, the props of culture. Here there were only swinging picks and rumbling machinery and sloshing concrete and the clatter of tools and the wheezing of troffies. Why? For five dollars an hour and keep?

Manue, raised in a back-country society that was almost a folk-culture, felt deep thirst for a goal. His father had been a stonemason, and he had labored lovingly to help build the new cathedral, to build houses and mansions and commercial buildings, and his blood was mingled in their mortar. He had built for the love of his community and the love of the people and their customs, and their gods. He knew his own ends, and the ends of those around him. But what sense was there in this endless scratching at the face of Mars? Did they think they could make it into a second Earth, with pine forests and lakes and snow-capped mountains and small country villages? Man was not that strong. No, if he were laboring for any cause at all, it was to build a world so unearthlike that he could not love it.

The foundation was finished. There was very little more to be done until the drillers struck pay. Manue sat around the camp and worked at breathing. It was becoming a conscious effort now, and if he stopped thinking about it for a few minutes, he found himself inspiring shallow, meaningless little sips of air that scarcely moved his diaphragm. He kept the aerator as low as possible, to make himself breathe great gasps that hurt his chest, but it made him dizzy, and he had to increase the oxygenation lest he faint.

Sam Donnell, the troffie mech-repairman, caught him about to slump dizzily from his perch atop a heap of rocks, pushed him erect, and turned his oxy back to normal. It was late afternoon, and the drillers were about to change shifts. Manue sat shaking his head for a moment, then gazed at Donnell gratefully.

"That's dangerous, kid," the troffie wheezed. "Guys can go psycho doing that. Which you rather have: sick lungs or sick mind?"

"Neither."

"I know, but—"

"I don't want to talk about it."

Donnell stared at him with a faint smile. Then he shrugged and sat down on the rock heap to watch the drilling.

"Oughta be hitting the tritium ice in a couple of days," he said pleasantly. "Then we'll see a big blow."

Manue moistened his lips nervously. The troffies always made him feel uneasy. He stared aside.

"Big blow?"

"Lotta pressure down there, they say. Something about the way Mars got formed. Dust cloud hypothesis."

Manue shook his head. "I don't understand."

"I don't either. But I've heard them talk. Couple of billion years ago, Mars was supposed to be a moon of Jupiter. Picked up a lot of ice crystals over a rocky core. Then it broke loose and picked up a rocky crust—from another belt of the dust cloud. The pockets of tritium ice catch a few neutrons from uranium ore—down under. Some of the tritium goes into helium. Frees oxygen. Gases form pressure. Big blow."

"What are they going to do with the ice?"

The troffie shrugged. "The engineers might know."

Manue snorted and spat. "They know how to make money."

"Hey! Sure, everybody's gettin' rich."

The Peruvian stared at him speculatively for a moment. "Señor Donnell, I—"

"Sam'll do."

"I wonder if anybody knows why . . . well . . . why we're really here."

Donnell glanced up to grin, then waggled his head. He fell thoughtful for a moment, and leaned forward to write in the earth. When he finished, he read it aloud.

"A plow plus a horse plus land equals the necessities of life." He glanced up at Manue. "Fifteen Hundred A.D."

The Peruvian frowned with bewilderment. Donnell rubbed out what he had written and wrote again.

"A factory plus steam turbines plus raw materials equals necessities plus luxuries. Nineteen Hundred A.D."

He rubbed it out and repeated the scribbling. "All those things plus nuclear power and computer controls equals a surplus of everything. Twenty-One Hundred A.D."

"So?"

"So, it's either cut production or find an outlet. Mars is an outlet for surplus energies, manpower, money. Mars Project keeps money turning over, keeps everything turning over. Economist told me that. Said if the Project folded, surplus would pile up—big depression on Earth."

The Peruvian shook his head and sighed. It didn't sound right somehow. It sounded like an explanation somebody figured out after the whole thing started. It wasn't the kind of goal he wanted.

Two days later, the drill hit ice, and the "big blow" was only a fizzle. There was talk around the camp that the whole operation had been a waste of time. The hole spewed a frosty breath for several hours, and the drill crews crowded around to stick their faces in it and breathe great gulps of the helium oxygen mixture. But then the blow subsided, and the hole leaked only a wisp of steam.

Technicians came, and lowered sonar "cameras" down to the ice. They spent a week taking internal soundings and plotting the extent of the ice-dome on their charts.

They brought up samples of ice and tested them. The engineers worked late into the Martian nights.

Then it was finished. The engineers came out of their huddles and called to the foremen of the labor gangs. They led the foremen around the site, pointing here, pointing there, sketching with chalk on the foundation, explaining in solemn voices. Soon the foremen were bellowing at their crews.

"Let's get the derrick down!"

"Start that mixer going!"

"Get that steel over here!"

"Unroll that dip-wire!"

"Get a move on! Shovel that fill!"

Muscles tightened and strained, machinery clamored and rang. Voices grumbled and shouted. The operation was starting again. Without knowing why, Manue shoveled fill and stretched dip-wire and poured concrete for a big floor slab to be run across the entire hundred-yard square, broken only by the big pipe-casing that stuck up out of the ground in the center and leaked a thin trail of steam.

The drill crew moved their rig half a mile across the plain to a point specified by the geologists and began sinking another hole. A groan went up from the structural boys: "Not *another* one of these things!"

But the supervisory staff said, "No, don't worry about it."

There was much speculation about the purpose of the whole operation, and the men resented the quiet secrecy connected with the project. There could be no excuse for secrecy, they felt, in time of peace. There was a certain arbitrariness about it, a hint that the Commission thought of its employees as children, or enemies, or servants. But the supervisory staff shrugged off all questions with: "You know there's tritium ice down there. You know it's what we've been looking for. Why? Well—what's the difference? There are lots of uses for it. Maybe we'll use it for one thing, maybe for something else. Who knows?"

Such a reply might have been satisfactory for an

iron mine or an oil well or a stone quarry, but tritium suggested hydrogen-fusion. And no transportation facilities were being installed to haul the stuff away—no pipelines nor railroad tracks nor glider ports.

Manue quit thinking about it. Slowly he came to adopt a grim cynicism toward the tediousness, the back-breaking labor of his daily work; he lived from day to day like an animal, dreaming only of a return to Earth when his contract was up. But the dream was painful because it was distant, as contrasted with the immediacies of Mars: the threat of atrophy, coupled with the discomforts of continued breathing, the nightmares, the barrenness of the landscape, the intense cold, the harshness of men's tempers, the hardship of labor and the lack of a cause.

A warm, sunny Earth was still over four years distant, and tomorrow would be another back-breaking, throat-parching, heart-tormenting, chest-hurting day. Where was there even a little pleasure in it? It was so easy, at least, to leave the oxy turned up all night, and get a pleasant restful sleep. Sleep was the only recourse from harshness, and fear robbed sleep of its quiet sensuality—unless a man just surrendered and quit worrying about his lungs.

Manue decided that it would be safe to give himself two completely restful nights a week.

Concrete was run over the great square and troweled to a rough finish. A glider train from the Mare Erythraeum brought in several huge crates of machinery, cut-stone masonry for building a wall, a shipful of new personnel, and a real rarity: lumber, cut from the first Earth-trees to be grown on Mars.

A building began going up, with the concrete square for foundation and floor. Structures could be flimsier on Mars; because of the light gravity, compression-stresses were smaller. Hence, the work progressed rapidly, and as the flat-roofed structure was completed, the technicians began uncrating new machinery and moving it into the building. Manue noticed that several of the units were computers. There was also a small steam-turbine generator driven by an atomic-fired boiler.

Months passed. The building grew into an integrated mass of power and control systems. Instead of using the well for pumping, the technicians were apparently going to lower something into it. A bomb-shaped cylinder was slung vertically over the hole. The men guided it into the mouth of the pipe casing, then let it down slowly from a massive cable. The cylinder's butt was a multi-contact socket like the female receptacle for a hundred-pin electron tube. Hours passed while the cylinder slipped slowly down beneath the hide of Mars. When it was done, the men hauled out the cable and began lowering stiff sections of pre-wired conduit, fitted with a receptacle at one end and a male plug at the other, so that as the sections fell into place, a continuous bundle of control cables was built up from "bomb" to surface.

Several weeks were spent in connecting circuits, setting up the computers, and making careful tests. The drillers had finished the second well hole, half a mile from the first, and Manue noticed that while the testing was going on, the engineers sometimes stood atop the building and stared anxiously toward the steel skeleton in the distance. Once while the tests were being conducted, the second hole began squirting a jet of steam high in the thin air, and a frantic voice bellowed from the roof top.

"Cut it! Shut it off! Sound the danger whistle!"

The jet of steam began to shriek a low-pitched whine acoss the Martian desert. It blended with the rising and falling *OOOO-awwww* of the danger siren. But gradually it subsided as the men in the control station shut down the machinery. All hands came up cursing from their hiding places, and the engineers stalked out to the new hold carrying Geiger counters. They came back wearing pleased grins.

The work was nearly finished. The men began crating up the excavating machinery and the drill rig and the tools. The control-building devices were entirely automatic, and the camp would be deserted when the station began operation. The men were disgruntled. They had spent a year of hard labor on what they had thought to be a tritium well, but now that it was done, there were no facilities for pumping the stuff or hauling it away. In fact, they had pumped various solutions *into* the ground through the second hole, and the control station shaft was fitted with pipes that led from lead-lined tanks down into the earth.

Manue had stopped trying to keep his oxy properly adjusted at night. Turned up to a comfortable level, it was like a drug, insuring comfortable sleep—and like addict or alcoholic, he could no longer endure living without it. Sleep was too precious, his only comfort. Every morning he awoke with a still, motionless chest, felt frightening remorse, sat up gasping, choking, sucking at the thin air with whining rattling lungs that had been idle too long. Sometimes he coughed violently, and bled a little. And then for a night or two he would correctly adjust the oxy, only to wake up screaming and suffocating. He felt hope sliding grimly away.

He sought out Sam Donnell, explained the situation, and begged the troffie for helpful advice. But the mech-repairman neither helped nor consoled nor joked about it. He only bit his lip, muttered something noncommittal, and found an excuse to hurry away. It was then that Manue knew his hope was gone. Tissue was withering, tubercules forming, tubes growing closed. He knelt abjected beside his cot, hung his face in his hands, and cursed softly, for there was no other way to pray an unanswerable prayer.

A glider train came in from the north to haul away the disassembled tools. The men lounged around the barracks or wandered across the Martian desert, gathering strange bits of rock and fossils, searching idly for a glint of metal or crystal in the wan sunshine of early fall. The lichens were growing brown and yellow, and the landscape took on the hues of Earth's autumn if not the forms.

There was a sense of expectancy around the camp. It could be felt in the nervous laughter, and the easy voices, talking suddenly of Earth and old friends and the smell of food in a farm kitchen, and old half-forgotten tastes for which men hungered: ham searing in a skillet, a cup of frothing cider from a fermenting crock, iced melon with honey and a bit of lemon, onion gravy on homemade bread. But someone always remarked, "What's the matter with you guys? We ain't going home. Not by a long shot. We're going to another place just like this."

And the group would break up and wander away, eyes tired, eyes haunted with nostalgia.

"What're we waiting for?" men shouted at the supervisory staff. "Get some transportation in here. Let's get rolling."

Men watched the skies for glider trains or jet transports, but the skies remained empty, and the staff remained closemouthed. Then a dust column appeared on the horizon to the north, and a day later a convoy of tractor-trucks pulled into camp.

"Start loading aboard, men!" was the crisp command.

Surly voices: "You mean we don't go by air? We gotta ride those kidney-bouncers? It'll take a week to get to Mare Ery! Our contract says—"

"Load aboard! We're not going to Mare Ery yet!"

Grumbling, they loaded their baggage and their weary bodies into the trucks, and the trucks thundered and clattered across the desert, rolling toward the mountains.

The convoy rolled for three days toward the mountains, stopping at night to make camp, and driving on at sunrise. When they reached the first slopes of the foothills, the convoy stopped again. The deserted encampment lay a hundred and fifty miles behind. The going had been slow over the roadless desert.

"Everybody out!" barked the messenger from the lead truck. "Bail out! Assemble at the foot of the hill."

Voices were growling among themselves as the men moved in small groups from the trucks and collected in a milling tide in a shallow basin, overlooked by a low cliff and a hill. Manue saw the staff climb out of a cab and slowly work their way up the cliff. They carried a portable public address system.

"Gonna get a preaching," somebody snarled.

"Sit down, please!" barked the loud-speaker. "You men sit down there! Quiet—quiet, please!"

The gathering fell into a sulky silence. Will Kinley stood looking out over them, his eyes nervous, his hand holding the mike close to his mouth so that they could hear his weak troffie voice.

"If you men have questions," he said, "I'll answer them now. Do you want to know what you've been doing during the past year?"

An affirmative rumble arose from the group.

"You've been helping to give Mars a breathable atmosphere." He glanced briefly at his watch, then looked back at his audience. "In fifty minutes, a controlled chain reaction will start in the tritium ice. The computers will time it and try to control it. Helium and oxygen will come blasting up out of a second hole."

A rumble of disbelief arose from his audience. Someone shouted: "How can you get air to blanket a planet from one hole?"

"You can't," Kinley replied crisply. "A dozen others are going in, just like that one. We plan three hundred, and we've already located the ice pockets. Three hundred wells, working for eight centuries, can get the job done."

"Eight centuries! What good—"

"Wait!" Kinley barked. "In the meantime, we'll build pressurized cities close to the wells. If everything pans out, we'll get a lot of colonists here, and gradually condition them to live in a seven or eight psi atmosphere—which is about the best we can hope to get. Colonists from the Andes and the Himalayas—they wouldn't need much conditioning."

"*What about us?*"

There was a long plaintive silence. Kinley's eyes scanned the group sadly, and wandered toward the Martian horizon, gold and brown in the late afternoon. "Nothing—about us," he muttered quietly.

"Why did we come here?"

"Because there's danger of the reaction getting out of

hand. We can't tell anyone about it, or we'd start a panic." He looked at the group sadly. "I'm telling you now, because there's nothing you could do. In thirty minutes—"

There were angry murmurs in the crowd. "You mean there may be an explosion?"

"There *will* be a limited explosion. And there's very little danger of anything more. The worst danger is in having ugly rumors start in the cities. Some fool with a slip-stick would hear about it, and calculate what would happen to Mars if five cubic miles of tritium ice detonated in one split second. It would probably start a riot. That's why we've kept it a secret."

The buzz of voices was like a disturbed beehive. Manue Nanti sat in the midst of it, saying nothing, wearing a dazed and weary face, thoughts jumbled, soul drained of feeling.

Why should men lose their lungs that after eight centuries of tomorrows, other men might breathe the air of Mars as the air of Earth?

Other men around him echoed his thoughts in jealous mutterings. They had been helping to make a world in which they would never live.

An enraged scream arose near where Manue sat. "They're going to blow us up! They're going to blow up Mars."

"Don't be a fool!" Kinley snapped.

"Fools they call us! We *are* fools! For ever coming here! We got sucked in! Look at *me!*" A pale dark-haired man came wildly to his feet and tapped his chest. "Look! I'm losing my lungs! We're all losing our lungs! Now they take a chance on killing everybody."

"Including ourselves," Kinley called coldly.

"We oughta take him apart. We oughta kill every one who knew about it—and Kinley's a good place to start!"

The rumble of voices rose higher, calling both agreement and dissent. Some of Kinley's staff were looking nervously toward the trucks. They were unarmed.

"You men sit down!" Kinley barked.

Rebellious eyes glared at the supervisor. Several men

who had come to their feet dropped to their haunches again. Kinley glowered at the pale upriser who called for his scalp.

"Sit down, Handell!"

Handell turned his back on the supervisor and called out to the others. "Don't be a bunch of cowards! Don't let him bully you!"

"You men sitting around Handell. Pull him down."

There was no response. The men, including Manue, stared up at the wild-eyed Handell gloomily, but made no move to quiet him. A pair of burly foremen started through the gathering from its outskirts.

"Stop!" Kinley ordered. "Turpin, Schultz—get back. Let the men handle this themselves."

Half a dozen others had joined the rebellious Handell. They were speaking in low tense tones among themselves.

"For the last time, men! Sit down!"

The group turned and started grimly toward the cliff. Without reasoning why, Manue slid to his feet quietly as Handell came near him. "Come on, fellow, let's get him," the leader muttered.

The Peruvian's fist chopped a short stroke to Handell's jaw, and the dull *thud* echoed across the clearing. The man crumpled, and Manue crouched over him like a hissing panther. "Get back!" he snapped at the others. "Or I'll jerk his hoses out."

One of the others cursed him.

"Want to fight, fellow?" the Peruvian wheezed. "I can jerk several hoses out before you drop me!"

They shuffled nervously for a moment.

"The guy's crazy!" one complained in a high voice.

"Get back or he'll kill Handell!"

They sidled away, moved aimlessly in the crowd, then sat down to escape attention. Manue sat beside the fallen man and gazed at the thinly smiling Kinley.

"Thank you, son. There's a fool in every crowd." He looked at his watch again. "Just a few minutes, men. Then you'll feel the Earth-tremor, and the explosion, and the wind. You can be proud of that wind, men. It's new air for Mars, and you made it."

"But we can't breathe it!" hissed a troffie.

Kinley was silent for a long time, as if listening to the distance. "What man ever made his own salvation?" he murmured.

They packed up the public address amplifier and came down the hill to sit in the cab of a truck, waiting.

It came as an orange glow in the south, and the glow was quickly shrouded by an expanding white cloud. Then, minutes later the ground pulsed beneath them, quivered and shook. The quake subsided, but remained as a hint of vibration. Then after a long time, they heard the dull-throated roar thundering across the Martian desert. The roar continued steadily, grumbling and growling as it would do for several hundred years.

There was only a hushed murmur of awed voices from the crowd. When the wind came, some of them stood up and moved quietly back to the trucks, for now they could go back to a city for reassignment. There were other tasks to accomplish before their contracts were done.

But Manue Nanti still sat on the ground, his head sunk low, desperately trying to gasp a little of the wind he had made, the wind out of the ground, the wind of the future. But lungs were clogged, and he could not drink of the racing wind. His big callused hand clutched slowly at the ground, and he choked a brief sound like a sob.

A shadow fell over him. It was Kinley, come to offer his thanks for the quelling of Handell. But he said nothing for a moment as he watched Manue's desperate Gethsemane.

"Some sow, others reap," he said.

"Why?" the Peruvian choked.

The supervisor shrugged. "What's the difference? But if you can't be both, which would you rather be?"

Nani looked up into the wind. He imagined a city to the south, a city built on tear-soaked ground, filled with people who had no ends beyond their culture, no goal but within their own society. It was a good sensible question: Which would he rather be—sower or reaper?"

Pride brought him slowly to his feet, and he eyed Kinley questioningly. The supervisor touched his shoulder.

"Go on to the trucks."

Nanti nodded and shuffled away. He had wanted something to work for, hadn't he? Something more than the reasons Donnell had given. Well, he could smell a reason, even if he couldn't breathe it.

Eight hundred years was a long time, but then—long time, big reason. The air smelled good, even with its clouds of boiling dust.

He knew now what Mars was—not a ten-thousand-a-year job, not a garbage can for surplus production. But an eight-century passion of human faith in the destiny of the race of Man.

He paused short of the truck. He had wanted to travel, to see the sights of Earth, the handiwork of Nature and of history, the glorious places of his planet.

He stooped, and scooped up a handful of the red-brown soil, letting it sift slowly between his fingers. Here was Mars—his planet now. No more of Earth, not for Manue Nanti. He adjusted his aerator more comfortably and climbed into the waiting truck.

FOUR IN ONE

GALAXY SCIENCE FICTION, FEBRUARY
DAMON KNIGHT (1922-   )

The multi-talented Damon Knight returns to the pages of this series (see "To Serve Man" in Vol. 12) with this stunning story. Quietly, without fanfare, this man played an enormous role in shaping modern science fiction as an innovative and excellent editor (of several magazines in the early 1950s and of the Orbit series of original anthologies in the sixties and seventies), as a critic who was perhaps the first insider who systematically demanded more than a sense of wonder in sf, as an organizer and teacher, a founder of the Science Fiction Writers of America and of the legendary Milford Writers Workshop, and not least, as an excellent anthologist. These activities have caused him to be somewhat undervalued as a writer, but his roughly 100 stories, especially but not exclusively those written in the fifties, broke new ground and influenced a whole generation of writers. His story "Babel II" (Beyond, July), narrowly missed inclusion in this book.

Isaac, what are we going to do? We have reached a point in the series where it would take two volumes to accommodate all the worthy stories.

—MHG

In general, chemistry deals with more complex systems than physics does, and biology deals with more complex systems than chemistry does. That's why we know more about physics than about chemistry and more about chemistry than biology (in the deep, what-makes-things-tick sense).

It's not surprising then that a good story involving biology is so much harder to write (and to find) than one involving chemistry or physics. Finding a biological is therefore a special delight and Damon is very good at it. It seems to me that no one can read this story without having it pounded into his consciousness for the rest of his life.

As to your question at the end, Marty, I'm afraid we're stuck. At the present time, we're publishing two of these books each year, which means we're gaining one year per year and in 2050, we'll do The Best of 2049 *and* The Best of 2050 *and our long task will be finished. Of course, neither of us will be alive and nobody else can possibly do the good job we do.*

If now we decided to do two volumes for each year, either DAW Books has to put out a total of four volumes per year or we'll stay forever behind by a fixed number of years. If we decide eventually to divide each year into three volumes or four (think of the number of good science fiction stories published each year now*) we'll start falling behind faster and faster.*

Of course, if we could arrange to live forever—

—IA

I

GEORGE MEISTER HAD once seen the nervous system of a man—a display specimen achieved by coating the smaller fibers until they were coarse enough to be seen, then dissolving all the unwanted tissue and re-placing it by clear plastic. A marvelous job; that fellow on Torkas III had done it. What was his name. . . ? At any rate, having seen the specimen, Meister knew what he himself must look like at the present moment.

Of course, there were distortions. For example, he was almost certain that the distance between his visual center and his eyes was now at least thirty centimeters. Also, no doubt, the system as a whole was curled up and spread out rather oddly, since the musculature it had originally controlled was gone; and he had noticed certain other changes which might or might not be reflected by gross structural differences. The fact remained that he—all that he could still call *himself*—was nothing more than a brain, a pair of eyes, a spinal cord, and a spray of neurons.

George closed his eyes for a second. It was a feat he had learned to do only recently and he was proud of it. That first long period, when he had had no control whatever, had been very bad. He had decided later that the paralysis had been due to the lingering effects of some anesthetic—the agent, whatever it was, that had kept him unconscious while his body was—

Well.

Either that or the neuron branches had simply not yet knitted firmly in their new positions. Perhaps he could verify one or the other supposition at some future time. But at first, when he had only been able to see and not to move, knowing nothing beyond the moment when he had fallen face-first into that mottled green and brown puddle of gelatin . . . that had been upsetting.

He wondered how the others were taking it. There were others, he knew, because occasionally he would feel a sudden acute pain down where his legs used to be, and at the same instant the motion of the landscape would stop with a jerk. That could only be some other brain, trapped like his, trying to move their common body in another direction.

Usually the pain stopped immediately, and George could go on sending messages down to the nerve-endings which had formerly belonged to his fingers and toes, and the gelatinous body would go on creeping slowly forward. When the pains continued, there was nothing to do but stop moving until the other brain quit—in which case George would feel like an unwilling passenger in a very slow vehicle—or try to alter his own movements to coincide, or at least produce a vector with the other brains.

He wondered who else had fallen in. Vivian Bellis? Major Gumbs? Miss McCarty? All three of them? There ought to be some way of finding out.

He tried looking down once more and was rewarded with a blurry view of a long, narrow strip of mottled green and brown, moving sluggishly along the dry stream bed they had been crossing for the last hour or more. Twigs and shreds of dry vegetable matter were stuck to the dusty, translucent surface.

He was improving; the last time, he had only been able to see the thinnest possible edge of his new body.

When he looked up again, the far side of the stream bed was perceptibly closer. There was a cluster of stiff-looking, dark-brown vegetable shoots just beyond, on the rocky shoulder; George was aiming slightly to the left of it. It had been a plant very much like that one that he'd been reaching for when he lost his balance and got himself into this situation.

He might as well have a good look at it, anyhow.

The plant would probably turn out to be of little interest. It would be out of all reason to expect every new life-form to be a startling novelty; and George Meister was convinced that he had already stumbled into the most interesting organism on this planet. Something-or-other *meisterii*, he thought, named after him, of course. He had not settled on a generic term—he would have to learn more about it before he decided—but *meisterii* certainly. It was his discovery and nobody could take it away from him. Or, unhappily, him away from it. Ah, well!

It was a really lovely organism, though. Primitive—less structure of its own than a jellyfish, and only on a planet with light surface gravity like this one could it ever have hauled itself up out of the sea. No brain, no nervous system at all, apparently. But it had the perfect survival mechanism. It simply let its rivals develop highly organized nervous tissue, sat in one place (looking exactly like a deposit of leaves and other clutter) until one of them fell into it, and then took all the benefit.

It wasn't parasitism, either. It was a true sysmbiosis, on a higher level than any other planet, so far as George knew, had ever developed. The captive brain was nourished by the captor; wherefore it served the captive's interest to move the captor toward food and away from danger. *You steer me, I feed you.* It was fair.

They were close to the plant, almost touching it. George inspected it. As he had thought, it was a common grass type.

Now his body was tilting itself up a ridge he knew to be low, although from his eye-level it looked tremendous. He climbed it laboriously and found himself looking down into still another gully. This could probably go on indefinitely. The question was—did he have any choice?

He looked at the shadows cast by the low-hanging sun. He was heading approximately northwest, directly away from the encampment. He was only a few hundred meters away; even at a crawl, he could make the distance easily enough . . . if he turned back.

He felt uneasy at the thought and didn't know why. Then it struck him that his appearance was not obviously that of a human being in distress. The chances were that he looked like a monster which had eaten and partially digested one or more people.

If he crawled into camp in his present condition, it was a certainly that he would be shot at before any questions were asked, and only a minor possibility that narcotic gas would be used instead of a machine rifle.

No, he decided, he was on the right course. The idea was to get away from camp, so that he wouldn't be found by the relief party which was probably searching for him now. Get away, bury himself in the forest, and study his new body: find out how it worked and what he could do with it, whether there actually were others in it with him, and if so, whether there was any way of communicating with them.

It would take a long time, he realized, but he could do it.

Limply, like a puddle of mush oozing over the edge of a tablecloth, George started down into the gully.

Briefly, the circumstances leading up to George's fall into the Something-or-other *meisterii* were as follows:

Until as late as the mid-twenty-first century, a game invented by the ancient Japanese was still played by millions in the eastern hemisphere of earth. The game was called *go*. Although its rules were almost childishly simple, its strategy included more permutations and was more difficult to master than chess.

Go was played at the height of development—just before the geological catastrophe that wiped out most of its devotees—on a board with nine hundred shallow holes, using small pill-shaped counters. At each turn, one of the two players placed a counter on the board, wherever he chose, the object being to capture as much territory as possible by surrounding it completely.

There were no other rules; and yet it had taken the Japanese almost a thousand years to work up to that thirty-by-thirty board, adding perhaps one rank and file per century. A hundred years was not too long to explore all the possibilities of that additional rank and file.

At the time George Meister fell into the gelatinous green-and-brown monster, toward the end of the twenty-third century A.D., a kind of *go* was being played in a three-dimensional field which contained more than ten billion positions. The Galaxy was the board, the positions were star-systems, men were the counters. The loser's penalty was annihilation.

The Galaxy was in the process of being colonized by two opposing federations, both with the highest aims and principles. In the early stages of this conflict, planets had been raided, bombs dropped, and a few battles had even been fought by fleets of spaceships. Later, that haphazard sort of warfare became impossible. Robot fighters, carrying enough armament to blow each other into dust, were produced by the trillion. In the space around the outer stars of a cluster belonging to one side or the other, they swarmed like minnows.

Within such a screen, planets were safe from attack and from any interference with their commerce . . . unless the enemy succeeded in colonizing enough of the surrounding star-systems to set up and maintain a second screen outside the first. It was *go*, played for desperate stakes and under impossible conditions.

Everyone was in a hurry; everyone's ancestors for seven generations had been in a hurry. You got your education in a speeded-up, capsulized form. You mated early and bred frantically. And if you were assigned to an advance ecological term, as George was, you had to work without proper preparation.

The sensible, the obvious thing to do in opening up a new planet with unknown life-forms would have been to begin with at least ten years of immunological study conducted from the inside of a sealed station. After the worst bacteria and viruses had been conquered, you might proceed to a little cautious field work and exploration. Finally—total elapsed time fifty years, say—the colonists would be shipped in.

There simply wasn't that much time.

Five hours after the landing, Meister's team had unloaded fabricators and set up barracks enough to house its 2,628 members.

An hour after that, Meister, Gumbs, Bellis and McCarty had started out across the level cinder and ash left by the transport's tail jets to the nearest living vegetation, six hundred meters away. They were to trace a spiral path outward from the camp site to a distance of a thousand meters, and then return with their specimens—providing nothing too large and hungry to be stopped by machine rifle had previously eaten them.

Meister, the biologist, was so hung down with collecting boxes that his slender torso was totally invisible. Major Gumbs had a survival kit, binoculars and a machine rifle. Vivian Bellis, who knew exactly as much mineralogy as had been contained in the three-month course prescribed for her rating, and no more, carried a light rifle, a hammer and a specimen sack. Miss McCarty—no one knew her first name—had no scientific function. She was the group's Loyalty Monitor. She wore two squat pistols and a bandolier bristling with cartridges. Her only job was to blow the cranium off any team member caught using an unauthorized communicator, or in any other way behaving oddly.

All of them were heavily gloved and booted, and their heads were covered by globular helmets, sealed to their tunic collars. They breathed through filtered respirators, so finely meshed that—in theory—nothing larger than an oxygen molecule could get through.

On their second circuit of the camp, they had struck a low ridge and a series of short, steep gullies, most of them choked with the dusty-brown stalks of dead vegetation. As they started down into one of these, George, who was third in line—Gumbs leading, then Bellis, and McCarty behind George—stepped out onto a protruding slab of stone to examine a cluster of plant stalks rooted on its far side.

His weight was only a little more than twenty kilograms on this planet, and the slab looked as if it were firmly cemented into the wall of the gully. Just the same, he felt it shift under him as soon as his weight was fully on it. He found himself falling, shouted, and caught a flashing glimpse of Gumbs and Bellis, standing as if caught by a high-speed camera. He heard a rattling of stones as he went by. Then he saw what looked like a shabby blanket of leaves and dirt floating toward him, and he remembered thinking, *It looks like a soft landing, anyhow. . . .*

That was all, until he woke up feeling as if he had been prematurely buried, with no part of him alive but his eyes.

Much later, his frantic efforts to move had resulted in the first fractional success. From then on, his field of vision had advanced fairly steadily, perhaps a meter

every fifty minutes, not counting the times when someone else's efforts had interfered with his own.

His conviction that nothing remained of the old George
Meister except a nervous system was not supported by
observation, but the evidence was regrettably strong.
To begin with, the anesthesia of the first hours had
worn off, but his body was not reporting the position of
the torso, head and four limbs he had formerly owned.
He had, instead, a vague impression of being flattened
and spread out over an enormous area. When he tried
to move his fingers and toes, the response he got was so
multiplied that he felt like a centipede.

He had no sense of cramped muscles, such as would
normally be expected after a long period of paralysis—
and he was not breathing. Yet his brain was evidently
being well supplied with food and oxygen; he felt clear-
headed, at ease and healthy.

He wasn't hungry, either, although he had been using energy steadily for a long time. There were, he
thought, two possible reasons for that, depending on
how you looked at it. One, that he wasn't hungry
because he no longer had any stomach lining to contract; two, that he wasn't hungry because the organism
he was riding in had been well nourished by the superfluous tissues George had contributed.

Two hours later, when the sun was setting, it began
to rain. George saw the big, slow falling drops and felt
their dull impacts on his "skin." He didn't know whether
rain would do him any damage or not, but crawled
under a bush with large, fringed leaves just to be on the
safe side. When the rain stopped, it was night and he
decided he might as well stay where he was until morning. He did not feel tired, and it occurred to him to
wonder whether he still needed to sleep. He composed
himself as well as he could to wait for the answer.

He was still wakeful after a long time had passed, but
had made no progress toward deciding whether this
answered the question or prevented it from being answered, when he saw a pair of dim lights coming slowly
and erratically toward him.

*   *   *

George watched them with an attentiveness compounded of professional interest and apprehension. Gradually, as they came closer, he made out that the lights were attached to long, thin stalks which grew from an ambiguous shape below—either light organs, like those of some deep-sea fish, or simply luminescent eyes.

George noted a feeling of tension in himself which seemed to suggest that adrenaline or an equivalent was being released somewhere in his system. He promised himself to follow this lead at the first possible moment; meanwhile, he had a more urgent problem to consider. Was this approaching organism the kind which the Something *meisterii* ate, or the kind which devoured the Something *meisterii?* If the latter, what could he do about it?

For the present, at any rate, sitting where he was seemed to be indicated. The body he inhabited made use of camouflage in its natural, or untenanted state, and was not equipped for speed. So George held still and watched, keeping his eyes half-closed, while he considered the possible nature of the approaching animal.

The fact that it was nocturnal, he told himself, meant nothing. Moths were nocturnal; so were bats—no, the devil with bats, they were carnivores.

The light-bearing creature came nearer, and George saw the faint gleam of a pair of long, narrow eyes below the two stalks.

Then the creature opened its mouth.

It had a great many teeth.

George found himself crammed into some kind of crevice in a wall of rock, without any clear recollection of how he had got there. He remembered a flurry of branches as the creature sprang at him, and a moment's furious pain, and nothing but vague, starlit glimpses of leaves and soil.

How had he got away?

He puzzled over it until dawn came, and then, looking down at himself, he saw something that had not been there before. Under the smooth edge of gelatinous flesh, three or four projections of some kind were visible. It struck George that his sensation of contact with the stone underneath him had changed, too. He seemed to be standing on a number of tiny points instead of lying flat.

He flexed one of the projections experimentally, then thrust it out straight ahead of him. It was a lumpy, single-jointed caricature of a finger or a leg.

II

Lying still for a long time, George Meister thought about it with as much coherence as he could muster. Then he waggled the limb again. It was there, and so were all the others, as solid and real as the rest of him.

He moved forward experimentally, sending the same messages down to his finger-and-toe nerve-ends as before. His body lurched out of the cranny with a swiftness that very nearly tumbled him down over the edge of a minor precipice.

Where he had crawled like a snail before, he now scuttled like an insect.

But how? No doubt, in his terror when the thing with the teeth attacked, he had unconsciously tried to run as if he still had legs. Was that all there was to it?

George thought of the carnivore again, and of the stalks supporting the organs which he had thought might be eyes. That would do as an experiment. He closed his eyes and imagined them rising outward, imagined the mobile stalks growing, growing. . . . He tried to convince himself that he had eyes like that, had always had them, that everyone who was anyone had eyes on stalks.

Surely, something was happening.

George opened his eyes again and found himself looking straight down at the ground, getting a view so close that it was blurred, out of focus. Impatiently, he tried to look up. All that happened was that his field of vision moved forward a matter of ten or twelve centimeters.

It was at this point that a voice shattered the stillness. It sounded like someone trying to shout through half a meter of lard. "Urghh! Lluhh! *Eeraghh!*"

George leaped convulsively, executed a neat turn and swept his eyes around a good two hundred and forty degrees of arc. He saw nothing but rocks and lichens. On a closer inspection, it appeared that a small green and orange larva or grub of some kind was moving past him. George regarded it with suspicion for a long moment, until the voice broke out again:

"Ellfff! Elffneee!"

The voice, somewhat higher this time, came from behind. George whirled again, swept his eyes around—

Around an impossibly wide circuit. His eyes *were* on stalks, and they were mobile whereas a moment ago he had been staring at the ground, unable to look up. George's brain clattered into high gear. He had grown stalks for his eyes, all right, but they'd been limp, just extensions of the jellylike mass of his body, without a stiffening cell-structure or muscular tissue to move them. Then, when the voice had startled him, he'd got the stiffening and the muscles in a hurry.

That must have been what had happened the previous night. Probably the process would have been completed, but much more slowly, if he hadn't been frightened. A protective mechanism, obviously. As for the voice—

George rotated once more, slowly, looking all around him. There was no question about it; he was alone. The voice, which had seemed to come from someone or something standing just behind him, must in fact have issued from his own body.

The voice started again, at a less frantic volume. It burbled a few times, then said quite clearly in a high tenor, "Whass happen? Wheh am I?"

George was floundering in enough bewilderment. He was in no condition to adapt quickly to more new circumstances, and when a large, dessicated lump fell from a nearby bush and bounced soundlessly to within a meter of him, he simply stared at it.

He looked at the hard-shelled object and then at the laden bush from which it had dropped. Slowly, painfully, he worked his way through to a logical conclusion. The dried fruit had fallen without a sound. This was natural, because he had been totally deaf ever since his metamorphosis. But he had heard a voice!

Ergo, hallucination or telepathy.

The voice began again. "Help! Oh, dear, I wish someone would answer!"

Vivian Bellis. Gumbs, even if he affected that tenor voice, wouldn't say, "Oh, dear." Neither would Miss McCarty.

George's shaken nerves were returning to normal. He thought intently, *I get scared, grow legs. Bellis gets scared, grows a telepathic voice. That's reasonable, I guess—her first and only impulse would be to yell*.

George tried to put himself into a yelling mood. He shut his eyes and imagined himself cooped up in a terrifyingly alien medium, without any control or knowledge of his predicament. He tried to shout: "Vivian!"

He went on trying, while the girl's voice continued at intervals. Finally she stopped abruptly in the middle of a sentence.

George said, "Can you hear me?"

"Who's that? What do you want?"

"This is George Meister, Vivian. Can you understand what I'm saying?"

"What—"

George kept at it. His pseudo-voice, he judged, was a little garbled, just as Bellis's had been at first. At last the girl said, "Oh, George—I mean Mr. Meister!" Oh, I've been so frightened. Where are you?"

George explained, apparently not very tactfully, because Bellis shrieked when he was through and then went back to burbling.

George sighed, and said, "Is there anyone else on the premises? Major Gumbs? Miss McCarty? Can you hear me?"

A few minutes later two sets of weird sounds began

almost simultaneously. When they became coherent, it was no trouble to identify the voices.

Gumbs, the big, red-faced professional soldier, shouted, "Why the hell don't you watch where you're going, Meister? If you hadn't started that rock-slide, we wouldn't be in this mess!"

Miss McCarty, who had a grim white face, a jutting jaw, and eyes the color of mud, said coldly, "Meister, all of this will be reported. *All* of it."

It appeared that only Meister and Gumbs had kept the use of their eyes. All four of them had some muscular control, though Gumbs was the only one who had made any serious attempt to interfere with George's locomotion. Miss McCarty, not to George's surprise, had managed to retain a pair of functioning ears.

But Bellis had been blind, deaf and dumb all through the afternoon and night. The only terminal sense-organs she had been able to use had been those of the skin— the perceptors of touch, heat and cold, and pain. She had heard nothing, seen nothing, but she had felt every leaf and stalk they had brushed against, the cold impact of every rain drop, and the pain of the toothy monster's bite. George's opinion of her went up several notches when he learned this. She had been terrified, but she hadn't been driven into hysteria or insanity.

It further appeared that nobody was doing any breathing and nobody was aware of a heartbeat.

George would have liked nothing better than to continue this discussion, but the other three were united in believing that what had happened to them after they got in was of less importance than how they were going to get out.

"We can't get *out*," said George. "At least, I don't see any possibility of it in the present state of our knowledge. If we—"

"But we've got to get out!" Vivian cried.

"We'll go back to camp," said McCarty coldly. "Immediately. And you'll explain to the Loyalty Committee why you didn't return as soon as you regained consciousness."

"That's right," Gumbs put in self-consciously. "If you can't do anything, Meister, maybe the other technical fellows can."

George patiently explained his theory of their probable reception by the guards at the camp. McCarty's keen mind detected a flaw. "You grew legs, and stalks for your eyes, according to your own testimony. If you aren't lying, you can also grow a mouth. We'll announce ourselves as we approach."

"That may not be easy," George told her. "We couldn't get along with just a mouth. We'd need teeth, tongue, hard and soft palates, lungs or the equivalent, vocal cords, and some kind of substitute for a diaphragm to power the whole business. I'm wondering if it's possible at all because when Miss Bellis finally succeeded in making herself heard, it was by the method we're using now. She didn't—"

"You talk too much," McCarty interrupted. "Major Gumbs, Miss Bellis, you and I will try to form a speak-apparatus. The first to succeed will receive a credit mark on his record. Commence."

George, being left out of the contest by implication, used his time trying to restore his hearing. It seemed to him likely that the Whatever-it-was *meisterii* had some sort of diversion of labor built into it, since Gumbs and he—the first two to fall in—had kept their sight without making any special effort, while matters like hearing and touch had been left for the latecomers. This was fine in principle, and George approved of it, but he didn't like the idea of Miss McCarty's being the sole custodian of any part of the apparatus whatever.

Even if he were able to persuade the other two to follow his lead—and at the moment this prospect seemed dim—McCarty was certain to be a holdout. And it might easily be vital to all of them, at some time in the near future, to have their hearing hooked into the circuit.

He was distracted at first by muttered comments

between Gumbs and Vivian—"Getting anywhere?" I don't think so. Are you?"—interspersed between yawps, humming sounds and other irritating noises as they tried unsuccessfully to switch over from mental to vocal communication. Finally McCarty snapped, "Concentrate on forming the necessary organs instead of braying like jackasses."

George settled down to work, using the same technique he had found effective before. With his eyes shut, he imagined that the thing with all the teeth was approaching in darkness—*tap; slither; tap; click.* He wished valiantly for ears to catch those faint approaching sounds. After a long time he thought he was beginning to succeed—or were those mental sounds, unconsciously emitted by one of the other three? *Click. Slither. Swish. Scrape.*

George opened his eyes, genuinely alarmed. A hundred meters away, facing him across the shallow slope of rocky ground, was a uniformed man just emerging from a stand of black vegetation spears. As George raised his eye-stalks, the man paused, stared back at him, then shouted and raised his rifle.

George ran. Instantly there was a babble of voices inside him, and the muscles of his "legs" went into wild spasms.

"Run, dammit!" he said frantically. "There's a trooper with—"

The rifle went off with a deafening roar and George felt a sudden hideous pain aft of his spine. Vivian Bellis screamed. The struggle for possession of their common legs stopped and they scuttled full speed ahead for the cover of a nearby boulder.

The rifle roared again. George heard rock splinters screeching through the foliage overhead. Then they were plunging down the side of a gully, up the other slope, over a low hummock and into a forest of tall, bare-limbed trees.

George spotted a leaf-filled hollow and headed for it, fighting somebody else's desire to keep on running in a straight line. They plopped into the hollow and crouched there while three running men went past them.

Vivian was moaning steadily. Raising his eye-stalks cautiously, George was able to see that several jagged splinters of stone had penetrated the monster's gelatinous flesh near the far rim. They had been very lucky. The shot had apparently been a near miss—accountable only on the grounds that the trooper had been shooting downhill at a moving target—and had shattered the boulder behind them.

Looking more closely, George observed something which excited his professional interest. The whole surface of the monster appeared to be in constant slow ferment, tiny pits opening and closing as if the flesh were boiling . . . except that here the bubbles of air were not forcing their way outward, but were being engulfed at the surface and pressed down into the interior.

He could also see, deep under the mottled surface of the huge lens-shaped body, four vague clots of darkness which must be the living brains of Gumbs, Bellis, McCarty—and Meister.

Yes, there was one which was radially opposite his own eye-stalks. It was an odd thing, George reflected, to be looking at your own brain. He hoped he could get used to it in time.

The four dark spots were arranged close together in an almost perfect square at the center of the lens. The spinal cords, barely visible, crossed between them and rayed outward from the center.

Pattern, George thought. The thing was designed to make use of more than one nervous system. It arranged them in an orderly fashion, with the brains inward for greater protection—and perhaps for another reason. Maybe there was even a provision for conscious cooperation among the passengers: a matrix that somehow promoted the growth of communication cells between the separate brains. If that were so, it would account for their ready success with telepathy. George wished acutely that he could get inside and find out.

Vivian's pain was diminishing. Hers was the brain opposite George's and she had taken most of the effect of the rock splinters. But the fragments were sinking now, slowly, through the gelid substance of the monster's tissues. Watching carefully, George could see them move. When they got to the bottom, they would be excreted, no doubt, just as the indigestible parts of their clothing and equipment had been.

George wondered idly which of the remaining two brains was McCarty's and which was Gumb's. The answer proved easy to find. To George's left, as he looked back toward the center of the mound, was a pair of blue eyes set flush with the surface. They had lids apparently grown from the monster's substance, but thickened and opaque.

To his right, George could make out two tiny openings, extending a few centimeters into the body, which could only be Miss McCarty's ears. George had an impulse to see if he could devise a method of dropping dirt into them.

Anyhow, the question of returning to camp had been settled, at least for the moment. McCarty said nothing more about growing a set of speech organs, although George was sure she was determined to keep on trying.

He didn't think she would succeed. Whatever the mechanism was by which these changes in bodily structure were accomplished, amateurs like themselves probably could succeed only under the pressure of considerable emotional strain, and then just with comparatively simple tasks which involved one new structure at a time. And as he had already told McCarty, the speech organs in Man were extraordinarily diverse and complicated.

It occurred to George that speech might be achieved by creating a thin membrane to serve as a diaphragm, and an air chamber behind it, with a set of muscles to produce the necessary vibrations and modulate them.

He kept the notion to himself, though, because he didn't want to go back.

George was a rare bird: a scientist who was actually fitted for his work and loved it for its own sake. And right now he was sitting squarely in the middle of the most powerful research tool that had ever existed in his field: a protean organism, with the observer *inside* it, able to order its structure and watch the results; able to devise theories of function and test them on the tissues of what was effectively his own body—able to construct new organs, new adaptations to environment!

George saw himself at the point of an enormous cone of new knowledge and some of the possibilities he glimpsed humbled and awed him.

He *couldn't* go back, even if it were possible to do it without getting killed. If only he alone had fallen in— No, then the others would have pulled him out and killed the monster.

There were, he felt, too many problems demanding solutions all at once. It was hard to concentrate; his mind kept slipping maddeningly out of focus.

Vivian, whose pain had stopped some time ago, began to wail again. Gumbs snapped at her. McCarty cursed both of them. George himself felt that he had had very nearly all he could take, cooped up with three idiots who had no more sense than to squabble among themselves.

"Wait a minute," he said. "Do you all feel the same way? Irritable? Jumpy? As if you'd been working for sixty hours straight and were too tired to sleep?"

"Stop talking like a video ad," Vivian said angrily. "Haven't we got enough trouble without—"

"We're hungry," George interrupted. "We didn't realize it, because we haven't got the organs that usually signal hunger. But the last thing this body ate was *us*, and that was a whole day ago. We've got to find something to ingest. And soon, I'd say."

"Good Lord, you're right," said Gumbs. "But if this thing only eats people—I mean to say—"

"It never met people until we landed," George replied curtly. "Any protein should do."

He started off in what he hoped was the direction they had been following all along—directly away from camp. At least, he thought, if they put enough distance behind them, they might get thoroughly lost.

III

They moved out of the trees and down the long slope of a valley, over a wiry carpet of dead grasses, until they reached a watercourse in which a thin trickle was still flowing. Far down the bank, partly screened by clumps of skeletal shrubbery, George saw a group of animals that looked vaguely like miniature pigs. He told the others about it, and started cautiously in that direction.

"Which way is the wind blowing, Vivian?" he asked. "Can you feel it?"

She said, "No, I could before, when we were going downhill, but now I think we're facing into it."

"Good. We may be able to sneak up on them."

"But we're not going to eat *animals*, are we?"

"Yes, how about it, Meister?" Gumbs put in. "I don't say I'm a squeamish fellow, but after all—"

George, who felt a little squeamish himself—like all the others, he had been brought up on a diet of yeasts and synthetic protein—said testily, "What else can we do? You've got eyes; you can see that it's autumn here. Autumn after a hot summer, at that. Trees bare, streams dried up. We eat meat or go without—or would you rather hunt for insects?"

Gumbs, shocked to the core, muttered for a while and then gave up.

Seen at closer range, the animals looked less porcine and even more unappetizing than before. They had lean, segmented, pinkish-gray bodies, four short legs, flaring ears, and blunt scimitar-like snouts with which they were rooting in the ground, occasionally turning up something which they gulped, ears flapping.

George counted thirty of them, grouped fairly closely in a little space of clear ground between the bushes and the river. They moved slowly, but their short legs looked powerful; he guessed that they could run fast enough when they had to.

He inched forward, keeping his eye-stalks low, stopping instantly whenever one of the beasts looked up. Moving with increasing caution, he had approached to within ten meters of the nearest when McCarty said abruptly:

"Meister, has it occurred to you to wonder just *how* we are going to eat these animals?"

"Don't be foolish," he said irritably. "We'll just—" He stopped, baffled.

Did the things normal method of assimilation stop as soon as it got a tenant? Were they supposed to grow fangs and a gullet and all the rest of the apparatus? Impossible; they'd starve to death first. But on the other hand—*damn* this fuzzy-headed feeling—wouldn't it have to stop, to prevent the tenant from being digested with his first meal?

"Well?" McCarty demanded.

That guess was wrong, George knew, but he couldn't say why; and it was a distinctly unpleasant thought. Or, even worse, suppose the meal became the tenant, and the tenant the meal?

The nearest animal's head went up, and four tiny red eyes stared directly at George. The floppy ears snapped to attention. It was no time for speculation.

"He's seen us!" George shouted mentally. *"Run!"*

One instant they were lying still in the prickly dry grass; the next thing they were skimming across the ground, with the herd galloping away straight ahead of them. The hams of the nearest beast loomed up closer and closer, bounding furiously; then they had run it down and vaulted over it.

Casting an eye backward, George saw that it was lying motionless in the grass—unconscious or dead.

They ran down another one. *The anesthetic,* George

thought lucidly. *One touch does it*. And another, and another. *Of course we can digest them*, he thought, with relief. *It has to be selective to begin with or it couldn't have separated out our nervous tissue*.

Four down. Six down. Three more together as the herd bunched between the last arm of the thicket and the steep river bank; then two that tried to double back; then four stragglers, one after the other.

The rest of the herd disappeared into the tall grass up the slope, but fifteen bodies were strewn behind them.

Taking no chances, George went back to the beginning of the line and edged the monster's body under the first carcass.

"Crouch down, Gumbs," he said. "We have to slide under it . . . that's far enough. Leave the head hanging over."

"What for?" barked the soldier.

"You don't want his brain in here with us, do you? We don't know how many this thing is equipped to take. It might even like this one better than any of ours. But I can't see it bothering to keep the rest of the nervous system, if we make sure not to eat the head."

"Oh!" said Vivian.

"I beg your pardon, Miss Bellis," George said contritely. "It shouldn't be too unpleasant, though, if we don't let it bother us. It isn't as if we had taste buds or—"

"It's all right," she said. "Just please let's not talk about it."

"I should think not," Gumbs put in. "A little more tact, don't you think, Meister?"

Accepting this reproof, George turned his attention to the corpse that lay on the monster's glabrous surface, between his section and Gumbs'. It was sinking, just visibly, into the flesh. A cloud of opacity was spreading around it.

When it was almost gone and the neck had been severed, they moved on to the next. This time, at George's suggestion, they took aboard two at once.

Gradually their irritable mood faded; they began to feel at ease and cheerful, and George found it possible to think consecutively without having vital points slip out of his reach.

They were on their eighth and ninth courses, and George was happily engaged in an intricate chain of speculation as to the monster's circulatory system, when Miss McCarty broke a long silence to announce:

"I have now perfected a method by which we can return to camp safely. We will begin at once."

Startled and dismayed, George turned his eyes toward McCarty's quadrant of the monster. Protruding from the rim was a stringy, jointed something that looked like—yes, it was!—a grotesque but recognizable arm and hand. As he watched, the lumpy fingers fumbled with a blade of grass, tugged, uprooted it.

"Major Gumbs!" said McCarty. "It will be your task to locate the following articles as quickly as possible. One, a surface suitable for writing. I suggest a large leaf, light in color, dry but not brittle, or a tree from which a large section of bark can be easily peeled. Two, a pigment. No doubt you will be able to discover berries yielding suitable juice. If not, mud will do. Three, a twig or reed for use as a pen. When you have directed me to all these essential items, I will employ them to write a message outlining our predicament. You will read the result and point out any errors, which I will then correct. When the message is completed, we will return with it to the camp, approaching at night, and deposit it in a conspicuous place. We will retire until daybreak, and when the message has been read, we will approach again. Begin, Major."

"Well, yes," said Gumbs, "that ought to work, except—I suppose you've figured out some system for holding the pen, Miss McCarty?"

"Fool!" she replied. "I have made a hand, of course."

"Well, in that case, by all means. Let's see, I believe we might try this thicket first—" Their common body gave a lurch in that direction.

George held back. "Wait a minute," he said desperately. "Let's at least have the common sense to finish this meal before we go. There's no telling when we'll get another."

McCarty demanded, "How large are these creatures, Major?"

"About six centimeters long, I should say."

"And we have consumed nine of them, is that correct?"

"Nearer eight," George corrected. "These two are only half gone."

"In other words," McCarty said, "we have had two apiece. That should be ample. Don't you agree, Major?"

George said earnestly, "Miss McCarty, you're thinking in terms of human food requirements, whereas this organism has a different metabolic rate and at least three times the mass of four human beings. Look at it this way—the four of us together had a mass of about three hundred kilos, and yet twenty hours after this thing absorbed us, it was hungry again. Well, these animals wouldn't weigh much more than twenty kilos apiece at one G—and according to your scheme, we've got to hold out until after daybreak tomorrow."

"Something in that," Gumbs agreed. "Yes, on the whole, Miss McCarty, I think we had better forage while we can. It won't take us more than half an hour longer, at this rate."

"Very well. Be as quick as you can, though."

They moved on to the next pair of victims. George's brain was working furiously. It was no good arguing with McCarty. If he could only convince Gumbs, then Bellis would fall in with the majority—maybe. It was the only hope he had.

"Gumbs," he said, "have you given any thought to what's going to happen to us when we get back?"

"Not my line, you know. I leave that to the technical fellows like yourself."

"No, that isn't what I mean. Suppose you were the C.O. of this team, and four other people had fallen into this organism instead of us—"

"What? What? I don't follow."

George patiently repeated it.

"Yes, I see what you mean. So?"

"What orders would you give?"

Gumbs thought a moment. "Turn the thing over to the bio section, I suppose."

"You don't think you might order it destroyed as a possible menace?"

"Good Lord, I suppose I might. No, but you see, we'll be careful what we say in the note. We'll point out that we're a valuable specimen and so on. Handle with care."

"All right," George said, "suppose that works, then what? Since it's out of your line, I'll tell you. Nine chances out of ten, bio section will classify us as a possible biological enemy weapon. That means, first of all, that we'll go through a full-dress interrogation and I don't have to tell you what that can be like—"

"Major Gumbs," said McCarthy stridently, "Meister will be executed for disloyalty at the first opportunity. You are forbidden to talk to him, under the same penalty."

"But she can't stop you from listening to me," George said tensely. "In the second place, Gumbs, they'll take samples. Without anesthesia. Finally, they'll either destroy us just the same, or they'll send us back to the nearest strong point for more study. We will then be Federation property, Gumbs, in a top-secret category, and since nobody in Intelligence will ever dare to take the responsibility of clearing us, we'll *stay* there.

"Gumbs, this *is* a valuable specimen, but it will never do anybody any good if we go back to camp. Whatever we discover about it, even if it's knowledge that could save billions of lives, that will be top-secret, too, and it'll never get past the walls of Intelligence. . . . If you're still hoping that they can get you out of this, you're wrong. This isn't like limb grafts. *Your whole body has been destroyed,* Gumbs, everything but your nervous system and your eyes. The only new body we'll get is the one we make ourselves."

"Major Gumbs," said McCarty, "I think we have

wasted quite enough time. Begin your search for the materials I need."

For a moment, Gumbs was silent and their collective body did not move.

Then he said: "Miss McCarty—unofficially, of course—there's one point I'd like your opinion on. Before we begin. That is to say, they'll be able to patch together some sort of bodies for us, don't you think? I mean one technical fellow says one thing, another says the opposite. Do you see what I'm driving at?"

George had been watching McCarty's new limb uneasily. It was flexing rhythmically and, he was almost certain, gradually growing larger. The fingers groped in the dry grass, plucking first a single blade, then two together, finally a whole tuft. Now she said: "I have no opinion, Major. The question is irrelevant. Our duty is to return to camp. That is all we need to know."

"Oh, I quite agree with you there," said Gumbs. "And besides," he added, "there really isn't any alternative, is there?"

George, staring down at one of the fingerlike projections visible below the rim of the monster, was passionately willing it to turn into an arm. He had, he suspected, started much too late.

"The alternative," he said, "is simply to keep on going as we are. Even if the Federation holds this planet for a century, there'll be places on it that will never be explored. We'll be safe."

"I mean to say," Gumbs went on as if he had only paused for thought, "a fellow can't very well cut himself off from civilization, can he?" There was a thoughtful tone to his voice.

Again George felt a movement toward the thicket; again he resisted it. Then he found himself overpowered as another set of muscles joined themselves to Gumbs's. Quivering, crabwise, the Something-or-other *meisterii* moved half a meter. Then it stopped, straining.

"I believe you, Mr. Meister—George," Vivian Bellis

said. "I don't want to go back. Tell me what you want me to do."

"You're doing beautifully right now," George assured her after a speechless instant. "Except if you can grow an arm, I imagine that will be useful."

"Now we know where we stand," said McCarty to Gumbs.

"Yes. Quite right."

"Major Gumbs," she said crisply, "you are opposite me, I believe?"

"Am I?" asked Gumbs doubtfully.

"Never mind. I believe you are. Now is Meister to your right or left?"

"Left. I know that, anyhow. Can see his eye-stalks out of the corner of my eye."

"Very well." McCarty's arm rose, with a sharp-pointed fragment of rock clutched in the blobby fingers.

Horrified, George watched it bend backward across the curve of the monster's body. The long, knife-sharp point probed tentatively at the surface three centimeters short of the area over his brain. Then the fist made an abrupt up-and-down movement and a fierce stab of pain shot through him.

"Not quite long enough, I think," McCarty said. She flexed the arm, then brought it back. "Major Gumbs, after my next attempt, you will tell me if you notice any reaction in Meister's eye-stalks."

The pain was still throbbing along George's nerves. With one half-blinded eye, he watched the embryonic arm that was growing, too slowly, under the rim; with the other, fascinated, he watched McCarty's arm lengthen slowly toward him.

It was growing visibly, he suddenly realized, but it wasn't getting any nearer. In fact, incredibly enough it seemed to be losing ground.

The monster's flesh was flowing away under it, expanding in both directions.

McCarty stabbed again, with vicious strength. This time the pain was less acute.

"Major?" she asked. "Any result?"

"No," said Gumbs, "no, I think not. We seem to be moving forward a bit, though, Miss McCarty."

"A ridiculous error," she replied. "We are being forced *back*. Pay attention, Major."

"No, really," he protested. "That is to say, we're moving toward the thicket. Forward to me, backward to you."

"Major Gumbs, *I* am moving forward, *you* are moving back."

They were both right, George discovered. The monster's body was no long circular; it was extending itself along the axis. A suggestion of concavity was becoming visible in the center. Below the surface, too, there was motion.

The four brains now formed an oblong, not a square.

The positions of the spinal cords had shifted. His own and Vivian's seemed to be about where they were, but Gumbs' now passed under McCarty's brain, and vice versa.

Having increased its mass by some two hundred kilos, the Something-or-other *meisterii* was fissioning into two individuals—and tidily separating its tenants, two to each. Gumbs and Meister in one, McCarty and Bellis in the other.

Next time it happened, he realized, each product of the fission would be reduced to one brain—and the time after that, one of the new individuals out of each pair would be a monster in the primary state, quiescent, camouflaged, waiting to be stumbled over.

But that meant that, like the common amoeba, this fascinating organism was immortal, barring accidents. It simply grew and divided.

Not the tenants, though, unfortunately. Their tissues would wear out and die.

Or would they? Human nervous tissue didn't regenerate, but neither did it proliferate as George's and Miss McCarty's had done; neither did *any* human tissue build new cells fast enough to account for George's eye-stalks or Miss McCarty's arm.

There was no question about it: none of that new tissue could possibly be human; it was all counterfeit, produced by the monster from its own substance according to the structural "blueprints" in the nearest genuine cells. And it was a perfect counterfeit: the new tissues knit with the old, axones coupled with dendrites, muscles contracted or expanded on command.

And therefore, when nerve cells wore out, they could be replaced. Eventually the last human cell would go, the human tenant would have become totally monster— but "a difference that makes no difference is no difference." Effectively, the tenant would still be human and he would be immortal.

Barring accidents.

Or murder.

Miss McCarty was saying, "Major Gumbs, you are being ridiculous. The explanation is quite obvious. Unless you are deliberately deceiving me, for what reason I cannot imagine, then our efforts to move in opposing directions must be pulling this creature apart."

McCarty was evidently confused in her geometry. Let her stay that way—it would keep her off balance until the fission was complete. No, that was no good. George himself was out of her reach already and getting farther away, but how about Bellis? Her brain and McCarty's were, if anything, closer together. . . .

What was he to do? If he warned the girl, that would only draw McCarty's attention to her sooner.

There wasn't much time left, he realized abruptly. If some physical linkage between the brains actually had occurred to make communication possible, those cells couldn't hold out much longer; the gap between the two pairs of brains was widening steadily. He had to keep McCarty from discovering how the four of them would be paired.

"Vivian!" he said.

"Yes, George?"

"Listen, we're not pulling this body apart. It's splitting. That's the way it reproduces. You and I will be in one half, Gumbs and McCarty in the other," he lied convincingly. "If they don't give us any trouble, we can all go where we please."

"Oh, I'm so glad!" What a warm voice she had. . . .

"Yes," said George nervously, "but we may have to fight them; it's up to them. So *grow an arm*, Vivian."

"I'll try," she said uncertainly.

McCarty's voice cut across hers. "Major Gumbs, since you have eyes, it will be your task to see to it that those two do not escape. Meanwhile, I suggest that you also grow an arm."

"Doing my best," said Gumbs.

Puzzled, George glanced downward, past his own half-formed arm. There, almost out of sight, a fleshy bulge appeared under Gumbs' section of the rim! The Major had been working on it in secret, keeping it hidden . . . and it was already better-developed than George's.

"Oh-oh," said Gumbs abruptly. "Look here, Miss McCarty, Meister's been leading you up the garden path. Deceiving you, you understand. Clever, I must say. I mean you and I aren't going to be in the same half. How could we be? We're on *opposite sides* of the blasted thing. It's going to be you and Miss Bellis, me and Meister."

The monster was developing a definite waistline. The spinal cords had rotated now, so that there was clear space between them in the center.

"Yes," said McCarty faintly. "*Thank* you, Major Gumbs."

"George!" came Vivian's frightened voice, distant and weak. "What shall I do?"

"Grow an arm!" he shouted.

There was no reply.

IV

Frozen, George watched McCarty's arm, the rock-fragment still clutched at the end of it, rise into view and swing leftward at full stretch over the bubbling surface of the monster. He had time to see it bob up and viciously down again; time to think. *Still short, thank God—that's McCarty's right arm, it's farther from Vivian's brain than it was from mine;* time, finally, to realize that he could not possibly help Vivian before McCarty lengthened the arm the few centimeters more that were necessary. The fission was only half complete, yet he could no more move to where he wanted to be than a Siamese twin could walk around his brother.

Then his time was up. A flicker of motion warned him, and he looked back to see a lumpy, distorted pseudo-hand clutching for his eye-stalks.

Instinctively he brought his own up, grasped the other's wrist and hung on desperately. It was half again the size of his, and so strongly muscled that although his leverage was better, he couldn't force it back or hold it away. He could only keep the system oscillating up and down, adding his strength to Gumbs' so that the mark was overshot.

Gumbs began to vary the force and rhythm of his movements, trying to catch him off guard. A thick finger brushed the base of one eye-stalk.

"Sorry about this, Meister," said Gumbs. "No hard feelings, you understand. Between us [oof] I don't fancy that McCarty woman much—but [ugh! almost had you that time] way I see it, I've got to look after myself. Mean to say [ugh] if I don't, who will? See what I mean?"

George did not reply. Astonishingly enough, he was no longer afraid, either for himself or for Vivian; he was simply overpoweringly, ecstatically, monomanically angry. Power from somewhere was surging into his arm. Fiercely concentrating, he thought *Bigger! Stronger! Longer! More arm!*

The arm grew. Visibly, it added substance to itself, it lengthened, thickened, bulked with muscle. So did Gumbs', however.

He began another arm. So did Gumbs.

All around him the surface of the monster was bubbling violently. And, George realized, the lenticular bulk of it was perceptibly shrinking. Its curious breathing system was inadequate; the thing was cannibalizing itself, destroying its own tissues to make up the difference.

How small could it get and still support two human tenants?

And which brain would it dispense with first?

He had no leisure to think about it. Scrabbling in the grass with his second hand, Gumbs had failed to find anything that would serve as a weapon. Now, with a sudden lurch, he swung their entire body around.

The fission was complete.

That thought reminded George of Vivian and McCarty. He risked a split-second's glance behind him, saw nothing but a featureless ovoid mound, and looked back in time to see Gumbs' half-grown right fist pluck up a long, sharp-pointed dead branch and drive it murderously at his eyes.

The lip of the river-bank was a meter away to the left. George made it in one abrupt surge. Their common body slipped, tottered, hesitated, hands clutching wildly—and toppled, end over end, hurtling in a cloud of dust and pebbles down the breakneck slope to a meaty smash at the bottom.

The universe made one more giant turn around them and came to rest. Half-blinded, George groped for the hold he had lost, found the wrist and seized it.

"Oh, Lord!" said Gumbs. "I'm hurt, Meister. Go on, man, finish it, will you? Don't waste time."

George stared at him suspiciously, without relaxing his grip. "What's the matter with you?"

"Paralyzed. I can't move."

They had fallen onto a small boulder, George saw, one of many with which the riverbed was strewn. This one was roughly conical; they were draped over it, and the blunt point was directly under Gumbs's spinal cord, a few centimeters from the brain.

"Gumbs, that may not be as bad as you think. If I can show you it isn't, will you give up and put yourself under my orders?"

"How do you mean? My spine's crushed."

"Never mind that now. Will you or won't you?"

"Why, yes," agreed Gumbs. "That's very decent of you, Meister, matter of fact. You have my word, for what it's worth."

"All right," said George. Straining hard, he managed to get their body off the boulder. Then he stared up at the slope down which they had tumbled. Too steep; he'd have to find an easier way back. He turned and started off to eastward, paralleling the thin stream that flowed in the center of the watercourse.

"What's up now?" Gumbs asked after a moment.

"We've got to find a way up to the top," George said impatiently. "I may still be able to help Vivian."

"Ah, yes. Afraid I was thinking about myself, Meister. If you don't mind telling me, what's the damage?"

She couldn't still be alive, George was thinking despondently, but if there were any small chance—

"You'll be all right," he said. "If you were still in your old body, that would be a fatal injury, or permanently disabling, anyhow, but not in this thing. You can repair yourself as easily as you can grow a new limb."

"Stupid of me not to think of that," said Gumbs. "But does that mean we were simply wasting our time trying to kill one another?"

"No. If you'd crushed my brain, I think the organism would have digested it and that would have been the end of me. But short of anything that drastic, I believe we're immortal."

"Immortal? That does rather put another face on it, doesn't it?"

The bank was becoming a little lower, and at one point, where the raw ground was thickly seeded with boulders, there was a talus slope that looked as if it could be climbed. George started up it.

"Meister," said Gumbs after a moment.

"What do you want?"

"You're right, you know—I'm getting some feeling back already. Look here, is there anything this beast *can't* do? I mean, for instance, do you suppose we could put ourselves back together the way we were, with all the—appendages, and so on?"

"It's possible," George said curtly. It was a thought that had been in the back of his mind, but he didn't feel like discussing it with Gumbs just now.

They were halfway up the slope.

"Well, in that case," said Gumbs meditatively, "the thing has *military* possibilities, you know. Man who brought a thing like that direct to the War Department could write his own ticket, more or less."

"After we split up," George offered, "you can do whatever you please."

"But dammit," said Gumbs in an irritated tone, "that won't do."

"Why not?"

"Because," said Gumbs, "they might find you." His hands reached up abruptly, pried out a small boulder before George could stop him.

The large boulder above it trembled, dipped and leaned ponderously outward. George, directly underneath, found that he could move neither forward nor back.

"Sorry again," he heard Gumbs saying, with what sounded like genuine regret. "But you know the Loyalty Committee. I simply can't take the chance."

The boulder seemed to take forever to fall. George tried twice more, with all his strength, to move out of its path. Then, instinctively, he put his arms up straight under it.

It struck.

George felt his arms breaking like twigs, and saw a looming grayness that blotted out the sky; he felt a sledge impact that made the ground shudder beneath him.

He heard a splattering sound.

And he was still alive. That astonishing fact kept him fully occupied for a long time after the boulder had clattered its way down the slope into silence. Then, at last, he looked down to his right.

The resistance of his stiffened arms, even while they broke, had been enough to lever the falling boulder over, a distance of some thirty centimeters. The right half of the monster was a flattened, shattered ruin. He could see a few flecks of pasty gray matter, melting now into green-brown translucence as the mass flowed slowly together again.

In twenty minutes, the last remnants of a superfluous spinal cord had been absorbed, the monster had collected itself back into its normal lens shape, and George's pain was diminishing. In five minutes more, his mended arms were strong enough to use.

They were also more convincingly shaped and colored than before—the tendons, the fingernails, even the wrinkles of the skin were in good order. In ordinary circumstances this discovery would have left George happily bemused for hours. Now, in his impatience, he barely noticed it. He climbed to the top of the bank.

Thirty meters away, a humped green-brown body like his own lay motionless on the dry grass.

It contained, of course, only one brain. Whose?

McCarty's, almost certainly; Vivian hadn't had a chance. But then how did it happen that there was no visible trace of McCarty's arm?

Unnerved, George walked around the creature for a closer inspection.

On the far side, he encountered two dark-brown eyes, with an oddly unfinished appearance. They focused on him after an instant and the whole body quivered slightly, moving toward him.

Vivian's eyes had been brown; George remembered them distinctly. Brown eyes with heavy dark lashes in a tapering slender face. But did that prove anything? What color had McCarty's eyes been? He couldn't remember.

George moved closer, hoping fervently that the Something-or-other *meisterii* was at least advanced enough to conjugate, instead of trying to devour members of its own species. . . .

The two bodies touched, clung and began to flow together. Watching, George saw the fissioning process reverse itself. From paired lenses, the alien flesh melted into a slipper-shape, to an ovoid, to a lens-shape again. His brain and the other drifted closer together, the spinal cords crossing at right angles.

And it was only then that he noticed an oddity about the other brain. It seemed to be more solid and compact than his, the outline sharper.

"Vivian?" he said worriedly. "Is that you?"

No answer. He tried again; and again.

Finally:

"George! Oh, dear—I want to cry, but I don't seem able to do it."

"No lachrymal glands," George said automatically. "Uh, Vivian?"

"Yes, George?" That warm voice again. . . .

"What happened to Miss McCarty? How did you—"

"I don't know. She's gone, isn't she? I haven't heard her for a long time."

"Yes," said George, "she's gone. You mean you don't *know?* Tell me what you did."

"Well, I wanted to make an arm, because you told me to, but I didn't think I had time enough. So I made a skull instead. And those things to cover my spine—"

"Vertebrae." *Now why*, he thought discontentedly, *didn't I think of that?* "And then?"

"I think I'm crying now," she said. "Yes, I am. It's such a relief— And then, after that, nothing. She was still hurting me, and I just lay still and thought how wonderful it would be if she weren't in here with me. After a while, she wasn't. And then I grew eyes to look for you."

The explanation, it seemed to George, was more perplexing than the enigma. Staring around in a vague search for enlightenment, he caught sight of something he hadn't noticed before. Two meters to his left, just visible in the grass, was a damp-looking grayish lump, with a suggestion of a stringy extension trailing off from it.

There must, he decided suddenly, be some mechanism in the Something-or-other *meisterii* for disposing of tenants who failed to adapt themselves—brains that went into catatonia, or hysteria, or suicidal frenzy. An eviction clause in the lease.

Somehow, Vivian had managed to stimulate that mechanism—to convince the organism that McCarty's brain was not only superfluous but dangerous—"Toxic" was the word.

It was the ultimate ignominy. Miss McCarty had not been digested. She'd been excreted.

By sunset, twelve hours later, they had made a good deal of progress. They had reached an understanding very agreeable to them both. They had hunted down another herd of the pseudo-pigs for their noon meal. They had not once quarreled or even irritated each other. And for divergent reasons—on George's side because the monster's normal metabolism was unsatisfactory when it had to move quickly, and on Vivian's because she refused to believe that any man could be attracted to her in her present condition—they had begun a serious attempt to reshape themselves.

The first trials were extraordinarily difficult, the rest surprisingly easy. Again and again, they had to let themselves collapse back into an ameboid shape, victims of some omitted or malfunctioning organ, but each failure smoothed the road. They were at last able to stand breathless but breathing, swaying but stable, face to face—two preliminary sketches of self-made Man.

They had also put thirty kilometers between themselves and the Federation camp. Standing on the crest of a rise and looking southward across the shallow valley, George could see a faint funereal glow: the mining machines, chewing out metals to feed the fabricators that would spawn lethal spaceships.

"We'll never go back there, will we?" begged Vivian.

"No," said George confidently. "We'll let them find us. When they do, they'll be a lot more disconcerted than we will. We can make ourselves anything we want to be, remember."

"I want you to want me, so I'm going to be beautiful."

"More beautiful than any woman ever was," he agreed, "and both of us will have super-intelligence. I don't see why not. We can direct our growth in any way we choose. We'll be more than human."

"I'd like that," said Vivian.

"They won't. The McCartys and the Gumbses and all the rest would never have a chance against us. We're the future."

There was one thing more, a small matter, but important to George, because it marked his sense of accomplishment, of one phase ended and a new one begun. He had finally completed the name of his discovery.

It wasn't Something-or-other *meisterii* at all.

It was *Spes hominis*—Man's hope.

SAUCER OF LONELINESS

THEODORE STURGEON (1918–1985)
GALAXY SCIENCE FICTION, FEBRUARY

We welcome back Theodore Sturgeon to these pages with considerable sadness, since he is dead only a few weeks as these words are written. Although he was largely silent for the last fifteen years, his work helped to center this field and will certainly outlive him. We miss you, Ted.

Theodore Sturgeon wrote only a few novels during his career, but one of them, published in 1953, is one of the seminal works in the field. More Than Human *is an expansion of his 1952* Galaxy *novella, "Baby Is Three" and is a fine study of gestalt psychology and speculation into parapsychology, as a group of "linked" children form the beginning of a new humanity, that of homo gestalt.*

1953 was also at the center of one of Ted Sturgeon's most productive periods, and "Saucer of Loneliness" is the first of two stories by him in this volume.

—MHG

This is again a mood piece. Ted was particularly good at such things and when he was really on a roll, what he wrote was virtually poetry.

There's a risk to that, of course, for if you aim for poetry and miss, even by a little, you can end up with an awful mess. Personally, I have never had the cour-

*age to try for it, or the talent, and I've been aiming
carefully at serviceable prose and nothing more.*

*It's the difficulty of hitting the bull's eye—that tiny
bull's eye—of beautiful writing that may account for the
fact that Ted had dry periods now and then, because if
you lose that Robin-Hood aim and are satisfied with
nothing else, then you have to hang up your bow for a
time.*

*It may also account for why Ted wrote so little in the
way of novels. It is hard to maintain a mood for several
hundred pages and Ted wouldn't compromise.*

*And, let's face it, novels are where fame, and suc-
cess, and money is. Short-story collections do not receive the same kind of warm editorial claspings-to-the-
bosom; they don't do as well once published; they don't
ricochet off the various subsidiary-rights walls as frequently. And so Ted never got the fame and success and
money he deserved. But the reading-gourmet knew about
him, and I think he knew that.*

—IA

IF SHE'S DEAD, I thought, I'll never find her in this
white flood of moonlight on the white sea, with the surf
seething in and over the pale, pale sand like a great
shampoo. Almost always, suicides who stab themselves
or shoot themselves in the heart carefully bare their
chests; the same strange impulse generally makes the
sea-suicide go naked.

A little earlier, I thought, or later, and there would
be shadows for the dunes and the breathing toss of the
foam. Now the only real shadow was mine, a tiny thing
just under me, but black enough to feed the blackness
of the shadow of a blimp.

A little earlier, I thought, and I might have seen her
plodding up the silver shore, seeking a place lonely
enough to die in. A little later and my legs would rebel
against this shuffling trot through sand, the maddening
sand that could not hold and would not help a hurrying
man.

My legs did give way then and I knelt suddenly,

sobbing—not for her; not yet—just for air. There was such a rush about me: wind, and tangled spray, and colors upon colors and shades of colors that were not colors at all but shifts of white and silver. If light like that were sound, it would sound like the sea on sand, and if my ears were eyes, they would see such a light.

I crouched there, gasping in the swirl of it, and a flood struck me, shallow and swift, turning up and outward like flower petals where it touched my knees, then soaking me to the waist in its bubble and crash. I pressed my knuckles to my eyes so they would open again. The sea was on my lips with the taste of tears and the whole white night shouted and wept aloud.

And there she was.

Her white shoulders were a taller curve in the sloping foam. She must have sensed me—perhaps I yelled—for she turned and saw me kneeling there. She put her fists to her temples and her face twisted, and she uttered a piercing wail of despair and fury, and then plunged seaward and sank.

I kicked off my shoes and ran into the breakers, shouting, hunting, grasping at flashes of white that turned to sea-salt and coldness in my fingers. I plunged right past her, and her body struck my side as a wave whipped my face and tumbled both of us. I gasped in solid water, opened my eyes beneath the surface and saw a greenish-white distorted moon hurtle as I spun. Then there was sucking sand under my feet again and my left hand was tangled in her hair.

The receding wave towed her away and for a moment she streamed out from my hand like steam from a whistle. In that moment I was sure she was dead, but as she settled to the sand, she fought and scrambled to her feet.

She hit my ear, wet, hard, and a huge, pointed pain lanced into my head. She pulled, she lunged away from me, and all the while my hand was caught in her hair. I couldn't have freed her if I had wanted to. She spun to me with the next wave, battered and clawed at me, and we went into deeper water.

"Don't . . . don't . . . I can't swim!" I shouted, so she clawed me again.

"Leave me alone," she shrieked. "Oh, dear God, why can't you *leave*" (said her fingernails) "*me . . .*" (said her fingernails) "*alone!*" (said her small hard fist).

So by her hair I pulled her head down tight to her white shoulder; and with the edge of my free hand I hit her neck twice. She floated again, and I brought her ashore.

I carried her to where a dune was between us and the sea's broad noisy tongue, and the wind was above us somewhere. But the light was as bright. I rubbed her wrists and stroked her face and said, "It's all right," and, "There!" and some names I used to have for a dream I had long, long before I ever heard of her.

She lay still on her back with the breath hissing between her teeth, with her lips in a smile which her twisted-tight, wrinkled-sealed eyes made not a smile but a torture. She was well, and conscious for many moments and still her breath hissed and her closed eyes twisted.

"Why couldn't you leave me alone?" she asked at last. She opened her eyes and looked at me. She had so much misery that there was no room for fear. She shut her eyes again and said, "You know who I am."

"I know," I said.

She began to cry.

I waited, and when she stopped crying, there were shadows among the dunes. A long time.

She said, "You don't know who I am. Nobody knows who I am."

I said, "It was in all the papers."

"That!" She opened her eyes slowly and her gaze traveled over my face, my shoulders, stopped at my mouth, touched my eyes for the briefest second. She curled her lips and turned away her head. "Nobody knows who I am."

I waited for her to move or speak, and finally I said, "Tell *me*."

"Who are you?" she asked, with her head still turned away.

"Someone who. . . ."

"Well?"

"Not now," I said. "Later, maybe."

She sat up suddenly and tried to hide herself. "Where are my clothes?"

"I didn't see them."

"Oh," she said. "I remember. I put them down and kicked sand over them, just where a dune would come and smooth them out, hide them as if they never were. . . . I hate sand. I wanted to drown in the sand, but it wouldn't let me. . . . You mustn't look at me!" she shouted. "I hate to have you looking at me!" She threw her head from side to side, seeking. "I can't stay here like this! What can I do? Where can I go?"

"Here," I said.

She let me help her up and then snatched her hand away, half-turned from me. "Don't touch me. Get away from me."

"Here," I said again, and walked down the dune where it curved in the moonlight, tipped back into the wind and down and became not dune but beach. "Here," I pointed behind the dune.

At last she followed me. She peered over the dune where it was chest-high, and again where it was knee-high. "Back there?"

I nodded.

"So dark. . . ." She stepped over the low dune and into the aching black of those moon-shadows. She moved away cautiously, feeling tenderly with her feet, back to where the dune was higher. She sank down into the blackness and disappeared there. I sat on the sand in the light. "Stay away from me," she spat.

I rose and stepped back. Invisible in the shadows, she breathed, "Don't go away." I waited, then saw her hand press out of the clean-cut shadows. "There," she said, "over there. In the dark. Just be a. . . . Stay away from me now. . . . Be a—voice."

I did as she asked, and sat in the shadows perhaps six feet from her.

She told me about it. Not the way it was in the papers.

She was perhaps seventeen when it happened. She was in Central Park in New York. It was too warm for such an early spring day, and the hammered brown slopes had a dusting of green of precisely the consistency of that morning's hoar frost on the rocks. But the frost was gone and the grass was brave and tempted some hundreds of pairs of feet from the asphalt and concrete to tread on it.

Hers were among them. The sprouting soil was a surprise to her feet, as the air was to her lungs. Her feet ceased to be shoes as she walked, her body was consciously more than clothes. It was the only kind of day which in itself can make a city-bred person raise his eyes. She did.

For a moment she felt separated from the life she lived, in which there was no fragrance, no silence, in which nothing ever quite fit nor was quite filled. In that moment the ordered disapproval of the buildings around the pallid park could not reach her; for two, three clean breaths it no longer mattered that the whole wide world really belonged to images projected on a screen; to gently groomed goddesses in these steel and glass towers; that it belonged, in short, always, always to someone else.

So she raised her eyes, and there above her was the saucer.

It was beautiful. It was golden, with a dusty finish like that of an unripe Concord grape. It made a faint sound, a chord composed of two tones and a blunted hiss like the wind in tall wheat. It was darting about like a swallow, soaring and dropping. It circled and dropped and hovered like a fish, shimmering. It was like all these living things, but with that beauty it had all the loveliness of things turned and burnished, measured, machined, and metrical.

At first she felt no astonishment, for this was so different from anything she had ever seen before that it had to be a trick of the eye, a false evaluation of size and speed and distance that in a moment would resolve itself into a sun-flash on an airplane or the lingering glare of a welding arc.

She looked away from it and abruptly realized that many other people saw it—saw *something*—too. People all around her had stopped moving and speaking and were craning upward. Around her was a globe of silent astonishment, and outside it she was aware of the life-noise of the city, the hard-breathing giant who never inhales.

She looked up again, and at last began to realize how large and how far away the saucer was. No: rather, how small and how very near it was. It was just the size of the largest circle she might make with her two hands, and it floated not quite eighteen inches over her head.

Fear came then. She drew back and raised a forearm, but the saucer simply hung there. She bent far side-ways, twisted away, leaped forward, looked back and upward to see if she had escaped it. At first she couldn't see it; then as she looked up and up, there it was, close and gleaming, quivering and crooning, right over her head.

She bit her tongue.

From the corner of her eye, she saw a man cross himself. *He did that because he saw me standing here with a halo over my head, she thought*. And that was the greatest single thing that had ever happened to her. No one had ever looked at her and made a respectful gesture before, not once, not ever. Through terror, through panic and wonderment, the comfort of that thought nestled into her, to wait to be taken out and looked at again in lonely times.

The terror was uppermost now, however. She backed away, staring upward, stepping a ludicrous cakewalk. She should have collided with people. There were plenty of people there, gasping and craning, but she reached

none. She spun around and discovered to her horror
that she was the center of a pointing, pressing crowd.
Its mosaic of eyes all bulged and its inner circle braced
its many legs to press back and away from her.

The saucer's gentle note deepened. It tilted, dropped
an inch or so. Someone screamed, and the crowd broke
away from her in all directions, milled about, and settled again in a new dynamic balance, a much larger
ring, as more and more people raced to thicken it
against the efforts of the inner circle to escape.

The saucer hummed and tilted, tilted. . . .

She opened her mouth to scream, fell to her knees,
and the saucer struck.

It dropped against her forehead and clung there. It
seemed almost to lift her. She came erect on her knees,
made one effort to raise her hands against it, and then
her arms stiffened down and back, her hands not reaching the ground. For perhaps a second and a half the
saucer held her rigid, and then it passed a single ecstatic quiver to her body and dropped it. She plumped
to the ground, the backs of her thighs heavy and painful
on her heels and ankles.

The saucer dropped beside her, rolled once in a
small circle, one just around its edge, and lay still. It lay
still and dull and metallic, different and dead.

Hazily, she lay and gazed at the gray-shrouded blue
of the good spring sky, and hazily she heard whistles.

And some tardy screams.

And a great stupid voice bellowing "Give her air!"
which made everyone press closer.

Then there wasn't so much sky because of the blueclad
bulk with its metal buttons and its leatherette notebook. "Okay, okay, what's happened here stand back
figods sake."

And the widening ripples of observation, interpreta-
tion and comment: "It knocked her down." "Some guy
knocked her down." "He knocked her down and—"
"Some guy knocked her down and—" "Right in broad
daylight this guy. . . ." "The park's gettin' to be. . . ."

onward and outward, the adulteration of fact until it
was lost altogether because excitement is so much more
important.

Somebody with a harder shoulder than the rest bull-
ing close, a notebook here, too, a witnessing eye over
it, ready to change ". . . a beautiful brunette . . ." to
"an attractive brunette" for the afternoon editions, because "attractive" is as dowdy as any woman is allowed
to get if she is a victim in the news.

The glittering shield and the florid face bending close:
"You hurt bad, sister?" And the echoes, back and back
through the crowd, "Hurt bad, hurt bad, badly injured,
he beat the hell out of her, broad daylight. . . ."

And still another man, slim and purposeful, tan gabardine, cleft chin and beard-shadow: "Flyin' saucer,
hm? Okay, Officer, I'll take over here."

"And who the hell might you be, takin' over?"

The flash of a brown leather wallet, a face so close
behind that its chin was pressed into the gabardine
shoulder. The face said, awed: "F.B.I." and that rippled outward, too. The policeman nodded—the entire
policeman nodded in one single bobbing genuflection.

"Get some help and clear this area," said the gabardine.

"Yes, *sir!*" said the policeman.

"F.B.I., F.B.I.," the crowd murmured and there was
more sky to look at above her.

She sat up and there was glory in her face. "The
saucer talked to me," she sang.

"You shut up," said the policeman. "My God, this
mob could be full of Communists."

"You shut up, too," said the gabardine.

Someone in the crowd told someone else a Communist beat up this girl, while someone else was saying
she got beat up because she was a Communist.

She started to rise, but solicitous hands forced her
down again. There were thirty police there by that
time.

"I can walk," she said.

"Now you just take it easy," they told her.

They put a stretcher down beside her and lifted her onto it and covered her with a big blanket.

"I can walk," she said as they carried her through the crowd.

A woman went white and turned away moaning, "Oh, my God, how awful!"

A small man with round eyes stared and stared at her and licked and licked his lips.

The ambulance. They slid her in. The gabardine was already there.

A white-coated man with very clean hands: "How did it happen, miss?"

"No questions," said the gabardine. "Security."

The hospital.

She said, "I got to get back to work."

"Take your clothes off," they told her.

She had a bedroom to herself then for the first time in her life. Whenever the door opened, she could see a policeman outside. It opened very often to admit the kind of civilians who were very polite to military people, and the kind of military people who were even more polite to certain civilians. She did not know what they all did nor what they wanted. Every single day they asked her four million, five hundred thousand questions. Apparently they never talked to each other because each of them asked her the same questions over and over.

"What is your name?"

"How old are you?"

"What year were you born?"

Sometimes they would push her down strange paths with their questions.

"Now your uncle. Married a woman from Middle Europe, did he? Where in Middle Europe?"

"What clubs or fraternal organizations did you belong to? Ah! Now about that Rinkeydinks gang on 63rd Street. Who was *really* behind it?"

But over and over again, "What did you mean when you said the saucer talked to you?"

And she would say, "It talked to me."

And they would say, "And it said—"

And she would shake her head.

There would be a lot of shouting ones, and then a lot of kind ones. No one had ever been so kind to her before, but she soon learned that no one was being kind to *her*. They were just getting her to relax, to think of other things, so they could suddenly shoot that question at her: "What do you mean it talked to you?"

Pretty soon it was just like Mom's or school or any place, and she used to sit with her mouth closed and let them yell. Once they sat her on a hard chair for hours and hours with a light in her eyes and let her get thirsty. Home, there was a transom over the bedroom door and Mom used to leave the kitchen light glaring through it all night, every night, so she wouldn't get the horrors. So the light didn't bother her at all.

They took her out of the hospital and put her in jail. Some ways it was good. The food. The bed was all right, too. Through the window she could see lots of women exercising in the yard. It was explained to her that they all had much harder beds.

"You are a very important young lady, you know."

That was nice at first, but as usual it turned out they didn't mean her at all. They kept working on her. Once they brought the saucer in to her. It was inside a big wooden crate with a padlock, and a steel box inside that with a Yale lock. It only weighed a couple of pounds, the saucer, but by the time they got it packed, it took two men to carry it and four men with guns to watch them.

They made her act out the whole thing just the way it happened with some soldiers holding the saucer over her head. It wasn't the same. They'd cut a lot of chips and pieces out of the saucer and, besides, it was that dead gray color. They asked her if she knew anything about that and for once she told them.

"It's empty now," she said.

The only one she would ever talk to was a little man with a fat belly who said to her the first time he was alone with her, "Listen, I think the way they've been treating you stinks. Now get this: I have a job to do. My job is to find out *why* you won't tell what the saucer said. I don't want to know what it said and I'll never ask you. I don't even want you to tell me. Let's just find out why you're keeping it a secret."

Finding out why turned out to be hours of just talking about having pneumonia and the flower pot she made in second grade that Mom threw down the fire escape and getting left back in school and the dream about holding a wine glass in both hands and peeping over it at some man.

And one day she told him why she wouldn't say about the saucer, just the way it came to her: "Because it was talking to *me*, and it's just nobody else's business."

She even told him about the man crossing himself that day. It was the only other thing she had of her own.

He was nice. He was the one who warned her about the trial. "I have no business saying this, but they're going to give you the full dress treatment. Judge and jury and all. And just say what you want to say, no less and no more, hear? And don't let 'em get your goat. You have a right to own something."

He got up and swore and left.

First a man came and talked to her for a long time about how maybe this Earth would be attacked from outer space by beings much stronger and cleverer than we are, and maybe she had the key to a defense. So she owed it to the whole world. And then even if the Earth wasn't attacked, just think of what an advantage she might give this country over its enemies. Then he shook his finger in her face and said that what she was doing amounted to working *for* the enemies of her country. And he turned out to be the man that was defending her at the trial.

The jury found her guilty of contempt of court and the judge recited a long list of penalties he could give her. He gave her one of them and suspended it. They put her back in jail for a few more days, and one fine day they turned her loose.

That was wonderful at first. She got a job in a restaurant, and a furnished room. She had been in the papers so much that Mom didn't want her back home. Mom was drunk most of the time and sometimes used to tear up the whole neighborhood, but all the same she had very special ideas about being respectable, and being in the papers all the time for spying was not her idea of being decent. So she put her maiden name on the mailbox downstairs and told her daughter not to live there any more.

At the restaurant she met a man who asked her for a date. The first time. She spent every cent she had on a red handbag to go with her red shoes. They weren't the same shade, but anyway they were both red. They went to the movies and afterward he didn't try to kiss her or anything, he just tried to find out what the flying saucer told her. She didn't say anything. She went home and cried all night.

Then some men sat in a booth talking and they shut up and glared at her every time she came past. They spoke to the boss, and he came and told her that they were electronics engineers working for the government and they were afraid to talk shop while she was around— wasn't she some sort of spy or something? So she got fired.

Once she saw her name on a juke box. She put in a nickel and punched that number, and the record was all about "the flyin' saucer came down one day, and taught her a brand new way to play, and what it was I will not say, but she took me out of this world." And while she was listening to it, someone in the juke-joint recognized her and called her by her name. Four of them followed her home and she had to block the door shut.

Sometimes she'd be all right for months on end, and then someone would ask for a date. Three times out of five, she and the date were followed. Once the man she was with arrested the man who was tailing them. Twice the man who was tailing them arrested the man she was

with. Five times out of five, the date would try to find
out about the saucer. Sometimes she would go out with
someone and pretend that it was a real date, but she
wasn't very good at it.

So she moved to the shore and got a job cleaning at
night in offices and stores. There weren't many to clean,
but that just meant there weren't many people to remember her face from the papers. Like clockwork, every
eighteen months, some feature writer would drag it all
out again in a magazine or a Sunday supplement; and
every time anyone saw a headlight on a mountain or a
light on a weather balloon it had to be a flying saucer,
and there had to be some tired quip about the saucer
wanting to tell secrets. Then for two or three weeks
she'd stay off the streets in the daytime.

Once she thought she had it whipped. People didn't
want her, so she began reading. The novels were all
right for a while until she found out that most of them
were like the movies—all about the pretty ones who
really own the world. So she learned things—animals,
trees. A lousy little chipmunk caught in a wire fence bit
her. The animals didn't want her. The trees didn't care.

Then she hit on the idea of the bottles. She got all
the bottles she could and wrote on papers which she
corked into the bottles. She'd tramp miles up and down
the beaches and throw the bottles out as far as she
could. She knew that if the right person found one, it
would give that person the only thing in the world that
would help. Those bottles kept her going for three solid
years. Everyone's got to have a secret little something
he does.

And at last the time came when it was no use any
more. You can go on trying to help someone who
maybe exists; but soon you can't pretend there is such a
person any more. And that's it. The end.

"Are you cold?" I asked when she was through telling me.
The surf was quieter and the shadows longer.

"No," she answered from the shadows. Suddenly she
said, "Did you think I was mad at you because you saw
me without my clothes?"

"Why shouldn't you be?"

"You know, I don't care? I wouldn't have wanted . . . wanted you to see me even in a ball gown or overalls. You can't cover up my carcass. It shows; it's there whatever. I just didn't want you to *see* me. At all."

"Me, or anyone?"

She hesitated. "You."

I got up and stretched and walked a little, thinking. "Didn't the F.B.I. try to stop you throwing your bottles?"

"Oh, sure. They spent I don't know how much tax-payers' money gathering 'em up. They still make a spot check every once in a while. They're getting tired of it, though. All the writing in the bottles is the same." She laughed. I didn't know she could.

"What's funny?"

"All of 'em—judges, jailers, juke-boxes—people. Do you know it wouldn't have saved me a minute's trouble if I'd told 'em the whole thing at the very beginning?"

"No?"

"No. They wouldn't have believed me. What they wanted was a new weapon. Super-science from a super-race, to slap hell out of the super-race if they ever got a chance, or out of our own if they don't. All those brains," she breathed, with more wonder than scorn, "all that brass. They think 'super-race' and it comes out 'super-science'. Don't they ever imagine a super-race has super-feelings, too—super-laughter, maybe, or super-hunger?" She paused. "Isn't it time you asked me what the saucer said?"

"I'll tell you," I blurted.

> *"There is in certain living souls*
> *A quality of loneliness unspeakable,*
> *So great it must be shared*
> *As company is shared by lesser beings.*
> *Such a loneliness is mine; so know by this*
> *That in immensity*
> *There is one lonelier than you."*

"Dear Jesus," she said devoutly, and began to weep. "And how is it addressed?"

"To the loneliest one . . ."

"How did you know?" she whispered.

"It's what you put in the bottles, isn't it?"

"Yes," she said. "Whenever it gets to be too much, that no one cares, that no one ever did . . . you throw a bottle into the sea, and out goes a part of your own loneliness. You sit and think of someone somewhere finding it . . . learning for the first time that the worst there is can be understood."

The moon was setting and the surf was hushed. We looked up and out to the stars. She said, "We don't know what loneliness is like. People thought the saucer was a saucer, but it wasn't. It was a bottle with a message inside. It had a bigger ocean to cross—all of space—and not much chance of finding anybody. Loneliness? We don't know loneliness."

When I could, I asked her why she had tried to kill herself.

"I've had it good," she said, "with what the saucer told me. I wanted to . . . pay back. I was bad enough to be helped; I had to know I was good enough to help. No one wants me? Fine. But don't tell me no one, anywhere, wants my help. I can't stand that."

I took a deep breath. "I found one of your bottles two years ago. I've been looking for you ever since. Tide charts, current tables, maps and . . . wandering. I heard some talk about you and the bottles hereabouts. Someone told me you'd quit doing it, you'd taken to wandering the dunes at night. I knew why. I ran all the way."

I needed another breath now. "I got a club foot. I think right, but the words don't come out of my mouth the way they're inside my head. I have this nose. I never had a woman. Nobody ever wanted to hire me to work where they'd have to look at me. You're beautiful," I said. "You're beautiful."

She said nothing, but it was as if a light came from her, more light and far less shadow than ever the practiced moon could cast. Among the many things it meant was that even to loneliness there is an end, for those who are lonely enough, long enough.

THE LIBERATION OF EARTH

WILLIAM TENN (PHILIP KLASS; 1920–   )
FUTURE SCIENCE FICTION, MAY

Here is Philip Klass, Professor of English at Penn State University, at his darkly humorous best. "The Liberation of Earth" is one of those strangely prophetic stories that might have appeared a decade and a half later, written by someone like Russell Baker or Art Buchwald. The good Professor had two other excellent stories published in 1953, "The Custodian" in Worlds Of If *and "The Deserter" in* Fred Pohl's Star Science Fiction Stories.

Future Science Fiction has an incredibly complex history, since it was published under some seven different names over a period of twenty-one years. There were, in order (I think): Future Fiction, Future Combined With Science Fiction, Future Fantasy and Science Fiction, Science Fiction Stories, Future Combined With Science Fiction Stories, Future Science Fiction Stories, *and finally,* Future Science Fiction.

Some business!

—MHG

There is something oxymoronic about Marty's phrase "darkly humorous." There are a number of ways of saying it, all seemingly self-contradictory: "black humor," "gallows humor." At its worst, it degenerates into "sarcasm" which itself comes from a Greek word meaning "to tear flesh."

Ordinary humor may be enjoyable, but it is almost always trivial. It is there to give pleasure rather than to make a point. Darken it, however; make it a bit savage; and it can drive deep. The pleasure becomes dubious, but the point made can be permanent.

Marty says the story is "strangely prophetic." I haven't asked him what he meant by that, but here is the strange prophecy I see in it. A decade and a half later, American forces were fighting in Vietnam. An American officer, as he set fire to the miserable thatched huts of a small village (using his cigarette lighter) said, "It is sometimes necessary to destroy a village to save it."

I suppose he meant it quite seriously, and even believed it (after all, it wasn't his village), but I suspect that that remark—which was widely publicized—helped enormously in turning American public opinion against the war.

—IA

THIS THEN, is the story of our liberation. Suck air and grab clusters. Heigh-ho, here is the tale.

August was the month, a Tuesday in August. These words are meaningless now, so far have we progressed; but many things known and discussed by our primitive ancestors, our unliberated, unreconstructed forefathers, are devoid of sense to our free minds. Still the tale must be told, with all of its incredible place names and vanished points of reference.

Why must it be told? Have any of you a *better* thing to do? We have had water and weeds and lie in a valley of gusts. So rest, relax and listen. And suck air, suck air.

On a Tuesday in August, the ship appeared in the sky over France in a part of the world then known as Europe. Five miles long the ship was, and word has come down to us that it looked like an enormous silver cigar.

The tale goes on to tell of the panic and consternation among our forefathers when the ship abruptly materialized in the summer-blue sky. How they ran, how they shouted, how they pointed!

How they excitedly notified the United Nations, one of their chiefest institutions, that a strange metal craft of incredible size had materialized over their land. How they sent an order *here* to cause military aircraft to surround it with loaded weapons, gave instructions *there* for hastily grouped scientists, with signaling apparatus, to approach it with friendly gestures. How, under the great ship, men with cameras took pictures of it; men with typewriters wrote stories about it; and men with concessions sold models of it.

All these things did our ancestors, enslaved and unknowing, do.

Then a tremendous slab snapped up in the middle of the ship and for the first of the aliens stepped out in the complex tripodal gait that all humans were shortly to know and love so well. He wore a metallic garment to protect him from the effects of our atmospheric peculiarities, a garment of the opaque, loosely folded type that these, the first of our liberators, wore throughout their stay on Earth.

Speaking in a language none could understand, but booming deafeningly through a huge mouth about halfway up his twenty-five feet of height, the alien discoursed for exactly one hour, waited politely for a response when he had finished, and, receiving none, retired into the ship.

That night, the first of our liberation! Or the first of our first liberation, should I say? *That* night, anyhow! Visualize our ancestors scurrying about their primitive intricacies: playing ice hockey, televising, smashing atoms, red-baiting, conducting giveaway shows and signing affidavits—all the incredible minutiae that made the olden times such a frightful mass of cumulative detail in which to live—as compared with the breathless and majestic simplicity of the present.

The big question, of course, was—what had the alien

said? Had he called on the human race to surrender? Had he announced that he was on a mission of peaceful trade and, having made what he considered a reasonable offer—for, let us say, the north polar ice cap—politely withdrawn so that we could discuss his terms among ourselves in relative privacy? Or, possibly, had he merely announced that he was the newly appointed ambassador to Earth from a friendly and intelligent race—and would we please direct him to the proper authority so that he might submit his credentials?

Not to know was quite maddening.

Since decision rested with the diplomats, it was the last possibility which was held, very late that night, to be most likely; and early the next morning, accordingly, a delegation from the United Nations waited under the belly of the motionless starship. The delegation had been instructed to welcome the aliens to the outermost limits of its collective linguistic ability. As an additional earnest of mankind's friendly intentions, all military craft patrolling the air about the great ship were ordered to carry no more than one atom bomb in their racks, and to fly a small white flag—along with the U.N. banner and their own national emblem. Thus did our ancestors face this, the ultimate challenge of history.

When the alien came forth a few hours later, the delegation stepped up to him, bowed, and, in the three official languages of the United Nations—English, French and Russian—asked him to consider this planet his home. He listened to them gravely, and then launched into his talk of the day before—which was evidently as highly charged with emotion and significance to him as it was completely incomprehensible to the representatives of world government.

Fortunately, a cultivated young Indian member of the secretariat detected a suspicious similarity between the speech of the alien and an obscure Bengali dialect whose anomalies he had once puzzled over. The reason, as we all know now, was that the last time Earth had been visited by aliens of this particular type, humanity's most advanced civilization lay in a moist valley in Bengal; extensive dictionaries of that language had been written, so that speech with the natives of Earth would present no problem to any subsequent exploring party.

However, I move ahead of my tale, as one who would munch on the succulent roots before the dryer stem. Let me rest and suck air for a moment. Heigh-ho, truly those were tremendous experiences for our kind.

You, sir, now you sit back and listen. You are not yet of an age to Tell the Tale. I remember, *well enough do I remember* how my father told it, and his father before him. You will wait your turn as I did; you will listen until too much high land between water holes blocks me off from life.

Then *you* may take your place in the juiciest weed patch and, reclining gracefully between sprints, recite the great epic of our liberation to the carelessly exercising young.

Pursuant to the young Hindu's suggestions, the one professor of comparative linguistics in the world capable of understanding and conversing in this peculiar version of the dead dialect was summoned from an academic convention in New York where he was reading a paper he had been working on for eighteen years: *An Initial Study of Apparent Relationships Between Several Past Participles in Ancient Sanscrit and an Equal Number of Noun Substantives in Modern Szechuanese*.

Yea, verily, all these things—and more, many more— did our ancestors in their besotted ignorance contrive to do. May we not count our freedom indeed?

The disgruntled scholar, minus—as he kept insisting bitterly—some of his most essential word lists, was flown by fastest jet to the area south of Nancy which, in those long-ago days, lay in the enormous black shadow of the alien spaceship.

Here he was acquainted with his task by the United Nations delegation, whose nervousness had not been allayed by a new and disconcerting development. Several more aliens had emerged from the ship carrying great quantities of immense, shimmering metal which they proceeded to assemble into something that was obviously a machine—though it was taller than any skyscraper man had ever built, and seemed to make noises to itself like a talkative and sentient creature. The first alien still stood courteously in the neighborhood of the profusely perspiring diplomats; ever and anon he would go through his little speech again, in a language that had been almost forgotten when the cornerstone of the library of Alexandria was laid. The men from the U.N. would reply, each one hoping desperately to make up for the alien's lack of familiarity with his own tongue by such devices as hand gestures and facial expressions. Much later, a commission of anthropologists and psychologists brilliantly pointed out the difficulties of such physical, gestural communication with creatures possessing—as these aliens did—five manual appendages and a single, unwinking compound eye of the type the insects rejoice in.

The problem and agonies of the professor as he was trundled about the world in the wake of the aliens, trying to amass a usable vocabulary in a language whose peculiarities he could only extrapolate from the limited samples supplied him by one who must inevitably speak it with the most outlandish of foreign accents—these vexations were minor indeed compared to the disquiet felt by the representatives of world government. They beheld the extraterrestrial visitors move every day to a new site on their planet and proceed to assemble there a titanic structure of flickering metal which muttered nostalgically to itself, as if to keep alive the memory of those faraway factories which had given it birth.

True, there was always the alien who would pause in his evidently supervisory labors to release the set little speech; but not even the excellent manners he displayed, in listening to upward of fifty-six replies in as many languages, helped dispel the panic caused whenever a human scientist, investigating the shimmering machines, touched a projecting edge and promptly shrank into a disappearing pinpoint. This, while not a frequent occurrence, happened often enough to cause chronic indigestion and insomnia among human administrators.

Finally, having used up most of his nervous system as fuel, the professor collated enough of the language to make conversation possible. He—and, through him, the world—was thereupon told the following:

The aliens were members of a highly advanced civilization which had spread its culture throughout the entire galaxy. Cognizant of the limitations of the as yet underdeveloped animals who had latterly become dominant upon Earth, they had placed us in a sort of benevolent ostracism. Until either we or our institutions had evolved to a level permitting, say, at least *associate* membership in the galactic federation (under the sponsoring tutelage, for the first few millennia, of one of the older, more widespread and more important species in that federation)—until that time, all invasions of our privacy and ignorance—except for a few scientific expeditions conducted under conditions of great secrecy—had been strictly forbidden by universal agreement.

Several individuals who had violated this ruling—at great cost to our racial sanity, and enormous profit to our reigning religions—had been so promptly and severely punished that no known infringements had occurred for some time. Our recent growth curve had been satisfactory enough to cause hopes that a bare thirty or forty centuries more would suffice to place us on applicant status with the federation.

Unfortunately, the peoples of this stellar community were many, and varied as greatly in their ethical outlook as their biological composition. Quite a few species lagged a considerable social distance behind the Dendi, as our visitors called themselves. One of these, a race of horrible, wormlike organisms known as the Troxxt—almost as advanced technologically as they were retarded in moral development—had suddenly volunteered for the position of sole and absolute ruler of the galaxy. They had seized control of several key suns, with their attendant planetary systems, and, after a calculated decimation of the races thus captured, had announced their intention of punishing with a merciless extinction all species unable to appreciate from these object lessons the value of unconditional surrender.

In despair, the galactic federation had turned to the Dendi, one of the oldest, most selfless, and yet most powerful of races in civilized space, and commissioned them, as the military arm of the federation, to hunt down the Troxxt, defeat them wherever they had gained illegal suzerainty, and destroy forever their power to wage war.

This order had come almost too late. Everywhere the Troxxt had gained so much the advantage of attack, that the Dendi were able to contain them only by enormous sacrifice. For centuries now, the conflict had careened across our vast island universe. In the course of it, densely populated planets had been disintegrated; suns had been blasted into novae; and whole groups of stars ground into swirling cosmic dust.

A temporary stalemate had been reached a short while ago, and, reeling and breathless, both sides were using the lull to strengthen weak spots in their perimeter.

Thus, the Troxxt had finally moved into the till-then peaceful section of space that contained our solar system—among others. They were thoroughly uninterested in our tiny planet with its meager resources; nor did they care much for such celestial neighbors as Mars or Jupiter. They established their headquarters on a planet of Proxima Centaurus, the star nearest our own sun, and proceeded to consolidate their offensive-defensive network between Rigel and Aldebaran. At this point in their explanation, the Dendi pointed out, the exigencies of interstellar strategy tended to become too complicated for anything but three-dimensional maps; let us here accept the simple statement, they suggested, that it became immediately vital for them to strike rapidly, and make the Troxxt position on Proxima Centaurus untenable—to establish a base inside their lines of communication.

The most likely spot for such a base was Earth.

The Dendi apologized profusely for intruding on our development, an intrusion which might cost us dear in our delicate developmental state. But, as they explained—in impeccable pre-Bengali—before their arrival we had, in effect, become (all unknowingly) a satrapy of the awful Troxxt. We could now consider ourselves liberated.

We thanked them much for that.

Besides, their leader pointed out proudly, the Dendi were engaged in a war for the sake of civilization itself, against an enemy so horrible, so obscene in its nature, and so utterly filthy in its practices, that it was unworthy of the label of intelligent life. They were fighting, not only for themselves, but for every loyal member of the galactic federation; for every small and helpless species; for every obscure race too weak to defend itself against a ravaging conquerer. Would humanity stand aloof from such a conflict?

There was just a slight bit of hesitation as the information was digested. Then: *"No!"* humanity roared back through such mass-communication media as television, newspapers, reverberating jungle drums, and mule-mounted backwoods messenger. *"We will not stand aloof! We will help you destroy this menace to the very fabric of civilization! Just tell us what you want us to do!"*

Well, nothing in particular, the aliens replied with some embarrassment. Possibly in a little while there might *be* something—*several* little things, in fact—which could be *quite* useful; but, for the moment, if we would concentrate on not getting in their way when they serviced their gunmounts, they would be very grateful, really. . . .

This reply tended to create a large amount of uncertainty among the two billion of Earth's human population. For several days afterward, there was a planetwide tendency—the legend has come down to us—of people failing to meet each other's eyes.

But then man rallied from this substantial blow to his pride. He would be useful, be it ever so humble, to the race which had liberated him from potential subjugation by the ineffably ugly Troxxt. For this, let us remember well our ancestors! Let us hymn their sincere efforts amid their ignorance!

All standing armies, all air and sea fleets, were reorganized into guard patrols around the Dendi weapons: no human might approach within two miles of the murmuring machinery, without a pass countersigned by the Dendi. Since they were never known to sign such a pass during the entire period of their stay on this planet, however, this loophole provision was never exercised as far as is known; and the immediate neighborhood of the extraterrestrial weapons became and remained henceforth wholesomely free of two-legged creatures.

Cooperation with our liberators took precedence over all other human activities. The order of the day was a slogan first given voice by a Harvard professor of government in a querulous radio round table on "Man's Place in a Somewhat Overcivilized Universe."

"Let us forget our individual egos and collective conceits," the professor cried at one point. "Let us subordinate everything—to the end that the freedom of the solar system in general, and Earth in particular, must and shall be preserved!"

Despite its mouth-filling qualities, this slogan was repeated everywhere. Still, it was difficult sometimes to know exactly what the Dendi wanted—partly because of the limited number of interpreters available to the heads of the various sovereign states, and partly because of their leader's tendency to vanish into his ship after ambiguous and equivocal statements, such as the curt admonition to "Evacuate Washington!"

On that occasion, both the Secretary of State and the American President perspired fearfully through five hours of a July day in all the silk-hatted, stiff-collared, dark-suited diplomatic regalia that the barbaric past demanded of political leaders who would deal with the representatives of another people. They waited and wilted beneath the enormous ship—which no human had ever been invited to enter, despite the wistful hints constantly thrown out by university professors and aeronautical designers—they waited patiently and wetly for the Dendi leader to emerge and let them know whether he had meant the State of Washington or Washington, D.C.

The tale comes down to us at this point as a tale of glory. The capitol building taken apart in a few days, and set up almost intact in the foothills of the Rocky Mountains; the missing Archives, that were later to turn up in the children's room of a public library in Duluth, Iowa; the bottles of Potomac River water carefully borne westward and ceremoniously poured into the circular concrete ditch built around the President's mansion (from which unfortunately it was to evaporate within a week because of the relatively low humidity of the region)—all these are proud moments in the galactic history of our species, from which not even the later knowledge that the Dendi wished to build no gun site on the spot, nor even an ammunition dump, but merely a recreation hall for their troops, could remove any of the grandeur of our determined cooperation and most willing sacrifice.

There was no denying, however, that the ego of our race was greatly damaged by the discovery, in the course of a routine journalistic interview, that the aliens totaled no more powerful a group than a squad; and that their leader, instead of the great scientist and key military strategist that we might justifiably have expected the Galactic Federation to furnish for the protection of Terra, ranked as the interstellar equivalent of a buck sergeant.

That the President of the United States, the Commander-in-Chief of the Army and the Navy, had waited in such obeisant fashion upon a mere noncommissioned officer was hard for us to swallow; but that the impending Battle of Earth was to have a historical dignity only slightly higher than that of a patrol action was impossibly humiliating.

And then there was the matter of "lendi."

The aliens, while installing or servicing their planet-wide weapon system, would occasionally fling aside an evidently unusable fragment of the talking metal. Separated from the machine of which it had been a component, the substance seemed to lose all those qualities which were deleterious to mankind and retain several which were quite useful indeed. For example, if a portion of the strange material was attached to any terrestrial metal and insulated carefully from contact with other substances it would, in a few hours, itself become exactly the metal that it touched, whether that happened to be zinc, gold, or pure uranium.

This stuff—"lendi," men have heard the aliens call it—was shortly in frantic demand in an economy ruptured by constant and unexpected emptyings of its most important industrial centers.

Everywhere the aliens went, to and from their weapon sites, hordes of ragged humans stood chanting—well outside the two-mile limit—"Any lendi, Dendi?" All attempts by law enforcement agencies of the planet to put a stop to this shameless, wholesale begging were useless, especially since the Dendi themselves seemed to get some unexplainable pleasure out of scattering tiny pieces of lendi to the scrabbling multitude. When policemen and soldiery began to join the trampling, murderous dash to the corner of the meadows wherein had fallen the highly versatile and garrulous metal, governments gave up.

Mankind almost began to hope for the attack to come, so that it would be relieved of the festering consideration of its own patent inferiorities. A few of the more fanatically conservative among our ancestors probably even began to regret liberation.

They did, children; they did! Let us hope that these would-be troglodytes were among the very first to be dissolved and melted down by the red flameballs. One cannot, after all, turn one's back on progress!

Two days before the month of September was over, the aliens announced that they had detected activity upon one of the moons of Saturn. The Troxxt were evidently threading their treacherous way inward through the solar system. Considering their vicious and deceitful propensities, the Dendi warned, an attack from these wormlike monstrosities might be expected at any moment.

Few humans went to sleep as the night rolled up to and past the meridian on which they dwelt. Almost all eyes were lifted to a sky carefully denuded of clouds by watchful Dendi. There was a brisk trade in cheap telescopes and bits of smoked glass in some sections of the planet; while other portions experienced a substantial boom in spells and charms of the all-inclusive, or omnibus, variety.

The Troxxt attacked in three cylindrical black ships simultaneously; one in the southern hemisphere, and two in the northern. Great gouts of green flame roared out of their tiny craft; and everything touched by this imploded into a translucent, glasslike sand. No Dendi was hurt by these, however, and from each of the now-writhing gunmounts there bubbled forth a series of scarlet clouds which pursued the Troxxt hungrily, until forced by a dwindling velocity to fall back upon Earth.

Here they had an unhappy aftereffect. Any populated area into which these pale pink cloudlets chanced to fall was rapidly transformed into a cemetery—a cemetery, if the truth be told as it has been handed down to us that had more the odor of the kitchen than the grave. The inhabitants of these unfortunate localities were subjected to enormous increases of temperature. Their skin reddened, then blackened; their hair and nails shriveled; their very flesh turned into liquid and boiled off their bones. Altogether a disagreeable way for one-tenth of the human race to die.

The only consolation was the capture of a black cylinder by one of the red clouds. When, as a result of this, it had turned white-hot and poured its substance down in the form of a metallic rainstorm, the two ships assaulting the northern hemisphere abruptly retreated to the asteroids into which the Dendi, because of severely limited numbers, steadfastly refused to pursue them.

In the next twenty-four hours the aliens—*resident* aliens, let us say—held conferences, made repairs to their weapons and commiserated with us. Humanity buried its dead. This last was a custom of our forefathers that was most worthy of note; and one that has not, of course, survived into modern times.

By the time the Troxxt returned, man was ready for them. He could not, unfortunately, stand to arms as he most ardently desired to do; but he could and did stand to optical instrument and conjurer's oration.

Once more the little red clouds burst joyfully into the upper reaches of the statosphere; once more the green flames wailed and tore at the chattering spires of lendi; once more men died by the thousands in the boiling backwash of war. But this time, there was a slight difference: the green flames of the Troxxt abruptly changed color after the engagement had lasted three hours; they became darker, more bluish. And, as they did so, Dendi after Dendi collapsed at his station and died in convulsions.

The call for retreat was evidently sounded. The survivors fought their way to the tremendous ship in which they had come. With an explosion from her stern jets that blasted a red-hot furrow southward through France, and kicked Marseilles into the Mediterranean, the ship roared into space and fled home ignominiously.

Humanity steeled itself for the coming ordeal of horror under the Troxxt.

They were truly wormlike in form. As soon as the two night-black cylinders had landed, they strode from their ships, their tiny segmented bodies held off the ground by a complex harness supported by long and slender metal crutches. They erected a domelike fort around each ship—one in Australia and one in the Ukraine—captured the few courageous individuals who had ventured close to their landing sites, and disappeared back into the dark craft with their squirming prizes.

While some men drilled about nervously in the ancient military patterns, others pored anxiously over scientific texts and records pertaining to the visit of the

Dendi, in the desperate hope of finding a way of preserving terrestrial independence against this ravening conqueror of the star-spattered galaxy.

And yet all this time, the human captives inside the artifically darkened spaceships (the Troxxt, having no eyes, not only had little use for light but the more sedentary individuals among them actually found such radiation disagreeable to their sensitive, unpigmented skins) were not being tortured for information—nor vivisected in the earnest quest of knowledge on a slightly higher level—but educated.

Educated in the Troxxtian language, that is.

True it was that a large number found themselves utterly inadequate for the task which the Troxxt had set them, and temporarily became servants to the more successful students. And another, albeit smaller, group developed various forms of frustration hysteria—ranging from mild unhappiness to complete catatonic depression—over the difficulties presented by a language whose every verb was irregular, and whose myriads of prepositions were formed by noun-adjective combinations derived from the subject of the previous sentence. But, eventually, eleven human beings were released, to blink madly in the sunlight as certified interpreters of Troxxt.

These liberators, it seemed, had never visited Bengal in the heyday of its millennia-past civilization.

Yes, these *liberators*. For the Troxxt had landed on the sixth day of the ancient, almost mythical month of October. And October the Sixth is, of course, the Holy Day of the Second Liberation. Let us remember, let us revere. (If only we could figure out which day it is on our calendar!)

The tale the interpreters told caused men to hang their heads in shame and gnash their teeth at the deception they had allowed the Dendi to practice upon them.

True, the Dendi had been commissioned by the Galactic Federation to hunt the Troxxt down and destroy them. This was largely because the Dendi *were* the Galactic Federation. One of the first intelligent arrivals on the interstellar scene, the huge creatures had organized a vast police force to protect them and their power against any contingency of revolt that might arise in the future. This police force was ostensibly a congress of all thinking life forms throughout the galaxy; actually, it was an efficient means of keeping them under rigid control.

Most species thus far discovered were docile and tractable, however; the Dendi had been ruling from time immemorial, said they—very well, then, let the Dendi continue to rule. Did it make that much difference?

But, throughout the centuries, opposition to the Dendi grew; and the nuclei of the opposition were the protoplasm-based creatures. What, in fact, had come to be known as the Protoplasmic League.

Though small in number, the creatures whose life cycles were derived from the chemical and physical properties of protoplasm varied greatly in size, structure, and specialization. A galactic community deriving the main wells of its power from them would be a dynamic instead of a static place, where extragalactic travel would be encouraged, instead of being inhibited, as it was at present because of Dendi fears of meeting a superior civilization. It would be a true democracy of species—a real biological republic—where all creatures of adequate intelligence and cultural development would enjoy a control of their destinies at present experienced by the silicon-based Dendi alone.

To this end, the Troxxt, the only important race which had steadfastly refused the complete surrender of armaments demanded of all members of the Federation, had been implored by a minor member of the Protoplasmic League to rescue it from the devastation which the Dendi intended to visit upon it, as punishment for an unlawful exploratory excursion outside the boundaries of the galaxy.

Faced with the determination of the Troxxt to defend their cousins in organic chemistry, and the suddenly aroused hostility of at least two-thirds of the interstellar peoples, the Dendi had summoned a rump meeting of the Galactic Council; declared a state of revolt in being; and proceeded to cement their disintegrating rule with the blasted life forces of a hundred worlds. The Troxxt, hopelessly outnumbered and outequipped, had been able to continue the struggle only because of the great ingenuity and selflessness of other members of the Protoplasmic League, who had risked extinction to supply them with newly developed secret weapons.

Hadn't we guessed the nature of the beast from the enormous precautions it had taken to prevent the exposure of any part of its body to the intensely corrosive atmosphere of Earth? Surely the seamless, barely translucent suits which our recent visitors had worn for every moment of their stay on our world should have made us suspect a body chemistry developed from complex silicon compounds rather than those of carbon?

Humanity hung its collective head and admitted that the suspicion had never occurred to it.

Well, the Troxxt admitted generously, we were extremely inexperienced and possibly a little too trusting. Put it down to that. Our naiveté, however costly to them, our liberators, would not be allowed to deprive us of that complete citizenship which the Troxxt were claiming as the birthright of all.

But as for our leaders, our probably corrupted, certainly irresponsible leaders. . . .

The first executions of U.N. officials, heads of states, and pre-Bengali interpreters as "Traitors to Protoplasm" —after some of the lengthiest and most nearly perfectly fair trials in the history of Earth—were held a week after G-J Day, the inspiring occasion on which, amidst gorgeous ceremonies, humanity was invited to join, first the Protoplasmic League and thence the New and Democratic Galactic Federation of All Species, All Races.

Nor was that all. Whereas the Dendi had contemptuously shoved us to one side as they went about their business of making our planet safe for tyranny, and had, in all probability, built special devices which made the very touch of their weapons fatal for us, the Troxxt—

with the sincere friendliness which had made their name a byword for democracy and decency wherever living creatures came together among the stars—our Second Liberators, as we lovingly called them, actually *preferred* to have us help them with the intensive, accelerating labor of planetary defense.

So men's intestines dissolved under the invisible glare of the forces used to assemble the new, incredibly complex weapons; men sickened and died, in scrabbling hordes, inside the mines which the Troxxt had made deeper than any we had dug hitherto; men's bodies broke open and exploded in the undersea oil-drilling sites which the Troxxt had declared were essential.

Children's schooldays were requested, too, in such collecting drives as "Platinum Scrap for Procyon" and "Radioactive Debris for Deneb." Housewives also were implored to save on salt whenever possible—this substance being useful to the Troxxt in literally dozens of incomprehensible ways—and colorful posters reminded: "*Don't salinate—sugarfy!*"

And over all, courteously caring for us like an intelligent parent, were our mentors, taking their giant supervisory strides on metallic crutches, while their pale little bodies lay curled in the hammocks that swung from each paired length of shining leg.

Truly, even in the midst of a complete economic paralysis caused by the concentration of all major productive facilities on otherworldly armaments, and despite the anguished cries of those suffering from peculiar industrial injuries which our medical men were totally unequipped to handle, in the midst of all this mind-wracking disorganization, it was yet very exhilarating to realize that we had taken our lawful place in the future government of the galaxy and were even now helping to make the universe safe for democracy.

But the Dendi returned to smash this idyll. They came in their huge, silvery spaceships and the Troxxt, barely warned in time, just managed to rally under the blow and fight back in kind. Even so, the Troxxt ship in the Ukraine was almost immediately forced to flee to its base in the depths of space. After three days, the only Troxxt on Earth were the devoted members of a little band guarding the ship in Australia. They proved, in three or more months, to be as difficult to remove from the face of our planet as the continent itself; and since there was now a state of close and hostile siege, with the Dendi on one side of the globe, and the Troxxt on the other, the battle assumed frightful proportions.

Seas boiled; whole steppes burned away; the climate itself shifted and changed under the gruelling pressure of the cataclysm. By the time the Dendi solved the problem, the planet Venus had been blasted from the skies in the course of a complicated battle maneuver, and Earth had wobbled over as orbital substitute.

The solution was simple: since the Troxxt were too firmly based on the small continent to be driven away, the numerically superior Dendi brought up enough firepower to disintegrate all Australia into an ash that muddied the Pacific. This occurred on the twenty-fourth of June, the Holy Day of First Reliberation. A day of reckoning for what remained of the human race, however.

How could we have been so naive, the Dendi wanted to know, as to be taken in by the chauvinistic protoplasm progaganda? Surely, if physical characteristics were to be the criteria of our racial empathy, we would not orient ourselves on a narrow chemical basis! The Dendi life plasma was based on silicon instead of carbon, true, but did not vertebrates—*appendaged* vertebrates, at that, such as we and the Dendi—have infinitely more in common, in spite of a *minor* biochemical difference or two, then vertebrates and legless, armless, slime-crawling creatures who happened, quite accidentally, to possess an identical organic substance?

As for this fantastic picture of life in the galaxy . . . *well!* The Dendi shrugged their quintuple shoulders as they went about the intricate business of erecting their noisy weapons all over the rubble of our planet. Had we ever seen a representative of these protoplasmic races the Troxxt were supposedly protecting? No, nor would we. For as soon as a race-animal, vegetable or mineral—developed enough to constitute even a *potential* danger to the sinuous aggressors, its civilization was systematically dismantled by the watchful Troxxt. We were in so primitive a state that they had not considered it at all risky to allow us the outward seeming of full participation.

Could we say we had learned a single useful piece of information about Troxxt technology, for all of the work we had done on their machines, for all of the lives we had lost in the process? No, of course not! We had merely contributed our mite to the enslavement of far-off races who had done us no harm.

There was much that we had cause to feel guilty about, the Dendi told us gravely—once the few surviving interpreters of the pre-Bengali dialect had crawled out of hiding. But our collective onus was as nothing compared to that borne by "vermicular collaborationists" —those traitors who had supplanted our martyred former leaders. And then there were the unspeakable human interpreters who had had linguistic traffic with creatures destroying a two-million-year-old galactic peace! Why, killing was almost too good for them, the Dendi murmured as they killed them.

When the Troxxt ripped their way back into possession of Earth some eighteen months later, bringing us the sweet fruits of the Second Reliberation—as well as a complete and most convincing rebuttal of the Dendi— there were few humans found who were willing to accept with any real enthusiasm the responsibilities of newly opened and highly paid positions in language, science, and government.

Of course, since the Troxxt, in order to reliberate Earth, had found it necessary to blast a tremendous chunk out of the northern hemisphere, there were very few humans to be found in the first place. . . .

Even so, many of these committed suicide rather than assume the title of Secretary General of the United

Nations when the Dendi came back for the glorious Re-Reliberation, a short time after that. This was the liberation, by the way, which swept the deep collar of matter off our planet, and gave it what our forefathers came to call a pear-shaped look.

Possibly it was at this time—possibly a liberation or so later—that the Troxxt and the Dendi discovered the Earth had become far too eccentric in its orbit to possess the minimum safety conditions demanded of a combat zone. The battle, therefore, zigzagged coruscatingly and murderously away in the direction of Aldebaran.

That was nine generations ago, but the tale that has been handed down from parent to child, to child's child, has lost little in the telling. You hear it now from me almost exactly as *I* heard it. From my father I heard it as I ran with him from water puddle to distant water puddle, across the searing heat of yellow sand. From my mother I heard it as we sucked air and frantically grabbed at clusters of thick green weed, whenever the planet beneath us quivered in omen of a geological spasm that might bury us in its burned-out body, or a cosmic gyration threatened to fling us into empty space.

Yes, even as we do now did we do then, telling the same tale, running the same frantic race across the miles of unendurable heat for food and water; fighting the same savage battles with the giant rabbits for each other's carrion—and always, ever and always, sucking desperately at the precious air, which leaves our world in greater quantities with every mad twist of its orbit.

Naked, hungry, and thirsty came we into the world, and naked, hungry, and thirsty do we scamper our lives out upon it, under the huge and never-changing sun.

The same tale it is, and the same traditional ending it has as that I had from my father and his father before him. Suck air, grab clusters, and hear the last holy observation of our history:

"Looking about us, we can say with pardonable pride that we have been about as thoroughly liberated as it is possible for a race and a planet to be!"

LOT

WARD MOORE (1903–1978)
THE MAGAZINE OF FANTASY AND SCIENCE FICTION MAY

At the risk of overusing this phrase, I think that Ward Moore is one of the most shamefully neglected science fiction writers of all time. It is true that his great alternate world novel in which the South wins the Civil War—Bring The Jubilee, (1953) is highly regarded and generally well-known, but the book is currently out-of-print, as are all of his novels, including the excellent Greener Than You Think (1947, and probably his best book).

Born in rural New Jersey, he worked at a variety of jobs including construction, publishing, and chicken farming before and after the publication of his first (non-sf) novel Breathe The Air Again (1942). He was a man who ultimately felt that science fiction was bad for him, a ghetto that kept his work from being better known. He died before publishing realities made science fiction less of a problem in this regard.

While he did not produce a huge number of short stories, these are uniformly excellent and it is a small tragedy that he has never had a collection. In addition to "Lot" and its sequel "Lot's Daughter," we would bring your attention to "Frank Merriwell in the White House," a terrific satirical commentary on American politics, and "The Fellow Who Married the Maxill Girl."

"Lot," one of the very best post-holocaust stories,

123

was loosely adapted for the screen in the forgettable
Panic In The Year Zero *(1962).*

—MHG

Here is a perfect example of what I consider a perfect title. If you look at the title before starting the story, it may seem meaningless. What does it mean? Great deal? A plot of ground on which to build a house? A device with which to make a random choice? One's destiny?

Read the story, however, and then look at the title again. Not only does the meaning of the title become clear, but it illuminates the story and puts it in a very stark light.

Incidentally, I always bristle at anyone who talks of a science fiction "ghetto."

In the first place, those of us who began our career in the era of John Campbell never thought of sf as a "ghetto." It was where we wanted to be. We wouldn't dream of writing anything else.

In the second place, any science fiction writer who seriously wanted to get out and write something else could do so. Kurt Vonnegut, John D. MacDonald, and John Jakes are all cases in point.

In the third place, the day finally came when science fiction became wildly remunerative and it's everything else that's the "ghetto."

—IA

MR. JIMMON even appeared elated, like a man about to set out on a vacation.

"Well, folks, no use waiting any longer. We're all set. So let's go."

There was a betrayal here; Mr. Jimmon was not the kind of man who addressed his family as "folks."

"David, you're sure. . . ?"

Mr. Jimmon merely smiled. This was quite out of character; customarily he reacted to his wife's habit of posing unfinished questions—after seventeen years the unuttered and larger part of the queries were always instantly known to him in some mysterious way, as

though unerringly projected by the key in which the
introduction was pitched, so that not only the full word-
ing was communicated to his mind, but the shades and
implications which circumstance and humor attached to
them—with sharp and querulous defense. No matter
how often he resolved to stare quietly or use the still
more effective, Afraid I didn't catch your meaning,
dear, he had never been able to put his resolution into
force. Until this moment of crisis. Crisis, reflected Mr.
Jimmon, still smiling and moving suggestively toward
the door, crisis changes people. Brings out underlying
qualities.

It was Jir who answered Molly Jimmon, with the
adolescent's half-whine of exasperation. "Aw furcrysay
Mom, what's the idea? The highways'll be clogged tight.
What's the good figuring out everything heada time and
having everything all set if you're going to start all over
again at the last minute? Get a grip on yourself and let's
go."

Mr. Jimmon did not voice the reflexive, That's no
way to talk to your Mother. Instead he thought, not
unsympathetically, of woman's slow reaction time. As-
set in childbirth, liability behind the wheel. He knew
Molly was thinking of the house and all the things in it:
her clothes and Erika's, the TV set—so sullenly ugly
now, with the electricity gone—the refrigerator in which
the food would soon begin to rot and stink, the dead
stove, the cellarful of cases of canned stuff for which
there was no room in the station wagon. And the
Buick, blocked up in the garage, with the air thoughtfully let out of the tires and the battery hidden.

Of course the house would be looted. But they had
known that all along. When they—or rather he, for it
was his executive's mind and training which were responsible for the Jimmons' preparation against this
moment—planned so carefully and providentially, he
had weighed property against life and decided on life.
No other decision was possible.

"Aren't you at least going to phone Pearl and Dan?"

Now why in the world, thought Mr. Jimmon, completely above petty irritation, should I call Dan Davisson? (Because of course it's *Dan* she means—My Old Beau. Oh, he was nobody then, just an impractical dreamer without a penny to his name; it wasn't for years that he was recognized as a Mathematical Genius; now he's a professor and all sorts of things—but she automatically says Pearl-and-Dan, not Dan.) What can Dan do with the square root of minus nothing to offset M equals whatever it is, at this moment? Or am I supposed to ask if Pearl has all her diamonds? Query, why doesn't Pearl wear pearls? Only diamonds? My wife's friends, heh heh, but even the subtlest intonation won't label them when you're entertaining an important client and Pearl and Dan.

And why should I? What sudden paralysis afflicts her? Hysteria?

"No," said Mr. Jimmon.

Then he added, relenting, "Phone's been out since."

"But," said Molly.

She's hardly going to ask me to drive into town. He selected several answers in readiness. But she merely looked toward the telephone helplessly (she ought to have been fat, thought Mr. Jimmon, really she should, or anyway plump; her thinness gives her that air of competence, or at least *attempt*), so he amplified gently, "They're unquestionably all right. As far away from It as we are."

Wendell was already in the station wagon. With Waggie hidden somewhere. Should have sent the dog to the humane society; more merciful to have it put to sleep. Too late now; Waggie would have to take his chance. There were plenty of rabbits in the hills above Malibu, he had often seen them quite close to the house. At all events there was no room for a dog in the wagon, already loaded within a pound of its capacity.

Erika came in briskly from the kitchen, her brown jodhpurs making her appear at first glance even younger than fourteen. But only at first glance; then the swell of hips and breast denied the childishness the jodhpurs seemed to accent.

"The water's gone, Mom. There's no use sticking around any longer."

Molly looked incredulous. "The water?"

"Of course the water's gone," said Mr. Jimmon, not impatiently, but rather with satisfaction in his own foresight. "If It didn't get the aqueduct, the mains depend on pumps. Electric pumps. When the electricity went, the water went too."

"But the water," repeated Molly, as though this last catastrophe was beyond all reason—even the outrageous logic which It brought in its train.

Jir slouched past them and outside. Erika tucked in a strand of hair, pulled her jockey cap downward and sideways, glanced quickly at her mother and father, then followed. Molly took several steps, paused, smiled vaguely in the mirror and walked out of the house.

Mr. Jimmon patted his pockets; the money was all there. He didn't even look back before closing the front door and rattling the knob to be sure the lock had caught. It had never failed, but Mr. Jimmon always rattled it anyway. He strode to the station wagon, running his eye over the springs to reassure himself again that they really hadn't overloaded it.

The sky was overcast; you might have thought it one of the regular morning high fogs if you didn't know. Mr. Jimmon faced southeast, but It had been too far away to see anything now. Erika and Molly were in the front seat; the boys were in the back, lost amid the neatly packed stuff. He opened the door on the driver's side, got in, turned the key and started the motor. Then he said casually over his shoulder, "Put the dog out, Jir."

Wendell protested, too quickly, "Waggie's not here."

Molly exclaimed, "Oh, David. . . ."

Mr. Jimmon said patiently, "We're losing pretty valuable time. There's no room for the dog; we have no food for him. If we had room we could have taken more essentials; those few pounds might mean the difference."

"Can't find him," muttered Jir.

"He's not here. I tell you he's not here," shouted Wendell, tearful voiced.

"If I have to stop the motor and get him myself we'll be wasting still more time and gas." Mr. Jimmon was still detached, judicial. "This isn't a matter of kindness to animals. It's life and death."

Erika said evenly, "Dad's right, you know. It's the dog or us. Put him out, Wend."

"I tell you—" Wendell began.

"Got him!" exclaimed Jir. "OK, Waggie! Outside and good luck."

The spaniel wriggled ecstatically as he was picked up and put out through the open window. Mr. Jimmon raced the motor, but it didn't drown out Wendell's anguish. He threw himself on his brother, hitting and kicking. Mr. Jimmon took his foot off the gas, and as soon as he was sure the dog was away from the wheels, eased the station wagon out of the driveway and down the hill toward the ocean.

"Wendell, Wendell, stop," pleaded Molly. "Don't hurt him, Jir."

Mr. Jimmon clicked on the radio. After a preliminary hum, clashing static crackled out. He pushed all five buttons in turn, varying the quality of unintelligible sound. "Want me to try?" offered Erika. She pushed the manual button and turned the knob slowly. Music dripped out.

Mr. Jimmon grunted. "Mexican station. Try something else. Maybe you can get Ventura."

They rounded a tight curve. "Isn't that the Warbinn's?" asked Molly.

For the first time since It happened Mr. Jimmon had a twinge of impatience. There was no possibility, even with the unreliable eye of shocked excitement, of mistaking the Warbinn's blue Mercury. No one else on Rambla Catalina had one anything like it, and visitors would be most unlikely now. If Molly would apply the most elementary logic!

Besides, Warbinn had stopped the blue Mercury in the Jimmon driveway five times every week for the past two months—ever since they had decided to put the Buick up and keep the wagon packed and ready against this moment—for Mr. Jimmon to ride with him to the city. Of course it was the Warbinn's.

"... advised not to impede the progress of the military. Adequate medical staffs are standing by at all hospitals. Local civilian defense units are taking all steps in accordance ..."

"Santa Barbara," remarked Jir, nodding at the radio with an expert's assurance.

Mr. Jimmon slowed, prepared to follow the Warbinns down to 101, but the Mercury halted and Mr. Jimmon turned out to pass it. Warbinn was driving and Sally was in the front seat with him; the back seat appeared empty except for a few things obviously hastily thrown in. No foresight, thought Mr. Jimmon.

Warbinn waved his hand vigorously out the window and Sally shouted something.

"... panic will merely slow rescue efforts. Casualties are much smaller than originally reported ..."

"How do they know?" asked Mr. Jimmon, waving politely at the Warbinns.

"Oh David, aren't you going to stop? They want something."

"Probably just to talk."

"... to retain every drop of water. Emergency power will be in operation shortly. There is no cause for undue alarm. General ..."

Through the rear-view mirror Mr. Jimmon saw the blue Mercury start after them. He had been right then, they only wanted to say something inconsequential. At a time like this.

At the junction with U.S. 101 five cars blocked Rambla Catalina. Mr. Jimmon set the handbrake, and steadying himself with the open door, stood tiptoe twistedly, trying to see over the cars ahead. 101 was solid with traffic which barely moved. On the southbound side of the divided highway a stream of vehicles flowed illegally north.

"Thought everybody was figured to go east," gibed Jir over the other side of the car.

Mr. Jimmon was not disturbed by his son's sarcasm.

How right he'd been to rule out the trailer. Of course the bulk of the cars were headed eastward as he'd calculated; this sluggish mass was nothing compared with the countless ones which must now be blocking the roads to Pasadena, Alhambra, Garvey, Norwalk. Even the northbound refugees were undoubtedly taking 99 or regular 101—the highway before them was really 101 Alternate—he had picked the most feasible exit.

The Warbinns drew up alongside. "Hurry didn't do you much good," shouted Warbinn, leaning forward to clear his wife's face.

Mr. Jimmon reached in and turned off the ignition. Gas was going to be precious. He smiled and shook his head at Warbinn; no use pointing out that he'd got the inside lane by passing the Mercury, with a better chance to seize the opening on the highway when it came. "Get in the car, Jir, and shut the door. Have to be ready when this breaks."

"If it ever does," said Molly. "All that rush and bustle. We might just as well. . . ."

Mr. Jimmon was conscious of Warbinn's glowering at him and resolutely refused to turn his head. He pretended not to hear him yell, "Only wanted to tell you you forgot to pick up your bumper-jack. It's in front of our garage."

Mr. Jimmon's stomach felt empty. What if he had a flat now? Ruined, condemned. He knew a burning hate for Warbinn—incompetent borrower, bad neighbor, thoughtless, shiftless, criminal. He owed it to himself to leap from the station wagon and seize Warbinn by the throat. . . .

"What did he say, David? What is Mr. Warbinn saying?"

Then he remembered it was the jack from the Buick; the station wagon's was safely packed where he could get at it easily. Naturally he would never have started out on a trip like this without checking so essential an item. "Nothing," he said, "nothing at all."

"*. . . plane dispatches indicate target was the Signal Hill area. Minor damage was done to Long Beach,*"

Wilmington and San Pedro. All non-military air traffic warned from Mines Field . . ."

The smash and crash of bumper and fender sounded familiarly on the highway. From his lookout station he couldn't see what had happened, but it was easy enough to reconstruct the impatient jerk forward that had caused it. Mr. Jimmon didn't exactly smile, but he allowed himself a faint quiver of internal satisfaction. A crash up ahead would make things worse, but a crash behind—and many of them were inevitable—must eventually create a gap.

Even as he thought this, the first car at the mouth of Rambla Catalina edged on to the shoulder of the highway. Mr. Jimmon slid back in and started the motor, inching ahead after the car in front, gradually leaving the still uncomfortable proximity of the Warbinns.

"Got to go to the toilet," announced Wendell abruptly.

"Didn't I tell you—! Well, hurry up! Jir, keep the door open and pull him in if the car starts to move."

"I can't go here."

Mr. Jimmon restrained his impulse to snap, Hold it in then. Instead he said mildly, "This is a crisis, Wendell. No time for niceties. Hurry."

". . . the flash was seen as far north as Ventura and as far south as Newport. An eyewitness who has just arrived by helicopter . . ."

"That's what we should of had," remarked Jir. "You thought of everything except that."

"That's no way to speak to your father," admonished Molly.

"Aw heck, Mom, this is a crisis. No time for niceties."

"You're awful smart, Jir," said Erika. "Big, tough, brutal mans."

"Go drown, brat," returned Jir, "your nose needs wiping."

"As a matter of record," Mr. Jimmon said calmly, "I thought of both plane and helicopter and decided against them."

"I can't go. Honest, I just can't go."

"Just relax, darling," advised Molly. "No one is looking."

. . . fires reported in Compton, Lynwood, Southgate, Harbor City, Lomita and other spots are now under control. Residents are advised not to attempt to travel on the overcrowded highways as they are much safer in their homes or places of employment. The civilian defense . . ."

The two cars ahead bumped forward. "Get in," shouted Mr. Jimmon.

He got the left front tire of the station wagon on the asphalt shoulder—the double lane of concrete was impossibly far ahead—only to be blocked by the packed procession. The clock on the dash said 11:04. Nearly five hours since It happened, and they were less than two miles from home. They could have done better walking. Or on horseback.

". . . All residents of the Los Angeles area are urged to remain calm. Local radio service will be restored in a matter of minutes, along with electricity and water. Reports of fifth column activities have been greatly exaggerated. The FBI has all known subversives under . . ."

He reached over and shut it off. Then he edged a daring two inches further on the shoulder, almost grazing an aggressive Cadillac packed solid with cardboard cartons. On his left a Model A truck shivered and trembled. He knew, distantly and disapprovingly, that it belonged to two painters who called themselves man and wife. The truckbed was loaded high with household goods; poor, useless things no looter would bother to steal. In the cab the artists passed a quart beer bottle back and forth. The man waved it genially at him; Mr. Jimmon nodded discouragingly back.

The thermometer on the mirror showed 90. Hot all right. Of course if they ever got rolling. I'm thirsty, he thought; probably suggestion. If I hadn't seen the thermometer. Anyway I'm not going to paw around in back for the canteen. Forethought. Like the arms. He cleared his throat. "Remember there's an automatic in the glove compartment. If anyone tries to open the door on your side, use it."

"Oh, David, I. . . ."

Ah, humanity. Non-resistance. Gandhi. I've never shot at anything but a target. At a time like this. But they don't understand.

"I could use the rifle from back here," suggested Jir. "Can I, Dad?"

"I can reach the shotgun," said Wendell. "That's better at close range."

"Gee, you men are brave," jeered Erika. Mr. Jimmon said nothing; both shotgun and rifle were unloaded. Foresight again.

He caught the hiccupping pause in the traffic instantly, gratified at his smooth coordination. How far he could proceed on the shoulder before running into a culvert narrowing the highway to the concrete he didn't know. Probably not more than a mile at most, but at least he was off Rambla Catalina and on 101.

He felt tremendously elated. Successful.

"Here we go!" He almost added, Hold on to your hats.

Of course the shoulder too was packed solid, and progress, even in low gear, was maddening. The gas consumption was something he did not want to think about; his pride in the way the needle of the gauge caressed the F shrank. And gas would be hard to come by in spite of his pocketful of ration coupons. Black market.

"Mind if I try the radio again?" asked Erika, switching it on.

Mr. Jimmon, following the pattern of previous success, insinuated the left front tire on to the concrete, eliciting a disapproving squawk from the Pontiac alongside ". . . *sector was quiet. Enemy losses are estimated . . .*"

"Can't you get something else?" asked Jir. "Something less dusty?"

"Wish we had TV in the car," observed Wendell. "Joe Tellifer's old man put a set in the back seat of their Chrysler."

"Dry up, squirt," said Jir. "Let the air out of your head."

"Jir!"

"Oh, Mom, don't pay attention! Don't you see that's what he wants?"

"Listen, brat, if you weren't a girl I'd spank you."

"You mean, if I wasn't your sister. You'd probably enjoy such childish sex-play with any other girl."

"Erika!"

Where do they learn it? marveled Mr. Jimmon. These progressive schools. Do you suppose. . . ?

He edged the front wheel further in exultantly, taking advantage of a momentary lapse of attention on the part of the Pontiac's driver. Unless the other went berserk with frustration and rammed into him, he practically had a cinch on a car-length of the concrete now.

"Here we go!" he gloried. "We're on our way."

"Aw, if I was driving we'd be halfway to Oxnard by now."

"Jir, that's no way to talk to your father."

Mr. Jimmon reflected dispassionately that Molly's ineffective admonitions only spurred Jir's sixteen-year-old brashness, already irritating enough in its own right. Indeed, if it were not for Molly, Jir might. . . .

It was of course possible—here Mr. Jimmon braked just short of the convertible ahead—Jir wasn't just going through a "difficult" period (What was particularly difficult about it? he inquired, in the face of all the books Molly suggestively left around on the psychological problems of growth. The boy had everything he could possibly want!) but was the type who, in different circumstances drifted into—well, perhaps not exactly juvenile delinquency, but. . . .

"*. . . in the Long Beach-Wilmington-San Pedro area. Comparison with that which occurred at Pittsburgh reveals that this morning's was in every way less serious. All fires are now under control and all the injured are now receiving medical attention . . .*"

"I don't think they're telling the truth," stated Mrs. Jimmon.

He snorted. He didn't think so either, but by what process had she arrived at that conclusion?

"I want to hear the ball game. Turn on the ball game, Rick," Wendell demanded.

Eleven sixteen, and rolling northward on the highway. Not bad, not bad at all. Foresight. Now if he could only edge his way leftward to the southbound strip they'd be beyond the Santa Barbara bottleneck by 2 o'clock.

"The lights," exclaimed Molly, "the faucets!"

Oh no, thought Mr. Jimmon, not that too. Out of the comic strips.

"Keep calm," advised Jir. "Electricity and water are both off—remember?"

"I'm not quite an imbecile yet, Jir. I'm quite aware everything went off. I was thinking of the time it went back on."

"Furcrysay, Mom, you worrying about next month's bills *now*?"

Mr. Jimmon, nudging the station wagon ever leftward, formed the sentence: You'd never worry about bills, young man, because you never have to pay them. Instead of saying it aloud, he formed another sentence: Molly, your talent for irrelevance amounts to genius. Both sentences gave him satisfaction.

Miraculously the traffic gathered speed briefly, and he took advantage of the spurt to get solidly in the left hand lane, right against the long island of concrete dividing the north from the southbound strips. "That's using the old bean, Dad," approved Wendell.

Whatever slight pleasure he might have felt in his son's approbation was overlaid with exasperation. Wendell, like Jir, was more Manville than Jimmon; they carried Molly's stamp on their faces and minds. Only Erika was a true Jimmon. Made in my own image, he thought pridelessly.

"I can't help but think it would have been at least courteous to get in touch with Pearl and Dan. At least *try*. And the Warbinns. . . ."

The gap in the concrete divider came sooner than he anticipated and he was on the comparatively unclogged southbound side. His foot went down on the accelerator and the station wagon grumbled earnestly ahead. For the first time Mr. Jimmon became aware how tightly he'd been gripping the wheel; how rigid the muscles in his arms, shoulders and neck had been. He relaxed partway as he adjusted to the speed of the cars ahead and the speedometer needle hung just below 45, but resentment against Molly (at least courteous), Jir (no time for niceties), and Wendell (got to go), rode up in the saliva under his tongue. Dependent. Helpless. Everything on him. Parasites.

At intervals Erika switched on the radio. News was always promised immediately, but little was forthcoming, only vague, nervous attempts to minimize the extent of the disaster and soothe listeners with allusions to civilian defense, military activities on the ever advancing front, and comparison with the destruction of Pittsburgh, so vastly much worse than the comparatively harmless detonation at Los Angeles. Must be pretty bad, thought Mr. Jimmon; cripple the war effort. . . .

"I'm hungry," said Wendell.

Molly began stirring around, instructing Jir where to find the sandwiches. Mr. Jimmon thought grimly of how they'd have to adjust to the absence of civilized niceties: bread and mayonnaise and lunch meat. Live on rabbit, squirrel, abalone, fish. When Wendell got hungry he'd have to get his own food. Self-sufficiency. Hard and tough.

At Oxnard the snarled traffic slowed them to a crawl again. Beyond, the juncture with the main highway north kept them at the same infuriating pace. It was long after 2 when they reached Ventura, and Wendell, who had been fidgeting and jumping up and down in the seat for the past hour, proclaimed, "I'm tired of riding."

Mr. Jimmon set his lips. Molly suggested, ineffectually, "Why don't you lie down, dear?"

"Can't. Way this crate is packed, ain't room for a grasshopper."

"Verry funny. Verrrry funny," said Jir.

"Now, Jir, leave him alone! He's just a little boy."

At Carpenteria the sun burst out. You might have

thought it the regular dissipation of the fog, only it was almost time for the fog to come down again. Should he try the San Marcos Pass after Santa Barbara, or the longer, better way? Flexible plans, but. . . . Wait and see.

It was 4 when they got to Santa Barbara and Mr. Jimmon faced concerted though unorganized rebellion. Wendell was screaming with stiffness and boredom; Jir remarked casually to no one in particular that Santa Barbara was the place they were going to beat the bottleneck oh yeh; Molly said, Stop at the first clean-looking gas station. Even Erika added, "Yes, Dad, you'll really have to stop."

Mr. Jimmon was appalled. With every second priceless and hordes of panic-stricken refugees pressing behind, they would rob him of all the precious gains he'd made by skill, daring, judgment. Stupidity and short-sightedness. Unbelievable. For their own silly comfort— good lord, did they think they had a monopoly on bodily weaknesses? He was cramped as they and wanted to go as badly. Time and space which could never be made up. Let them lose this half hour and it was quite likely they'd never get out of Santa Barbara.

"If we lose a half hour now we'll never get out of here."

"Well, now, David, that wouldn't be utterly disastrous, would it? There are awfully nice hotels here and I'm sure it would be more comfortable for everyone than your idea of camping in the woods, hunting and fishing. . . ."

He turned off State; couldn't remember name of the parallel street, but surely less traffic. He controlled his temper, not heroically, but desperately. "May I ask how long you would propose to stay in one of these awfully nice hotels?"

"Why, until we could go home."

"My dear Molly. . . ." What could he say? My dear Molly, we are never going home, if you mean Malibu? Or: My dear Molly, you just don't understand what is happening?

The futility of trying to convey the clear picture in his mind. Or any picture. If she could not of herself see the endless mob pouring, pouring out of Los Angeles, searching frenziedly for escape and refuge, eating up the substance of the surrounding country in ever-widening circles, crowding, jam-packing, over-flowing every hotel, boarding-house, lodging or private home into which they could edge, agonizedly bidding up the price of everything until the chaos they brought with them was indistinguishable from the chaos they were fleeing—if she could not see all this instantly and automatically, she could not be brought to see it at all. Any more than the other aimless, planless, improvident fugitives could see it.

So, my dear Molly: nothing.

Silence gave consent only continued expostulation. "David, do you really mean you don't intend to stop at *all*?"

Was there any point in saying, Yes I do? He set his lips still more tightly and once more weighed San Marcos Pass against the coast route. Have to decide now.

"Why, the time we're waiting here, just waiting for the cars up ahead to move would be enough."

Could you call her stupid? He weighed the question slowly and justly, alert for the first jerk of the massed cars all around. Her reasoning was valid and logical if the laws of physics and geometry were suspended. (Was that right—physics and geometry? Body occupying two different positions at the same time?) It was the facts which were illogical—not Molly. She was just exasperating.

By the time they were halfway to Gaviota or Goleta— Mr. Jimmon could never tell them apart—foresight and relentless sternness began to pay off. Those who had left Los Angeles without preparation and in panic were dropping out or slowing down, to get gas or oil, repair tires, buy food, seek rest rooms. The station wagon was steadily forging ahead.

He gambled on the old highway out of Santa Barbara. Any kind of obstruction would block its two lanes; if it didn't he would be beating the legions on the wider, straighter road. There were stretches now where he could hit 50; once he sped a happy half mile at 65.

Now the insubordination crackling all around gave indications of simultaneous explosion. "I really," began Molly, and then discarded this for a fresher, firmer start. "David, I don't understand how you can be so utterly selfish and inconsiderate."

Mr. Jimmon could feel the veins in his forehead begin to swell, but this was one of those rages that didn't show.

"But, Dad, would ten minutes ruin everything?" asked Erika.

"Monomania," muttered Jir. "Single track. Like Hitler."

"I want my dog," yelped Wendell. "Dirty old dog-killer."

"Did you ever hear of cumulative—" Erika had addressed him reasonably; surely he could make her understand? "Did you ever hear of cumulative. . . ." What was the word? Snowball rolling downhill was the image in his mind. "Oh, what's the use?"

The old road rejoined the new; again the station wagon was fitted into the traffic like parquetry. Mr. Jimmon, from an exultant, unfettered—almost—65 was imprisoned in a treadmill set at 38. Keep calm; you can do nothing about it, he admonished himself. Need all your nervous energy. Must be wrecks up ahead. And then, with a return of satisfaction: If I hadn't used strategy back there we'd have been with those making 25. A starting-stopping 25.

"It's fantastic," exclaimed Molly. "I could almost believe Jir's right and you've lost your mind."

Mr. Jimmon smiled. This was the first time Molly had ever openly shown disloyalty before the children or sided with them in their presence. She was revealing herself. Under pressure. Not the pressure of events; her incredible attitude at Santa Barbara had demonstrated her incapacity to feel that. Just pressure against the bladder.

"No doubt those left behind can console their last moments with pride in their sanity." The sentence came out perfectly formed, with none of the annoying pauses or interpolated "ers" or "mmphs" which could, as he knew from unhappy experience, flaw the most crushing rejoinders.

"Oh, the end can always justify the means for those who want it that way."

"Don't they restrain people—"

"That's enough, Jir!"

Trust Molly to return quickly to fundamental hypocrisy; the automatic response—his mind felicitously grasped the phrase, conditioned reflex—to the customary stimulus. She had taken an explicit stand against his common sense, but her rigid code—honor thy father; iron rayon the wrong side; register and vote; avoid scenes; only white wine with fish; never re-hire a discharged servant—quickly substituted pattern for impulse. Seventeen years.

The road turned away from the ocean, squirmed inland and uphill for still slower miles; abruptly widened into a divided, four lane highway. Without hesitation Mr. Jimmon took the southbound side; for the first time since they had left Rambla Catalina his foot went down to the floorboards and with a sigh of relief the station wagon jumped into smooth, ecstatic speed.

Improvisation and strategy again. And, he acknowledged generously, the defiant example this morning of those who'd done the same thing in Malibu. Now, out of re-established habit the other cars kept to the northbound side even though there was nothing coming south. Timidity, routine, inertia. Pretty soon they would realize sheepishly that there was neither traffic nor traffic cops to keep them off, but it would be miles before they had another chance to cross over. By that time he would have reached the comparatively uncongested stretch.

"It's dangerous, David."

Obey the law. No smoking. Keep off the grass. Please adjust your clothes before leaving. Trespassers will be.

Picking California wildflowers or shrubs is forbidden. Parking 45 min. Do not.

She hadn't put the protest in the more usual form of a question. Would that technique have been more irritating? Isn't it *dan*gerous, Day-vid? His calm conclusion: it didn't matter.

"No time for niceties," chirped Jir.

Mr. Jimmon tried to remember Jir as a baby. All the bad novels he had read in the days when he read anything except *Time* and the *New Yorker*, all the movies he'd seen before they had a TV set, always prescribed such retrospection as a specific for softening the present. If he could recall David Alonzo Jimmon, junior, at six months, helpless and lovable, it should make Jir more acceptable by discovering some faint traces of the one in the other.

But though he could recreate in detail the interminable, disgusting, trembling months of that initial pregnancy (had he really been afraid she would die?) he was completely unable to reconstruct the appearance of his first-born before the age of. . . . It must have been at 6 that Jir had taken his baby sister out for a walk and lost her. (Had Molly permitted it? He still didn't know for sure.) Erika hadn't been found for four hours.

The tidal screeching of sirens invaded and destroyed his thoughts. What the devil. . . ? His foot lifted from the gas pedal as he slewed obediently to the right, ingrained reverence surfacing at the sound.

"I told you it wasn't safe! Are you really trying to kill us all?"

Whipping over the rise ahead, a pair of motorcycles crackled. Behind them snapped a long line of assorted vehicles, fire-trucks and ambulances mostly, interspersed here and there with olive drab army equipment. The cavalcade flicked down the central white line, one wheel in each lane. Mr. Jimmon edged the station wagon as far over as he could; it still occupied too much room to permit the free passage of the onrush without compromise.

The knees and elbows of the motorcycle policemen

stuck out widely, reminding Mr. Jimmon of grasshoppers. The one on the near side was headed straight for the station wagon's left front fender; for a moment Mr. Jimmon closed his eyes as he plotted the unswerving course, knifing through the crust-like steel, bouncing lightly on the tires, and continuing unperturbed. He opened them to see the other officer shoot past, mouth angrily open in his direction while the one straight ahead came to a skidding stop.

"Going to get it now," gloated Wendell.

An old-fashioned parent, one of the horrible examples held up to shuddering moderns like himself, would have reached back and relieved his tension by clouting Wendell across the mouth. Mr. Jimmon merely turned off the motor.

The cop was not indulging in the customary deliberate and ominous performance of slowly dismounting and striding toward his victim with ever more menacing steps. Instead he got off quickly and covered the few feet to Mr. Jimmon's window with unimpressive speed.

Heavy goggles concealed his eyes; dust and stubble covered his face. "Operator's license!"

Mr. Jimmon knew what he was saying, but the sirens and the continuous rustle of the convoy prevented the sound from coming through. Again the cop deviated from the established routine; he did not take the proffered license and examine it incredulously before drawing out his pad and pencil, but wrote the citation, glancing up and down from the card in Mr. Jimmon's hand.

Even so, the last of the vehicles—*San Jose F.D.* —passed before he handed the summons through the window to be signed. "Turn around and proceed in the proper direction," he ordered curtly, pocketing the pad and buttoning his jacket briskly.

Mr. Jimmon nodded. The officer hesitated, as though waiting for some limp excuse. Mr. Jimmon said nothing.

"No tricks," said the policeman over his shoulder. "Turn around and proceed in the proper direction."

He almost ran to his motorcycle, and roared off, twisting his head for a final stern frown as he passed, siren wailing. Mr. Jimmon watched him dwindle in the rearview mirror and then started the motor. "Gonna lose a lot more than you gained," commented Jir.

Mr. Jimmon gave a last glance in the mirror and moved ahead, shifting into second. "David!" exclaimed Molly horrified, "you're not turning around!"

"Observant," muttered Mr. Jimmon, between his teeth.

"Dad, you can't get away with it," Jir decided judicially.

Mr. Jimmon's answer was to press the accelerator down savagely. The empty highway stretched invitingly ahead; a few hundred yards to their right they could see the northbound lanes ant-clustered. The sudden motion stirred the traffic citation on his lap, floating it down to the floor. Erika leaned forward and picked it up.

"Throw it away," ordered Mr. Jimmon.

Molly gasped. "You're out of your mind."

"You're a fool," stated Mr. Jimmon calmly. "Why should I save that piece of paper?"

"Isn't what you told the cop." Jir was openly jeering now.

"I might as well have, if I'd wanted to waste conversation. I don't know why I was blessed with such a stupid family—"

"Maybe something in heredity after all."

If Jir had said it out loud, reflected Mr. Jimmon, it would have passed casually as normal domestic repartee, a little ill-natured perhaps, certainly callow and trite, but not especially provocative. Muttered, so that it was barely audible, it was an ultimate defiance. He had read that far back in pre-history, when the young males felt their strength, they sought to overthrow the rule of the Old Man and usurp his place. No doubt they uttered a preliminary growl or screech as challenge. They were not very bright, but they acted in a pattern; a pattern Jir was apparently following.

Refreshed by placing Jir in proper Neanderthal setting, Mr. Jimmon went on, "—none of you seem to have the slightest initiative or ability to grasp reality.

Tickets, cops, judges, juries mean nothing any more.
There is no law now but the law of survival."

"Aren't you being dramatic, David?" Molly's tone
was deliberately aloof adult to excited child.

"I could hear you underline words, Dad," said Erika,
but he felt there was no malice in her gibe.

"You mean we can do anything we want now? Shoot
people? Steal cars and things?" asked Wendell.

"There, David! You see?"

Yes, I see. Better than you. Little savage. This is the
pattern. What will Wendell—and the thousands of other
Wendells (for it would be unjust to suppose Molly's
genes and domestic influence unique)—be like after six
months of anarchy? Or after six years?

Survivors, yes. And that will be about all: naked,
primitive, ferocious, superstitious savages. Wendell can
read and write (but not so fluently as I or any of our
generation at his age); how long will he retain the tags
and scraps of progressive schooling?

And Jir? Detachedly Mr. Jimmon foresaw the fate of
Jir. Unlike Wendell who would adjust to the new conditions, Jir would go wild in another sense. His values
were already set; they were those of television, high
school dating, comic strips, law and order. Released
from civilization, his brief future would be one of guilty
rape and pillage until he fell victim to another youth or
gang bent the same way. Molly would disintegrate and
perish quickly, Erika. . . .

The station wagon flashed along the comparatively
unimpeded highway. Having passed the next cross-
over, there were now other vehicles on the southbound
strip, but even on the northbound one, crowding had
eased.

Furiously Mr. Jimmon determined to preserve the
civilization in Erika. [He would teach her everything he
knew (including the insurance business?)] . . . ah, if he
were some kind of scientist, now—not the Dan Davisson kind, whose abstract speculations seemed always to
prepare the way for some new method of destruction,
but the . . . Franklin? Jefferson? Watt? protect her

night and day from the refugees who would be roaming the hills south of Monterey. The rifle ammunition, properly used—and he would see that no one but himself used it—would last years. After it was gone—presuming fragments and pieces of a suicidal world hadn't pulled itself miraculously together to offer a place to return to—there were the two hunting bows whose steel-tipped shafts could stop a man as easily as a deer or mountain lion. He remembered debating long, at the time he had first begun preparing for It, how many bows to order, measuring their weight and bulk against the other precious freight and deciding at last that two was the satisfactory minimum. It must have been in his subconscious mind all along that of the whole family Erika was the only other person who could be trusted with a bow.

"There will be," he spoke in calm and solemn tones, not to Wendell, whose question was now left long behind, floating on the gas-greasy air of a sloping valley growing with liveoaks, but to a larger, impalpable audience. "There will be others who will think that because there is no longer law or law enforcement— "

"You're being simply fantastic!" She spoke more sharply than he had ever heard her in front of the children. "Just because It happened to Los Angeles—"

"And Pittsburgh."

"All right. And Pittsburgh, doesn't mean that the whole United States has collapsed and everyone in the country is running frantically for safety."

"Yet," added Mr. Jimmon firmly, "Yet. Do you suppose they are going to stop with Los Angeles and Pittsburgh, and leave Gary and Seattle standing? Or even New York and Chicago? Or do you imagine Washington will beg for armistice terms while there is the least sign of organized life left in the country?"

"We'll wipe Them out first," insisted Jir in patriotic shock. Wendell backed him up with a machine gun "Brrrrr."

"Undoubtedly. But it will be the last gasp. At any rate it will be years, if at all in my lifetime, before stable communities are re-established—"

"David, you're raving."

"Re-established," he repeated. "So there will be many others who'll also feel that the dwindling of law and order is license to kill people and steal cars 'and things.' Naked force and cunning will be the only means of self-preservation. That was why I picked out a spot where I felt survival would be easiest; not only because of wood and water, game and fish, but because it's nowhere near the main highways, and so unlikely to be chosen by any great number."

"I wish you'd stop harping on that insane idea. You're just a little too old and flabby for pioneering. Even when you were younger you were hardly the rugged, outdoor type."

No, thought Mr. Jimmon, I was the sucker type. I would have gotten somewhere if I'd stayed in the bank, but like a bawd you pled your belly; the insurance business brought in the quick money for you to give up your job and have Jir and the proper home. If you'd got rid of it as I wanted. Flabby *Flabby*! Do you think your scrawniness is so enticing?

Controlling himself, he said aloud, "We've been through all this. Months ago. It's not a question of physique, but of life."

"Nonsense. Perfect nonsense. Responsible people who really know Its effects. . . . Maybe it was advisable to leave Malibu for a few days or even a few weeks. And perhaps it's wise to stay away from the larger cities. But a small town or village, or even one of those ranches where they take boarders—"

"Aw, Mom, you agreed. You know you did. What's the matter with you anyway? Why are you acting like a drip?"

"I want to go and shoot rabbits and bears like Dad said," insisted Wendell.

Erika said nothing, but Mr. Jimmon felt he had her sympathy; the boys' agreement was specious. Wearily he debated going over the whole ground again, patiently pointing out that what Molly said might work in the Dakotas or the Great Smokies but was hardly operative anywhere within refugee range of the Pacific Coast. He had explained all this many times, including the almost certain impossibility of getting enough gasoline to take them into any of the reasonably safe areas; that was why they'd agreed on the region below Monterey, on California State Highway 1, as the only logical goal.

A solitary car decorously bound in the legal direction interrupted his thoughts. Either crazy or has mighty important business, he decided. The car honked disapprovingly as it passed, hugging the extreme right side of the road.

Passing through Buellton the clamor again rose for a pause at a filling station. He conceded inwardly that he could afford ten or fifteen minutes without strategic loss since by now they must be among the leaders of the exodus; ahead lay little more than the normal travel. However he had reached such a state of irritated frustration and consciousness of injustice that he was willing to endure unnecessary discomfort himself in order to inflict a longer delay on them. In fact it lessened his own suffering to know the delay was needless, that he was doing it, and that his action was a just—if inadequate—punishment.

"We'll stop this side of Santa Maria," he said. "I'll get gas there."

Mr. Jimmon knew triumph: his forethought, his calculations, his generalship had justified themselves. Barring unlikely mechanical failure—the station wagon was in perfect shape—or accident—and the greatest danger had certainly passed—escape was now practically assured. For the first time he permitted himself to realize how unreal, how romantic the whole project had been. As any attempt to evade the fate charted for the multitude must be. The docile mass perished; the headstrong (but intelligent) individual survived.

Along with triumph went an expansion of his prophetic vision of life after reaching their destination. He had purposely not taxed the cargo capacity of the wagon with transitional goods; there was no tent, canned luxuries, sleeping-bags, lanterns, candles or any of the paraphernalia of camping midway between the urban and nomadic life. Instead, besides the weapons, tackle and utensils, there was in miniature the List For Life On A Desert Island: shells and cartridges, lures, hooks, nets, gut, leaders, flint and steel, seeds, traps, needles and thread, government pamphlets on curing and tanning hides and the recognition of edible weeds and fungi, files, nails, a judicious stock of simple medicines. A pair of binoculars to spot intruders. No coffee, sugar, flour; they would begin living immediately as they would have to in a month or so in any case, on the old, half-forgotten human cunning.

"Cunning," he said aloud.

"What?"

"Nothing. Nothing."

"I still think you should have made an effort to reach Pearl and Dan."

"The telephone was dead, Mother."

"At the moment, Erika. You can hardly have forgotten how often the lines have been down before. And it never takes more than half an hour till they're working again."

"Mother, Dan Davisson is quite capable of looking after himself."

Mr. Jimmon shut out the rest of the conversation so completely he didn't know whether there was any more to it or not. He shut out the intense preoccupation with driving, with making speed, with calculating possible gains. In the core of his mind, quite detached from everything about him, he examined and marveled.

Erika. The cool, inflexible, adult tone. Almost indulgent, but so dispassionate as not to be. One might have expected her to be exasperated by Molly's silliness, to have answered impatiently, or not at all.

Mother. Never in his recollection had the children ever called her anything but Mom. The "Mother" implied—oh, it implied a multitude of things. An entirely new relationship, for one. A relationship of aloofness, of propriety without emotion. The ancient stump of the umbilical cord, black and shriveled, had dropped off painlessly.

She had not bothered to argue about the telephone or point out the gulf between "before" and now. She had not even tried to touch Molly's deepening refusal of reality. She had been . . . *indulgent.*

Not "Uncle Dan," twitteringly imposed false avuncularity, but striking through it (and the façade of "Pearl and") and aside (when I was a child I . . . something . . . but now I have put aside childish things); the wealth of implicit assertion. Ah yes, Mother, we all know the pardonable weakness and vanity; we excuse you for your constant reminders, but Mother, with all deference, we refuse to be forced any longer to be parties to middle-age's nostalgic flirtatiousness. One could almost feel sorry for Molly.

. . . middle-age's nostalgic flirtatiousness . . .

. . .*nostalgic* . . .

Metaphorically Mr. Jimmon sat abruptly upright. The fact that he was already physically in this position made the transition, while invisible, no less emphatic. The nostalgic flirtatiousness of middle-age implied—might imply—memory of something more than mere coquetry. Molly and Dan. . . .

It all fitted together so perfectly it was impossible to believe it untrue. The impecunious young lovers, equally devoted to Dan's genius, realizing marriage was out of the question (he had never denied Molly's shrewdness; as for Dan's impracticality, well, impracticality wasn't necessarily uniform or consistent. Dan had been practical enough to marry Pearl and Pearl's money) could have renounced. . . .

Or not renounced at all?

Mr. Jimmon smiled; the thought did not ruffle him. Cuckoo, cuckoo. How vulgar, how absurd. Suppose Jir were Dan's? A blessed thought.

Regretfully he conceded the insuperable obstacle of Molly's conventionality. Jir was the product of his own loins. But wasn't there an old superstition about the image in the woman's mind at the instant of conception? So, justly and rightly Jir was not his. Nor Wendy, for that matter. Only Erika, by some accident. Mr. Jimmon felt free and lighthearted.

"Get gas at the next station," he bulletined.

"The next one with a clean rest room," Molly corrected.

Invincible. The Earth-Mother, using men for her purposes: reproduction, clean rest rooms, nourishment, objects of culpability, *Homes & Gardens.* The bank was my life; I could have gone far but: Why David—they pay you less than the janitor! It's ridiculous. And: I can't understand why you hesitate; it isn't as though it were a different type of work.

No, no different; just more profitable. Why didn't she tell Dan Davisson to become an accountant; that was the same type of work, just more profitable? Perhaps she had and Dan had simply been less befuddled. Or amenable. Or stronger in purpose? Mr. Jimmon probed his pride thoroughly and relentlessly without finding the faintest twinge of retrospective jealousy. Nothing like that mattered now. Nor, he admitted, had it for years.

Two close-peaked hills gulped the sun. He toyed with the idea of crossing over to the northbound side now that it was uncongested and there were occasional southbound cars. Before he could decide the divided highway ended.

"I hope you're not planning to spend the night in some horrible motel," said Molly. "I want a decent bath and a good dinner."

Spend the night. Bath. Dinner. Again calm sentences formed in his mind, but they were blown apart by the unbelievable, the monumental obtuseness. How could you say, It is absolutely essential to drive till we get there? When there were no absolutes, no essentials in her concepts? My dear Molly, I.

"No," he said, switching on the lights.

Wendy, he knew, would be the next to kick up a fuss. Till he fell mercifully asleep. If he did. Jir was probably debating the relative excitements of driving all night and stopping in a strange town. His voice would soon be heard.

The lights of the combination wayside store and filling-station burned inefficiently, illuminating the deteriorating false-front brightly and leaving the gas pumps in shadow. Swallowing regret at finally surrendering to mechanical and human need, and so losing the hardwon position; relaxing, even for a short while, the fierce initiative that had brought them through in the face of all probability, he pulled the station wagon alongside the pumps and shut off the motor. About halfway—the worst half, much the worst half—to their goal. Not bad.

Molly opened the door on her side with stiff dignity. "I certainly wouldn't call this a *clean* station." She waited for a moment, hand still on the window, as though expecting an answer.

"Crummy joint," exclaimed Wendell, clambering awkwardly out.

"Why not?" asked Jir. "No time for niceties." He brushed past his mother who was walking slowly into the shadows.

"Erika," began Mr. Jimmon, in a half-whisper.

"Yes, Dad?"

"Oh . . . never mind. Later."

He was not himself quite sure what he had wanted to say; what exclusive, urgent message he had to convey. For no particular reason he switched on the interior light and glanced at the packed orderliness of the wagon. Then he slid out from behind the wheel.

No sign of the attendant, but the place was certainly not closed. Not with the lights on and the hoses ready. He stretched, and walked slowly, savoring the comfortably painful uncramping of his muscles, toward the crude outhouse labeled MEN. Molly, he thought, must be furious.

When he returned, a man was leaning against the station wagon. "Fill it up with ethyl," said Mr. Jimmon pleasantly, "and check the oil and water."

The man made no move. "That'll be five bucks a

gallon." Mr. Jimmon thought there was an uncertain tremor in his voice.

"Nonsense; I've plenty of ration coupons."

"OK." The nervousness was gone now, replaced by an ugly truculence. "Chew'm up and spit'm in your gas tank. See how far you can run on them."

The situation was not unanticipated. Indeed, Mr. Jimmon thought with satisfaction of how much worse it must be closer to Los Angeles; how much harder the gouger would be on later supplicants as his supply of gasoline dwindled. "Listen," he said, and there was reasonableness rather than anger in his voice, "we're not out of gas. I've got enough to get to Santa Maria, even to San Luis Obispo."

"OK. Go on then. Ain't stopping you."

"Listen. I understand your position. You have a right to make a profit in spite of government red tape."

Nervousness returned to the man's speech. "Look, whyn't you go on? There's plenty other stations up ahead."

The reluctant bandit. Mr. Jimmon was entertained. He had fully intended to bargain, to offer $2 a gallon, even to threaten with the pistol in the glove compartment. Now it seemed mean and niggling even to protest. What good was money now? "All right," he said, "I'll pay you $5 a gallon."

Still the other made no move. "In advance."

For the first time Mr. Jimmon was annoyed; time was being wasted. "Just how can I pay you in advance when I don't know how many gallons it'll take to fill the tank?"

The man shrugged.

"Tell you what I'll do. I'll pay for each gallon as you pump it. In advance." He drew out a handful of bills; the bulk of his money was in his wallet, but he'd put the small bills in his pockets. He handed over a five. "Spill the first one on the ground or in a can if you've got one."

"How's that?"

Why should I tell him; give him ideas? As if he

hadn't got them already. "Just call me eccentric," he said. "I don't want the first gallon from the pump. Why should you care? It's just five dollars more profit."

For a moment Mr. Jimmon thought the man was going to refuse, and he regarded his foresight with new reverence. Then he reached behind the pump and produced a flat-sided tin in which he inserted the flexible end of the hose. Mr. Jimmon handed over the bill, the man wound the handle round and back—it was an ancient gas pump such as Mr. Jimmon hadn't seen for years—and lifted the drooling hose from the can.

"Minute," said Mr. Jimmon.

He stuck two fingers quickly and delicately inside the nozzle and smelled them. Gas all right, not water. He held out a ten dollar bill. "Start filling."

Jir and Wendell appeared out of the shadows. "Can we stop at a town where there's a movie tonight?"

The handle turned, a cogtoothed rod crept up and retreated, gasoline gurgled into the tank. Movies, thought Mr. Jimmon, handing over another bill; movies, rest rooms, baths, restaurants. Gouge apprehensively lest a scene be made and propriety disturbed. In a surrealist daydream he saw Molly turning the crank, grinding him on the cogs, pouring his essence into insatiable Jir and Wendell. He held out $20.

Twelve gallons had been put in when Molly appeared. "You have a phone here?" he asked casually. Knowing the answer from the blue enameled sign not quite lost among less sturdy ones advertising soft drinks and cigarettes.

"You want to call the cops?" He didn't pause in his pumping.

"No. Know if the lines to L.A."—Mr. Jimmon loathed the abbreviation—"are open yet?" He gave him another ten.

"How should I know?"

Mr. Jimmon beckoned his wife around the other side of the wagon, out of sight. Swiftly but casually he extracted the contents of his wallet. The 200 dollar bills made a fat lump. "Put this in your bag," he said. "Tell you why later. Meantime why don't you try and get Pearl and Dan on the phone? See if they're OK?"

He imagined the puzzled look on her face. "Go on," he urged. "We can spare a minute while he's checking the oil."

He thought there was a hint of uncertainty in Molly's walk as she went toward the store. Erika joined her brothers. The tank gulped; gasoline splashed on the concrete. "Guess that's it."

The man became suddenly brisk as he put up the hose, screwed the gascap back on. Mr. Jimmon had already disengaged the hood; the man offered the radiator a squirt of water, pulled up the oil gauge, wiped it, plunged it down, squinted at it under the light and said, "Oil's OK."

"All right," said Mr. Jimmon. "Get in Erika."

Some of the light shone directly on her face. Again he noted how mature and self-assured she looked. Erika would survive—and not as a savage either. The man started to wipe the windshield. "Oh, Jir," he said casually, "run in and see if your mother is getting her connection. Tell her we'll wait."

"Aw furcrysay, I don't see why I always—"

"And ask her to buy a couple of boxes of candy bars if they've got them. Wendell, go with Jir, will you?"

He slid in behind the wheel and closed the door gently. The motor started with hardly a sound. As he put his foot on the clutch and shifted into low he thought Erika turned to him with a startled look. As the station wagon moved forward, he was sure of it.

"It's all right, Erika," said Mr. Jimmon, "I'll explain later."

He'd have lots of time to do it.

Afterword
I didn't want to give any hints in the headnote, but if you're still puzzled by the title, please refer to the Bible—Genesis 19:30-38

—*IA*

THE NINE BILLION NAMES OF GOD

ARTHUR C. CLARKE (1917–   )
STAR SCIENCE FICTION STORIES

Star Science Fiction Stories *was the pioneer "original anthology" series in science fiction.*

This is a term that has always left me cold, for an anthology should refer to carefully chosen, reprinted material. I suppose that the one-time only collections of original stories by different hands could qualify as an anthology, but a series *is really a magazine in book form.*

Before Star, *a few single shots did appear, like Raymond J. Healy's* New Tales of Space and Time *in 1951, but as far as I know no one had attempted a series of these books before Fred Pohl. This effort was very successful, ultimately producing seven volumes including one of novellas,* Star Short Novels. *The material was so rich that a best of book,* Star of Stars *appeared in 1960.*

"The Nine Billion Names of God" is probably the most famous story from the series.

—MHG

This is one of the classics of short science fiction. I doubt that anyone would have the hardihood to deny it.

It is absolutely unforgettable, and although it has been endlessly reprinted, it is never at a loss for an audience. Anyone who has managed not to read it

155

*before is struck hard by it. Anyone who has read it
before can always manage to read it again.*

*And apart from that, it's got one of the greatest last
lines anyone has ever written. (No—on the odd chance
that you don't know the last line—don't look at it now.)*

What else is there to say?

—IA

"THIS IS A SLIGHTLY unusual request," said Dr. Wagner,
with what he hoped was commendable restraint. "As far
as I know, it's the first time anyone's been asked to
supply a Tibetan monastery with an Automatic Sequence
Computer. I don't wish to be inquisitive, but I should
hardly have thought that your—ah—establishment had
much use for such a machine. Could you explain just
what you intend to do with it?"

"Gladly," replied the Lama, readjusting his silk robe
and carefully putting away the slide rule he had been
using for currency conversions. "Your Mark V Computer can carry out any routine mathematical operation
involving up to ten digits. However, for our work we
are interested in *letters*, not numbers. As we wish you
to modify the output circuits, the machine will be printing words, not columns of figures."

"I don't quite understand. . . ."

"This is a project on which we have been working for
the last three centuries—since the lamasery was founded,
in fact. It is somewhat alien to your way of thought, so I
hope you will listen with an open mind while I explain
it."

"Naturally."

"It is really quite simple. We have been compiling a
list which shall contain all the possible names of God."

"I beg your pardon?"

"We have reason to believe," continued the Lama
imperturbably, "that all such names can be written with
not more than nine letters in an alphabet we have
devised."

"And you have been doing this for three centuries?"

"Yes: we expected it would take us about fifteen thousand years to complete the task."

"Oh." Dr. Wagner looked a little dazed. "Now I see why you wanted to hire one of our machines. But exactly what is the purpose of this project?"

The Lama hesitated for a fraction of a second and Wagner wondered if he had offended him. If so, there was no trace of annoyance in the reply.

"Call it ritual, if you like, but it's a fundamental part of our belief. All the many names of the Supreme Being—God, Jehovah, Allah, and so on—they are only man-made labels. There is a philosophical problem of some difficulty here, which I do not propose to discuss, but somewhere among all the possible combinations of letters which can occur are what one may call the *real* names of God. By systematic permutation of letters, we have been trying to list them all."

"I see. You've been starting at AAAAAAAAA . . . and working up to ZZZZZZZZZ. . . ."

"Exactly—though we use a special alphabet of our own. Modifying the electromatic typewriters to deal with this is, of course, trivial. A rather more interesting problem is that of devising suitable circuits to eliminate ridiculous combinations. For example, no letter must occur more than three times in succession."

"Three? Surely you mean two."

"Three is correct: I am afraid it would take too long to explain why, even if you understood our language."

"I'm sure it would," said Wagner hastily. "Go on."

"Luckily, it will be a simple matter to adapt your Automatic Sequence Computer for this work, since once it has been programmed properly it will permute each letter in turn and print the result. What would have taken us fifteen thousand years it will be able to do in a hundred days."

Dr. Wagner was scarcely conscious of the faint sounds from the Manhattan streets far below. He was in a different world, a world of natural, not man-made mountains. High up in their remote aeries these monks had been patiently at work, generation after generation, compiling their lists of meaningless words. Was there any limit to the follies of mankind? Still, he must give no hint of his inner thoughts. The customer was always right. . . .

"There's no doubt," replied the doctor, "that we can modify the Mark V to print lists of this nature. I'm much more worried about the problem of installation and maintenance. Getting out to Tibet, in these days, is not going to be easy."

"We can arrange that. The components are small enough to travel by air—that is one reason why we chose your machine. If you can get them to India, we will provide transport from there."

"And you want to hire two of our engineers?"

"Yes, for the three months which the project should occupy."

"I've no doubt that Personnel can manage that." Dr. Wagner scribbled a note on his desk pad. "There are just two other points—"

Before he could finish the sentence the Lama had produced a small slip of paper.

"This is my certified credit balance at the Asiatic Bank."

"Thank you. It appears to be—ah—adequate. The second matter is so trivial that I hesitate to mention it—but it's surprising how often the obvious gets overlooked. What source of electrical energy have you?"

"A diesel generator providing 50 kilowatts at 110 volts. It was installed about five years ago and is quite reliable. It's made life at the lamasery much more comfortable, but of course it was really installed to provide power for the motors driving the prayer wheels."

"Of course," echoed Dr. Wagner. "I should have thought of that."

The view from the parapet was vertiginous, but in time one gets used to anything. After three months, George Hanley was not impressed by the two-thousand-foot swoop into the abyss or the remote checkerboard of fields in the valley below. He was leaning against the wind-smoothed stones and staring morosely at the distant mountains whose names he had never bothered to discover.

This, thought George, was the craziest thing that had ever happened to him. "Project Shangri-La," some wit at the labs had christened it. For weeks now the Mark V had been churning out acres of sheets covered with gibberish. Patiently, inexorably, the computer had been rearranging letters in all their possible combinations, exhausting each class before going on to the next. As the sheets had emerged from the electromatic typewriters, the monks had carefully cut them up and pasted them into enormous books. In another week, heaven be praised, they would have finished. Just what obscure calculations had convinced the monks that they needn't bother to go on to words of ten, twenty, or a hundred letters, George didn't know. One of his recurring nightmares was that there would be some change of plan, and that the High Lama (whom they'd naturally called Sam Jaffe, though he didn't look a bit like him) would suddenly announce that the project would be extended to approximately 2060 A.D. They were quite capable of it.

George heard the heavy wooden door slam in the wind as Chuck came out on to the parapet beside him. As usual, Chuck was smoking one of the cigars that made him so popular with the monks—who, it seemed, were quite willing to embrace all the minor and most of the major pleasures of life. That was one thing in their favor: they might be crazy, but they weren't bluenoses. Those frequent trips they took down to the village, for instance. . . .

"Listen, George," said Chuck urgently. "I've learned something that means trouble."

"What's wrong? Isn't the machine behaving?" That was the worst contingency George could imagine. It might delay his return, than which nothing could be more horrible. The way he felt now, even the sight of a TV commercial would seem like manna from heaven. At least it would be some link with home.

"No—it's nothing like that." Chuck settled himself on

the parapet, which was unusual because normally he was scared of the drop. "I've just found what all this is about."

"What d'ya mean—I thought we knew."

"Sure—we know what the monks are trying to do. But we didn't know why. It's the craziest thing—"

"Tell me something new," growled George.

"—but old Sam's just come clean with me. You know the way he drops in every afternoon to watch the sheets roll out. Well, this time he seemed rather excited, or at least as near as he'll ever get to it. When I told him that we were on the last cycle he asked me, in that cute English accent of his, if I'd ever wondered what they were trying to do. I said 'Sure'—and he told me."

"Go on: I'll buy it."

"Well, they believe that when they have listed all His names—and they reckon that there are about nine billion of them—God's purpose will be achieved. The human race will have finished what it was created to do, and there won't be any point in carrying on. Indeed, the very idea is something like blasphemy."

"Then what do they expect us to do? Commit sucide?"

"There's no need for that. When the list's completed, God steps in and simply winds things up . . . bingo!"

"Oh, I get it. When we finish our job, it will be the end of the world."

Chuck gave a nervous little laugh.

"That's just what I said to Sam. And do you know what happened? He looked at me in a very queer way, like I'd been stupid in class, and said 'It's nothing as trivial as *that*.'"

George thought this over for a moment.

"That's what I call taking the Wide View," he said presently. "But what d'ya suppose we should do about it? I don't see that it makes the slightest difference to us. After all, we already knew that they were crazy."

"Yes—but don't you see what may happen? When the list's complete and the Last Trump doesn't blow—or whatever it is they expect—we may get the blame. It's our machine they've been using. I don't like the situation one little bit."

"I see," said George slowly. "You've got a point there. But this sort of thing's happened before, you know. When I was a kid down in Louisiana we had a crackpot preacher who said the world was going to end next Sunday. Hundreds of people believed him—even sold their homes. Yet nothing happened, they didn't turn nasty as you'd expect. They just decided that he'd made a mistake in his calculations and went right on believing. I guess some of them still do."

"Well, this isn't Louisiana, in case you hadn't noticed. There are just two of us and hundreds of these monks. I like them, and I'll be sorry for old Sam when his lifework backfires on him. But all the same, I wish I was somewhere else."

"I've been wishing that for weeks. But there's nothing we can do until the contract's finished and the transport arrives to fly us out."

"Of course," said Chuck thoughtfully, "we could always try a bit of sabotage."

"Like hell we could! That would make things worse."

"Not the way I meant. Look at it like this. The machine will finish its run four days from now, on the present twenty-hours-a-day basis. The transport calls in a week. O.K.—then all we need do is to find something that wants replacing during one of the overhaul periods—something that will hold up the works for a couple of days. We'll fix it, of course, but not too quickly. If we time matters properly, we can be down at the airfield when the last name pops out of the register. They won't be able to catch us then."

"I don't like it," said George. "It will be the first time I ever walked out on a job. Besides, it would make them suspicious. No. I'll sit tight and take what comes."

"I *still* don't like it," he said, seven days later, as the tough little mountain ponies carried them down the winding road. "And don't you think I'm running away because I'm afraid. I'm just sorry for those poor old guys up there, and I don't want to be around when they find what suckers they've been. Wonder how Sam will take it?"

"It's funny," replied Chuck, "but when I said good-bye I got the idea he knew we were walking out on him—and that he didn't care because he knew the machine was running smoothly and that the job would soon be finished. After that—well, of course, for him there just isn't any After That. . . ."

George turned in his saddle and stared back up the mountain road. This was the last place from which one could get a clear view of the lamasery. The squat, angular buildings were silhouetted against the afterglow of the sunset: here and there, lights gleamed like portholes in the sides of an ocean liner. Electric lights, of course, sharing the same circuit as the Mark V. How much longer would they share it, wondered George. Would the monks smash up the computer in their rage and disappointment? Or would they just sit down quietly and begin their calculations all over again?

He knew exactly what was happening up on the mountain at this very moment. The High Lama and his assistants would be sitting in their silk robes, inspecting the sheets as the junior monks carried them away from the typewriters and pasted them into the great volumes. No one would be saying anything. The only sound would be the incessant patter, the never-ending rainstorm, of the keys hitting the paper, for the Mark V itself was utterly silent as it flashed through its thousands of calculations a second. Three months of this, thought George, was enough to start anyone climbing up the wall.

"There she is!" called Chuck, pointing down into the valley. "Ain't she beautiful!"

She certainly was, thought George. The battered old DC 3 lay at the end of the runway like a tiny silver cross. In two hours she would be bearing them away to freedom and sanity. It was a thought worth savoring like a fine liqueur. George let it roll round his mind as the pony trudged patiently down the slope.

The swift night of the high Himalayas was now almost upon them. Fortunately the road was very good, as roads went in this region, and they were both carrying torches. There was not the slightest danger, only a certain discomfort from the bitter cold. The sky overhead was perfectly clear and ablaze with the familiar, friendly stars. At least there would be no risk, thought George, of the pilot being unable to take off because of weather conditions. That had been his only remaining worry.

He began to sing, but gave it up after a while. This vast arena of mountains, gleaming like whitely hooded ghosts on every side, did not encourage such ebullience. Presently George glanced at his watch.

"Should be there in an hour," he called back over his shoulder to Chuck. Then he added, in an afterthought: "Wonder if the computer's finished its run? It was due about now."

Chuck didn't reply, so George swung round in his saddle. He could just see Chuck's face, a white oval turned toward the sky.

"Look," whispered Chuck, and George lifted his eyes to heaven. (There is always a last time for everything.)

Overhead, without any fuss, the stars were going out.

WARM

ROBERT SHECKLEY (1928–   )
GALAXY SCIENCE FICTION, JUNE

There are some stories that have images that stay with you for years, that sneak up on you at odd times of the day or night. I have remembered this story since the moment I read it on a steamy Miami Beach day when I was twelve. Those of you who are about to read it for the first time are in for a real treat.

Robert Sheckley appeared all over the place from 1952 through the late fifties, so prolific that his very special stories all seemed to run together and lack unique-ness, and he was undervalued until somewhat later. While one can find themes in Sheckley like alienation and cynicism, he is actually much more difficult to categorize. Let's just say that he was and is one hell of a writer who greatly enriched science fiction and influenced a whole generation of its practitioners.

—MHG

On occasion, I've thought of reading all the stories in the world (science fiction and everything else) and trying to divide them up into classes and subclasses and sub-subclasses and so on, the way biologists have divided up all the living organisms they know about, existent and extinct. (But then I shake my head vigorously until the thought goes away.)

If, however, I were to do so, I would find a rather

*small group of stories that would be what I might call
"cyclic" which invariably have a powerful effect on me.
This is one of them.*

*Incidentally, Bob Sheckley along with Bob Silverberg
were the first writers who made me feel like an "old-
timer." I clung to my opinion of myself as a bright
young newcomer in the field for about fifteen years.
Then along came the two Bobs and they were obviously
so much younger, and just as obviously entered the
field with such a rocket-whoosh that I fell into the
ranks of the superannuated at once.*

*I considered killing them, of course, but I couldn't
think of a good way.*

—IA

ANDERS LAY ON HIS BED, fully dressed except for his
shoes and black bow tie, contemplating, with a certain
uneasiness, the evening before him. In twenty minutes
he would pick up Judy at her apartment, and that was
the uneasy part of it.

He had realized, only seconds ago, that he was in
love with her.

Well, he'd tell her. The evening would be memora-
ble. He would propose, there would be kisses, and the
seal of acceptance would, figuratively speaking, be
stamped across his forehead.

Not too pleasant an outlook, he decided. It really
would be much more comfortable not to be in love.
What had done it? A look, a touch, a thought? It didn't
take much, he knew, and stretched his arms for a
thorough yawn.

"Help me!" a voice said.

His muscles spasmed, cutting off the yawn in mid-
moment. He sat upright on the bed, then grinned and
lay back again.

"You must help me!" the voice insisted.

Anders sat up, reached for a polished shoe and fitted
it on, giving his full attention to the tying of the laces.

'Can you hear me?" the voice asked. "You can, can't
you?"

That did it. "Yes, I can hear you," Anders said, still in a high good humor. "Don't tell me you're my guilty subconscious, attacking me for a childhood trauma I never bothered to resolve. I suppose you want me to join a monastery."

"I don't know what you're talking about," the voice said. "I'm no one's subconscious. I'm *me*. Will you help me?"

Anders believed in voices as much as anyone; that is, he didn't believe in them at all, until he heard them. Swiftly he catalogued the possibilities. Schizophrenia was the best answer, of course, and one in which his colleagues would concur. But Anders had a lamentable confidence in his own sanity. In which case—

"Who are you?" he asked.

"I don't know," the voice answered.

Anders realized that the voice was speaking within his own mind. Very suspicious.

"You don't know who you are," Anders stated. "Very well. *Where* are you?"

"I don't know that, either." The voice paused, and went on. "Look, I know how ridiculous this must sound. Believe me, I'm in some sort of limbo. I don't know how I got here or who I am, but I want desperately to get out. Will you help me?"

Still fighting the idea of a voice speaking within his head, Anders knew that his next decision was vital. He had to accept—or reject—his own sanity.

He accepted it.

"All right," Anders said, lacing the other shoe. "I'll grant that you're a person in trouble, and that you're in some sort of telepathic contact with me. Is there anything else you can tell me?"

"I'm afraid not," the voice said, with infinite sadness. "You'll have to find out for yourself."

"Can you contact anyone else?"

"No."

"Then how can you talk with me?"

"I don't know."

Anders walked to his bureau mirror and adjusted his

black bow tie, whistling softly under his breath. Having just discovered that he was in love, he wasn't going to let a little thing like a voice in his mind disturb him.

"I really don't see how I can be of any help," Anders said, brushing a bit of lint from his jacket. "You don't know where you are, and there don't seem to be any distinguishing landmarks. How am I to find you?" He turned and looked around the room to see if he had forgotten anything.

"I'll know when you're close," the voice said. "You were warm just then."

"Just then?" All he had done was look around the room. He did so again, turning his head slowly. Then it happened.

The room, from one angle, looked different. It was suddenly a mixture of muddled colors, instead of the carefully blended pastel shades he had selected. The lines of wall, floor and ceiling were strangely off proportion, zigzag, unrelated.

Then everything went back to normal.

"You were *very* warm," the voice said.

Anders resisted the urge to scratch his head, for fear of disarranging his carefully combed hair. What he had seen wasn't so strange. Everyone sees one or two things in his life that make him doubt his normality, doubt sanity, doubt his very existence. For a moment the orderly Universe is disarranged and the fabric of belief is ripped.

But the moment passes.

Anders remembered once, as a boy, awakening in his room in the middle of the night. How strange everything had looked! Chairs, table, all out of proportion, swollen in the dark. The ceiling pressing down, as in a dream.

But that also had passed.

"Well, old man," he said, "if I get warm again, tell me."

"I will," the voice in his head whispered. "I'm sure you'll find me."

"I'm glad you're so sure," Anders said gaily, switched off the lights and left.

Lovely and smiling, Judy greeted him at the door. Looking at her, Anders sensed her knowledge of the moment. Had she felt the change in him, or predicted it? Or was love making him grin like an idiot?

"Would you like a before-party drink?" she asked.

He nodded, and she led him across the room, to the improbable green-and-yellow couch. Sitting down, Anders decided he would tell her when she came back with the drink. No use in putting off the fatal moment. A lemming in love, he told himself.

"You're getting warm again," the voice said.

He had almost forgotten his invisible friend. Or fiend, as the case could well be. What would Judy say if she knew he was hearing voices? Little things like that, he reminded himself, often break up the best of romances.

"Here," she said, handing him a drink.

Still smiling, he noticed. The number two smile—to a prospective suitor, provocative and understanding. It had been preceded, in their relationship, by the number one nice-girl smile, the don't-misunderstand-me smile, to be worn on all occasions, until the correct words have been mumbled.

"That's right," the voice said. "It's in how you look at things."

Look at what? Anders glanced at Judy, annoyed at his thoughts. If he was going to play the lover, let him play it. Even through the astigmatic haze of love, he was able to appreciate her blue-gray eyes, her fine skin (if one overlooked a tiny blemish on the left temple), her lips, slightly reshaped by lipstick.

"How did your classes go today?" she asked.

Well, of course she'd ask that, Anders thought. Love is marking time.

"All right," he said. "Teaching psychology to young apes— "

"Oh, come now!"

"Warmer," the voice said.

What's the matter with me, Anders wondered. She
really is a lovely girl. The *gestalt* that is Judy, a pattern
of thoughts, expressions, movements, making up the
girl I—

I what?

Love?

Anders shifted his long body uncertainly on the couch.
He didn't quite understand how this train of thought
had begun. It annoyed him. The analytical young in-
structor was better off in the classroom. Couldn't science wait until 9:10 in the morning?

"I was thinking about you today," Judy said, and
Anders knew that she had sensed the change in his
mood.

"Do you see?" the voice asked him. "You're getting
much better at it."

"I don't see anything," Anders thought, but the voice
was right. It was as though he had a clear line of
inspection into Judy's mind. Her feelings were nakedly
apparent to him, as meaningless as his room had been
in that flash of undistorted thought.

"I really was thinking about you," she repeated.

"Now look," the voice said.

Anders, watching the expression on Judy's face, felt
the strangeness descend on him. He was back in the
nightmare perception of that moment in his room. This
time it was as though he were watching a machine in a
laboratory. The object of this operation was the evoca-
tion and preservation of a particular mood. The machine
goes through a searching process, invoking trains of
ideas to achieve the desired end.

"Oh, were you?" he asked, amazed at his new
perspective.

"Yes . . . I wondered what you were doing at noon,"
the reactive machine opposite him on the couch said,
expanding its shapely chest slightly.

"Good," the voice said, commending him for his
perception.

"Dreaming of you, of course," he said to the flesh-
clad skeleton behind the total *gestalt* Judy. The flesh

machine rearranged its limbs, widened its mouth to denote pleasure. The mechanism searched through a complex of fears, hopes, worries, through half-remembrances of analogous situations, analogous solutions.

And this was what he loved. Anders saw too clearly and hated himself for seeing. Through his new nightmare perception, the absurdity of the entire room struck him.

"Were you really?" the articulating skeleton asked him.

"You're coming closer," the voice whispered.

To what? The personality? There was no such thing. There was no true cohesion, no depth, nothing except a web of surface reactions, stretched across automatic visceral movements.

He was coming closer to the truth.

"Sure," he said sourly.

The machine stirred, searching for a response.

Anders felt a quick tremor of fear at the sheer alien quality of his viewpoint. His sense of formalism had been sloughed off, his agreed-upon reactions by-passed. What would be revealed next?

He was seeing clearly, he realized, as perhaps no man had ever seen before. It was an oddly exhilarating thought.

But could he still return to normality?

"Can I get you a drink?" the reaction machine asked.

At that moment Anders was as thoroughly out of love as a man could be. Viewing one's intended as a depersonalized, sexless piece of machinery is not especially conducive to love. But it is quite stimulating, intellectually.

Anders didn't want normality. A curtain was being raised and he wanted to see behind it. What was it some Russian scientist—Ouspensky, wasn't it—had said?

"Think in other categories."

That was what he was doing, and would continue to do.

"Good-by," he said suddenly.

The machine watched him, open-mouthed, as he

walked out the door. Delayed circuit reactions kept it silent until it heard the elevator door close.

"You were very warm in there," the voice within his head whispered, once he was on the street. "But you still don't understand everything."

"Tell me, then," Anders said, marveling a little at his equanimity. In an hour he had bridged the gap to a completely different viewpoint, yet it seemed perfectly natural.

"I can't," the voice said. "You must find it yourself."

"Well, let's see now," Anders began. He looked around at the masses of masonry, the convention of streets cutting through the architectural piles. "Human life," he said, "is a series of conventions. When you look at a girl, you're supposed to see—a pattern, not the underlying formlessness."

"That's true," the voice agreed, but with a shade of doubt.

"Basically, there is no form. Man produces *gestalts*, and cuts form out of the plethora of nothingness. It's like looking at a set of lines and saying that they represent a figure. We look at a mass of material, extract it from the background and say it's a man. But in truth, there is no such thing. There are only the humanizing features that we—myopically—attach to it. Matter is conjoined, a matter of viewpoint."

"You're not seeing it now," said the voice.

"Damn it," Anders said. He was certain that he was on the track of something big, perhaps something ultimate. "Everyone's had the experience. At some time in his life, everyone looks at a familiar object and can't make any sense out of it. Momentarily, the *gestalt* fails, but the true moment of sight passes. The mind reverts to the superimposed pattern. Normalcy continues."

The voice was silent. Anders walked on, through the *gestalt* city.

"There's something else, isn't there?" Anders asked.

"Yes."

What could that be, he asked himself. Through clearing eyes, Anders looked at the formality he had called his world.

He wondered momentarily if he would have come to this if the voice hadn't guided him. Yes, he decided after a few moments, it was inevitable.

But who was the voice? And what had he left out?

"Let's see what a party looks like now," he said to the voice.

The party was a masquerade; the guests were all wearing their faces. To Anders, their motives, individually and collectively, were painfully apparent. Then his vision began to clear further.

He saw that the people weren't truly individual. They were discontinuous lumps of flesh sharing a common vocabulary, yet not even truly discontinuous.

The lumps of flesh were a part of the decoration of the room and almost indistinguishable from it. They were one with the lights, which lent their tiny vision. They were joined to the sounds they made, a few feeble tones out of the great possibility of sound. They blended into the walls.

The kaleidoscopic view came so fast that Anders had trouble sorting his new impressions. He knew now that these people existed only as patterns, on the same basis as the sounds they made and the things they thought they saw.

Gestalts, sifted out of the vast, unbearable real world.

"Where's Judy?" a discontinuous lump of flesh asked him. This particular lump possessed enough nervous mannerisms to convince the other lumps of his reality. He wore a loud tie as further evidence.

"She's sick," Anders said. The flesh quivered into an instant sympathy. Lines of formal mirth shifted to formal woe.

"Hope it isn't anything serious," the vocal flesh remarked.

"You're warmer," the voice said to Anders.

Anders looked at the object in front of him.

"She hasn't long to live," he stated.

The flesh quivered. Stomach and intestines contracted

in sympathetic fear. Eyes distended, mouth quivered.
The loud tie remained the same.

'My God! you don't mean it!"

"What are you?" Anders asked quietly.

"What do you mean?" the indignant flesh attached to
the tie demanded. Serene within its reality, it gaped at
Anders. Its mouth twitched, undeniable proof that it
was real and sufficient. "You're drunk," it sneered.

Anders laughed and left the party.

"There is still something you don't know," the voice
said. "But you were hot! I could feel you near me."

"What are you?" Anders asked again.

"I don't know," the voice admitted. "I am a person. I
am I. I am trapped."

"So are we all," Anders said. He walked on asphalt,
surrounded by heaps of concrete, silicates, aluminum
and iron alloys. Shapeless, meaningless heaps that made
up the *gestalt* city.

And then there were the imaginary lines of demarca-
tion dividing city from city, the artificial boundaries of
water and land.

All ridiculous.

"Give me a dime for some coffee, mister?" something
asked, a thing indistinguishable from any other thing.

"Old Bishop Berkeley would give a nonexistent dime
to your nonexistent presence," Anders said gaily.

"I'm really in a bad way," the voice whined, and
Anders perceived that it was no more than a series of
modulated vibrations.

"Yes! Go on!" the voice commanded.

"It you could spare me a quarter—" the vibrations
said, with a deep pretense at meaning.

No, what was there behind the senseless patterns?
Flesh, mass. What was that? All made up of atoms.

"I'm really hungry," the intricately arranged atoms
muttered.

All atoms. Conjoined. There were no true separa-
tions between atom and atom. Flesh was stone, stone
was light. Anders looked at the masses of atoms that
were pretending to solidity, meaning and reason.

"Can't you help me?" a clump of atoms asked. But the clump was identical with all the other atoms. Once you ignored the superimposed patterns, you could see the atoms were random, scattered.

"I don't believe in you," Anders said.

The pile of atoms was gone.

"Yes!" the voice cried. "Yes!"

"I don't believe in any of it," Anders said. After all, what was an atom?

"Go on!" the voice shouted. "You're hot! Go on!"

What was an atom? An empty space surrounded by an empty space.

Absurd!

"Then it's all false!" Anders said. And he was alone under the stars.

"That's right!" the voice within his head screamed. "Nothing!"

But stars, Anders thought. How can one believe—

The stars disappeared. Anders was in a gray nothingness, a void. There was nothing around him except shapeless gray.

Where was the voice?

Gone.

Anders perceived the delusion behind the grayness, and then there was nothing at all.

Complete nothingness, and himself within it.

Where was he? What did it mean? Anders' mind tried to add it up.

Impossible. *That* couldn't be true.

Again the score was tabulated, but Anders' mind couldn't accept the total. In desperation, the overloaded mind erased the figures, eradicated the knowledge, erased itself.

"Where am I?"

In nothingness, Alone.

Trapped.

"Who am I?"

A voice.

The voice of Anders searched the nothingness, shouted, "Is there anyone here?"

No answer.

But there was someone. All directions were the same, yet moving along one he could make contact . . . with someone. The voice of Anders reached back to someone who could save him, perhaps.

"Save me," the voice said to Anders, lying fully dressed on his bed, except for his shoes and black bow tie.

IMPOSTOR

PHILIP K. DICK (1928–1982)
ASTOUNDING SCIENCE FICTION, JUNE

Here at last we can greet the wonderful Philip K. Dick, who broke into the science fiction magazines one year earlier with "Beyond Lies the Wub." Dick was a man who crammed drugs, several wives, more than fifty novels (some of which are just now being published), considerable poverty, and much love into a thirty-year career that has left an enormous impact on the sf field. Long proclaimed a master of speculative fiction in France, he was finally receiving the recognition and wealth due him at the time of his early death, just as the film Bladerunner, *loosely based on his 1968 novel* Do Androids Dream of Electric Sheep? *was being released.*

His rich legacy includes the Hugo-Award winning novel The Man In The High Castle *(1963),* Time Out Of Joint *(1959),* The Three Stigmata Of Palmer Eldritch *(1965),* Flow My Tears, The Policeman Said *(1974), and* Valis *(1981). All of his work is at least a little bit autobiographical, and his fascinating life and art is currently the subject of numerous books and articles.*

"Impostor" captures the essence of his work—the real, the maybe real, and the unreal—for few things are what they appear in any story with his name on it. He wasn't the first to ask "what is the nature of reality" in an sf work, a question now quite fashionable in the

field, but no one ever asked it better than Phil did in this powerful and unforgettable story.

—MHG

I never met Philip Dick, but I heard that, at least early in his career, he experimented with what some people call "mind-expanding" drugs. I found that distasteful.

I have heard it said that such drugs help the creative process. Having never touched them myself, I can't say, out of personal experience, whether they do or not—but I am convinced (out of instinct? intuition?) that they do not. Nor do I consider the drugs "mind-expanding." "Mind-distorting" is what I think they are.

A writer's prime tool is his brain, obviously. A secondary tool is, let us say, a typewriter or a word-processor. I have never heard of any writer who persistently banged his typewriter with a hammer under the conviction that this would enable it to do its work better. Why, then, should the persistent banging of a brain with a chemical hammer make it work any better?

—IA

"ONE OF THESE DAYS I'm going to take time off," Spence Olham said at first-meal. He looked around at his wife. "I think I've earned a rest. Ten years is a long time."

"And the project?"

"The war will be won without me. This ball of clay of ours isn't really in much danger." Olham sat down at the table and lit a cigarette. "The news-machines alter dispatches to make it appear the Outspacers are right on top of us. You know what I'd like to do on my vacation? I'd like to take a camping trip in those mountains outside of town, where we went that time. Remember? I got poison oak and you almost stepped on a gopher snake."

"Sutton Wood?" Mary began to clear away the food dishes. "The wood was burned a few weeks ago. I thought you knew. Some kind of a flash fire."

Olham sagged. "Didn't they even try to find the cause?" His lips twisted. "No one cares any more. All they can think of is the war." He clamped his jaws together, the whole picture coming up in his mind, the Outspacers, the war, the needle-ships.

"How can we think about anything else?"

Olham nodded. She was right, of course. The dark little ships out of Alpha Centauri had bypassed the Earth cruisers easily, leaving them like helpless turtles. It had been one-way fights, all the way back to Terra.

All the way, until the protec-bubble was demonstrated by Westinghouse Labs. Thrown around the major Earth cities and finally the planet itself, the bubble was the first real defense, the first legitimate answer to the Outspacers—as the news-machines labeled them.

But to win the war, that was another thing. Every lab, every project was working night and day, endlessly, to find something more: a weapon for positive combat. His own project, for example. All day long, year after year.

Olham stood up, putting out his cigarette. "Like the Sword of Damocles. Always hanging over us. I'm getting tired. All I want to do is take a long rest. But I guess everybody feels that way."

He got his jacket from the closet and went out on the front porch. The shoot would be along any moment, the fast little bug that would carry him to the project.

"I hope Nelson isn't late." He looked at his watch. "It's almost seven."

"Here the bug comes," Mary said, gazing between the rows of houses. The sun glittered behind the roofs, reflecting against the heavy lead plates. The settlement was quiet; only a few people were stirring. "I'll see you later. Try not to work beyond your shift, Spence."

Olham opened the car door and slid inside, leaning back against the seat with a sigh. There was an older man with Nelson.

"Well?" Olham said, as the bug shot ahead. "Heard any interesting news?"

"The usual," Nelson said. "A few Outspace ships hit; another asteriod abandoned for strategic reasons."

"It'll be good when we get the project into final stage. Maybe it's just the propaganda from the news-machines, but in the last month I've gotten weary of all this. Everything seems so grim and serious, no color to life."

"Do you think the war is in vain?" the older man said suddenly. "You are an integral part of it, yourself."

"This is Major Peters," Nelson said. Olham and Peters shook hands. Olham studied the older man.

"What brings you along so early?" he said. "I don't remember seeing you at the project before."

"No, I'm not with the project," Peters said, "but I know something about what you're doing. My own work is altogether different."

A look passed between him and Nelson. Olham noticed it and he frowned. The bug was gaining speed, flashing across the barren, lifeless ground toward the distant rim of the project buildings.

"What is your business?" Olham said. "Or aren't you permitted to talk about it?"

"I'm with the government," Peters said. "With FSA, the security organ."

"Oh?" Olham raised an eyebrow. "Is there any enemy infiltration in this region?"

"As a matter of fact I'm here to see you, Mr. Olham."

Olham was puzzled. He considered Peter's words, but he could make nothing of them. "To see me? Why?"

"I'm here to arrest you as an Outspace spy. That's why I'm up so early this morning. *Grab him, Nelson. . . .*"

The gun drove into Olham's ribs. Nelson's hands were shaking, trembling with released emotion, his face pale. He took a deep breath and let it out again.

"Shall we kill him now?" he whispered to Peters. "I think we should kill him now. We can't wait."

Olham stared into his friend's face. He opened his mouth to speak, but no words came. Both men were staring at him steadily, rigid and grim with fright. Olham felt dizzy. His head ached and spun.

"I don't understand," he murmured.

At that moment the shoot car left the ground and rushed up, heading into space. Below them the project fell away, smaller and smaller, disappearing. Olham shut his mouth.

"We can wait a little," Peters said. "I want to ask him some questions, first."

Olham gazed dully ahead as the bug rushed through space.

"The arrest was made all right," Peters said into the vidscreen. On the screen the features of the security chief showed. "It should be a load off everyone's mind."

"Any complications?"

"None. He entered the bug without suspicion. He didn't seem to think my presence was too unusual."

"Where are you now?"

"On our way out, just inside the protec-bubble. We're moving at a maximum speed. You can assume that the critical period is past. I'm glad the takeoff jets in this craft were in good working order. If there had been any failure at that point. . . ."

"Let me see him," the security chief said. He gazed directly at Olham where he sat, his hands in his lap, staring ahead.

"So that's the man." He looked at Olham for a time. Olham said nothing. At last the chief nodded to Peters. "All right. That's enough." A faint trace of disgust wrinkled his features. "I've seen all I want. You've done something that will be remembered for a long time. They're preparing some sort of citation for both of you."

"That's not necessary," Peters said.

"How much danger is there now? Is there still much chance that. . . ?"

"There is some chance, but not too much. According to my understanding, it requires a verbal key phrase. In any case we'll have to take the risk."

"I'll have the moon base notified you're coming."

"No." Peters shook his head. "I'll land the ship outside, beyond the base. I don't want it in jeopardy."

"Just as you like." The chief's eyes flickered as he

glanced again at Olham. Then his image faded. The screen blanked.

Olham shifted his gaze to the window. The ship was already through the protec-bubble, rushing with greater and greater speed all the time. Peters was in a hurry; below him, rumbling under the floor, the jets were wide open. They were afraid, hurrying frantically, because of him.

Next to him on the seat, Nelson shifted uneasily. "I think we should do it now," he said. "I'd give anything if we could get it over with."

"Take it easy," Peters said. "I want you to guide the ship for a while so I can talk to him."

He slid over beside Olham, looking into his face. Presently he reached out and touched him gingerly on the arm and then on the cheek.

Olham said nothing. *If I could let Mary know*, he thought again. *If I could find some way of letting her know*. He looked around the ship. How? The vidscreen? Nelson was sitting by the board, holding the gun. There was nothing he could do. He was caught, trapped.

But why?

"Listen," Peters said, "I want to ask you some questions. You know where we're going. We're moving moonward. In an hour we'll land on the far side, on the desolate side. After we land you'll be turned over immediately to a team of men waiting there. Your body will be destroyed at once. Do you understand that?" He looked at his watch. "Within two hours your parts will be strewn over the landscape. There won't be anything left of you."

Olham struggled out of his lethargy. "Can't you tell me. . . ."

"Certainly, I'll tell you." Peters nodded. "Two days ago we received a report that an Outspace ship had penetrated the protec-bubble. The ship let off a spy in the form of a humanoid robot. The robot was to destroy a particular human being and take his place."

Peters looked calmly at Olham.

"Inside the robot was a U-bomb. Our agent did not know how the bomb was to be detonated, but he conjectured that it might be by a particular spoken phrase, a certain group of words. The robot would live the life of the person he killed, entering into his usual activities, his job, his social life. He had been constructed to resemble that person. No one would know the difference."

Olham's face went sickly chalk.

"The person whom the robot was to impersonate was Spence Olham, a high-ranking official at one of the research projects. Because this particular project was approaching crucial stage, the presence of an animate bomb, moving toward the center of the project. . . ."

Olham stared down at his hands. *"But I'm Olham!"*

"Once the robot had located and killed Olham, it was a simple matter to take over his life. The robot was probably released from the ship eight days ago. The substitution was probably accomplished over the last weekend when Olham went for a short walk in the hills."

"But I'm Olham." He turned to Nelson, sitting at the controls. "Don't you recognize me? You've known me for twenty years. Don't you remember how we went to college together?" He stood up. "You and I were at the university. We had the same room." He went toward Nelson.

"Stay away from me!" Nelson snarled.

"Listen. Remember our second year? Remember that girl? What was her name. . . ." He rubbed his forehead. "The one with the dark hair. The one we met over at Ted's place."

"Stop!" Nelson waved the gun frantically. "I don't want to hear any more. You killed him! You . . . machine."

Olham looked at Nelson. "You're wrong. I don't know what happened, but the robot never reached me. Something must have gone wrong. Maybe the ship crashed." He turned to Peters. "I'm Olham. I know it. No transfer was made. I'm the same as I've always been."

He touched himself, running his hands over his body.

"There must be some way to prove it. Take me back to Earth. An X-ray examination, a neurological study, anything like that will show you. Or maybe we can find the crashed ship."

Neither Peters nor Nelson spoke.

"I am Olham," he said again. "I know I am. But I can't prove it."

"The robot," Peters said, "would be unaware that he was not the real Spence Olham. He would become Olham in mind as well as body. He was given an artificial memory system, false recall. He would look like him, have his memories, his thoughts and interests, perform his job.

"But there would be one difference. Inside the robot is a U-bomb, ready to explode at the trigger phrase." Peters moved a little away. "That's the one difference. That's why we're taking you to the moon. They'll disassemble you and remove the bomb. Maybe it will explode, but it won't matter, not there."

Olham sat down slowly.

"We'll be there soon," Nelson said.

He lay back, thinking frantically, as the ship dropped slowly down. Under them was the pitted surface of the moon, the endless expanse of ruin. What could he do? What would save him?

"Get ready," Peters said.

In a few minutes he would be dead. Down below he could see a tiny dot, a building of some kind. There were men in the building, the demolition team, waiting to tear him to bits. They would rip him open, pull off his arms and legs, break him apart. When they found no bomb they would be surprised; they would know, but it would be too late.

Olham looked around the small cabin. Nelson was still holding the gun. There was no chance there. If he could get to a doctor, have an examination made—that was the only way. Mary could help him. He thought frantically, his mind racing. Only a few minutes, just a little time left. If he could contact her, get word to her some way.

"Easy," Peters said. The ship came down slowly, bumping on the rough ground. There was silence.

"Listen," Olham said thickly. "I can prove I'm Spence Olham. Get a doctor. Bring him here. . . ."

"There's the squad." Nelson pointed. "They're coming." He glanced nervously at Olham. "I hope nothing happens."

"We'll be gone before they start work," Peters said. "We'll be out of here in a moment." He put on his pressure suit. When he had finished he took the gun from Nelson. "I'll watch him for a moment."

Nelson put on his pressure suit, hurrying awkwardly. "How about him?" He indicated Olham. "Will he need one?"

"No." Peters shook his head. "Robots probably don't require oxygen."

The group of men were almost to the ship. They halted, waiting. Peters signaled to them.

"Come on!" He waved his hand and the men approached warily, stiff, grotesque figures in their inflated suits.

"If you open the door," Olham said, "it means my death. It will be murder."

"Open the door," Nelson said. He reached for the handle.

Olham watched him. He saw the man's hand tighten around the metal rod. In a moment the door would swing back, the air in the ship would rush out. He would die, and presently they would realize their mistake. Perhaps at some other time, when there was no war, men might not act this way, hurrying an individual to his death because they were afraid. Everyone was frightened, everyone was willing to sacrifice the individual because of the group fear.

He was being killed because they could not wait to be sure of his guilt. There was not enough time.

He looked at Nelson. Nelson had been his friend for years. They had gone to school together. He had been best man at his wedding. Now Nelson was going to kill him. But Nelson was not wicked; it was not his fault. It was the times. Perhaps it had been the same way during the plagues. When men had shown a spot they probably had been killed, too, without a moment's hesitation, without proof, on suspicion alone. In times of danger there was no other way.

He did not blame them. But he had to live. His life was too precious to be sacrificed. Olham thought quickly. What could he do? Was there anything? He looked around.

"Here goes," Nelson said.

"You're right," Olham said. The sound of his own voice surprised him. It was the strength of desperation. "I have no need of air. Open the door."

They paused, looking at him in curious alarm.

"Go ahead. Open it. It makes no difference." Olham's hand disappeared inside his jacket. "I wonder how far you two can run."

"Run?"

"You have fifteen seconds to live." Inside his jacket his fingers twisted, his arm suddenly rigid. He relaxed, smiling a little. "You were wrong about the trigger phrase. In that respect you were mistaken. Fourteen seconds, now."

Two shocked faces stared at him from the pressure suits. Then they were struggling, running, tearing the door open. The air shrieked out, spilling into the void. Peters and Nelson bolted out of the ship. Olham came after them. He grasped the door and dragged it shut. The automatic pressure system chugged furiously, restoring the air. Olham let his breath out with a shudder.

One more second. . . .

Beyond the window the two men had joined the group. The group scattered, running in all directions. One by one they threw themselves down, prone on the ground. Olham seated himself at the control board. He moved the dials into place. As the ship rose up into the air the men below scrambled to their feet and stared up, their mouths open.

"Sorry," Olham murmured, "but I've got to get back to Earth."

He headed the ship back the way it had come.

It was night. All around the ship crickets chirped, disturbing the chill darkness. Olham bent over the vidscreen. Gradually the image formed; the call had gone through without trouble. He breathed a sigh of relief.

"Mary," he said. The woman stared at him. She gasped.

"Spence! Where are you? What's happened?"

"I can't tell you. Listen, I have to talk fast. They may break this call off any minute. Go to the project grounds and get Dr. Chamberlain. If he isn't there, get any doctor. Bring him to the house and have him stay there. Have him bring equipment, X-ray, fluoroscope, everything."

"But. . . ."

"Do as I say. Hurry. Have him get it ready in an hour." Olham leaned toward the screen. "Is everything all right? Are you alone?"

"Alone?"

"Is anyone with you? Has . . . has Nelson or anyone contacted you?"

"No. Spence, I don't understand."

"All right. I'll see you at the house in an hour. And don't tell anyone anything. Get Chamberlain there on any pretext. Say you're very ill."

He broke the connection and looked at his watch. A moment later he left the ship, stepping down into the darkness. He had a half-mile to go.

He began to walk.

One light showed in the window, the study light. He watched it, kneeling against the fence. There was no sound, no movement of any kind. He held his watch up and read it by starlight. Almost an hour had passed.

Along the street a shoot bug came. It went on.

Olham looked toward the house. The doctor should have already come. He should be inside, waiting with

Mary. A thought struck him. Had she been able to leave the house? Perhaps they had intercepted her. Maybe he was moving into a trap.

But what else could he do?

With a doctor's records, photographs and reports, there was a chance, a chance of proof. If he could be examined, if he could remain alive long enough for them to study him. . . .

He could prove it that way. It was probably the only way. His one hope lay inside the house. Dr. Chamberlain was a respected man. He was the staff doctor for the project. He would know, his word on the matter would have meaning. He could overcome their hysteria, their madness, with facts.

Madness—that was what it was. If only they would wait, act slowly, take their time. But they could not wait. He had to die, die at once, without proof, without any kind of trial or examination. The simplest test would tell, but they had not time for the simplest test. They could think only of the danger. Danger, and nothing more.

He stood up and moved toward the house. He came up on the porch. At the door he paused, listening. Still no sound. The house was absolutely still.

Too still.

Olham stood on the porch, unmoving. They were trying to be silent inside. Why? It was a small house; only a few feet away, beyond the door, Mary and Dr. Chamberlain should be standing. Yet he could hear nothing, no sound of voices, nothing at all. He looked at the door. It was a door he had opened and closed a thousand times, every morning and every night.

He put his hand on the knob. Then, all at once, he reached out and touched the bell instead. The bell pealed, off some place in the back of the house. Olham smiled. He could hear movement.

Mary opened the door. As soon as he saw her face he knew.

He ran, throwing himself into the bushes. A security officer shoved Mary out of the way, firing past her. The bushes burst apart. Olham wriggled around the side of the house. He leaped up and ran, racing frantically into the darkness. A searchlight snapped on, a beam of light circling past him.

He crossed the road and squeezed over a fence. He jumped down and made his way across a backyard. Behind him men were coming, Security officers, shouting to each other as they came. Olham gasped for breath, his chest rising and falling.

Her face—he had known at once. The set lips, the terrified, wretched eyes. Suppose he had gone ahead, pushed open the door and entered! They had tapped the call and come at once, as soon as he had broken off. Probably she believed their account. No doubt she thought he was the robot, too.

Olham ran on and on. He was losing the officers, dropping them behind. Apparently they were not much good at running. He climbed a hill and made his way down the other side. In a moment he would be back at the ship. But where to, this time? He slowed down, stopping. He could see the ship already, outlined against the sky, where he had parked it. The settlement was behind him; he was on the outskirts of the wilderness between the inhabited places, where the forests and desolation began. He crossed a barren field and entered the trees.

As he came toward it, the door of the ship opened.

Peters stepped out, framed against the light. In his arms was a heavy boris-gun. Olham stopped, rigid. Peters stared around him, into the darkness. "I know you're there, someplace," he said. "Come on up here, Olham. There are security men all around you."

Olham did not move.

"Listen to me. We will catch you very shortly. Apparently you still do not believe you're the robot. Your call to the woman indicates that you are still under the illusion created by your artificial memories.

"But you *are* the robot. You are the robot, and inside you is the bomb. Any moment the trigger phrase may be spoken, by you, by someone else, by anyone. When that happens the bomb will destroy everything for miles around. The project, the woman, all of us will be killed. Do you understand?"

Olham said nothing. He was listening. Men were moving toward him, slipping through the woods.

"If you don't come out, we'll catch you. It will be only a matter of time. We no longer plan to remove you to the moon base. You will be destroyed on sight, and we will have to take the chance that the bomb will detonate. I have ordered every available security officer into the area. The whole country is being searched, inch by inch. There is no place you can go. Around this wood is a cordon of armed men. You have about six hours left before the last inch is covered."

Olham moved away. Peters went on speaking; he had not seen him at all. It was too dark to see anyone. But Peters was right. There was no place he could go. He was beyond the settlement, on the outskirts where the woods began. He could hide for a time, but eventually they would catch him.

Only a matter of time.

Olham walked quietly through the wood. Mile by mile, each part of the county was being measured off, laid bare, searched, studied, examined. The cordon was coming all the time, squeezing him into a smaller and smaller space.

What was there left? He had lost the ship, the one hope of escape. They were at his home; his wife was with them, believing, no doubt, that the real Olham had been killed. He clenched his fists. Someplace there was a wrecked Outspace needle-ship, and in it the remains of the robot. Somewhere nearby the ship had crashed, crashed and broken up.

And the robot lay inside, destroyed.

A faint hope stirred him. What if he could find the remains? If he could show them the wreckage, the remains of the ship, the robot. . . .

But where? Where would he find it?

He walked on, lost in thought. Someplace, not too far

off, probably. The ship would have landed close to the project; the robot would have expected to go the rest of the way on foot. He went up the side of a hill and looked around. Crashed and burned. Was there some clue, some hint? Had he read anything, heard anything? Someplace close by, within walking distance. Some wild place, a remote spot where there would be no people.

Suddenly Olham smiled. Crashed and burned. . . .

Sutton Wood.

He increased his pace.

It was morning. Sunlight filtered down through the broken trees onto the man crouching at the edge of the clearing. Olham glanced up from time to time, listening. They were not far off, only a few minutes away. He smiled.

Down below him, strewn across the clearing and into the charred stumps that had been Sutton Wood, lay a tangled mass of wreckage. In the sunlight it glittered a little, gleaming darkly. He had not had too much trouble finding it. Sutton Wood was a place he knew well; he had climbed around it many times in his life, when he was younger. He had known where he would find the remains. There was one peak that jutted up suddenly without warning.

A descending ship, unfamiliar with the wood, had little chance of missing it. And now he squatted, looking down at the ship, or what remained of it.

Olham stood up. He could hear them, only a little distance away, coming together, talking in low tones. He tensed himself. Everything depended on who first saw him. If it were Nelson, he had no chance. Nelson would fire at once. He would be dead before they saw the ship. But if he had time to call out, hold them off for a moment—that was all he needed. Once they saw the ship he would be safe.

But if they fired first. . . .

A charred branch cracked. A figure appeared, coming forward uncertainly. Olham took a deep breath. Only a few seconds remained, perhaps the last seconds of his life. He raised his arms, peering intently.

It was Peters.

"Peters!" Olham waved his arms. Peters lifted his gun, aiming. "Don't fire!" His voice shook. "Wait a minute. Look past me, across the clearing."

"I've found him," Peters shouted. Security men came pouring out of the burned woods around him.

"Don't shoot. Look past me. The ship, the needle-ship. The Outspace ship. Look!"

Peters hesitated. The gun wavered.

"It's down there," Olham said rapidly. "I knew I'd find it here. The burned wood. Now you believe me. You'll find the remains of the robot in the ship. Look, will you?"

"There is something down there," one of the men said nervously.

"Shoot him!" a voice said. It was Nelson.

"Wait." Peters turned sharply. "I'm in charge. Don't anyone fire. Maybe he's telling the truth."

"Shoot him," Nelson said. "He killed Olham. Any minute he may kill us all. If the bomb goes off. . . ."

"Shut up." Peters advanced toward the slope. He stared down. "Look at that." He waved two men up to him. "Go down there and see what that is."

The men raced down the slope, across the clearing. They bent down, poking in the ruins of the ship.

"Well?" Peters called.

Olham held his breath. He smiled a little. It must be there; he had not had time to look, himself, but it had to be there. Suddenly doubt assailed him. Suppose the robot had lived long enough to wander away? Suppose his body had been completely destroyed, burned to ashes by the fire?

He licked his lips. Perspiration came out on his forehead. Nelson was staring at him, his face still livid. His chest rose and fell.

"Kill him," Nelson said. "Before he kills us."

The two men stood up.

"What have you found?" Peters said. He held the gun steady. "Is there anything there?"

"Looks like something. It's a needle-ship, all right. There's something beside it."

"I'll look." Peters strode past Olham. Olham watched him go down the hill and up to the men. The others were following after him, peering to see.

"It's a body of some sort," Peters said. "Look at it!"

Olham came along with them. They stood around in a circle, staring down.

On the ground, bent and twisted into a strange shape, was a grotesque form. It looked human, perhaps; except that it was bent so strangely, the arms and legs flung off in all directions. The mouth was open, the eyes stared glassily.

"Like a machine that's run down," Peters murmured.

Olham smiled feebly. "Well?" he said.

Peters looked at him. "I can't believe it. You were telling the truth all the time."

"The robot never reached me," Olham said. He took out a cigarette and lit it. "It was destroyed when the ship crashed. You were all too busy with the war to wonder why an out-of-the-way woods would suddenly catch fire and burn. Now you know."

He stood smoking, watching the men. They were dragging the grotesque remains from the ship. The body was stiff, the arms and legs rigid.

"You'll find the bomb, now," Olham said. The men laid the body on the ground. Peters bent down.

"I think I see the corner of it." He reached out, touching the body.

The chest of the corpse had been laid open. Within the gaping tear something glinted, something metal. The men stared at the metal without speaking.

"That would have destroyed us all, if it had lived," Peters said. "That metal box, there."

There was silence.

"I think we owe you something," Peters said to Olham.

"This must have been a nightmare to you. If you hadn't escaped, we would have. . . ." He broke off.

Olham put out his cigarette. "I knew, of course, that the robot had never reached me. But I had no way of proving it. Sometimes it isn't possible to prove a thing right away. That was the whole trouble. There wasn't any way I could demonstrate that I was myself."

"How about a vacation?" Peters said. "I think we might work out a month's vacation for you. You could take it easy, relax."

"I think right now I want to go home," Olham said.

"All right, then," Peters said. "Whatever you say."

Nelson had squatted down on the ground beside the corpse. He reached out toward the glint of metal visible within the chest.

"Don't touch it," Olham said. "It might still go off. We better let the demolition squad take care of it later on."

Nelson said nothing. Suddenly he grabbed hold of the metal, reaching his hand inside the chest. He pulled.

"What are you doing?" Olham cried.

Nelson stood up. He was holding onto the metal object. His face was blank with terror. It was a metal knife, an Outspace needle-knife, covered with blood.

"This killed him," Nelson whispered. "My friend was killed with this." He looked at Olham. "You killed him with this and left him beside the ship."

Olham was trembling. His teeth chattered. He looked from the knife to the body. "This can't be Olham," he said. His mind spun, everything was whirling. "Was I wrong?"

He gaped.

"But if that's Olham, then I must be. . . ."

He did not complete the sentence, only the first phrase. The blast was visible all the way to Alpha Centauri.

THE WORLD WELL LOST

THEODORE STURGEON
UNIVERSE SCIENCE FICTION, JUNE

"The World Well Lost" appeared in Universe Science
Fiction, *one of Ray Palmer's stable of publications (which
of course included* Amazing Stories *and* Fantastic*) although he was not the editor who bought the story—
this honor goes to George Bell, of whom I know nothing.
The magazine's name was changed to* Other Worlds *in
1955. The publication of this story broke an important
taboo in science fiction, and it ended up in Universe
only because it had been rejected by most or all of the
higher paying markets.*

—MHG

Ted is gone now; he has left us. It is sad to think that
such things must happen. As we proceed along this
series of books, the vital statistic (1918–   ) with that
comfortable blank in second place, tells us that all is not
over, that more stories may appear, that more work
may be done. And then comes the day when it is
changed to (1918–1985) and we know that the curtain
has come down.

Ted's last years, I believe, were sad. His writing
never seemed to come easy, and it never brought him
quite the degree of fame and success (and money) that
other, lesser writers achieved.

Perhaps in the end he thought as he wearily turned

194

his face to the wall that the world was well lost, but none of us who knew him and read him can ever think that Ted was well lost.

Ave atque vale, Ted. You have left us, but your stories remain.

—IA

ALL THE WORLD knew them as loverbirds, though they were certainly not birds, but humans. Well, say humanoids. Featherless bipeds. Their stay on earth was brief, a nine-day wonder. Any wonder that lasts nine days on an earth of orgasmic trideo shows; time-freezing pills; synapse-inverter fields which make it possible for a man to turn a sunset to perfumes, a masochist to a fur-feeler; and a thousand other euphorics—why, on such an earth, a nine-day wonder is a wonder indeed.

Like a sudden bloom across the face of the world came the peculiar magic of the loverbirds. There were loverbird songs and loverbird trinkets, loverbird hats and pins, bangles and baubles, coins and quaffs and tidbits. For there was that about the loverbirds which made a deep enchantment. No one can be told about a loverbird and feel this curious delight. Many are immune even to a solidograph. But watch loverbirds, only for a moment, and see what happens. It's the feeling you had when you were twelve, and summer-drenched, and you kissed a girl for the very first time and knew a breathlessness you were sure could never happen again. And indeed it never could—unless you watched loverbirds. Then you are spellbound for four quiet seconds, and suddenly your very heart twists, and incredulous tears sting and stay; and the very first move you make afterward, you make on tiptoe, and your first word is a whisper.

This magic came over very well on trideo, and everyone had trideo; so for a brief while the earth was enchanted.

There were only two loverbirds. They came down out of the sky in a single brassy flash, and stepped out of their ship, hand in hand. Their eyes were full of wonder, each at the other, and together at the world. They seemed frozen in a full-to-bursting moment of discovery; they made way for one another gravely and with courtesy, they looked about them and in the very looking gave each other gifts—the color of the sky, the taste of the air, the pressures of things growing and meeting and changing. They never spoke. They simply *were* together. To watch them was to know of their awestruck mounting of staircases of bird notes, of how each knew the warmth of the other as their flesh supped silently on sunlight.

They stepped from their ship, and the tall one threw a yellow powder back to it. The ship fell in upon itself and became a pile of rubble, which collapsed into a pile of gleaming sand, which slumped compactly down to dust and then to an airblown emulsion so fine that Brownian movement itself hammered it up and out and away. Anyone could see that they intended to stay. Anyone could know by simply watching them that next to their wondrous delight in each other came their delighted wonder at earth itself, everything and everybody about it.

Now, if terrestrial culture were a pyramid, at the apex (where the power is) would sit a blind man, for so constituted are we that only by blinding ourselves, bit by bit, may we rise above our fellows. The man at the apex has an immense preoccupation with the welfare of the whole, because he regards it as the source and structure of his elevation, which it is, and as an extension of himself, which it is not. It was such a man who, in the face of immeasurable evidence, chose to find a defense against loverbirds, and fed the matrices and coordinates of the loverbird image into the most marvelous calculator that had ever been built.

The machine sucked in symbols and raced them about, compared and waited and matched and sat still while its bulging memory, cell by cell, was silent, was silent—and suddenly, in a far corner, resonated. It grasped this resonance in forceps made of mathematics, snatched it

out (translating furiously as it snatched) and put out a
fevered tongue of paper on which was typed:

DIRBANU

Now this utterly changed the complexion of things.
For earth ships had ranged the cosmos far and wide,
with few hindrances. Of these hindrances, all could be
understood but one, and that one was Dirbanu, a
transgalactic planet which shrouded itself in impenetrable fields of force whenever an earthship approached.
There were other worlds which could do this, but in
each case the crews knew why it was done. Dirbanu,
upon discovery, had prohibited landings from the very
first until an ambassador could be sent to Terra. In due
time one did arrive (so reported the calculator, which
was the only entity that remembered the episode) and
it was obvious that Earth and Dirbanu had much in
common. The ambassador, however, showed a most
uncommon disdain of Earth and all its works, curled his
lip and went wordlessly home, and ever since then
Dirbanu had locked itself tight away from the questing
Terrans.

Dirbanu thereby became of value, and fair game, but
we could do nothing to ripple the bland face of her
defenses. As this impregnability repeatedly proved itself, Dirbanu evolved in our group mind through the
usual stages of being: the Curiosity, the Mystery, the
Challenge, the Enemy, the Enemy, the Enemy, the
Mystery, the Curiosity, and finally That-which-is-too-
far-away-to-bother-with, or the Forgotten.

And suddenly, after all this time, Earth had two
genuine natives of Dirbanu aboard, entrancing the pop-
ulace and giving no information. This intolerable circumstance began to make itself felt throughout the
world—but slowly, for this time the blind men's din
was cushioned and soaked by the magic of the loverbirds.
It might have taken a very long time to convince the
poeple of the menace in their midst had there not been
a truly startling development:

A direct message was received from Dirbanu.

The collective impact of loverbird material emanating from transmitters on Earth had attracted the attention of Dirbanu, which promptly informed us that the loverbirds were indeed their nationals, that in addition they were fugitives, that Dirbanu would take it ill if Earth should regard itself as a sanctuary for the criminals of Dirbanu but would, on the other hand, find it in its heart to be very pleased if Earth saw fit to return them.

So from the depths of its enchantment, Terra was able to calculate a course of action. Here at last was an opportunity to consort with Dirbanu on a friendly basis— great Dirbanu which, since it had force fields which Earth could not duplicate, must of necessity have many other things Earth could use; mighty Dirbanu before whom we could kneel in supplication (with purely-for-defense bombs hidden in our pockets) with lowered heads (making invisible the knife in our teeth) and ask for crumbs from their table (in order to extrapolate the location of their kitchens).

Thus the loverbird episode became another item in the weary procession of proofs that Terra's most reasonable intolerance can conquer practically anything, even magic.

Especially magic.

So it was that the loverbirds were arrested, that the *Starmite* 439 was fitted out as a prison ship, that a most carefully screened crew was chosen for her, and that she struck starward with the cargo that would gain us a world.

Two men were the crew—a colorful little rooster of a man and a great dun bull of a man. They were, respectively, Rootes, who was Captain and staff, and Grunty, who was midship and inboard corps. Rootes was cocky, springy, white and crisp. His hair was auburn and so were his eyes, and the eyes were hard. Grunty was a shambler with big gentle hands and heavy shoulders half as wide as Rootes was high. He should have worn a cowl and rope-belted habit. He should, perhaps, have worn a burnoose. He did neither, but the effect was there. Known only to him was the fact that words and pictures, concepts and comparisons were an endless swirling blizzard inside him. Known only to him and Rootes was the fact that he had books, and books, and books, and Rootes did not care if he had or not. Grunty he had been called since he first learned to talk, and Grunty was name enough for him. For the words in his head would not leave him except one or two at a time, with long moments between. So he had learned to condense his verbal messages to breathy grunts, and when they wouldn't condense, he said nothing.

They were primitives, both of them, which is to say that they were doers, while Modern Man is a thinker and/or a feeler. The thinkers compose new variations and permutations of euphoria, and the feelers repay the thinkers by responding to their inventions. The ships had no place for Modern Man, and Modern Man had only the most casual use for the ships.

Doers can cooperate like cam and pushrod, like ratchet and pawl, and such linkage creates a powerful bond. But Rootes and Grunty were unique among crews in that these machine parts were not interchangeable. Any good captain can command any good crew, surroundings being equivalent. But Rootes would not and could not ship out with anyone but Grunty, and Grunty was just that dependent. Grunty understood this bond, and the fact that the only way it could conceivably be broken would be to explain it to Rootes. Rootes did not understand it because it never occurred to him to try, and had he tried, he would have failed, since he was inherently non-equipped for the task. Grunty knew that their unique bond was, for him, a survival matter. Rootes did not know this, and would have rejected the idea with violence.

So Rootes regarded Grunty with tolerance and a modified amusement. The modification was an inarticulate realization of Grunty's complete dependability. Grunty regarded Rootes with . . . well, with the ceaseless, silent flurry of words in his mind.

There was, beside the harmony of functions and the other link, understood only by Grunty, a third adjunct to their phenomenal efficiency as a crew. It was organic, and it had to do with the stellar drive.

Reaction engines were long forgotten. The so-called "warp" drive was used only experimentally and on certain crash-priority war-craft where operating costs were not a factor. The *Starmite* 439 was, like most interstellar craft, powered by an RS plant. Like the transistor, the Referential Stasis generator is extremely simple to construct and very difficult indeed to explain. Its mathematics approaches mysticism and its theory contains certain impossibilities which are ignored in practice. Its effect is to shift the area of stasis of the ship and everything in it from one point of reference to another. For example, the ship at rest on the Earth's surface is in stasis in reference to the ground on which it rests. Throwing the ship into stasis in reference to the center of the earth gives it instantly an effective speed equal to the surface velocity of the planet around its core—some one thousand miles per hour. Stasis referential to the sun moves the Earth out from under the ship at the Earth's orbital velocity. GH stasis "moves" the ship at the angular velocity of the sun about the Galactic Hub. The galactic drift can be used, as can any simple or complex mass center in this expanding universe. There are resultants and there are multipliers, and effective velocities can be enormous. Yet the ship is constantly in stasis, so that there is never an inertia factor.

The one inconvenience of the RS drive is that shifts from one referent to another invariably black the crew out, for psychoneural reasons. The blackout period varies slightly between individuals, from one to two and a half hours. But some anomaly in Grunty's gigantic frame kept his blackout periods down to thirty or forty minutes, while Rootes was always out for two hours or more. There was that about Grunty which made moments of isolation a vital necessity, for a man must occasionally be himself, which in anyone's company Grunty was not. But after stasis shifts Grunty had an hour or so to himself while his commander lay numbly spread-eagled on the blackout couch, and he spent these in communions of his own devising. Sometimes this meant only a good book.

This, then, was the crew picked to man the prison ship. It had been together longer than any other crew in the Space Service. Its record showed a metrical efficiency and a resistance to physical and phychic debilitations previously unheard of in a trade where close confinement on long voyages had come to be regarded as hazards. In space, shift followed shift uneventfully, and planetfall was made on schedule and without incident. In port Rootes would roar off to the fleshpots, in which he would wallow noisily until an hour before takeoff, while Grunty found, first, the business office, and next, a bookstore.

They were pleased to be chosen for the Dirbanu trip. Rootes felt no remorse at taking away Earth's new delight, since he was one of the very few who was immune to it. ("Pretty," he said at his first encounter.) Grunty simply grunted, but then, so did everyone else. Rootes did not notice, and Grunty did not remark upon the obvious fact that though the loverbirds' expression of awestruck wonderment in each other's presence had, if anything, intensified, their extreme pleasure in Earth and the things of Earth had vanished. They were locked, securely but comfortably, in the after cabin behind a new transparent door, so that their every move could be watched from the main cabin and control console. They sat close, with their arms about one another, and though their radiant joy in the contact never lessened, it was a shadowed pleasure, a lachrymose beauty like the wrenching music of the wailing wall.

The RS drive laid its hand on the moon and they vaulted away. Grunty came up from blackout to find it very quiet. The loverbirds lay still in each other's arms. looking very human except for the high joining of their closed eyelids, which nictated upward rather than downward like a Terran's. Rootes sprawled limply on the other couch, and Grunty nodded at the sight. He deeply appreciated the silence, since Rootes had filled the small cabin with earthy chatter about his conquests in port, detail by hairy detail, for two solid hours preceding their departure. It was a routine which Grunty found particularly wearing, partly for its content, which interested him not at all, but mostly for its inevitability. Grunty had long ago noted that these recitations, for all their detail, carried the tones of thirst rather than of satiety. He had his own conclusions about it, and, characteristically, kept them to himself. But inside, his spinning gusts of words could shape themselves well to it, and they did. "And man, she moaned!" Rootes would chant. "And take money? She *gave* me money. And what did I do with it? Why, I bought up some more of the same." *And what you could buy with a shekel's worth of tenderness, my prince!* his silent words sang. ". . . across the floor and around the rug until, by damn, I thought we're about to climb the wall. Loaded, Grunty-boy, I tell you, I was loaded!" *Poor little one* ran the hushed susurrus, *thy poverty is as great as thy joy and a tenth as great as thine empty noise.* One of Grunty's greatest pleasures was taken in the fact that this kind of chuntering was limited to the first day out, with barely another word on the varied theme until the next departure, no matter how many months away that might be. *Squeak to me of love, dear mouse,* his words would chuckle. *Stand up on your cheese and nibble away at your dream.* Then, wearily, *But oh, this treasure I carry is too heavy a burden, in all its fullness, to be so tugged at by your clattering vacuum!*

Grunty left the couch and went to the controls. The preset courses checked against the indicators. He logged them and fixed the finder control to locate a certain mass-nexus in the Crab Nebula. It would chime when it was ready. He set the switch for final closing by the push-button beside his couch, and went aft to wait.

He stood watching the loverbirds because there was nothing else for him to do.

They lay quite still, but love so permeated them that their very poses expressed it. Their lax bodies yearned each to each, and the tall one's hand seemed to stream toward the fingers of his beloved, and then back again, like the riven tatters of a torn fabric straining toward oneness again. And as their mood was a sadness too, so their pose, each and both, together and singly expressed it, and singly each through the other silently spoke of the loss they had suffered, and how it ensured greater losses to come. Slowly the picture suffused Grunty's thinking, and his words picked and pieced and smoothed it down, and murmured finally. *Brush away the dusting of sadness from the future, bright ones. You've sadness enough for now. Grief should live only after it is truly born, and not before.*

His words sang,

> *Come fill the cup and in the fire of spring*
> *Your winter garment of repentance fling.*
> *The bird of time has but a little way*
> *To flutter—and the bird is on the wing.*

and added *Omar Khayyam, born circa 1073*, for this, too, was one of the words' functions.

And then he stiffened in horror; his great hands came up convulsively and clawed the imprisoning glass. . . .

They were smiling at him.

They were smiling, and on their faces and on and about their bodies there was no sadness.

They had *heard* him!

He glanced convulsively around at the Captain's unconscious form, then back to the loverbirds.

That they should recover so swiftly from blackout was, to say the least, an intrusion; for his moments of aloneness were precious and more than precious to Grunty, and would be useless to him under the scrutiny of those jeweled eyes. But that was a minor matter compared to this other thing, this terrible fact that they *heard*.

Telepathic races were not common, but they did

exist. And what he was now experiencing was what invariably happened when humans encountered one. He could only send; the loverbirds could only receive. And they *must not* receive him! No one must. No one must know what he was, what he thought. If anyone did, it would be a disaster beyond bearing. It would mean no more flights with Rootes. Which, of course, meant no flights with anyone. And how could he live— where could he go?

He turned back to the loverbirds. His lips were white and drawn back in a snarl of panic and fury. For a blood-thick moment he held their eyes. They drew closer to one another, and together sent him a radiant, anxious, friendly look that made him grind his teeth.

Then, at the console, the finder chimed.

Grunty turned slowly from the transparent door and went to his couch. He lay down and poised his thumb over the push-button.

He *hated* the loverbirds, and there was no joy in him. He pressed the button, the ship slid into a new stasis, and he blacked out.

The time passed.

"Grunty!"

"?"

"You feed them this shift?"

"Nuh."

"Last shift?"

"Nuh."

"What the hell's the matter with you, y'big dumb bastich? What you expect them to live on?"

Grunty sent a look of roiling hatred aft. "Love," he said.

"Feed'em," snapped Rootes.

Wordlessly Grunty went about preparing a meal for the prisoners. Rootes stood in the middle of the cabin, his hard small fists on his hips, his gleaming auburn head tilted to one side, and watched every move. "I didn't used to have to tell you anything," he growled, half pugnaciously, half worriedly. "You sick?"

Grunty shook his head. He twisted the tops of two cans and set them aside to heat themselves, and took down the water suckers.

"You got it in for these honeymooners or something?"

Grunty averted his face.

"We get them to Dirbanu alive and healthy, hear me? They get sick, you get sick, by God. I'll see to that. Don't give me trouble, Grunty. I'll take it out on you. I never whipped you yet, but I will."

Grunty carried the tray aft. "You hear me?" Rootes yelled.

Grunty nodded without looking at him. He touched the control and a small communication window slid open in the glass wall. He slid the tray through. The taller loverbird stepped forward and took it eagerly, gracefully, and gave him a dazzling smile of thanks. Grunty growled low in his throat like a carnivore. The loverbird carried the food back to the couch and they began to eat, feeding each other little morsels.

A new stasis, and Grunty came fighting up out of blackness. He sat up abruptly, glanced around the ship. The Captain was sprawled out across the cushions, his compact body and outflung arm forming the poured-out, spring-steel laxness usually seen only in sleeping cats. The loverbirds, even in deep unconsciousness, lay like hardly separate parts of something whole, the small one on the couch, the tall one on the deck, prone, reaching, supplicating.

Grunty snorted and hove to his feet. He crossed the cabin and stood looking down on Rootes.

The hummingbird is a yellow-jacket, said his words. *Buzz and dart, hiss and flash away. Swift and hurtful, hurtful. . . .*

He stood for a long moment, his great shoulder muscles working one against the other, and his mouth trembled.

He looked at the loverbirds, who were still motionless. His eyes slowly narrowed.

His words tumbled and climbed, and ordered themselves:

> *I through love have learned three things,*
> *Sorrow, sin and death it brings.*
> *Yet day by day my heart within*
> *Dares shame and sorrow, death and sin. . . .*

And dutifully he added *Samuel Ferguson, born 1810*. He glared at the loverbirds, and brought his fist into his palm with a sound like a club on an anthill. They had heard him again, and this time they did not smile, but looked into each other's eyes and then turned together to regard him, nodding gravely.

Rootes went through Grunty's books, leafing and casting aside. He had never touched them before. "Buncha crap," he jeered. "Garden of the Plynck. Wind in the Willows. Worm Ouroborous. Kid stuff."

Grunty lumbered across and patiently gathered up the books the Captain had flung aside, putting them one by one back into their places, stroking them as if they had been bruised.

"Isn't there nothing in here with pictures?"

Grunty regarded him silently for a moment and then took down a tall volume. The Captain snatched it, leafed through it. "Mountains," he growled. "Old houses." He leafed. "Damn boats." He smashed the book to the deck. "Haven't you got *any* of what I want?"

Grunty waited attentively.

"Do I have to draw a diagram?" the Captain roared. "Got that ol' itch, Grunty. You wouldn't know. I feel like looking at pictures, get what I mean?"

Grunty stared at him, utterly without expression, but deep within him a panic squirmed. The Captain never, *never* behaved like this in mid-voyage. It was going to get worse, he realized. Much worse. And quickly.

He shot the loverbirds a vicious, hate-filled glance. If they weren't aboard. . . .

There could be no waiting. Not now. Something had to be done. Something. . . .

"Come on, come on," said Rootes. "Goddlemighty Godfrey, even a deadbutt like you must have *something* for kicks."

Grunty turned away from him, squeezed his eyes closed for a tortured second, then pulled himself together. He ran his hand over the books, hesitated, and finally brought out a large, heavy one. He handed it to the Captain and went forward to the console. He slumped down there over the file of computer tapes, pretending to be busy.

The Captain sprawled onto Grunty's couch and opened the book. "Michelangelo, what the hell," he growled. He grunted, almost like his shipmate. "Statues," he half-whispered, in withering scorn. But he ogled and leafed at last, and was quiet.

The loverbirds looked at him with a sad tenderness, and then together sent beseeching glances at Grunty's angry back.

The matrix-pattern for Terra slipped through Grunty's fingers, and he suddenly tore the tape across, and across again. A filthy place, Terra. *There is nothing*, he thought, *like the conservatism of license.* Given a culture of sybaritics, with an endless choice of mechanical titillations, and you have a people of unbreakable and hidebound formality, a people with few but massive taboos, a shockable, narrow, prissy people obeying the rules—even the rules of their calculated depravities—and protecting their treasured, specialized pruderies. In such a group there are words one may not use for fear of their fanged laughter, colors one may not wear, gestures and intonations one must forego, on pain of being torn to pieces. The rules are complex and absolute, and in such a place one's heart may not sing lest, through its warm free joyousness, it betrays one.

And if you must have joy of such a nature, if you must be free to be your pressured self, then off to space . . . off to the glittering black lonelinesses. And let the days go by, and let the time pass, and huddle beneath your impenetrable integument, and wait, and wait, and every once in a long while you will have that moment of lonely consciousness when there is no one around to see; and then it may burst from you and you may dance, or cry, or twist the hair on your head till your eyeballs blaze, or do any of the other things your so unfashionable nature thirstily demands.

It took Grunty half a lifetime to find this freedom. No price would be too great to keep it. Not lives, nor interplanetary diplomacy, nor Earth itself were worth such a frightful loss.

He would lose it if anyone knew, and the loverbirds knew.

He pressed his heavy hands together until the knuckles crackled. Dirbanu, reading it all from the ardent minds of the loverbirds; Dirbanu flashing the news across the stars; the roar of reaction, and then Rootes, Rootes, when the huge and ugly impact washed over him. . . .

So let Dirbanu be offended. Let Terra accuse this ship of fumbling, even of treachery—anything but the withering news the loverbirds had stolen.

Another new stasis, and Grunty's first thought as he came alive in the silent ship was *It has to be soon.*

He rolled off the couch and glared at the unconscious loverbirds. The helpless loverbirds.

Smash their heads in.

Then Rootes . . . what to tell Rootes?

The loverbirds attacked him, tried to seize the ship?

He shook his head like a bear in a beehive. Rootes would never believe that. Even if the loverbirds could open the door, which they could not, it was more than ridiculous to imagine those two bright and slender things attacking anyone—especially not so rugged and massive an opponent.

Poison? No—there was nothing in the efficient, unfailingly beneficial food stores that might help.

His glance strayed to the Captain, and he stopped breathing.

Of *course!*

He ran to the Captain's personal lockers. He should have known that such a cocky little hound as Rootes could not live, could not strut and prance as he did unless he had a weapon. And if it was the kind of weapon that such a man would characteristically choose—

A movement caught his eye as he searched.

The loverbirds were awake.

That wouldn't matter.

He laughed at them, a flashing, ugly laugh. They cowered close together and their eyes grew very bright.

They knew.

He was aware that they were suddenly very busy, as busy as he. And then he found the gun.

It was a snug little thing, smooth and intimate in his hand. It was exactly what he had guessed, what he had hoped for—just what he needed. It was silent. It would leave no mark. It need not even be aimed carefully. Just a touch of its feral radiation and throughout the body, the axones suddenly refuse to propagate nerve impulses. No thought leaves the brain, no slightest contraction of heart or lung occurs again, ever. And afterward, no sign remains that a weapon has been used.

He went to the serving window with the gun in his hand. *When he wakes, you will be dead,* he thought. *Couldn't recover from stasis blackout. Too bad. But no one's to blame, hm? We never had Dirbanu passengers before. So how could we know?*

The loverbirds, instead of flinching, were crowding close to the window, their faces beseeching, their delicate hands signing and signaling, frantically trying to convey something.

He touched the control, and the panel slid back.

The taller loverbird held up something as if it would shield him. The other pointed at it, nodded urgently, and gave him one of those accursed, hauntingly sweet smiles.

Grunty put up his hand to sweep the thing aside, and then checked himself.

It was only a piece of paper.

All the cruelty of humanity rose up in Grunty. A

species that can't protect itself doesn't deserve to live. He raised the gun.

And then he saw the pictures.

Economical and accurate, and, for all their subject, done with the ineffable grace of the loverbirds themselves, the pictures showed three figures:

Grunty himself, hulking, impassive, the eyes glowing, the tree-trunk legs and hunched shoulders.

Rootes, in a pose so characteristic and so cleverly done that Grunty gasped. Crisp and clean, Rootes' image had one foot up on a chair, both elbows on the high knee, the head half turned. The eyes fairly sparkled from the paper.

And a girl.

She was beautiful. She stood with her arms behind her, her feet slightly apart, her face down a little. She was deep-eyed, pensive, and to see her was to be silent, to wait for those downcast lids to lift and break the spell.

Grunty frowned and faltered. He lifted a puzzled gaze from these exquisite renderings to the loverbirds, and met the appeal, the earnest, eager, hopeful faces.

The loverbird put a second paper against the glass.

There were the same three figures, identical in every respect to the previous ones, except for one detail; they were all naked.

He wondered how they knew human anatomy so meticulously.

Before he could react, still another sheet went up.

The loverbirds, this time—the tall one, the shorter one, hand in hand. And next to them a third figure, somewhat similar, but tiny, very round, and with grotesquely short arms.

Grunty stared at the three sheets, one after the other. There was something . . . something. . . .

And then the loverbird put up the fourth sketch, and slowly, slowly, Grunty began to understand. In the last picture, the loverbirds were shown exactly as before, except that they were naked, and so was the small creature beside them. He had never seen loverbirds naked before. Possibly no one had.

Slowly he lowered the gun. He began to laugh. He reached through the window and took both the loverbirds' hands in one of his, and they laughed with him.

Rootes stretched easily with his eyes closed, pressed his face down into the couch, and rolled over. He dropped his feet to the deck, held his head in his hands and yawned. Only then did he realize that Grunty was standing just before him.

"What's the matter with you?"

He followed Grunty's grim gaze.

The glass door stood open.

Rootes bounced to his feet as if the couch had turned white-hot. "Where—what—"

Grunty's crag of a face was turned to the starboard bulkhead. Rootes spun to it, balanced on the balls of his feet as if he were boxing. His smooth face gleamed in the red glow of the light over the airlock.

"The lifeboat . . . you mean they took the lifeboat? They got away?"

Grunty nodded.

Rootes held his head. "Oh, fine," he moaned. He whipped around to Grunty. "And where the hell were you when this happened?"

"Here."

"Well, what in God's name happened?" Rootes was on the trembling edge of foaming hysteria.

Grunty thumped his chest.

"You're not trying to tell me you let them go?"

Grunty nodded, and waited—not for very long.

"I'm going to burn you down," Rootes raged. "I'm going to break you so low you'll have to climb for twelve years before you get a barracks to sweep. And after I get done with you I'll turn you over to the Service. What do you think they'll do to you? What do you think they're going to do to *me?*"

He leapt at Grunty and struck him a hard, cutting blow to the cheek. Grunty kept his hands down and made no attempt to avoid the fist. He stood immovable, and waited.

"Maybe those were criminals, but they were Dirbanu nationals," Rootes roared when he could get his breath. "How are we going to explain this to Dirbanu? Do you realize this could mean war?"

Grunty shook his head.

"What do you mean? You know something. You better talk while you can. Come on, bright boy—what are we going to tell Dirbanu?"

Grunty pointed at the empty cell. "Dead," he said.

"What good will it do us to say they're dead? They're not. They'll show up again some day, and—"

Grunty shook his head. He pointed to the star chart. Dirbanu showed as the nearest body. There was no livable planet within thousands of parsecs.

"They didn't go to Dirbanu!"

"Nuh."

"Damn it, it's like pulling rivets to get anything out of you. In that lifeboat they go to Dirbanu—which they won't—or they head out, maybe for years, to the Rim stars. That's all they can do!"

Grunty nodded.

"And you think Dirbanu won't track them, won't bring 'em down?"

"No ships."

"They have ships!"

"Nuh."

"The loverbirds told you?"

Grunty agreed.

"You mean their own ship that they destroyed, and the one the ambassador used were all they had?"

"Yuh."

Rootes strode up and back. "I don't get it. I don't begin to get it. What did you do it for, Grunty?"

Grunty stood for a moment, watching Rootes' face. Then he went to the computing desk. Rootes had no choice but to follow. Grunty spread out the four drawings.

"What's this? Who drew these? *Them?* What do you know. *Damn!* Who is the chick?"

Grunty patiently indicated all of the pictures in one sweep. Rootes looked at him, puzzled, looked at one of

Grunty's eyes, then the other, shook his head, and applied himself to the pictures again. "This is more like it," he murmured. "Wish I'd a' known they could draw like this." Again Grunty drew his attention to all the pictures and away from the single drawing that fascinated him.

"There's you, there's me. Right? Then this chick. Now, here we are again, all buff naked. Damn, what a carcass. All right, all right, I'm going on. Now, this is the prisoners, right? And who's the little fat one?"

Grunty pushed the fourth sheet over. "Oh," said Rootes. "Here everybody's naked too. Hm."

He yelped suddenly and bent close. Then he rapidly eyed all four sheets in sequence. His face began to get red. He gave the fourth picture a long, close scrutiny. Finally he put his finger on the sketch of the round little alien. "This is . . . a . . . a Dirbanu—"

Grunty nodded. "Female."

"Then those two—they were—"

Grunty nodded.

"So that's it!" Rootes fairly shrieked in fury. "You mean we been shipped out all this time with a coupla God damned *fairies?* Why, if I'd a' known that I'd a' killed 'em!"

"Yuh."

Rootes looked up at him with a growing respect and considerable amusement. "So you got rid of 'em so's I wouldn't kill 'em and mess everything up?" He scratched his head. "Well, I'll be billy-be-damned. You got a think-tank on you after all. Anything I can't stand, it's a fruit."

Grunty nodded.

"God," said Rootes, "It figures. It really figures. Their females don't look anything like the males. Compared with them, our females are practically identical to us. So the ambassador comes, and sees what looks like a planet full of queers. He knows better but he can't stand the sight. So back he goes to Dirbanu, and Earth gets brushed off."

Grunty nodded.

"Then these pansies here run off to earth, figuring

they'll be at home. They damn near made it, too. But Dirbanu calls 'em back, not wanting the likes of them representing their planet. I don't blame 'em a bit. How would you feel if the only Terran on Dirbanu was a fluff? Wouldn't you want him out of there, but quick?"

Grunty said nothing.

"And now," said Rootes, "we better give Dirbanu the good news."

He went forward to the communicator.

It took a surprisingly short time to contact the shrouded planet. Dirbanu acknowledged and coded out a greeting. The decoder over the console printed the message for them:

GREETINGS STARMITE 439. ESTABLISH ORBIT. CAN YOU DROP PRISONERS TO DIRBANU? NEVER MIND PARACHUTE.

"Whew," said Rootes. "Nice people. Hey, you notice they don't say come on in. They never expected to let us land. Well, what'll we tell 'em about their lavender lads?"

"Dead," said Grunty.

"Yeah," said Rootes. "That's what they want anyway." He sent rapidly.

In a few minutes the response clattered out of the decoder.

STAND BY FOR TELEPATH SWEEP. WE MUST CHECK. PRISONERS MAY BE PRETENDING DEATH.

"Oh-oh," said the Captain. "This is where the bottom drops out."

"Nuh," said Grunty, calmly.

"But their detector will locate—oh—I see what you're driving at. No life, no signal! Same as if they weren't here at all."

"Yuh."

The coder clattered.

DIRBANU GRATEFUL. CONSIDER MISSION COMPLETE. DO NOT WANT BODIES. YOU MAY EAT THEM.

Rootes retched. Grunty said, "Custom."

The decoder kept clattering.

NOW READY FOR RECIPROCAL AGREEMENT WITH TERRA.

"We go home in a blaze of glory," Rootes exulted. He sent,

TERRA ALSO READY. WHAT DO YOU SUGGEST?

The decoder paused, then:

TERRA STAY AWAY FROM DIRBANU AND DIRBANU WILL STAY AWAY FROM TERRA. THIS IS NOT A SUGGESTION. TAKES EFFECT IMMEDIATELY.

"Why that bunch of bastards!"

Rootes pounded his codewriter, and although they circled the planet at a respectful distance for nearly four days, they received no further response.

The last thing Rootes had said before they established the first stasis on the way home was: "Well, anyway—it does me good to think of those two queens crawling away in that lifeboat. Why, they can't even starve to death. They'll be cooped up there for *years* before they get anywhere they can sit down."

It still rang in Grunty's mind as he shook off the blackout. He glanced aft to the glass partition and smiled reminiscently. "For years," he murmured. His words curled up and spun, and said,

> . . . *Yes; love requires the focal space*
> *Of recollection or of hope,*
> *Ere it can measure its own scope.*
> *Too soon, too soon comes death to show*
> *We love more deeply than we know!*

Dutifully, then, came the words: *Coventry Patmore, born 1823.*

He rose slowly and stretched, reveling in his precious privacy. He crossed to the other couch and sat down on the edge of it.

For a time he watched the Captain's unconscious face, reading it with great tenderness and utmost attention, like a mother with an infant.

His words said, *Why must we love where the lightning strikes, and not where we choose?*

And they said, *But I'm glad it's you, little prince. I'm glad it's you.*

He put out his huge hand and, with a feather touch, stroked the sleeping lips.

A BAD DAY FOR SALES

FRITZ LEIBER (1910–)
GALAXY SCIENCE FICTION, JULY

The science fiction of the 1950s was heavily influenced by men like Frederik Pohl, Horace Gold, and Ian Ballantine, all of whom had a strong interest in social problems and trends, and all of whom were in a position to encourage the writing of social satire and extrapolation. 1953 was the year that saw the book publication (by Ian Ballantine) of Pohl and Kornbluth's The Space Merchants, *one of the great commentaries on the production-consumption process. The pages of* Galaxy *and other magazines were filled with stories about television, advertising, and attacks on revered American institutions like insurance companies and lawyers, many carrying trends evident in American society to their logical (and sometimes) illogical conclusions.*

And 1953 was the year "A Bad Day For Sales" appeared, and indeed it was.

—MHG

I might also add to what Marty says that 1953 was the height and apex of Senator Joseph McCarthy's villainous career. It was the year in which, as never before, Americans were learning to keep their mouths shut, and to look at each other with uneasy suspicion. (It's not surprising that Dick's "Impostor" appeared in that year.)

It was at about this time that I heard Ted Sturgeon in a speech at a science fiction convention say that when censorship clamped down on science fiction stories, the last remnant of freedom would be gone. I took that to mean that censors who, by a process of self-selection, must be very stupid people (who, with an ounce of brains would want such a job or be able to endure it for long) would not recognize the sardonic satire in science fiction. If the pressures grew heavy enough, though, even sf would come under scrutiny as the last item.

Science fiction never did. All through the McCarthy era, science fiction writers said exactly what they wanted to say, and Fritz Leiber in this story cleverly juxtoposes the triviality of life and the reality thereof in a way that might well have displeased the super-patriots.

—IA

THE BIG BRIGHT DOORS parted with a *whoosh* and Robie glided suavely onto Times Square. The crowd that had been watching the fifty-foot tall clothing-ad girl get dressed, or reading the latest news about the Hot Truce scrawl itself in yard-high script, hurried to look.

Robie was still a novelty. Robie was fun. For a little while yet he could steal the show.

But the attention did not make Robie proud. He had no more vanity than the pink plastic giantess, and she did not even flicker her blue mechanical eyes.

Robie radared the crowd, found that it surrounded him solidly, and stopped. With a calculated mysteriousness, he said nothing.

"Say, ma, he doesn't look like a robot at all. He looks sort of like a turtle."

Which was not completely inaccurate. The lower part of Robie's body was a metal hemisphere hemmed with sponge rubber and not quite touching the sidewalk. The upper was a metal box with black holes in it. The box could swivel and duck.

A chromium-bright hoopskirt with a turret on top.

"Reminds me too much of the Little Joe Baratanks," a veteran of the Persian War muttered, and rapidly rolled himself away on wheels rather like Robie's.

His departure made it easier for some of those who knew about Robie to open a path in the crowd. Robie headed straight for the gap. The crowd whooped.

Robie glided very slowly down the path, deftly jogging aside whenever he got too close to ankles in skylon or sockassins. The rubber buffer on his hoopskirt was merely an added safeguard.

The boy who had called Robie a turtle jumped in the middle of the path and stood his ground, grinning foxily.

Robie stopped two feet short of him. The turret ducked. The crowd got quiet.

"Hello, youngster," Robie said in a voice that was smooth as that of a TV star, and was in fact a recording of one.

The boy stopped smiling. "Hello," he whispered.

"How old are you?" Robie asked.

"Nine. No, eight."

"That's nice," Robie observed. A metal arm shot down from his neck, stopped just short of the boy. The boy jerked back.

"For you," Robie said gently.

The boy gingerly took the red polly-lop from the neatly-fashioned blunt metal claws. A gray-haired woman whose son was a paraplegic hurried on.

After a suitable pause Robie continued, "And how about a nice refreshing drink of Poppy Pop to go with your polly-lop?" The boy lifted his eyes but didn't stop licking the candy. Robie wiggled his claws ever so slightly. "Just give me a quarter and within five seconds—"

A little girl wriggled out of the forest of legs. "Give me a polly-lop too, Robie," she demanded.

"Rita, come back here," a woman in the third rank of the crowd called angrily.

Robie scanned the newcomer gravely. His reference silhouettes were not good enough to let him distinguish the sex of children, so he merely repeated, "Hello, youngster."

"Rita!"

"Give me a polly-lop!"

Disregarding both remarks, for a good salesman is single-minded and does not waste bait, Robie said winningly, "I'll bet you read *Junior Space Killers*. Now I have here—"

"Uh-hhh, I'm a girl. *He* got a polly-lop."

At the word "girl" Robie broke off. Rather ponderously he said, "Then—" After another pause he continued, "I'll bet you read *Gee-Gee Jones, Space Stripper*. Now I have here the latest issue of that thrilling comic, not yet in the stationary vending machines. Just give me fifty cents and within five—"

"Please let me through. I'm her mother."

A young woman in the front rank drawled over her powder-sprayed shoulder, "I'll get her for you," and slithered out on six-inch platforms. "Run away, children," she said nonchalantly and lifting her arms behind her head, pirouetted slowly before Robie to show how much she did for her bolero half-jacket and her form-fitting slacks that melted into skylon just above the knees. The little girl glared at her. She ended the pirouette in profile.

At this age-level Robie's reference silhouettes permitted him to distinguish sex, though with occasional amusing and embarrassing miscalls. He whistled admiringly. The crowd cheered.

Someone remarked critically to his friend. "It would go better if he was built more like a real robot. You know, like a man."

The friend shook his head. "This way it's subtler."

No one in the crowd was watching the newscript overhead as it scribbled, "Ice Pack for Hot Truce? Vanadin hints Russ may yield on Pakistan."

Robie was saying, ". . . in the savage new glamor-tint we have christened Mars Blood, complete with spray applicator and fit-all fingerstalls that mask each finger completely except for the nail. Just give me five dollars— uncrumpled bills may be fed into the revolving rollers you see beside my arm—and within five seconds,—"

"No thanks, Robie," the young woman yawned.

"Remember," Robie persisted, "for three more weeks seductivising Mars Blood will be unobtainable from any other robot or human vendor."

"No thanks."

Robie scanned the crowd resourcefully. "Is there any gentleman here . . ." he began just as a woman elbowed her way through the front rank.

"I told you to come back!" she snarled at the little girl.

"But I didn't get my polly-lop!"

". . . who would care to . . ."

"Rita!"

"Robie cheated. Ow!"

Meanwhile the young woman in the half-bolero had scanned the nearby gentlemen on her own. Deciding that there was less than a fifty per cent chance of any of them accepting the proposition Robie seemed about to make, she took advantage of the scuffle to slither gracefully back into the ranks. Once again the path was clear before Robie.

He paused, however, for a brief recapitulation of the more magical properties of Mars Blood, including a telling phrase about "the passionate claws of a Martian sunrise."

But no one bought. It wasn't quite time yet. Soon enough silver coins would be clinking, bills going through the rollers faster than laundry, and five hundred people struggling for the privilege of having their money taken away from them by America's only genuine mobile sales-robot.

But now was too soon. There were still some tricks that Robie did free, and one certainly should enjoy those before starting the more expensive fun.

So Robie moved on until he reached the curb. The variation in level was instantly sensed by his underscanners. He stopped. His head began to swivel. The crowd watched in eager silence. This was Robie's best trick.

Robie's head stopped swiveling. His scanners had found the traffic light. It was green. Robie edged forward. But then it turned red. Robie stopped again, still on the curb. The crowd softly *ahhed* its delight.

Oh, it was wonderful to be alive and watching Robie on such a wonderful day. Alive and amused in the fresh, weather-controlled air between the lines of bright skyscrapers with their winking windows and under a sky so blue you could almost call it dark.

(But way, way up, where the crowd could not see, the sky was darker still. Purple-dark, with stars showing. And in that purple-dark, a silver-green something, the color of a bud, plunged downward at better than three miles a second. The silver-green was a paint that foiled radar.)

Robie was saying, "While we wait for the light there's time for you youngsters to enjoy a nice refreshing Poppy Pop. Or for you adults—only those over five feet are eligible to buy—to enjoy an exciting Poppy Pop fizz. Just give me a quarter or—I'm licensed to dispense intoxicating liquors—in the case of adults one dollar and a quarter and within five seconds. . . .

But that was not cutting it quite fine enough. Just three seconds later the silver-green bud bloomed above Manhattan into a globular orange flower. The skyscrapers grew brighter and brighter still, the brightness of the inside of the sun. The windows winked white fire.

The crowd around Robie bloomed too. Their clothes puffed into petals of flame. Their heads of hair were torches.

The orange flower grew, stem and blossom. The blast came. The winking windows shattered tier by tier, became black holes. The walls bent, rocked, cracked. A stony dandruff dribbled from their cornices. The flaming flowers on the sidewalk were all leveled at once. Robie was shoved ten feet. His metal hoopskirt dimpled, regained its shape.

The blast ended. The orange flower, grown vast, vanished overhead on its huge, magic beanstalk. It grew dark and very still. The cornice-dandruff pattered down. A few small fragments rebounded from the metal hoopskirt.

Robie made some small, uncertain movements, as if feeling for broken bones. He was hunting for the traffic light, but it no longer shone, red or green.

He slowly scanned a full circle. There was nothing anywhere to interest his reference silhouettes. Yet whenever he tried to move, his under-scanners warned him of low obstructions. It was very puzzling.

The silence was disturbed by moans and a crackling sound, faint at first as the scampering of rats.

A seared man, his charred clothes fuming where the blast had blown out the fire, rose from the curb. Robie scanned him.

"Good day, sir," Robie said. "Would you care for a smoke? A truly cool smoke? Now I have here a yet-unmarketed brand. . . ."

But the customer had run away, screaming, and Robie never ran after customers, though he could follow them at a medium brisk roll. He worked his way along the curb where the man had sprawled, carefully keeping his distance from the low obstructions, some of which writhed now and then, forcing him to jog. Shortly he reached a fire hydrant. He scanned it. His electronic vision, though it still worked, had been somewhat blurred by the blast.

"Hello, youngster," Robie said. Then, after a long pause, "Cat got your tongue? Well, I've got a little present for you. A nice, lovely polly-lop." His metal arm snaked down.

"Take it, youngster," he said after another pause. "It's for you. Don't be afraid."

His attention was distracted by other customers, who began to rise up oddly here and there, twisting forms that confused his reference silhouettes and would not stay to be scanned properly. One cried, "Water," but no quarter clinked in Robie's claws when he caught the word and suggested, "How about a nice refreshing drink of Poppy Pop?"

The rat-crackling of the flames had become a jungle muttering. The blink windows began to wink fire agaiin.

A little girl marched up, stepping neatly over arms

and legs she did not look at. A white dress and the once taller bodies around her had shielded her from the brilliance and the blast. Her eyes were fixed on Robie. In them was the same imperious confidence, though none of the delight, with which she had watched him earlier.

"Help me, Robie, she said. "I want my mother."

"Hello, youngster," Robie said. "What would you like? Comics? Candy?"

"Where is she, Robie? Take me to her."

"Balloons? Would you like to watch me blow up a balloon?"

The little girl began to cry. The sound triggered off another of Robie's novelty circuits.

"Is something wrong?" he asked. "Are you in trouble? Are you lost?"

"Yes, Robie. Take me to my mother."

"Stay right here," Robie said reassuringly, "and don't be frightened. I will call a policeman." He whistled shrilly, twice.

Time passed. Robie whistled again. The windows flared and roared. The little girl begged, "Take me away, Robie," and jumped onto a little step in his hoopskirt.

"Give me a dime," Robie said. The little girl found one in her pocket and put it in his claws.

"Your weight," Robie said, "is fifty-four and one-half pounds, exactly."

"Have you seen my daughter, have you seen her?" a woman was crying somewhere. "I left her watching that thing while I stepped inside—Rita!"

"Robie helped me," the little girl was telling her moments later. "He knew I was lost. He even called a policeman, but he didn't come. He weighed me too. Didn't you, Robie?"

But Robie had gone off to peddle Poppy Pop to the members of a rescue squad which had just come around the corner, more robot-like than he in their fireproof clothing.

COMMON TIME

JAMES BLISH (1921–1975)
SCIENCE FICTION QUARTERLY, AUGUST

*If you asked a reasonably young science fiction reader
about James Blish he/she would probably tell you that he
was that guy who wrote those collections of* Star Trek
adaptations. Such are the ironies of commercial publishing.

*But in a career cut short by cancer this intellectual,
somewhat cynical man produced several notable works
of science fiction that were important to the development of the field, including the "Okie" series that began with* Earthman, Come Home *in 1955 and that can
be found in the omnibus* Cities in Flight *(1970); the
novel* A Case of Conscience *(1958), one of the best
treatments of religion in sf; and the fix-up collection*
The Seedling Stars *(1957), still the outstanding por-
trayal of microcosmic life.*

*Blish was trained in science and read widely, with a
life-long interest in Ezra Pound and James Branch Cab-
ell. Along with Damon Knight, he was one of the most
perceptive literary critics of science fiction in the fifties
and sixties, publishing his criticism as by "William Ath-
eling, Jr." He supplemented his writing income (perhaps it was the other way around) by working in the
public relations field for long periods of time. He moved
to England, where he was an influential figure in British sf circles during the last years of his life.*

—MHG

In 1974, Janet and I visited England (by ship) and I saw Jim in London. It was the last time I saw him and he didn't look well. He had already been operated on for cancer.

My feeling has always been that it was tobacco that killed him, as it killed John Campbell.

Jim was a "hard" science fiction writer in the best sense of the word, for he labored to make his stories consistent with science, and self-consistent within themselves. His story "Surface Tension" has always been one of my favorites, and "Common Time" is another one.

Science fiction writers play games with time and a new game is hard to find. Jim found one here and I'll bet it took a lot of hard thought to explore the different angles of this particular game.

—IA

. . . the days went slowly round and round,
endless and uneventful as cycles in space.
Time, and time-pieces! How many centuries did
my hammock tell, as pendulum-like it swung
to the ship's dull roll, and ticked the hours.
and ages.—HERMAN MELVILLE, in *Mardi*

Don't move.

It was the first thought that came into Garrard's mind when he awoke, and perhaps it saved his life. He lay where he was, strapped against the padding, listening to the round hum of the engines. That in itself was wrong; he should be unable to hear the overdrive at all.

He thought to himself: *Has it begun already?*

Otherwise everything seemed normal. The DFC-3 had crossed over into interstellar velocity, and he was still alive, and the ship was still functioning. The ship should at this moment be traveling at 22.4 times the speed of light—a neat 4,157,000 miles per second.

Somehow Garrard did not doubt that it was. On both previous tries, the ships had whiffed away toward Alpha Centauri at the proper moment when the ovrdrive should have cut in; and the split second of residual image after they had vanished, subjected to spectroscopy, showed a Doppler shift which tallied with the acceleration predicted for that moment by Haertel.

The trouble was not that Brown and Cellini hadn't gotten away in good order. It was simply that neither of them had ever been heard from again.

Very slowly, he opened his eyes. His eyelids felt terrifically heavy. As far as he could judge from the pressure of the couch against his skin, the gravity was normal; nevertheless, moving his eyelids seemed almost an impossible job.

After long concentration, he got them fully open. The instrument chassis was directly before him, extended over his diaphragm on its elbow joint. Still without moving anything but his eyes—and those only with the utmost patience—he checked each of the meters. Velocity: 22.4c. Operating temperature: normal. Ship temperature: 37°C. Air pressure: 778mm. Fuel: No. 1 tank full, No. 2 tank full, No. 3 tank full, No. 4 tank nine-tenths full. Gravity: 1g. Calendar: stopped.

He looked at it closely, though his eyes seemed to focus very slowly, too. It was, of course, something more than a calendar—it was an all-purpose clock, designed to show him the passage of seconds, as well as of the ten months his trip was supposed to take to the double star. But there was no doubt about it: the second hand was motionless.

That was the second abnormality. Garrard felt an impulse to get up and see if he could start the clock again. Perhaps the trouble had been temporary and safely in the past. Immediately there sounded in his head the injunction he had drilled into himself for a full month before the trip had begun:

Don't move!

Don't move until you know the situation as far as it can be known without moving. Whatever it was that had snatched Brown and Cellini irretrievably beyond human ken was potent and totally beyond anticipation. They had both been excellent men, intelligent, resourceful, trained to the point of diminishing returns and not a micron beyond that point—the best men in the project. Preparations for every knowable kind of trouble had been built into their ships, as they had been built into the DFC-3. Therefore, if there was something wrong nevertheless, it would be something that might strike from some commonplace quarter—and strike only once.

He listened to the humming. It was even and placid and not very loud, but it disturbed him deeply. The overdrive was supposed to be inaudible, and the tapes from the first unmanned test vehicles had recorded no such hum. The noise did not appear to interfere with the overdrive's operation or to indicate any failure in it. It was just an irrelevancy for which he could find no reason.

But the reason existed. Garrard did not intend to do so much as draw another breath until he found out what it was.

Incredibly, he realized for the first time that he had not in fact drawn one single breath since he had first come to. Though he felt not the slightest discomfort, the discovery called up so overwhelming a flash of panic that he very nearly sat bolt upright on the couch. Luckily—or so it seemed, after the panic had begun to ebb—the curious lethargy which had affected his eyelids appeared to involve his whole body, for the impulse was gone before he could summon the energy to answer it. And the panic, poignant though it had been for an instant, turned out to be wholly intellectual. In a moment, he was observing that his failure to breathe in no way discommoded him as far as he could tell—it was just there, waiting to be explained. . . .

Or to kill him. But it hadn't, yet.

Engines humming; eyelids heavy; breathing absent; calendar stopped. The four facts added up to nothing. The temptation to move something—even if it were only a big toe—was strong, but Garrard fought it back. He had been awake only a short while—half an hour at most—and already had noticed four abnormalities. There were bound to be more, anomalies more subtle than these four; but available to close examination before he had to move. Nor was there anything in particular that he had to do, aside from caring for his own wants; the project, on the chance that Brown's and Cellini's failure to return had resulted from some tampering with the overdrive, had made everything in the DFC-3 subject only to the computer. In a very real sense, Garrard was just along for the ride. Only when the overdrive was off could he adjust. . . .

Pock.

It was a soft, low-pitched noise, rather like a cork coming out of a wine bottle. It seemed to have come just from the right of the control chassis. He halted a sudden jerk of his head on the cushions toward it with a flat fiat of will. Slowly, he moved his eyes in that direction.

He could see nothing that might have caused the sound. The ship's temperature dial showed no change, which ruled out a heat noise from differential contraction or expansion—the only possible explanation he could bring to mind.

He closed his eyes—a process which turned out to be just as difficult as opening them had been—and tried to visualize what the calendar had looked like when he had first come out of anesthesia. After he got a clear and—he was almost sure—accurate picture, Garrard opened his eyes again.

The sound had been the calendar, advancing one second. It was now motionless again, apparently stopped.

He did not know how long it took the second hand to make that jump, normally; the question had never come up. Certainly the jump, when it came at the end of each second, had been too fast for the eye to follow.

Belatedly, he realized what all this cogitation was costing him in terms of essential information. The calendar had moved. Above all and before anything else, he *must* know exactly how long it took it to move again. . . .

He began to count, allowing an arbitrary five seconds

lost. *One-and-a-six, one-and-a-seven, one-and-an eight*. . . .

Garrard had gotten only that far when he found himself plunged into hell.

First, and utterly without reason, a sickening fear flooded swiftly through his veins, becoming more and more intense. His bowels began to knot with infinite slowness. His whole body became a field of small, slow pulses—not so much shaking him as putting his limbs into contrary joggling motions and making his skin ripple gently under his clothing. Against the hum another sound became audible, a nearly subsonic thunder which seemed to be inside his head. Still the fear mounted, and with it came the pain, and the tenesmus—a board-like stiffening of his muscles, particularly across his abdomen and his shoulders, but affecting his forearms almost as grievously. He felt himself beginning, very gradually, to double at the middle, a motion about which he could do precisely nothing—a terrifying kind of dynamic paralysis. . . .

It lasted for hours. At the height of it, Garrard's mind, even his very personality, was washed out utterly; he was only a vessel of horror. When some few trickles of reason began to return over that burning desert of reasonless emotion, he found that he was sitting up on the cushions, and that with one arm he had thrust the control chassis back on its elbow so that it no longer jutted over his body. His clothing was wet with perspiration, which stubbornly refused to evaporate or to cool him. And his lungs ached a little, although he could still detect no breathing.

What under God had happened? Was it this that had killed Brown and Cellini? For it would kill Garrard, too—of that he was sure—if it happened often. It would kill him even if it happened only twice more, if the next two such things followed the first one closely. At the very best it would make a slobbering idiot of him; and though the computer might bring Garrard and the ship back to Earth, it would not be able to tell the project about his tornado of senseless fear.

The calendar said that the eternity in hell had taken

three seconds. As he looked at it in academic indigna-
tion, it said *pock* and condescended to make the total
seizure four seconds long. With grim determination,
Garrard began to count again.

He took care to establish the counting as an absolutely even, automatic process which would not stop at
the back of his mind no matter what other problem he
tackled along with it, or what emotional typhoons should
interrupt him. Really compulsive counting cannot be
stopped by anything—not the transports of love nor the
agonies of empires. Garrard knew the dangers in deliberately setting up such a mechanism in his mind, but
he also knew how desperately he needed to time that
clock tick. He was beginning to understand what had
happened to him—but he needed exact measurement
before he could put that understanding to use.

Of course there had been plenty of speculation on
the possible effect of the overdrive on the subjective
time of the pilot, but none of it had come to much. At
any speed below the velocity of light, subjective and
objective time were exactly the same as far as the pilot
was concerned. For an observer on Earth, time aboard
the ship would appear to be vastly slowed at near-light
speeds; but for the pilot himself there would be no
apparent change.

Since flight beyond the speed of light was impossible—
although for slightly differing reasons—by both the current theories of relativity, neither theory had offered
any clue as to what would happen on board a translight
ship. They would not allow that any such ship could
even exist. The Haertel transformation, on which, in
effect, the DFC-3 flew, was nonrelativistic: it showed
that the apparent elapsed time of a translight journey
should be identical in ship time and in the time of
observers at both ends of the trip.

But since ship and pilot were part of the same system, both covered by the same expression in Haertel's
equation, it had never occurred to anyone that the pilot
and the ship might keep different times. The notion
was ridiculous.

One-and-a-seven-hundred one, one-and-a-seven-hundred two, one-and-a-seven-hundred three, one-and-a-seven-hundred four. . . .

The ship was keeping ship time, which was identical with observer time. It would arrive at the Alpha Centauri system in ten months. But the pilot was keeping Garrard time, and it was beginning to look as though he wasn't going to arrive at all.

It was impossible, but there it was. Something—almost certainly an unsuspected physiological side effect of the overdrive field on human metabolism, an effect which naturally could not have been detected in the preliminary, robot-piloted tests of the overdrive—had speeded up Garrard's subjective apprehension of time and had done a thorough job of it.

The second hand began a slow, preliminary quivering as the calendar's innards began to apply power to it. *Seventy-hundred-forty-one, seventy-hundred-forty-two, seventy-hundred-forty-three. . . .*

At the count of 7,058 the second hand began the jump to the next graduation. It took it several apparent minutes to get across the tiny distance and several more to come completely to rest. Later still, the sound came to him:

Pock.

In a fever of thought, but without any real physical agitation, his mind began to manipulate the figures. Since it took him longer to count an individual number as the number became larger, the interval between the two calendar ticks probably was closer to 7,200 seconds than to 7,058. Figuring backward brought him quickly to the equivalence he wanted: one second in ship time was two hours in Garrard time.

Had he really been counting for what was, for him, two whole hours? There seemed to be no doubt about it. It looked like a long trip ahead.

Just how long it was going to be struck him with stunning force. Time had been slowed for him by a factor of 7,200. He would get to Alpha Centauri in just 72,000 months.

Which was . . .
Six thousand years!

II

Garrard sat motionless for a long time after that, the Nessus shirt of warm sweat swathing him persistently, refusing even to cool. There was, after all, no hurry.

Six thousand years. There would be food and water and air for all that time, or for sixty or six hundred thousand years; the ship would synthesize his needs, as a matter of course, for as long as the fuel lasted, and the fuel bred itself. Even if Garrard ate a meal every three seconds of objective, or ship, time (which, he realized suddenly, he wouldn't be able to do, for it took the ship several seconds of objective time to prepare and serve up a meal once it was ordered; he'd be lucky if he ate once a day, Garrard time), there would be no reason to fear any shortage of supplies. That had been one of the earliest of the possibilities for disaster that the project engineers had ruled out in the design of the DFC-3.

But nobody had thought to provide a mechanism which would indefinitely refurbish Garrard. After six thousand years, there would be nothing left of him but a faint film of dust on the DFC-3's dully gleaming horizontal surfaces. His corpse might outlast him awhile, since the ship itself was sterile—but eventually he would be consumed by the bacteria which he carried in his own digestive tract. He needed those bacteria to synthesize part of his B-vitamin needs while he lived, but they would consume him without compunction once he had ceased to be as complicated and delicately balanced a thing as a pilot—or as any other kind of life.

Garrard was, in short, to die before the DFC-3 had gotten fairly away from Sol; and when, after 12,000 apparent years, the DFC-3 returned to Earth, not even his mummy would be still aboard.

The chill that went through him at that seemed almost unrelated to the way he thought he felt about the discovery; it lasted an enormously long time, and insofar as he could characterize it at all, it seemed to be a chill of urgency and excitement—not at all the kind of chill he should be feeling at a virtual death sentence. Luckily it was not as intolerably violent as the last such emotional convulsion; and when it was over, two clock ticks later, it left behind a residuum of doubt.

Suppose that this effect of time-stretching was only mental? The rest of his bodily processes might still be keeping ship time; Garrard had no immediate reason to believe otherwise. If so, he would be able to move about only on ship time, too; it would take many apparent months to complete the simplest task.

But he would live, if that were the case. His mind would arrive at Alpha Centauri six thousand years older, and perhaps madder, than his body, but he would live.

If, on the other hand, his bodily movements were going to be as fast as his mental processes, he would have to be enormously careful. He would have to move slowly and exert as little force as possible. The normal human hand movement, in such a task as lifting a pencil, took the pencil from a state of rest to another state of rest by imparting to it an acceleration of about two feet per second—and, of course, decelerated it by the same amount. If Garrard were to attempt to impart to a two-pound weight, which was keeping ship time, an acceleration of 14,440 ft/sec^2 in his time, he'd have to exert a force of 900 pounds on it.

The point was not that it couldn't be done—but that it would take as much effort as pushing a stalled jeep. He'd never be able to lift that pencil with his forearm muscles alone; he'd have to put his back into the task.

And the human body wasn't engineered to maintain stresses of that magnitude indefinitely. Not even the most powerful professional weight lifter is forced to show his prowess throughout every minute of every day.

Pock.

That was the calendar again; another second had gone by. Or another two hours. It had certainly seemed longer than a second, but less than two hours, too.

Evidently subjective time was an intensively recomplicated measure. Even in this world of microtime—in which Garrard's mind, at least, seemed to be operating—he could make the lapses between calendar ticks seem a little shorter by becoming actively interested in some problem or other. That would help during the waking hours, but it would help only if the rest of his body was *not* keeping the same time as his mind. If it was not, then he would lead an incredibly active, but perhaps not intolerable, mental life during the many centuries of his awake time and would be mercifully asleep for nearly as long.

Both problems—that of how much force he could exert with his body and how long he could hope to be asleep in his mind—emerged simultaneously into the forefront of his consciousness while he still sat inertly on the hammock, their terms still much muddled together. After the single tick of the calendar, the ship—or the part of it that Garrard could see from here—settled back into complete rigidity. The sound of the engines, too, did not seem to vary in frequency or amplitude, at least as far as his ears could tell. He was still not breathing. Nothing moved, nothing changed.

It was the fact that he could still detect no motion of his diaphragm or his rib cage that decided him at last. His body had to be keeping ship time, otherwise he would have blacked out from oxygen starvation long before now. That assumption explained, too, those two incredibly prolonged, seemingly sourceless saturnalias of emotion through which he had suffered: they had been nothing more or less than the response of his endocrine glands to the purely intellectual reactions he had experienced earlier. He had discovered that he was not breathing, had felt a flash of panic and had tried to sit up. Long after his mind had forgotten those two impulses, they had inched their way from his brain down his nerves to the glands and muscles involved, and actual, *physical* panic had supervened. When that was over, he actually *was* sitting up, though the flood of adrenalin had prevented his noticing the motion as he had made it. The later chill—less violent and apparently associated with the discovery that he might die long before the trip was completed—actually had been his body's response to a much earlier mental command; the abstract fever of interest he had felt while computing the time differential had been responsible for it.

Obviously, he was going to have to be very careful with apparently cold and intellectual impulses of any kind—or he would pay for them later with a prolonged and agonizing glandular reaction. Nevertheless, the discovery gave him considerable satisfaction, and Garrard allowed it free play; it certainly could not hurt him to feel pleased for a few hours, and the glandular pleasure might even prove helpful if it caught him at a moment of mental depression. Six thousand years, after all, provided a considerable number of opportunities for feeling down at the mouth; so it would be best to encourage all pleasure moments, and let the after-reaction last as long as it might. It would be the instants of panic, of fear, of gloom, which he would have to regulate sternly the moment they came into his mind; it would be those which would otherwise plunge him into four, five, six, perhaps even ten Garrard hours of emotional inferno.

Pock.

There now, that was very good: there had been two Garrard hours which he had passed with virtually no difficulty of any kind and without being especially conscious of their passage. If he could really settle down and become used to this kind of scheduling, the trip might not be as bad as he had at first feared. Sleep would take immense bites out of it; and during the waking periods he could put in one hell of a lot of creative thinking. During a single day of ship time, Garrard could get in more thinking than any philosopher of Earth could have managed during an entire lifetime. Garrard could, if he disciplined himself sufficiently, devote his mind for a century to running down the consequences of a single thought, down to the last detail and still have millennia left to go on to the next thought. What panoplies of pure reason could he not have assembled by the time 6,000 years had gone by? With sufficient concentration, he might come up with the solution to the problem of evil between breakfast and dinner of a single ship's day, and in a ship's month might put his finger on the first cause!

Pock.

Not that Garrard was sanguine enough to expect that he would remain logical or even sane throughout the trip. The vista was still grim in much of its detail. But the opportunities, too, were there. He felt a momentary regret that it hadn't been Haertel, rather than himself, who had been given such an opportunity . . .

Pock.

. . . for the old man could certainly have made better use of it than Garrard could. The situation demanded someone trained in the highest rigors of mathematics to be put to the best conceivable use. Still and all Garrard began to feel . . .

Pock.

. . . that he would give a good account of himself, and it tickled him to realize that (as long as he held on to his essential sanity) he would return . . .

Pock.

. . . to Earth after ten Earth months with knowledge centuries advanced beyond anything . . .

Pock.

. . . that Haertel knew or that anyone could know . . .

Pock.

. . . who had to work within a normal lifetime. *Pck.* The whole prospect tickled him. *Pck.* Even the clock tick seemed more cheerful. *Pck.* He felt fairly safe now *Pck* in disregarding his drilled-in command *Pck* against moving *Pck*, since in any *Pck* event he *Pck* had already *Pck* moved *Pck* without *Pck* being *Pck* harmed *Pck Pck Pck Pck Pck pckpckpckpckpckpckpck.* . . .

He yawned, stretched, and got up. It wouldn't do to be too pleased, after all. There were certainly many problems that still needed coping with, such as how to keep the impulse toward getting a ship-time task performed going, while his higher centers were following the ramifications or some purely philosophical point. And besides . . .

And besides, he had just moved.

More than that, he had just performed a complicated maneuver with his body *in normal time!*

Before Garrard looked at the calendar itself, the message it had been ticking away at him had penetrated. While he had been enjoying the protracted, glandular backwash of his earlier feeling of satisfaction, he had failed to notice, at least consciously, that the calendar was accelerating.

Good-by, vast ethical systems which would dwarf the Greeks. Good-by, calculuses aeons advanced beyond the spinor calculus of Dirac. Good-by, cosmologies by Garrard which would allot the Almighty a job as third-assistant waterboy in an *n*-dimensional backfield.

Good-by, also, to a project he had once tried to undertake in college—to describe and count the positions of love, of which, according to under-the-counter myth, there were supposed to be at least forty-eight. Garrard had never been able to carry his tally beyond twenty, and he had just lost what was probably his last opportunity to try again.

The microtime in which he had been living had worn off, only a few objective minutes after the ship had gone into overdrive and he had come out of the anesthetic. The long intellectual agony, with its glandular counterpoint, had come to nothing. Garrard was now keeping ship time.

Garrard sat back down on the hammock, uncertain whether to be bitter or relieved. Neither emotion satisfied him in the end; he simply felt unsatisfied. Microtime had been bad enough while it lasted; but now it was gone, and everything seemed normal. How could so transient a thing have killed Brown and Cellini? They were stable men, more stable, by his own private estimation, than Garrard himself. Yet he had come through it. Was there more to it than this?

And if there was—what, conceivably could it be?

There was no answer. At his elbow, on the control chassis which he had thrust aside during that first moment of infinitely protracted panic, the calendar continued to tick. The engine noise was gone. His breath came and went in natural rhythm. He felt light and strong. The ship was quiet, calm, unchanging.

The calendar ticked, faster and faster. It reached and passed the first hour, ship time, of flight in overdrive.

Pock.

Garrard looked up in surprise. The familiar noise, this time, had been the hour hand jumping one unit. The minute hand was already sweeping past the past half-hour. The second hand was whirling like a propeller— and while he watched it, it speeded up to complete invisibility. . . .

Pock.

Another hour. The half-hour already passed. *Pock.* Another hour. *Pock.* Another, *Pock. Pock. Pock, Pock, Pock, Pock, pck-pck-pck-pck-pckpckpckpck.* . . .

The hands of the calendar swirled toward invisibility as time ran away with Garrard. Yet the ship did not change. It stayed there, rigid, inviolate, invulnerable. When the date tumblers reached a speed at which Garrard could no longer read them, he discovered that once more he could not move—and that, although his whole body seemed to be aflutter like that of a hummingbird, nothing coherent was coming to him through his senses. The room was dimming, becoming redder; or no, it was. . . .

But he never saw the end of the process, never was allowed to look from the pinnacle of macrotime toward which the Haertel overdrive was taking him.

Pseudo-death took him first.

III

That Garrard did not die completely, and within a comparatively short time after the DFC-3 had gone into overdrive, was due to the purest of accidents; but Garrard did not know that. In fact, he knew nothing at all for an indefinite period, sitting rigid and staring, his metabolism slowed down to next to nothing, his mind almost utterly inactive. From time to time, a single wave of low-level metabolic activity passed through him—what an electrician might have termed a "maintenance turnover"—in response to the urgings of some occult survival urge; but these were of so basic a nature as to reach his consciousness not at all. This was the pseudo-death.

When the observer actually arrived, however, Garrard woke. He could make very little sense out of what he saw or felt even now; but one fact was clear: the overdrive was off—and with it the crazy alterations in time rates—and there was strong light coming through one of the ports. The first leg of the trip was over. It had been these two changes in his environment which had restored him to life.

The thing (or things) which had restored him to consciousness, however, was—it was what? It made no sense. It was a construction, a rather fragile one, which completely surrounded his hammock. No, it wasn't a construction, but evidently something alive—a living being, organized horizontally, that had arranged itself in a circle about him. No, it was a number of beings. Or a combination of all of these things.

How it had gotten into the ship was a mystery, but there it was. Or there they were.

"How do you hear?" the creature said abruptly. Its voice, or their voices, came at equal volume from every point in the circle, but not from any particular point in it. Garrard could think of no reason why that should be unusual.

"I . . ." he said. "Or we—we hear with our ears. Here."

His answer, with its unintentionally long chain of open vowel sounds, rang ridiculously. He wondered why he was speaking such an odd language.

"We-they wooed to pitch you-yours thiswise," the creature said. With a thump, a book from the DFC-3's ample library fell to the deck beside the hammock.

"We wooed there and there and there for a many. You are the being-Garrard. We-they are the clinesterton beademung, with all of love."

"With all of love," Garrard echoed. The beademung's use of the language they both were speaking was odd; but again Garrard could find no logical reason why the beademung's usage should be considered wrong.

"Are—are you-they from Alpha Centauri?" he said hesitantly.

"Yes, we hear the twin radioceles, that show there beyond the gift-orifices. We-they pitched that the being-Garrard with most adoration these twins and had mind to them, soft and loud alike. How do you hear?"

This time the being-Garrard understood the question. "I hear Earth," he said. "But that is very soft, and does not show."

"Yes," said the beademung. "It is a harmony, not a first, as ours. The All-Devouring listens to lovers there, not on the radioceles. Let me-mine pitch you-yours so to have mind of the rodalent beademung and other brothers and lovers, along the channel which is fragrant to the being-Garrard."

Garrard found that he understood the speech without difficulty. The thought occurred to him that to understand a language on its own terms—without having to put it back into English in one's own mind—is an ability that is won only with difficulty and long practice. Yet, instantly his mind said, "But it *is* English," which of course it was. The offer the clinesterton beademung had just made was enormously hearted and he in turn was much minded and of love, to his own delighting as well as to the beademungen; that almost went without saying.

There were many matings of ships after that, and the being-Garrard pitched the harmonies of the beademungen, leaving his ship with the many gift-orifices in harmonic for the All-Devouring to love, while the beademungen made show of they-theirs.

He tried, also, to tell how he was out of love with the

overdrive, which wooed only spaces and times, and made featurelings. The rodalent beademung wooed the overdrive, but it did not pitch he-them.

Then the being-Garrard knew that all the time was devoured and he must hear Earth again.

"I pitch you-them to fullest love," he told the beademungen, "I shall adore the radioceles of Alpha and Proxima Centauri, 'on Earth as it is in heaven.' Now the overdrive my-other must woo and win me and make me adore a featureling much like silence."

"But you will be pitched again," the clinesterton beademung said. "After you have adored Earth. You are much loved by Time, the All-Devouring. We-they shall wait for this othering."

Privately Garrard did not faith as much, but he said, "Yes, we-they will make a new wooing of the beademungen at some other radiant. With all of love."

On this the beademungen made and pitched adorations, and in the midst the overdrive cut in. The ship with the many gift-orifices and the being-Garrard himother saw the twin radioceles sundered away.

Then, once more, came the pseudo-death.

IV

When the small candle lit in the endless cavern of Garrard's pseudo-dead mind, the DFC-3 was well inside the orbit of Uranus. Since the sun was still very small and distant, it made no spectacular display through the nearby port, and nothing called him from the postdeath sleep for nearly two days.

The computers waited patiently for him. They were no longer immune to his control; he could now tool the ship back to Earth himself if he so desired. But the computers were also designed to take into account the fact that he might be truly dead by the time the DFC-3 got back. After giving him a solid week, during which time he did nothing but sleep, they took over again. Radio signals began to go out, tuned to a special channel.

An hour later, a very weak signal came back. It was

only a directional signal, and it made no sound inside
the DFC-3—but it was sufficient to put the big ship in
motion again.

It was that which woke Garrard. His conscious mind
was still glazed over with the icy spume of the pseudo-
death; and as far as he could see the interior of the
cabin had not changed one whit, except for the book on
the deck. . . .

The book. The clinesterton beademung had dropped
it there. But what under God was a clinesterton
beademung? And what was he, Garrard, crying about?
It didn't make sense. He remembered dimly some kind
of experience out there by the Centauri twins . . .

. . . *the twin radioceles* . . .

There was another one of those words. It seemed to
have Greek roots, but he knew no Greek—and besides,
why would Centaurians speak Greek?

He leaned forward and actuated the switch which
would roll the shutter off the front port, actually a
telescope with a translucent viewing screen. It showed
a few stars, and a faint nimbus off on one edge which
might be the sun. At about one o'clock on the screen
was a planet about the size of a pea which had tiny
projections, like teacup handles, on each side. The
DFC-3 hadn't passed Saturn on its way out; at that time
it had been on the other side of the sun from the route
the starship had had to follow. But the planet was
certainly difficult to mistake.

Garrard was on his way home—and he was still alive
and sane. Or was he still sane? These fantasies about
Centaurians—which still seemed to have such a profound emotional effect upon him—did not argue very
well for the stability of his mind.

But they were fading rapidly. When he discovered,
clutching at the handiest fragments of the "memories,"
that the plural of *beademung* was *beademungen,* he
stopped taking the problem seriously. Obviously a race
of Centaurians who spoke Greek wouldn't also be forming weak German plurals. The whole business had obviously been thrown up by his unconscious.

But what *had* he found by the Centaurus stars?

There was no answer to that question but that incomprehensible garble about love, the All-Devouring and beademungen. Possibly, he had never seen the Centaurus stars at all, but had been lying here, cold as a mackerel, for the entire twenty months.

Or had it been 12,000 years? After the tricks the overdrive had played with time, there was no way to tell what the objective date was. Frantically Garrard put the telescope into action. Where was the Earth? After 12,000 years. . . .

The Earth was there. Which, he realized swiftly, proved nothing. The Earth had lasted for many millions of years; 12,000 years was nothing to a planet. The moon was there, too; both were plainly visible, on the far side of the sun—but not too far to pick them out clearly, with the telescope at highest power. Garrard could even see a clear sun highlight on the Atlantic Ocean, not far east of Greenland; evidently the computers were bringing the DFC-3 in on the Earth from about twenty-three degrees north of the plane of the ecliptic.

The moon, too, had not changed. He could even see on its face the huge splash of white, mimicking the sun highlight on Earth's ocean, which was the magnesium hydroxide landing beacon, which had been dusted over the Mare Vaporum in the earliest days of space flight, with a dark spot on its southern edge which could only be the crater Monilius.

But that again proved nothing. The moon never changed. A film of dust laid down by modern man on its face would last for millennia—what, after all, existed on the moon to blow it away? The Mare Vaporum beacon covered more than 4,000 square miles; age would not dim it, nor could man himself undo it—either accidentally or on purpose—in anything under a century. When you dust an area that large on a world without atmosphere, it stays dusted.

He checked the stars against his charts. They hadn't moved; why should they have, in only 12,000 years?

The pointer stars in the Dipper still pointed to Polaris. Draco, like a fantastic bit of tape, wound between the two Bears, and Cepheus and Cassiopeia, as it always had done. These constellations told him only that it was spring in the northern hemisphere of Earth.

But spring of what year?

Then, suddenly, it occurred to Garrard that he had a method of finding the answer. The moon causes tides in the Earth, and action and reaction are always equal and opposite. The moon cannot move things on Earth without itself being affected—and that effect shows up in the moon's angular momentum. The moon's distance from the Earth increases steadily by 0.6 inch every year. At the end of 12,000 years, it should be 600 feet farther away from the Earth.

Was it possible to measure? Garrard doubted it, but he got out his ephemeris and his dividers anyhow and took pictures. While he worked, the Earth grew nearer. By the time he had finished his first calculation—which was indecisive because it allowed a margin of error greater than the distances he was trying to check—Earth and moon were close enough in the telescope to permit much more accurate measurements.

Which were, he realized wryly, quite unnecessary. The computer had brought the DFC-3 back, not to an observed sun or planet, but simply to a calculated point. That Earth and moon would not be near that point when the DFC-3 returned was not an assumption that the computer could make. That the Earth was visible from here was already good and sufficient proof that no more time had elapsed than had been calculated for from the beginning.

This was hardly new to Garrard; it had simply been retired to the back of his mind. Actually he had been doing all this figuring for one reason and one reason only: because deep in his brain, set to work by himself, there was a mechanism that demanded counting. Long ago, while he was still trying to time the ship's calendar, he had initiated compulsive counting—and it appeared that he had been counting ever since. That had been one of the known dangers of deliberately starting such a mental mechanism; and now it was bearing fruit in these perfectly useless astronomical exercises.

The insight was healing. He finished the figures roughly, and that unheard moron deep inside his brain stopped counting at last. It had been pawing its abacus for twenty months now, and Garrard imagined that it was as glad to be retired as he was to feel it go.

His radio squawked and said anxiously, "DFC-3. DFC-3. Garrard, do you hear me? Are you still alive? Everybody's going wild down here. Garrard, if you hear me, call us!"

It was Haertel's voice. Garrard closed the dividers so convulsively that one of the points nipped into the heel of his hand. "Haertel, I'm here. DFC-3 to the project. This is Garrard." And then, without knowing quite why, he added: "With all of love."

Haertel, after all the hoopla was over, was more than interested in the time effects. "It certainly enlarges the manifold in which I was working," he said. "But I think we can account for it in the transformation. Perhaps even factor it out, which would eliminate it as far as the pilot is concerned. We'll see, anyhow."

Garrard swirled his highball reflectively. In Haertel's cramped old office in the project's administration shack, he felt both strange and as old, as compressed, constricted. He said, "I don't think I'd do that, Adolph. I think it saved my life.

"How?"

"I told you that I seemed to die after a while. Since I got home, I've been reading; and I've discovered that the psychologists take far less stock in the individuality of the human psyche than you and I do. You and I are physical scientists, so we think about the world as being all outside our skins—something which is to be observed, but which doesn't alter the essential 1. But evidently, that old solipsistic position isn't quite true. Our very personalities, really, depend in large part upon *all* the things in our environment, large and small, that exist outside our skins. If by some means you could cut a human being off from every sense impression that comes to him from outside, he would cease to exist as a personality within two or three minutes. Probably he would die.

"Unquote: Harry Stack Sullivan," Haertel said, dryly. "So?"

"So," Garrard said, "think of what a monotonous environment the inside of a spaceship is. It's perfectly rigid, still, unchanging, lifeless. In ordinary interplanetary flight, in such an environment, even the most hardened spaceman may go off his rocker now and then. You know the typical spaceman's psychosis as well as I do, I suppose. The man's personality goes rigid, just like his surroundings. Usually he recovers as soon as he makes port and makes contact with a more or less normal world again.

"But in the DFC-3, I was cut off from the world around me much more severely. I couldn't look outside the ports—I was in overdrive, and there was nothing to see. I couldn't communicate with home because I was going faster than light. And then I found I couldn't move either, for an enormous long while; and that even the instruments that are in constant change for the usual spaceman wouldn't be in motion for me. Even those were fixed.

"After the time rate began to pick up, I found myself in an even more impossible box. The instruments moved, all right, but they they moved too *fast* for me to read them. The whole situation was now utterly rigid—and, in effect, I died. I froze as solid as the ship around me and stayed that way as long as the overdrive was on."

"By that showing," Haertel said dryly, "the time effects were hardly your friends."

"But they were, Adolph. Look. Your engines act as subjective time; they keep it varying along continuous curves—from far-too-slow to far-too-fast—and, I suppose, back down again. Now, this is a *situation of continuous change*. It wasn't marked enough, in the long run, to keep me out of pseudo-death; but it was sufficient to protect me from being obliterated altogether, which I think is what happened to Brown and Cellini. Those men knew that they could shut down the overdrive if they could just get to it, and they killed themselves trying. But I knew that I just had to sit and take it—and, by my great good luck, your sine-curve time variation made it possible for me to survive."

"Ah, ah," Haertel said. "A point worth considering—though I doubt that it will make interstellar travel very popular!"

He dropped back into silence, his thin mouth pursed. Garrard took a grateful pull at his drink.

At last Haertel said, "Why are you in trouble over these Centaurians? It seems to me that you have done a good job. It was nothing that you were a hero—any fool can be brave—but I see also that you *thought*, where Brown and Cellini evidently only reacted. Is there some secret about what you found when you reached those two stars?"

Garrard said, "Yes, there is. But I've already told you what it is. When I came out of the pseudo-death, I was just a sort of plastic palimpsest upon which anybody could have made a mark. My own environment, my ordinary Earth environment, was a hell of a long way off. My present surroundings were nearly as rigid as they had ever been. When I met the Centaurians—if I did, and I'm not at all sure of that—*they* became the most important thing in my world, and my personality changed to accommodate and understand them. That was a change about which I couldn't do a thing.

"Possibly I did understand them. But the man who understood them wasn't the same man you're talking to now, Adolph. Now that I'm back on Earth, I don't understand that man. He even spoke English in a way that's gibberish to me. If I can't understand myself during that period—and I can't; I don't even believe that that man was the Garrard I know—what hope have I of telling you or the project about the Centaurians? They found me in a controlled environment, and they altered me by entering it. Now that they're gone, nothing comes through; I don't even understand why I think they spoke English!"

"Did they have a name for themselves?"

"Sure," Garrard said. "They were the beademungen."

"What did they look like?"

"I never saw them."

Haertel leaned forward. "Then. . . ."

"I heard them. I think." Garrard shrugged and tasted his Scotch again. He was home, and on the whole he was pleased.

But in his malleable mind he heard someone say, *On Earth, as it is in heaven;* and then, in another voice, which might also have been his own (why had he thought "him-other"?), *It is later than you think.*

"Adolph," he said, "is this all there is to it? Or are we going to go on with it from here? How long will it take to make a better starship, a DFC-4?"

"Many years," Haertel said, smiling kindly. "Don't be anxious, Garrard. You've come back, which is more than the others managed to do, and nobody will ask you to go out again. I really think that it's hardly likely that we'll get another ship built during your lifetime; and even if we do, we'll be slow to launch it. We really have very little information about what kind of playground you found out there."

"I'll go," Garrard said. "I'm not afraid to go back—I'd like to go. Now that I know how the DFC-3 behaves, I could take it out again, bring you back proper maps, tapes, photos."

"Do you really think," Haertel said, his face suddenly serious, "that we could let the DFC-3 go out again? Garrard, we're going to take that ship apart practically molecule by molecule; that's preliminary to the building of any DFC-4. And no more can we let you go. I don't mean to be cruel, but has it occurred to you that this desire to go back may be the result of some kind of posthypnotic suggestion? If so, the more badly you want to go back, the more dangerous to us all you may be. We are going to have to examine you just as thoroughly as we do the ship. If these beademungen wanted you to come back, they must have had a reason—and we have to know that reason."

Garrard nodded, but he knew that Haertel could see the slight movement of his eyebrows and the wrinkles forming in his forehead, the contractions of the small muscles which stop the flow of tears only to make grief patent on the rest of the face.

"In short," he said, *"don't move."*

Haertel looked politely puzzled. Garrard, however, could say nothing more. He had returned to humanity's common time and would never leave it again.

Not even, for all his dimly remembered promise, with all there was left in him of love.

TIME IS THE TRAITOR

ALFRED BESTER (1913–   )
THE MAGAZINE OF FANTASY AND SCIENCE FICTION,
SEPTEMBER

1953 saw the publication of Alfred Bester's novel The
Demolished Man, *one of the landmark books in the
history of modern science fiction. It was published by
Shasta, one of the pioneer fan-owned publishers who
also published* Who Goes There? *by John W. Campbell, Jr. and* Slaves of Sleep *by L. Ron Hubbard. Bester's
novel, a mystery in science fiction form, is set in a
future when murder is "impossible" because of telepathy and remains fascinating and fresh thirty plus years
after its appearance. It is also notable for its two main
characters, Ben Reich and Prefect Lincoln Powell, two
complex individuals who are among the most memora-
ble figures in the genre.*

*We would be remiss if we did not mention several
other Bester stories that merit rereading from 1953—
"Disappearing Act," "The Roller Coaster," and "Star
Light, Star Bright."*

—MHG

*For some years now, Alfie has lived in some hidden
corner of Pennsylvania and done his writing there. I
know other writers who also seem to find bucolic surroundings desirable and every once in a while I find
myself envying them.*

After all, there is peace and quiet and a sense of

*isolation with one's muse. One walks hand in hand with
nature and the pressures and tensions of the artificial
world that humanity has created are far away.*

*Why not? After all, a writer can turn out his material
anywhere as long as he can find an electric outlet for
his typewriter (or even without that if he'll use a manual) and a steady supply of pens, paper, and other
paraphernalia.*

*But then I think that that's not the way it works.
Temperaments differ and what is peace to one person
may be shrieking boredom to another. I live in a quiet
and fairly spacious apartment high above the city noise,
and with a panoramic view of park and highrise that is,
in itself, worth the expense, and even that's a little too
quiet for me.*

*At least once a week, and often twice, I find occasion
to visit publishers, not only to interact with my partners-
in-literature, but for the opportunity of threading the
canyons of Manhattan which are home to me and in
which I belong. I am as adapted to the noise and hurry
and traffic and crowding impersonality as ever Br'er
Rabbit was adapted to the thorns and scraggy branches
of his briar patch.*

*I work as peacefully in my surroundings as Alfie does
in his, and my envy leaves me.*

—IA

YOU CAN'T GO BACK and you can't catch up. Happy
endings are always bitter-sweet.

There was a man named John Strapp; the most valuable, the most powerful, the most legendary man in a
world containing 700 planets and 1700 milliards of peoples. He was prized for one quality alone. He could
make Decisions. Note the capital D. He was one of the
few men who could make Major Decisions in a world of
incredible complexity, and his Decisions were 87 per
cent correct. He sold his Decisions for high prices.

There would be an industry named . . . say . . .
Bruxton Biotics, with plants on Deneb Alpha, Mizar
III, Terra, and main offices on Alcor IV. Bruxton's gross

income was Cr. 270 millions. The involutions of Bruxton's trade relations with consumers and competitors required the specialized services of 200 company economists, each an expert on one tiny facet of the vast overall picture. No one was big enough to coordinate the entire picture.

Bruxton would need a Major Decision on policy. A research expert named E. T. A. Goland in the Deneb laboratories had discovered a new catalyst for biotic synthesis. It was an embryological hormone that rendered nucleonic molecules as plastic as clay. The clay could be modeled and developed in any direction. Query: Should Bruxton abandon the old culture methods and retool for this new technique? The Decision involved an infinite ramification of inter-reacting factors: cost, saving, time, supply, demand, training, patents, patent legislation, court actions, and so on. There was only one answer. Ask Strapp.

The initial negotiations were crisp. Strapp Associates replied that John Strapp's fee was Cr. 100,000 plus 1 per cent of the voting stock of Bruxton Biotics. Take it or leave it. Bruxton Biotics took it with pleasure.

The second step was more complicated. John Strapp was very much in demand. He was scheduled for Decisions at the rate of two a week straight through to the first of the year. Could Bruxton wait that long for an appointment? Bruxton could not. Bruxton was TT'd a list of John Strapp's future appointments and told to arrange a swap with any of the clients as best they could. Bruxton bargained, bribed, blackmailed and arranged a trade. John Strapp was to appear at the Alcor central plant on Monday, June 29, at noon precisely.

Then the mystery began. At 9 o'clock that Monday morning, Aldous Fisher, the acidulous liaison man for Strapp, appeared at Bruxton's offices. After a brief conference with old man Bruxton himself, the following announcement was broadcast through the plant: AT-TENTION! ATTENTION! URGENT! URGENT! ALL MALE PERSONNEL NAMED KRUGER REPORT TO CENTRAL. REPEAT. ALL MALE PERSONNEL

NAMED KRUGER REPORT TO CENTRAL. UR-
GENT! REPEAT. URGENT!

Forty-seven men named Kruger reported to Central
and were sent home with strict instructions to stay
home until further notice. The plant police organized a
hasty winnowing and, goaded by the irascible Fisher,
checked the identification cards of all the employees
they could reach. Nobody named Kruger should remain
in the plant, but it was impossible to comb out 2,500
men in three hours. Fisher burned and fumed like
nitric acid.

By 11:30, Bruxton Biotics was running a fever. Why
send home all the Krugers? What did it have to do with
the legendary John Strapp? What kind of a man was
Strapp? What did he look like? How did he act? He
earned Cr. 10 millions a year. He owned 1 per cent of
the world. He was so close to God in the minds of the
personnel that they expected angels and golden trum-
pets and a giant bearded creature of infinite wisdom
and compassion.

At 11:40 Strapp's personal bodyguard arrived; a security squad of ten men in plain-clothes who checked
doors and halls and *cul-de-sacs* with icy efficiency. They
gave orders. This had to be removed. That had to be
locked. Such and such had to be done. It was done. No
one argued with John Strapp. The security squad took
positions and waited. Bruxton Biotics held its breath.

Noon struck, and a silver mote appeared in the sky.
It approached with a high whine and landed with agonizing speed and precision before the main gate. The
door of the ship snapped open. Two burly men stepped
out alertly, their eyes busy. The chief of the security
squad made a sign. Out of the ship came two secretaries, brunette and redheaded, striking, chic, efficient.
After them came a thin, fortyish clerk in a baggy suit
with papers stuffed in his side pockets, wearing hornshell
spectacles and a harassed air. After him came a magnificent creature, tall, majestic, clean-shaven but of infinite
wisdom and compassion.

The burly men closed in on the beautiful man and

escorted him up the steps and through the main door. Bruxton Biotics sighed happily. John Strapp was no disappointment. He was indeed God, and it was a pleasure to have 1 per cent of yourself owned by him. The visitors marched down the main hall to old man Bruxton's office and entered. Bruxton had waited for them, poised majestically behind his desk. Now he leaped to his feet and ran forward. He grasped the magnificent man's hand fervently and exclaimed, "Mr. Strapp, sir, on behalf of my entire organization, I welcome you."

The clerk closed the door and said, "I'm Strapp." He nodded to his decoy who sat down quietly in a corner. "Where's your data?"

Old Man Bruxton pointed faintly to his desk. Strapp sat down behind it, picked up the fat folders and began to read. A thin man. A harassed man. A fortyish man. Straight black hair. China blue eyes. A good mouth. Good bones under the skin. One quality stood out . . . a complete lack of self-consciousness. But when he spoke there was a hysterical undercurrent in his voice that showed something violent and possessed deep inside him.

After two hours of breakneck reading and muttered comments to his secretaries who made cryptic notes in Whithead symbols, Strapp said, "I want to see the plant."

"Why?" Bruxton asked.

"To feel it," Strapp answered. "There's always the nuance involved in a Decision. It's the most important factor."

They left the office and the parade began. The security squad, the burly men, the secretaries, the clerk, the acidulous Fisher and the magnificent decoy. They marched everywhere. They saw everything. The "clerk" did most of the leg work for "Strapp." He spoke to workers, foremen, technicians, high, low and middle brass. He asked names, gossiped, introduced them to the great man, talked about their families, working conditions, ambitions. He explored, smelled and felt.

After four exhausting hours they returned to Bruxton's office. The "clerk" closed the door. The decoy stepped aside.

"Well?" Bruxton asked. "Yes or No?"

"Wait," Strapp said.

He glanced through his secretaries' notes, absorbed them, closed his eyes and stood still and silent in the middle of the office like a man straining to hear a distant whisper.

"Yes," he Decided, and was Cr. 100,000 and 1 per cent of the voting stock of Bruxton Biotics richer. In return, Bruxton had an 87 per cent assurance that the Decision was correct. Strapp opened the door again, the parade reassembled and marched out of the plant. Personnel grabbed its last chance to take photos and touch the great man. The clerk helped promote public relations with eager affability. He asked names, introduced and amused. The sound of voices and laughter increased as they reached the ship. Then the incredible happened.

"You!" the clerk cried suddenly. His voice screeched horribly. "You son of a bitch! You goddamned lousy murdering bastard! I've been waiting for this. I've waited ten years!" He pulled a flat gun from his inside pocket and shot a man through the forehead.

Time stood still. It took hours for the brains and blood to burst out of the back of the head and for the body to crumple. Then the Strapp staff leaped into action. They hurled the clerk into the ship. The secretaries followed, then the decoy. The two burly men leaped after them and slammed the door. The ship took off and disappeared with a fading whine. The ten men in plain-clothes quietly drifted off and vanished. Only Fisher, the Strapp liaison man, was left alongside the body in the center of the horrified crowd.

"Check his identification," Fisher snapped.

Someone pulled the dead man's wallet out and opened it.

"William F. Kruger, bio-mechanic."

"The damned fool!" Fisher said savagely. "We warned

him. We warned all the Krugers. All right. Call the police."

That was John Strapp's sixth murder. It cost exactly Cr. 500,000 to fix. The other five had cost the same, and half the amount usually went to a man desperate enough to substitute for the killer and plead temporary insanity. The other half went to the heirs of the deceased. There were six of these substitutes languishing in various penitentiaries, serving from twenty to 50 years, their families Cr. 250,000 richer.

In their suite in the Alcor Splendide, the Strapp staff consulted gloomily.

"Six in six years," Aldous Fisher said bitterly. "We can't keep it quiet much longer. Sooner or later somebody's going to ask why John Strapp always hires crazy clerks."

"Then we fix him too," the redheaded secretary said. "Strapp can afford it."

"He can afford a murder a month," the magnificent decoy murmured.

"No." Fisher shook his head sharply. "You can fix so far and no further. You reach a saturation point. We've reached it now. What are we going to do?"

"What the hell's the matter with Strapp anyway?" one of the burly men inquired.

"Who knows?" Fisher exclaimed in exasperation. "He's got a Kruger fixation. He meets a man named Kruger . . . any man named Kruger. He screams. He curses. He murders. Don't ask me why. It's something buried in his past."

"Haven't you asked him?"

"How can I? It's like an epileptic fit. He never knows it happened."

"Take him to a psychoanalyst," the decoy suggested.

"Out of the question."

"Why?"

"You're new," Fisher said. "You don't understand."

"Make me understand."

"I'll make an analogy. Back in the 1900's, people

played card games with 52 cards in the deck. Those were simple times. Today everything's more complex. We're playing with 5200 in the deck. Understand?"

"I'll go along with it."

"A mind can figure 52 cards. It can make decisions on that total. They had it easy in the 1900's. But no mind is big enough to figure 5200 . . . no mind except Strapp's."

"We've got computers."

"And they're perfect when only cards are involved. But when you have to figure 5200 cardplayers too . . . their likes, dislikes, motives, inclinations, prospects, tendencies, and so on . . . what Strapp calls the nuances, then Strapp can do what a machine can't do. He's unique, and we may destroy his uniqueness with psychoanalysis."

"Why?"

"Because it's an unconscious process in Strapp," Fisher explained irritably. "He doesn't know how he does it. If he did he'd be 100 per cent right instead of 87 per cent. It's an unconscious process and for all we know it may be linked up with the same abnormality that makes him murder Krugers. If we get rid of one we may destroy the other. We can't take the chance."

"Then what do we do?"

"Protect our property," Fisher said, looking around ominously. "Never forget that for a minute. We've put in too much work on Strapp to let it be destroyed. We protect our property!"

"I think he needs a friend," the brunette said.

"Why?"

"We could find out what's bothering him without destroying anything. People talk to their friends. Strapp might talk."

"We're his friends."

"No, we're not. We're his associates."

"Have you been to bed with him?"

"Of course."

"Has he talked to you?"

"No."

"You?" Fisher shot at the redhead.

She shook her head. "It isn't friendly going to bed with Strapp. It's a war."

"How?"

"He's looking for something he never finds."

"What?"

"A woman, I think. A special kind of woman."

"A woman named Kruger?"

"I don't know."

"Damn it, it doesn't make sense." Fisher thought a moment. "All right. We'll have to hire him a friend, and we'll have to ease off the schedule to give the friend a chance to make Strapp talk. From now on we cut the program to one Decision a week."

"My God!" the brunette exclaimed. "That's cutting five million a year." •

"It's got to be done," Fisher said grimly. "It's cut now or take a total loss later. We're rich enough to stand it."

"What are you going to do for a friend?" the decoy asked.

"I said we'd hire one. We'll hire the best. Get Terra on the TT. Tell them to locate Frank Alceste and put him through urgent."

"Frankie!" the redhead squealed. "I swoon."

"Ooh! Frankie!" The brunette fanned herself.

"You mean Fatal Frank Alceste? The heavyweight champ?" The burly man asked in awe. "I saw him fight Lonzo Jordan. Oh, man!"

"He's an actor now," the decoy explained. "I worked with him once. He sings. He dances. He—"

"And he's twice as fatal," Fisher interrupted. "We'll hire him. Make out a contract. He'll be Strapp's friend. As soon as Strapp meets him he'll—"

"Meets who?" Strapp appeared in the doorway of his bedroom, yawning, blinking in the light. He always slept deeply after his attacks. "Who am I going to meet?" He looked around, thin, graceful, but harassed and indubitably possessed.

"A man named Frank Alceste," Fisher said. "He

badgered us for an introduction and we can't hold him off any longer."

"Frank Alceste?" Strapp murmured. "Never heard of him."

Strapp could make Decisions; Alceste could make friends. He was a powerful man in his middle thirties, sandy-haired, freckle-faced, with a broken nose and deep-set gray eyes. His voice was high and soft. He moved with the athlete's lazy poise that is almost feminine. He charmed you without knowing how he did it, or even wanting to do it. He charmed Strapp, but Strapp also charmed him. They became friends.

"No, it really is friends," Alceste told Fisher when he returned the check that had been paid him. "I don't need the money, and old Johnny needs me. Forget you hired me original-like. Tear up the contract. I'll try to straighten Johnny out on my own."

Alceste turned to leave the suite in the Rigel Splendide and passed the great-eyed secretaries. "If I wasn't so busy, ladies," he murmured, "I'd sure like to chase you a little."

"Chase me, Frankie," the brunette blurted.

The redhead looked caught.

And as Strapp Associates zigzagged in slow tempo from city to city and planet to planet, making the one Decision a week, Alceste and Strapp enjoyed themselves while the magnificent decoy gave interviews and posed for pictures. There were interruptions when Frankie had to return to Terra to make a picture, but in between they golfed, tennised, brubaged, bet on horses, dogs and dowlens, and went to fights and routs. They hit the nightspots and Alceste came back with a curious report.

"Me, I don't know how close you folks been watching Johnny," he told Fisher, "but if you think he's been sleeping every night, safe in his little trundle, you better switch notions."

"How's that?" Fisher asked in surprise.

"Old Johnny, he's been sneaking out nights all along

when you folks thought he was getting his brain rest."

"How do you know?"

"By his reputation," Alceste told him sadly. "They know him everywhere. They know old Johnny in every bistro from here to Orion. And they know him the worst way."

"By name?"

"By nickname. Wasteland, they call him."

"Wasteland!"

"Uh huh. Mr. Devastation. He runs through women like a prairie fire. You don't know this?"

Fisher shook his head.

"Must pay off out of his personal pocket," Alceste mused and departed.

There was a terrifying quality to the possessed way that Strapp ran through women. He would enter a club with Alceste, take a table, sit down and drink. Then he would stand up and coolly survey the room, table by table, woman by woman. Upon occasion men would become angered and offer to fight. Strapp disposed of them coldly and viciously, in a manner that excited Alceste's professional admiration. Frankie never fought himself. No professional ever touches an amateur. But he tried to keep the peace, and failing that, at least kept the ring.

After the survey of the women guests, Strapp would sit down and wait for the show, relaxed, chatting, laughing. When the girls appeared, his grim possession would take over again and he would examine the line carefully and dispassionately. Very rarely he would discover a girl that interested him; always the identical type, a girl with jet hair, inky eyes and clear silken skin. Then the trouble began.

If it was an entertainer, Strapp went backstage after the show. He bribed, fought, blustered and forced his way into her dressing room. He would confront the astonished girl, examine her in silence, then ask her to speak. He would listen to her voice, then close in like a tiger and make a violent and unexpected pass. Sometimes there would be shrieks, sometimes a spirited defense, sometimes complaisance. At no time was Strapp satisfied. He would abandon the girl abruptly, pay off all complaints and damages like a gentleman, and leave to repeat the performance in club after club until curfew.

If it was one of the guests, Strapp immediately cut in, disposed of her escort, or if that was impossible, followed the girl home and there repeated the dressing room attack. Again he would abandon the girl, pay like a gentleman and leave to continue his possessed search.

"Me, I been around, but I'm scared by it," Alceste told Fisher. "I never saw such a hasty man. He could have most any woman agreeable if he'd slow down a little. But he can't. He's driven."

"By what?"

"I don't know. It's like he's working against time."

After Strapp and Alceste became intimate, Strapp permitted him to come along on a daytime quest that was even stranger. As Strapp Associates continued its round through the planets and industries, Strapp visited the Bureau of Vital Statistics in each city. There he bribed the Chief Clerk and presented a slip of paper. On it was written:

Height 5' 6"
Weight 110
Hair Black
Eyes Black
Bust 34
Waist 26
Hips 36
Size 12

"I want the name and address of every girl over twenty-one who fits this description," Strap would say. "I'll pay ten credits a name."

Twenty-four hours later would come the list, and off Strapp would chase on a possessed search, examining, talking, listening, sometimes making the terrifying pass, always paying off like a gentleman. The procession of tall, jet-haired, inky-eyed, busty girls made Alceste dizzy.

"He's got an *idée fixe*," Alceste told Fisher in the Cygnus Splendide, "and I got it figured this much. He's looking for a special particular girl and nobody comes up to specifications."

"A girl named Kruger?"

"I don't know if the Kruger business comes into it."

"Is he hard to please?"

"Well, I'll tell you. Some of those girls . . . me, I'd call them sensational. But he don't pay any mind to them. Just looks and moves on. Others . . . dogs, practically, he jumps like old Wasteland."

"What is it? A rape compulsion?"

"I think it's a kind of test. Something to make the girls react hard and natural. It ain't that kind of passion with old Wasteland. It's a cold-blooded trick so he can watch 'em in action."

"But what's he looking for?"

"I don't know yet," Alceste said, "but I'm going to find out. I got a little trick figured. It's taking a chance, but Johnny's worth it."

It happened in the Arena where Strapp and Alceste went to watch a pair of gorillas tear each other to pieces inside a glass cage. It was a bloody affair, and both men agreed that gorilla-fighting was no more civilized than cockfighting and left in disgust. Outside, in the empty concrete corridors, a shriveled man loitered. When Alceste signaled to him, he ran up to them like an autograph hound.

"Frankie!" the shriveled man shouted. "Good old Frankie! Don't you remember me?"

Alceste stared.

"I'm Blooper Davis. We was raised together in the old precinct. Don't you remember Blooper Davis?"

"Blooper!" Alceste's face lit up. "Sure enough. But it was Blooper Davidoff then."

"Sure," the shriveled man laughed. "And it was Frankie Kruger then."

"Kruger!" Strapp cried in the thin screeching voice.

"That's right," Frankie said. "Kruger. I changed my

name when I went into the fight game." He motioned sharply to the shriveled man who backed against the corridor wall and slid away.

"You son of a bitch!" Strapp cried. His face was white and twitched hideously. "You goddamned lousy murdering bastard! I've been waiting for this. I've waited ten years."

He whipped a flat gun from his inside pocket and fired. Alceste sidestepped barely in time and the slug ricocheted down the corridor with a high whine. Strapp fired again and the flame seared Alceste's cheek. He closed in, caught Strapp's wrist and paralyzed it with his powerful grip. He pointed the gun away and clinched. Strapp's breath was hissing. His eyes rolled. Overhead sounded the wild roars of the crowd.

"All right, I'm Kruger," Alceste grunted. "Kruger's the name, Mr. Strapp. So what? What are you going to do about it?"

"Son of a bitch!" Strapp screamed, struggling like one of the gorillas. "Killer! Murderer! I'll rip your guts out!"

"Why me? Why Kruger?" Exerting all his strength, Alceste dragged Strapp to a niche and slammed him into it. He caged him with his huge frame. "What did I ever do to you ten years ago?"

He got the story in hysterical animal outbursts before Strapp fainted.

After he put Strapp to bed, Alceste went out into the lush living room of the suite in the Indi Splendide and explained to the staff.

"Old Johnny was in love with a girl named Sima Morgan," he began. "She was in love with him. It was big romantic stuff. They were going to be married. Then Sima Morgan got killed by a guy named Kruger."

"Kruger! So that's the connection. How?"

"This Kruger was a drunken no-good. Society. He had a bad driving record. They took his license away from him, but that didn't make any difference to Kruger's kind of money. He bribed a dealer and bought a hot rod jet without a license. One day he buzzed a school for the hell of it. He smashed the roof in and killed thirteen children and their teacher. . . . This was on Terra in Berlin."

"Jesus," the burly man whispered.

"They never got Kruger. He started planet hopping and he's still on the lam. The family sends him money. The police can't find him. Strapp's looking for him because the school teacher was his girl, Sima Morgan."

There was a pause, then Fisher asked: "How long ago was this?"

"Near as I can figure, ten years eight months."

Fisher calculated intently. "And ten years three months ago, Strapp first showed he could make decisions. The Big Decisions. Up to then he was nobody. Then came the tragedy, and with it the hysteria and the ability. Don't tell me one didn't produce the other."

"Nobody's telling you anything."

"So he kills Kruger over and over again," Fisher said coldly. "Right. Revenge fixation. But what about the girls and the Wasteland business?"

Alceste smiled sadly. "You ever hear the expression, 'One girl in a million'?"

"Who hasn't?"

"If your girl was one in a million, that means there ought to be nine more like her in a city of ten million, yes?"

The Strapp staff nodded, wondering.

"Old Johnny's working on that idea. He thinks he can find Sima Morgan's duplicate."

"How?"

"He's worked it out arithmeticwise. He's thinking like so: There's one chance in 64 billion of fingerprints matching. But today there's 1700 billion people. That means there can be 26 with one matching print, and maybe more."

"Not necessarily."

"Sure not necessarily, but there's the chance and that's all old Johnny wants. He figures if there's 26 chances of one print matching there's an outside chance of one person matching. He thinks he can find Sima

Morgan's duplicate if he just keeps on looking hard enough."

"That's outlandish!"

"I didn't say it wasn't, but it's the only thing that keeps him going. It's a kind of life preserver made out of numbers. It keeps his head above water . . . the crazy notion that sooner or later he can pick up where death left him off ten years ago."

"Ridiculous!" Fisher snapped.

"Not to Johnny. He's still in love."

"Impossible."

"I wish you could feel it like I feel it," Alceste answered. "He's looking . . . looking. He meets girl after girl. He hopes. He talks. He makes the pass. If it's Sima's duplicate he knows she'll respond just the way he remembers Sima responding ten years ago. 'Are you Sima?' he asks himself. 'No,' he says, and moves on. It hurts, thinking about a lost guy like that. We ought to do something for him."

"No," Fisher said.

"We ought to help him find his duplicate. We ought to coax him into believing some girl's the duplicate. We ought to make him fall in love again."

"No," Fisher repeated emphatically.

"Why no?"

"Because the moment Strapp finds his girl, he heals himself. He stops being the great John Strapp, the Decider. He turns back into a nobody . . . a man in love."

"What's he care about being great? He wants to be happy."

"Everybody wants to be happy," Fisher snarled. "Nobody is. Strapp's no worse off than any other man, but he's a lot richer. We maintain the status quo."

"Don't you mean you're a lot richer?"

"We maintain the status quo," Fisher repeated. He eyed Alceste coldly. "I think we'd better terminate the contract. We have no further use for your services."

"Mister, we terminated when I handed back the check. You're talking to Johnny's friend, now."

"I'm sorry, Mr. Alceste, but Strapp won't have much time for his friends from now on. I'll let you know when he'll be free next year."

"You'll never pull it off. I'll see Johnny when and where I please."

"Do you want him for a friend?" Fisher smiled unpleasantly. "Then you'll see him when and where I please. Either you see him on those terms or Strapp sees the contract we gave you. I still have it in the files, Mr. Alceste. I did not tear it up. I never part with anything. How long do you imagine Strapp will believe in your friendship after he sees the contract you signed?"

Alceste clenched his fists. Fisher held his ground. For a moment they glared at each other, then Frankie turned away.

"Poor Johnny," he muttered. "It's like a man being run by his tapeworm. I'll say so long to him. Let me know when you're ready for me to see him again."

He went into the bedroom where Strapp was just awakening from his attack without the faintest memory, as usual. Alceste sat down on the edge of the bed.

"Hey, old Johnny," he grinned.

"Hey, Frankie," Strapp smiled.

They punched each other solemnly, which is the only way that men friends can embrace and kiss.

"What happened after that gorillafight?" Strapp asked. "I got fuzzy."

"Man, you got plastered. I never saw a guy take on such a load." Alceste punched Strapp again. "Listen, old Johnny, I got to get back to work. I got a three-picture-a-year contract and they're howling."

"Why, you took a month off six planets back," Strapp said in disappointment. "I thought you caught up."

"Nope. I'll be pulling out today, Johnny. Be seeing you real soon."

"Listen," Strapp said. "To hell with the pictures. Be my partner. I'll tell Fisher to draw up an agreement." He blew his nose. "This is the first time I've had laughs in—in a long time."

"Maybe later, Johnny. Right now I'm stuck with a

contract. Soon as I can get back, I'll come a-running. Cheers."

"Cheers," Strapp said wistfully.

Outside the bedroom, Fisher was waiting like a watch-dog. Alceste looked at him with disgust.

"One thing you learn in the fight game," he said slowly. "It's never won till the last round. I give you this one, but it isn't the last."

As he left, Alceste said, half to himself, half aloud, "I want him to be happy. I want every man to be happy. Seems like every man could be happy if we'd all just lend a hand."

Which is why Frankie Alceste couldn't help making friends.

So the Strapp staff settled back into the same old watchful vigilance of the murdering years, and stepped up Strapp's Decision appointments to two a week. They knew why Strapp had to be watched. They knew why the Krugers had to be protected. But that was the only difference. Their man was miserable, hysteric, almost psychotic; it made no difference. That was a fair price to pay for 1 per cent of the world.

But Frankie Alceste kept his own counsel, and visited the Deneb laboratories of Bruxton Biotics. There he consulted with one E.T.A. Goland, the research genius who had discovered that novel technique for molding life which first brought Strapp to Bruxton, and was indirectly responsible for his friendship with Alceste. Ernst Theodor Amadeus Goland was short, fat, asthmatic and enthusiastic.

"But yes, yes," he sputtered when the layman had finally made himself clear to the scientist. "Yes, indeed! A most ingenious notion. Why it never occurred to me, I cannot think. It could be accomplished without any difficulty. Without any difficulty whatsoever." He considered. "Except money," he added.

"You could duplicate the girl that died ten years ago?" Alceste asked.

"Without any difficulty, except money." Goland nodded emphatically.

"She'd look the same? Act the same? Be the same?"

"Up to 95 per cent plus or minus point nine seven five."

"Would that make any difference? I mean 95 per cent of a person as against 100 per cent."

"Ach! No. It is a most remarkable individual who is aware of more than 80 per cent of the total characteristics of another person. Above 90 per cent is unheard of."

"How would you go about it?"

"Ach? So. Empirically we have two sources. One: Complete psychological pattern of the subject in the Centaurus Master Files. They will TT a transcript upon application and payment of Cr. 100 through formal channels. I will apply."

"And I'll pay. Two?"

"Two: The embalmment process of modern times which—she is buried, yes?"

"Yes."

"Which is 98 per cent perfect. From remains and psychological pattern we reconstruct body and psyche by the equation sigma equals square root of minus two over—we do it without any difficulty, except money."

"Me, I've got the money," Frankie Alceste said. "You do the rest."

For the sake of his friend, Alceste paid Cr. 100 and expedited the formal application to the Master Files on Centaurus for the transcript of the complete psychological pattern of Sima Morgan, deceased. After it arrived, Alceste returned to Terra and a city called Berlin where he blackmailed a gimpster named Augenblick into turning graverobber. Augenblick visited the *Staats-Gottesacker* and removed the porcelain coffin from under the marble headstone that read SIMA MORGAN. It contained what appeared to be a black-haired, silken skinned girl in deep sleep. By devious routes, Alceste got the porcelain coffin through four customs barriers to Deneb.

One aspect of the trip of which Alceste was not aware

but which bewildered various police organizations, was the series of catastrophes which pursued him and never quite caught up. There was the jet liner explosion that destroyed the ship and an acre of docks half an hour after passengers and freight were discharged. There was a hotel holocaust ten minutes after Alceste checked out. There was the shuttle disaster which extinguished the pneumatic train for which Alceste had unexpectedly canceled passage. Despite all this he was able to present the coffin to biochemist Goland.

"Ach!" said Ernst Theodor Amadeus. "A beautiful creature. She is worth recreating. The rest now is simple, except money."

For the sake of his friend, Alceste arranged a leave of absence for Goland, bought him a laboratory and financed an incredibly expensive series of experiments. For the sake of his friend, Alceste poured forth money and patience until at last, eight months later, there emerged from the opaque maturation chamber, a black-haired, inky-eyed, silken skinned creature with long legs and a full bust. She answered to the name of Sima Morgan.

"I heard the jet coming down toward the school," Sima said, unaware that she was speaking eleven years later. "Then I heard a crash. What happened?"

Alceste was jolted. Up to this moment she had been an objective . . . a goal . . . unreal, unalive. This was a living woman. There was a curious hesitation in her speech, almost a lisp. Her head had an engaging tilt when she spoke. She arose from the edge of the table, and she was not fluid or graceful as Alceste had expected she would be. She moved boyishly. Suddenly she realized she was nude and blushed. It was the first time Alceste had ever seen a blushing nude, and he was inexpressibly moved to see the blush flood up from her waist to her bosom and then to her throat and face. He stepped forward quickly with a robe and put it around her.

"I'm Frank Alceste," he said quietly. He adjusted the robe, then took her shoulders. "I want you to look at me and make up your mind whether you can trust me."

Their eyes locked in a steady gaze. Sima examined him gravely. Again Alceste was jolted and moved. His hands began to tremble and he released the girl's shoulders in panic.

"Yes," Sima said. "I can trust you."

"No matter what I say, you must trust me. No matter what I tell you to do, you must trust me and do it."

"Why?"

"For the sake of Johnny Strapp."

Her eyes widened. "Something's happened to him," she said quickly. "What is it?"

"Not to him, Sima. To you. Be patient, honey. I'll explain. I had it in my mind to explain now, but I can't. I . . . I'd best wait until tomorrow."

They put her to bed and Alceste went out for a wrestling match with himself. The Deneb nights are soft and black as velvet, thick and sweet with romance . . . or so it seemed to Frankie Alceste that night.

"You can't be falling in love with her," he muttered. "It's crazy."

And later: "You saw hundreds like her when Johnny was hunting. Why didn't you fall for one of them?"

And last of all: "What are you going to do?"

He did the only thing an honorable man can do in a situation like that, and tried to turn his desire into friendship. He came into Sima's room the next morning, wearing tattered old jeans, needing a shave, with his hair standing on end. He hoisted himself up on the foot of her bed, and while she ate the first of the careful meals Goland had prescribed, Frankie chewed on a cigarette and explained what had happened to her. When she wept, he did not take her in his arms to console her, but thumped her on the back like a brother.

He ordered a dress for her. He had ordered the wrong size, and when she showed herself to him in it, she looked so adorable that he wanted to kiss her. Instead, he punched her, very gently and very solemnly, and took her out to buy a wardrobe. When she showed herself to him in proper clothes, she looked so enchanting that he had to punch her again. Then they went to a ticket office and booked immediate passage for Ross-Alpha III.

Alceste had intended delaying a few days to rest the girl, but he was compelled to rush for fear of himself. It was this alone that saved both from the explosion that destroyed the private home and private laboratory of biochemist Goland, and destroyed the biochemist too. Alceste never knew this. He was already on board ship with Sima, frantically fighting temptation.

One of the things that everybody knows about space travel but never mentions is its aphrodisiac quality. Like the ancient days when travelers crossed oceans on ships, the passengers are isolated in their own tiny world for a week. They're cut off from reality. A magic mood of freedom from ties and responsibilities pervades the jet liner. Everyone has a fling. There are thousands of jet romances every week . . . quick, passionate affairs that are enjoyed in complete safety and ended on landing day.

In this atmosphere, Frankie Alceste maintained a rigid self-control. He was not aided by the fact that he was a celebrity with tremendous animal magnetism. While a dozen handsome women threw themselves at him, he persevered in the role of the big brother and thumped and punched Sima until she protested.

"I know you're a wonderful friend to Johnny and me," she said on the last night out, "but you are exhausting, Frankie. I'm covered with bruises."

"Yeah. I know. It's habit. Some people, like Johnny, they think with their brains. Me, I think with my fists."

They were standing before the starboard crystal, bathed in the soft light of the approaching Ross-Alpha, and there is nothing more damnably romantic than the velvet of space illuminated by the white-violet of a distant sun. Sima tilted her head and looked at him.

"I was talking to some of the passengers," she said. "You're famous, aren't you?"

"More notorious like."

"There's so much to catch up on. But I must catch up on you first."

"Me?"

Sima nodded. "It's all been so sudden. I've been bewildered . . . and so excited, that I haven't had a chance to thank you, Frankie. I do thank you. I'm beholden to you forever."

She put her arms around his neck and kissed him with parted lips. Alceste began to shake.

"No," he thought. "No. She doesn't know what she's doing. She's so crazy happy at the idea of being with Johnny again that she doesn't realize. . . ."

He reached behind him until he felt the icy surface of the crystal which passengers are strictly enjoined from touching. Before he could give way, he deliberately pressed the backs of his hands against the sub-zero surface. The pain made him start. Sima released him in surprise, and when he pulled his hands away, he left six square inches of skin and blood behind.

So he landed on Ross-Alpha III with one girl in good condition and two hands in bad shape and he was met by the acid-faced Aldous Fisher accompanied by an official who requested Mr. Alceste to step into an office for a very serious private talk.

"It has been brought to our attention by Mr. Fisher," the official said, "that you are attempting to bring in a young woman of illegal status."

"How would Mr. Fisher know?" Alceste asked.

"You fool!" Fisher spat. "Did you think I would let it go at that? You were followed. Every minute."

"Mr. Fisher informs us," the official continued austerely, "that the woman with you is traveling under an assumed name. Her papers are fraudulent."

"How fraudulent?" Alceste said. "She's Sima Morgan. Her papers say she's Sima Morgan."

"Sima Morgan died eleven years ago," Fisher answered. "The woman with you can't be Sima Morgan."

"And unless the question of her true identity is cleared up," the official said, "she will not be permitted entry."

"I'll have the documentation on Sima Morgan's death

here within the week," Fisher added triumphantly.

Alceste looked at Fisher and shook his head wearily. "You don't know it, but you're making it easy for me," he said. "The one thing in the world I'd like to do is take her out of here and never let Johnny see her. I'm so crazy to keep her for myself that—" He stopped himself and touched the bandages on his hands. "Withdraw your charge, Fisher."

"No," Fisher snapped.

"You can't keep 'em apart. Not this way. Suppose she's interned? Who's the first man I subpoena to establish her identity? John Strapp. Who's the first man I call to come and see her? John Strapp. D'you think you could stop him?"

"That contract," Fisher began. "I'll—"

"To hell with the contract. Show it to him. He wants his girl, not me. Withdraw your charge, Fisher. And stop fighting. You've lost your meal ticket."

Fisher glared malevolently, then swallowed. "I withdraw the charge," he growled. Then he looked at Alceste with blood in his eyes. "It isn't the last round yet," he said, and stamped out of the office.

Fisher was prepared. At a distance of light-years he might be too late with too little. Here on Ross-Alpha III he was protecting his property. He had all the power and money of John Strapp to call on. The floater that Frankie Alceste and Sima took from the spaceport was piloted by a Fisher aide who unlatched the cabin door and performed steep banks to tumble his fares out into the air. Alceste smashed the glass partition and hooked a meaty arm around the driver's throat until he righted the floater and brought them safely to earth. Alceste was pleased to note Sima did not fuss more than necessary.

On the road level they were picked up by one of a hundred cars which had been pacing the floater from below. At the first shot, Alceste clubbed Sima into a doorway and followed her at the expense of a burst shoulder which he bound hastily with strips of Sima's lingerie. Her dark eyes were enormous but she made no complaint. Alceste complimented her with mighty thumps and took her up to the roof and down into the adjoining building where he broke into an apartment and telephoned for an ambulance.

When the ambulance arrived, Alceste and Sima descended to the street where they were met by uniformed policemen who had official instructions to pick up a couple answering to their description. Wanted: for floater robbery with assault. Dangerous. Shoot to kill. The police, Alceste disposed of, and also the ambulance driver and interne. He and Sima departed in the ambulance, Alceste driving like a fury, Sima operating the siren like a banshee.

They abandoned the ambulance in the downtown shopping district, entered a department store, and emerged 40 minutes later as a young valet in uniform pushing an old man in a wheelchair. Outside the difficulty of the bust, Sima was boyish enough to pass as a valet. Frankie was weak enough from assorted injuries to simulate the old man.

They checked into the Ross Splendide where Alceste barricaded Sima in a suite, had his shoulder attended to, and bought a gun. Then he went looking for John Strapp. He found him in the Bureau of Vital Statistics, briging the Chief Clerk and presenting him with a slip of paper that read:

Height 5′ 6″
Weight 110
Hair Black
Eyes Black
Bust 34
Waist 26
Hips 36
Size 12

"Hey, old Johnny," Alceste said.
"Hey, Frankie!" Strapp cried in delight.
They punched each other affectionately. With a happy grin, Alceste watched Strapp explain and offer further

bribes to the Chief Clerk for the names and addresses of all girls over twenty-one who fitted the description on the slip of paper. As they left, Alceste said: "I met a girl who might fit that, old Johnny."

That cold look came into Strapp's eyes. "Oh?" he said.

"She's got a kind of half lisp."

Strapp looked at Alceste strangely.

"And a funny way of tilting her head when she talks."

Strapp clutched Alceste's arm.

"Only trouble is, she isn't girlie-girlie like most. More like a fella. You know what I mean? Spunky-like."

"Show her to me, Frankie," Strapp said in a low voice.

They hopped a floater and were taxied to the Ross Splendide roof. They took the elevator down to the twentieth floor and walked to suite 20-M. Alceste code-knocked on the door. A girl's voice called, "Come in." Alceste shook Strapp's hand and said, "Cheers, Johnny." He unlocked the door, then walked down the hall to lean against the balcony balustrade. He drew his gun just in case Fisher might get around to last ditch interruptions. Looking out across the glittering city, he reflected that every man could be happy if everybody would just lend a hand; but sometimes that hand was expensive.

John Strapp walked into the suite. He shut the door, turned and examined the jet-haired inky-eyed girl, coldly, intently. She stared at him in amazement. Strapp stepped closer, walked around her, faced her again.

"Say something," he said.

"You're not John Strapp?" she faltered. "Not Johnny Strapp?"

"Yes."

"No!" she exclaimed. "No! My Johnny's young. My Johnny is—"

Strapp closed in like a tiger. His hands and lips savaged her while his eyes watched coldly and intently. The girl screamed and struggled, terrified by those strange eyes that were alien, by the harsh hands that were alien, by the alien compulsions of the creature who was once her Johnny Strapp but was now aching years of change apart from her.

"You're someone else!" she cried. "You're not Johnny Strapp. You're another man."

And Strapp, not so much eleven years older as eleven years other than the man whose memory he was fighting to fulfill, asked himself: "Are you my Sima? Are you my love . . . my lost dead love?" And the change within him answered: "No, this isn't Sima. This isn't your love yet. Move on, Johnny. Move on and search. You'll find her some day . . . the girl you lost."

He paid like a gentleman and departed.

From the balcony, Alceste saw him leave. He was so astonished he could not call to him. He went back to the suite and found Sima standing there, stunned, staring at a sheaf of money on a table. He realized what had happened at once. When Sima saw Alceste, she began to cry . . . not like a girl, but boyishly, with her fists clenched and her face screwed up.

"Frankie," she wept. "My God! Frankie!" She held out her arms to him in desperation. She was lost in a world that had passed her by.

He took a step, then hesitated. He made a last attempt to quench the love for this creature within him, searching for a way to bring her and Strapp together. Then he lost all control and took her in his arms.

"She doesn't know what she's doing," he thought. "She's so scared of being lost. She's not mine. Not yet. Maybe never."

And then: "Fisher's won, and I've lost."

And last of all: "We only remember the past; we never know it when we meet it. The mind goes back, but time goes on, and farewells should be forever."

THE WALL AROUND THE WORLD

THEODORE R. COGSWELL (1918–   )
BEYOND, SEPTEMBER

*Born in Pennsylvania, where he still lives, and holder
of degrees from the Universities of Colorado and Den-
ver, Ted Cogswell began publishing his sharp, ironic
stories in the science fiction magazines in 1952. Never
prolific, the bulk of his short fiction is available to us in
two collections—*The Wall Around The World *(1962)
and* The Third Eye *(1968). He is also the author of one
of the best* Star Trek *books,* Spock Messiah! *(1976).*

*Much of his career has been in higher education,
since 1965 as Professor at Keystone Junior College.
Science fiction professionals and fans also know him for
his activities on behalf of the Science Fiction Writers of
America, for whom he served as editor of the SFWA
FORUM and as Secretary. He possesses one of the
sharpest (and biting) senses of humor in the field.*

—MHG

*Every once in a while, life conspires to give you an
unexpected chance.*

*A couple of years ago, Janet was reading through a
collection of Ted Cogswell's short stories and said to
me, "Do you want to read a good story?" Of course, I
am always ready to read a good story, and she said,
"Read 'The Wall Around the World'."*

I had read it once when it first appeared but I was

perfectly willing to read it again and, indeed, I enjoyed it just as much the second time.

As you remember, in an earlier headnote I mentioned my scarcely repressed ambition to divide science fiction into classifications. If I did, one of the sub-classes would surely be what I would call "The Limited World." You'll see what I mean when you read the story.

Incidentally, there's one thing about Ted that Marty may not know about, even though he speaks of his sense of humor. There was once a time when Ted Cogswell was the presiding genius of an irregularly appearing periodical called "Proceedings of the Institute for Twenty-First Century Studies" (if memory serves me). It was referred to by the acronym PITFCS, which was pronounced—No, I think that, on second thought, I forget how it was pronounced.

In any case, Ted gave his sense of humor totally free reign and it was the wildest, maddest periodical that ever existed. I would gladly describe it in detail, if words existed that would make the description possible. Since the words don't exist, I won't waste my time trying. Sorry.

—*IA*

THE WALL THAT WENT ALL THE WAY AROUND the World had always been there, so nobody paid much attention to it—except Porgie.

Porgie was going to find out what was on the other side of it—assuming there was another side—or break his neck trying. He was going on fourteen, an age that tends to view the word *impossible* as a meaningless term invented by adults for their own peculiar purposes. But he recognized that there were certain practical difficulties involved in scaling a glassy-smooth surface that rose over a thousand feet straight up. That's why he spent a lot of time watching the eagles.

This morning, as usual, he was late for school. He lost time finding a spot for his broomstick in the crowded rack in the school yard, and it was exactly six minutes after the hour as he slipped guiltily into the classroom.

For a moment, he thought he was safe. Old Mr. Wickens had his back to him and was chalking a pentagram on the blackboard.

But just as Porgie started to slide into his seat, the schoolmaster turned and drawled, "I see Mr. Mills has finally decided to join us."

The class laughed, and Porgie flushed.

"What's your excuse this time, Mr. Mills?"

"I was watching an eagle," said Porgie lamely.

"How nice for the eagle. And what was he doing that was of such great interest?"

"He was riding up on the wind. His wings weren't flapping or anything. He was over the box canyon that runs into the East wall, where the wind hits the Wall and goes up. The eagle just floated in circles, going higher all the time. You know, Mr. Wickens, I'll bet if you caught a whole bunch of eagles and tied ropes to them, they could lift you right up to the top of the wall!"

"That," said Mr. Wickens, "is possible—if you could catch the eagles. Now, if you'll excuse me, I'll continue with the lecture. When invoking Elementals of the Fifth Order, care must be taken to . . ."

Porgie glazed his eyes and began to think up ways and means to catch some eagles.

The next period, Mr. Wickens gave them a problem in Practical Astrology. Porgie chewed his pencil and tried to work on it, but couldn't concentrate. Nothing came out right—and when he found he had accidentally transposed a couple of signs of the zodiac at the very beginning, he gave up and began to draw plans for eagle traps. He tried one, decided it wouldn't work, started another—

"Porgie!"

He jumped. Mr. Wickens, instead of being in front of the class, was standing right beside him. The schoolmaster reached down, picked up the paper Porgie had been drawing on, and looked at it. Then he grabbed Porgie by the arm and jerked him from his seat.

"Go to my study!"

As Porgie went out the door, he heard Mr. Wickens say, "The class is dismissed until I return!"

There was a sudden rush of large, medium, and small-sized boys out of the classroom. Down the corridor to the front door they pelted, and out into the bright sunshine. As they ran past Porgie, his cousin Homer skidded to a stop and accidentally on purpose jabbed an elbow into his ribs. Homer, usually called "Bull Pup" by the kids because of his squat build and pugnacious face, was a year older than Porgie and took his seniority seriously.

"Wait'll I tell Dad about this. You'll catch it tonight!" He gave Porgie another jab and then ran out into the schoolyard to take command of a game of Warlock.

Mr. Wickens unlocked the door to his study and motioned Porgie inside. Then he shut and locked it carefully behind him. He sat down in the high-backed chair behind his desk and folded his hands.

Porgie stood silently, hanging his head, filled with that helpless guilty anger that comes from conflict with superior authority.

"What were you doing instead of your lesson?" Mr. Wickens demanded.

Porgie didn't answer.

Mr. Wickens narrowed his eyes. The large hazel switch that rested on top of the bookcase baside the stuffed owl lifted lightly into the air, drifted across the room, and dropped into his hand.

"Well?" he said, tapping the switch on the desk.

"Eagle traps," admitted Porgie. "I was drawing eagle traps. I couldn't help it. The Wall made me do it."

"Proceed."

Porgie hesitated for a moment. The switch tapped. Porgie burst out, "I want to see what's on the other side! There's no magic that will get me over, so I've got to find something else!"

Tap, went the switch. "Something else?"

"If a magic way was in the old books, somebody would have found it already!"

Mr. Wickens rose to his feet and stabbed one bony

finger accusingly at Porgie. "Doubt is the mother of damnation!"

Porgie dropped his eyes to the floor and wished he was someplace else.

"I see doubt in you. Doubt is evil, Porgie, *evil!* There are ways permitted to men and ways forbidden. You stand on the brink of the fatal choice. Beware that the Black Man does not come for you as he did for your father before you. Now, bend over!"

Porgie bent. He wished he'd worn a heavier pair of pants.

"Are you ready?"

"Yes, sir," said Porgie sadly.

Mr. Wickens raised the switch over his head. Porgie waited. The switch slammed—but on the desk.

"Straighten up," Mr. Wickens said wearily. He sat down again. "I've tried pounding things into your head, and I've tried pounding things on your bottom, and one end is as insensitive as the other. Porgie, can't you understand that you aren't supposed to try and find out new things? The Books contain everything there is to know. Year by year, what is written in them becomes clearer to us."

He pointed out the window at the distant towering face of the Wall that went around the World. "Don't worry about what is on the other side of that! It may be a place of angels or a place of demons—the Books do not tell us. But no man will know until he is ready for that knowledge. Our broomsticks won't climb that high, our charms aren't strong enough. We need more skill at magic, more understanding of the strange unseen forces that surround us. In my grandfather's time the best of the broomsticks wouldn't climb over a hundred feet in the air. But Adepts in the Great Tower worked and worked until now, when the clouds are low, we can ride right up among them. Someday we will be able to soar all the way to the top of the Wall—"

"Why not now?" Porgie asked stubbornly. "With eagles."

"Because we're not *ready*," Mr. Wickens snapped.

"Look at mind-talk. It was only thirty years ago that the proper incantations were worked out, and even now there are only a few who have the skill to talk across the miles by just thinking out their words. Time, Porgie— it's going to take time. We were placed here to learn the Way, and everything that might divert us from the search is evil. Man can't walk two roads at once. If he tries, he'll split himself in half."

"Maybe so," said Porgie. "But birds get over the Wall, and they don't know any spells. Look, Mr. Wickens, if everything is magic, how come magic won't work on everything? Like this, for instance—"

He took a shiny quartz pebble out of his pocket and laid it on the desk.

Nudging it with his finger, he said:

> "*Stone fly,*
> *Rise on high,*
> *Over cloud*
> *And into sky.*"

The stone didn't move.

"You see, sir? If words work on broomsticks, they should work on stones, too."

Mr. Wickens stared at the stone. Suddenly it quivered and jumped into the air.

"That's different," said Porgie. "You took hold of it with your mind. Anybody can do that with little things. What I want to know is why the words won't work by themselves."

"We just don't know enough yet," said Mr. Wickens impatiently. He released the stone and it clicked on the desktop. "Every year we learn a little more. Maybe by your children's time we'll find the incantation that will make everything lift." He sniffed. "What do you want to make stones fly for, anyhow? You get into enough trouble just throwing them."

Porgie's brow furrowed. "There's a difference between *making* a thing do something, like when I lift it with my hand or mind, and putting a spell on it so it does the work by itself, like a broomstick."

There was a long silence in the study as each thought his own thoughts.

Finally Mr. Wickens said, "I don't want to bring up the unpleasant past, Porgie, but it would be well to remember what happened to your father. His doubts came later than yours—for a while he was my most promising student—but they were just as strong."

He opened a desk drawer, fumbled in it for a moment, and brought out a sheaf of papers yellow with age. "This is the paper that damned him—*An Enquiry into Non-Magical Methods of Levitation*. He wrote it to qualify for his Junior Adeptship." He threw the paper down in front of Porgie as if the touch of it defiled his fingers.

Porgie started to pick it up.

Mr. Wickens roared, "Don't touch it! It contains blasphemy!"

Porgie snatched back his hand. He looked at the top paper and saw a neat sketch of something that looked like a bird—except that it had two sets of wings, one in front and one in back.

Mr. Wickens put the papers back in the desk drawer. His disapproving eyes caught and held Porgie's as he said, "If you want to go the way of your father, none of *us* can stop you." His voice rose sternly, "But there is one who can. . . . Remember the Black Man, Porgie, for his walk is terrible! There are fires in his eyes and no spell may defend you against him. When he came for your father, there was darkness at noon and a high screaming. When the sunlight came back, they were gone—and it is not good to think where."

Mr. Wickens shook his head as if overcome at the memory and pointed toward the door. "Think before you act. Porgie. Think well!"

Porgie was thinking as he left, but more about the sketch in his father's paper than about the Black Man.

The orange crate with the two boards across it for wings had looked something like his father's drawing, but appearances had been deceiving. Porgie sat on the back steps of his house feeling sorry for himself and alternately rubbing two tender spots on his anatomy. Though they were at opposite ends, and had different immediate causes, they both grew out of the same thing. His bottom was sore as a result of a liberal application of his uncle's hand. His swollen nose came from an aerial crack-up.

He'd hoisted his laboriously contrived machine to the top of the woodshed and taken a flying leap in it. The expected soaring glide hadn't materialized. Instead, there had been a sickening fall, a splintering crash, a momentary whirling of stars as his nose banged into something hard.

He wished now he hadn't invited Bull Pup to witness his triumph, because the story'd gotten right back to his uncle—with the usual results.

Just to be sure the lesson was pounded home, his uncle had taken away his broomstick for a week—and just so Porgie wouldn't sneak out, he'd put a spell on it before locking it away in the closet.

"Didn't feel like flying, anyway," Porgie said sulkily to himself, but the pretense wasn't strong enough to cover up the loss. The gang was going over to Red Rocks to chase bats as soon as the sun went down, and he wanted to go along.

He shaded his eyes and looked toward the western Wall as he heard a distant halloo of laughing voices. They were coming in high and fast on their broomsticks. He went back to the woodshed so they wouldn't see him. He was glad he had when they swung low and began to circle the house yelling for him and Bull Pup. They kept hooting and shouting until Homer flew out of his bedroom window to join them.

"Porgie can't come," he yelled. "He got licked and Dad took his broom away from him. Come on, gang!"

With a quick looping climb, he took the lead and they went hedge-hopping off toward Red Rocks. Bull Pup had been top dog ever since he got his big stick. He'd zoom up to five hundred feet, hang from his broom by his knees and then let go. Down he'd plummet, his arms spread and body arched as if he were making a swan dive—and then, when the ground wasn't more than a hundred feet away, he'd call and his broomstick would arrow down after him and slide between his legs, lifting him up in a great sweeping arc that barely cleared the treetops.

"Showoff!" muttered Porgie and shut the woodshed door on the vanishing stick-riders.

Over on the work bench sat the little model of paper and sticks that had got him into trouble in the first place. He picked it up and gave it a quick shove into the air with his hands. It dove toward the floor and then, as it picked up speed, tilted its nose toward the ceiling and made a graceful loop in the air. Leveling off, it made a sudden veer to the left and crashed against the woodshed wall. A wing splintered.

Porgie went to pick it up. "Maybe what works for little things doesn't work for big ones," he thought sourly. The orange crate and the crossed boards had been as close an approximation of the model as he had been able to make. Listlessly, he put the broken glider back on his work bench and went outside. Maybe Mr. Wickens and his uncle and all the rest were right. Maybe there was only one road to follow.

He did a little thinking about it and came to a conclusion that brought forth a secret grin. He'd do it their way—but there wasn't any reason why he couldn't hurry things up a bit. Waiting for his grandchildren to work things out wasn't getting *him* over the wall.

Tomorrow, after school, he'd start working on his new idea, and this time maybe he'd find the way.

In the kitchen, his uncle and aunt were arguing about him. Porgie paused in the hall that led to the front room and listened.

"Do you think I like to lick the kid? I'm not some kind of an ogre. It hurt me more than it hurt him."

"I notice you were able to sit down afterward," said Aunt Olga dryly.

"Well, what else could I do? Mr. Wickens didn't come right out and say so, but he hinted that if Porgie didn't stop mooning around, he might be dropped from school altogether. He's having an unsettling effect on the other kids. Damn it, Olga, I've done everything for that boy I've done for my own son. What do you want me to do, stand back and let him end up like your brother?"

"You leave my brother out of this! No matter what Porgie does, you don't have to beat him. He's still only a little boy."

There was a loud snort. "In case you've forgotten, dear, he had his thirteenth birthday last March. He'll be a man pretty soon."

"Then why don't you have a man-to-man talk with him?"

"Haven't I tried? You know what happens every time. He gets off with those crazy questions and ideas of his and I lose my temper and pretty soon we're back where we started." He threw up his hands. "I don't know what to do with him. Maybe that fall he had this afternoon will do some good. I think he had a scare thrown into him that he won't forget for a long time. Where's Bull Pup?"

"Can't you call him Homer? It's bad enough having his friends call him by that horrible name. He went out to Red Rocks with the other kids. They're having a bat hunt or something."

Porgie's uncle grunted and got up. "I don't see why that kid can't stay at home at night for a change. I'm going in the front room and read the paper."

Porgie was already there, flipping the pages of his schoolbooks and looking studious. His uncle settled down in his easy chair, opened his paper, and lit his pipe. He reached out to put the charred match in the ashtray, and as usual the ashtray wasn't there.

"Damn that woman," he muttered to himself and raised his voice: "Porgie."

"Yes, Uncle Veryl?"

"Bring me an ashtray from the kitchen, will you please? Your aunt has them all out there again."

"Sure thing," said Porgie and shut his eyes. He thought

of the kitchen until a picture of it was crystal-clear in his mind. The beaten copper ashtray was sitting beside the sink where his aunt had left it after she had washed it out. He squinted the little eye inside his head, stared hard at the copper bowl, and whispered:

> "Ashtray fly,
> Follow eye."

Simultaneously he lifted with his mind. The ashtray quivered and rose slowly into the air.

Keeping it firmly suspended, Porgie quickly visualized the kitchen door and the hallway and drifted it through.

"Porgie!" came his uncle's angry voice.

Porgie jumped, and there was a crash in the hallway outside as the bowl was suddenly released and crashed to the floor.

"How many times have I told you not to levitate around the house? If it's too much work to go out to the kitchen, tell me and I'll do it myself."

"I was just practicing," mumbled Porgie defensively.

"Well, practice outside. You've got the walls all scratched up from banging things against them. You know you shouldn't fool around with telekinesis outside sight range until you've mastered full visualization. Now go and get me that ashtray."

Crestfallen, Porgie went out the door into the hall. When he saw where the ashtray had fallen, he gave a silent whistle. Instead of coming down the center of the hall, it had been three feet off course and heading directly for the hall table when he let it fall. In another second, it would have smashed into his aunt's precious black alabaster vase.

"Here it is, Uncle," he said, taking it into the front room. "I'm sorry."

His uncle looked at his unhappy face, sighed and reached out and tousled his head affectionately.

"Buck up, Porgie. I'm sorry I had to paddle you this afternoon. It was for your own good. Your aunt and I don't want you to get into any serious trouble. You know what folks think about machines." He screwed up his face as if he'd said a dirty word. "Now, back to your books—we'll forget all about what happened today. Just remember this, Porgie: If there's anything you want to know, don't go fooling around on your own. Come and ask me, and we'll have a man-to-man talk."

Porgie brightened. "There's something I have been wondering about."

"Yes?" said his uncle encouragingly.

"How many eagles would it take to lift a fellow high enough to see what was on the other side of the Wall?"

Uncle Veryl counted to ten—very slowly.

The next day Porgie went to work on his new project. As soon as school was out, he went over to the Public Library and climbed upstairs to the main circulation room.

"Little boys are not allowed in this section," the librarian said. "The children's division is downstairs."

"But I need a book," protested Porgie. "A book on how to fly."

"This section is only for adults."

Porgie did some fast thinking. "My uncle can take books from here, can't he?"

"I suppose so."

"And he could send me over to get something for him, couldn't he?"

The librarian nodded reluctantly.

Porgie prided himself on never lying. If the librarian chose to misconstrue his questions, it was her fault, not his.

"Well, then," he said, "do you have any books on how to make things fly in the air?"

"What kind of things?"

"Things like birds."

"Birds don't have to be made to fly. They're born that way."

"I don't mean real birds," said Porgie. "I mean birds you make."

"Oh, Animation. Just a second, let me visualize." She shut her eyes and a card catalogue across the room opened and shut one drawer after another. "Ah, that might be what he's looking for," she murmured after a moment, and concentrated again. A large brass-bound book came flying out of the stacks and came to rest on the desk in front of her. She pulled the index card out of the pocket in the back and shoved it toward Porgie. "Sign your uncle's name here."

He did and then, hugging the book to his chest, got out of the library as quickly as he could.

By the time Porgie had worked three-quarters of the way through the book, he was about ready to give up in despair. It was all grown-up magic. Each set of instructions he ran into either used words he didn't understand or called for unobtainable ingredients like powdered unicorn horns and the blood of red-headed female virgins.

He didn't know what a virgin was—all his uncle's encyclopedia had to say on the subject was that they were the only ones who could ride unicorns—but there was a red-head by the name of Dorothy Boggs who lived down the road a piece. He had a feeling, however, that neither she nor her family would take kindly to a request for two quarts of blood, so he kept on searching through the book. Almost at the very end he found a set of instructions he thought he could follow.

It took him two days to get the ingredients together. The only thing that gave him trouble was finding a toad—the rest of the stuff, though mostly nasty and odoriferous, was obtained with little difficulty. The date and exact time of the experiment was important and he surprised Mr. Wickens by taking a sudden interest in his Practical Astrology course.

At last, after laborious computations, he decided everything was ready.

Late that night, he slipped out of bed, opened his bedroom door a crack, and listened. Except for the usual night noises and resonant snores from Uncle Veryl's room, the house was silent. He shut the door carefully and got his broomstick from the closet—Uncle Veryl had relented about that week's punishment.

Silently he drifted out through his open window and across the yard to the woodshed.

Once inside, he checked carefully to see that all the windows were covered. Then he lit a candle. He pulled a loose floorboard up and removed the book and his assembled ingredients. Quickly, he made the initial preparations.

First there was the matter of molding the clay he had taken from the graveyard into a rough semblance of a bird. Then, after sticking several white feathers obtained from last Sunday's chicken into each side of the figure to make wings, he anointed it with a noxious mixture he had prepared in advance.

The moon was just setting behind the Wall when he began the incantation. Candlelight flickered on the pages of the old book as he slowly and carefully pronounced the difficult words.

When it came time for the business with the toad, he almost didn't have the heart to go through with it; but he steeled himself and did what was necessary. Then, wincing, he jabbed his forefinger with a pin and slowly dropped the requisite three drops of blood down on the crude clay figure. He whispered:

> *"Clay of graveyard,*
> *White cock's feather,*
> *Eye of toad,*
> *Rise together!"*

Breathlessly he waited. He seemed to be in the middle of a circle of silence. The wind in the trees outside had stopped and there was only the sound of his own quick breathing. As the candlelight rippled, the clay figure seemed to quiver slightly as it if were hunching for flight.

Porgie bent closer, tense with anticipation. In his mind's eye, he saw himself building a giant bird with wings powerful enough to lift him over the Wall around the World. Swooping low over the schoolhouse during recess, he would wave his hands in a condescending gesture of farewell, and then as the kids hopped on their sticks and tried to follow him, he would rise higher and higher until he had passed the ceiling of their brooms and left them circling impotently below him. At last he would sweep over the Wall with hundreds of feet to spare, over it and then down—down into the great unknown.

The candle flame stopped flickering and stood steady and clear. Beside it, the clay bird squatted, lifeless and motionless.

Minutes ticked by and Porgie gradually saw it for what it was—a smelly clod of dirt with a few feathers tucked in it. There were tears in his eyes as he picked up the body of the dead toad and said softly, "I'm sorry."

When he came in from burying it, he grasped the image of the clay bird tightly in his mind and sent it swinging angrily around the shed. Feathers fluttered behind it as it flew faster and faster until in disgust he released it and let it smash into the rough boards of the wall. It crumbled into a pile of foul-smelling trash and fell to the floor. He stirred it with his toe, hurt, angry, confused.

His broken glider still stood where he had left it on the far end of his work bench. He went over and picked it up.

"At least you flew by yourself," he said, "and I didn't have to kill any poor little toads to make you."

Then he juggled it in his hand, feeling its weight, and began to wonder. It had occurred to him that maybe the wooden wings on his big orange-box glider had been too heavy.

"Maybe if I could get some long, thin poles," he thought, "and some cloth to put across the wings. . . ."

During the next three months, there was room in Porgie's mind for only one thing—the machine he was building in the roomy old cave at the top of the long hill on the other side of Arnett's grove. As a result, he kept slipping further and further behind at school.

Things at home weren't too pleasant, either—Bull Pup felt it was his duty to keep his parents fully informed of Porgie's short-comings. Porgie didn't care, though. He was too busy. Every minute he could steal was spent in either collecting materials or putting them together.

The afternoon the machine was finally finished, he could hardly tear himself away from it long enough to go home for dinner. He was barely able to choke down his food, and didn't even wait for dessert.

He sat on the grass in front of the cave, waiting for darkness. Below, little twinkling lights marked the villages that stretched across the plain for a full forty miles. Enclosing them like encircling arms stretched the dark and forbidding mass of the Wall. No matter where he looked, it stood high against the night. He followed its curve with his eyes until he had turned completely around, and then he shook his fist at it.

Patting the ungainly mass of the machine that rested on the grass beside him, he whispered fiercely, "I'll get over you yet. Old *Eagle* here will take me!"

Old *Eagle* was an awkward, boxkite-like affair; but to Porgie she was a thing of beauty. She had an uncovered fuselage composed of four long poles braced together to make a rectangular frame, at each end of which was fastened a large wing.

When it was dark enough, he climbed into the open frame and reached down and grabbed hold of the two lower members. Grunting, he lifted until the two upper ones rested under his armpits. There was padding there to support his weight comfortably once he was airborne. The bottom of the machine was level with his waist and the rest of him hung free. According to his thinking, he should be able to control his flight by swinging his legs. If he swung forward, the shifting weight should tilt the nose down; if he swung back, it should go up.

There was only one way to find out if his ifs were right. The *Eagle* was a heavy contraption. He walked awkwardly to the top of the hill, the cords standing out on his neck. He was scared as he looked down the long steep slope that stretched out before him—so scared that he was having trouble breathing. He swallowed twice in a vain attempt to moisten his dry throat, and then lunged forward, fighting desperately to keep his balance as his wabbling steps gradually picked up speed.

Faster he went, and faster, his steps turning into leaps as the wing surfaces gradually took hold. His toes scraped through the long grass and then they were dangling in free air.

He was aloft.

Not daring to even move his head, he slanted his eyes down and to the left. The earth was slipping rapidly by a dozen feet below him. Slowly and cautiously, he swung his feet back. As the weight shifted, the nose of the glider rose. Up, up he went, until he felt a sudden slowing down and a clumsiness of motion. Almost instinctively, he leaned forward again, pointing the nose down in a swift dip to regain flying speed.

By the time he reached the bottom of the hill, he was a hundred and fifty feet up. Experimentally, he swung his feet a little to the left. The glider dipped slightly and turned. Soaring over a clump of trees, he felt a sudden lifting as an updraft caught him.

Up he went—ten, twenty, thirty feet—and then slowly began to settle again.

The landing wasn't easy. More by luck than by skill, he came down in the long grass of the meadow with no more damage than a few bruises. He sat for a moment and rested, his head spinning with excitement. He had flown like a bird, without his stick, without uttering a word. There *were* other ways than magic!

His elation suddenly faded with the realization that, while gliding down was fun, the way over the Wall was *up*. Also, and of more immediate importance, he was half a mile from the cave with a contraption so heavy and unwieldy that he could never hope to haul it all the way back up the hill by himself. If he didn't get it out of sight by morning, there was going to be trouble, serious trouble. People took an unpleasant view of machines and those who built them.

Broomsticks, he decided, had certain advantages, after all. They might not fly very high, but at least you didn't have to walk home from a ride.

"If I just had a great big broomstick," he thought, "I could lift the *Eagle* up with it and fly her home."

He jumped to his feet. It might work!

He ran back up the hill as fast as he could and finally, very much out of breath, reached the entrance of the cave. Without waiting to get back his wind, he jumped on his stick and flew down to the stranded glider.

Five minutes later, he stepped back and said:

> "*Broomstick fly,*
> *Rise on high*
> *Over cloud*
> *And into sky.*"

It didn't fly. It couldn't. Porgie had lashed it to the framework of the *Eagle*. When he grabbed hold of the machine and lifted, nine-tenths of its weight was gone, canceled out by the broomstick's lifting power.

He towed it back up the hill and shoved it into the cave. Then he looked uneasily at the sky. It was later than he had thought. He should be home and in bed— but when he thought of the feeling of power he had had in his flight, he couldn't resist hauling the *Eagle* back out again.

After checking the broomstick to be sure it was still fastened tightly to the frame, he went swooping down the hill again. This time when he hit the thermal over the clump of trees, he was pushed up a hundred feet before he lost it. He curved through the darkness until he found it again and then circled tightly within it.

Higher he went and higher, higher than any broomstick had ever gone!

When he started to head back, though, he didn't have such an easy time of it. Twice he was caught in downdrafts that almost grounded him before he was able to break loose from the tugging winds. Only the lifting power of his broomstick enabled him to stay aloft. With it bearing most of the load, the *Eagle* was so light that it took just a flutter of air to sweep her up again.

He landed the glider a stone's throw from the mouth of his cave.

"Tomorrow night!" he thought exultantly as he unleashed his broomstick. "Tomorrow night!"

There was a tomorrow night, and many nights after that. The *Eagle* was sensitive to every updraft, and with care he found he could remain aloft for hours, riding from thermal to thermal. It was hard to keep his secret, hard to keep from shouting the news, but he had to. He slipped out at night to practice, slipping back in again before sunrise to get what sleep he could.

He circled the day of his fourteenth birthday in red and waited. He had a reason for waiting.

In the World within the Wall, fourteenth birthdays marked the boundary between the little and the big, between being a big child and a small man. Most important, they marked the time when one was taken to the Great Tower where the Adepts lived and given a full-sized broomstick powered by the most potent of spells, sticks that would climb to a full six hundred feet, twice the height that could be reached by the smaller ones the youngsters rode.

Porgie needed a man-sized stick, needed that extra power, for he had found that only the strongest of updrafts would lift him past the three-hundred-foot ceiling where the lifting power of his little broomstick gave out. He had to get up almost as high as the Wall before he could make it across the wide expanse of flat plain that separated him from the box canyon where the great wind waited.

So he counted the slowly passing days and practiced flying during the rapidly passing nights.

The afternoon of his fourteenth birthday found Porgie sitting on the front steps expectantly, dressed in his best and waiting for his uncle to come out of the house. Bull Pup came out and sat down beside him.

"The gang's having a coven up on top of old Baldy tonight," he said. "Too bad you can't come."

"I can go if I want to," said Porgie.

"How?" said Bull Pup and snickered. "You going to

grow wings and fly? Old Baldy's five hundred feet up and your kid stick won't lift you that high."

"Today's my birthday."

"You think you're going to get a new stick?"

Porgie nodded.

"Well, you ain't. I heard Mom and Dad talking. Dad's mad because you flunked Alchemy. He said you had to be taught a lesson."

Porgie felt sick inside, but he wouldn't let Bull Pup have the satisfaction of knowing it.

"I don't care," he said. "I'll go to the coven if I want to. You just wait and see."

Bull Pup was laughing when he hopped on his stick and took off down the street. Porgie waited an hour, but his uncle didn't come out.

He went into the house. Nobody said anything about his new broomstick until after supper. Then his uncle called him into the living room and told him he wasn't getting it.

"But, Uncle Veryl, you promised!"

"It was a conditional promise, Porgie. There was a big if attached to it. Do you remember what it was?"

Porgie looked down at the floor and scuffed one toe on the worn carpet. "I tried."

"Did you really, son?" His uncle's eyes were stern but compassionate. "Were you trying when you fell asleep in school today? I've tried talking with you and I've tried whipping you and neither seems to work. Maybe this will. Now you run upstairs and get started on your studies. When you can show me that your marks are improving, we'll talk about getting you a new broomstick. Until then, the old one will have to do."

Porgie knew that he was too big to cry, but when he got to his room, he couldn't help it. He was stretched out on his bed with his face buried in the pillows when he heard a hiss from the window. He looked up to see Bull Pup sitting on his stick, grinning malevolently at him.

"What do you want?" sniffed Porgie.

"Only little kids cry," said Bull Pup.

"I wasn't crying. I got a cold."

"I just saw Mr. Wickens. He was coming out of that old cave back of Arnett's grove. He's going to get the Black Man, I'll bet."

"I don't know anything about that old cave," said Porgie, sitting bolt upright on his bed.

"Oh, yes, you do. I followed you up there one day. You got a machine in there. I told Mr. Wickens and he gave me a quarter. He was real interested."

Porgie jumped from his bed and ran toward the window, his face red and his fists doubled. "I'll fix you!"

Bull Pup backed his broomstick just out of Porgie's reach, and then stuck his thumbs in his ears and waggled his fingers. When Porgie started to throw things, he gave a final taunt and swooped away toward old Baldy and the coven.

Porgie's uncle was just about to go out in the kitchen and fix himself a sandwich when the doorbell rang. Grumbling, he went out into the front hall. Mr. Wickens was at the door. He came into the house and stood blinking in the light. He seemed uncertain as to just how to begin.

"I've got bad news for you," he said finally. "It's about Porgie. Is your wife still up?"

Porgie's uncle nodded anxiously.

"She'd better hear this, too."

Aunt Olga put down her knitting when they came into the living room.

"You're out late, Mr. Wickens."

"It's not of my own choosing."

"Porgie's done something again," said his uncle.

Aunt Olga sighed. "What is it this time?"

Mr. Wickens hesitated, cleared his throat, and finally spoke in a low, hushed voice: "Porgie's built a machine. The Black Man told me. He's coming after the boy tonight."

Uncle Veryl dashed up the stairs to find Porgie. He wasn't in his room.

Aunt Olga just sat in her chair and cried shrilly.

*   *   *

The moon stood high and silver-lit the whole countryside. Porgie could make out the world far below him almost as if it were day. Miles to his left, he saw the little flickering fires on top of old Baldy where the kids were holding their coven. He fought an impulse and then succumbed to it. He circled the *Eagle* over a clump of trees until the strong rising currents lifted him almost to the height of the Wall. Then he twisted his body and banked over toward the distant red glowing fires.

Minutes later, he went silently over them at eight hundred feet, feeling out the air currents around the rocks. There was a sharp downdraft on the far side of Baldy that dropped him suddenly when he glided into it, but he made a quick turn and found untroubled air before he fell too far. On the other side, toward the box canyon, he found what he wanted, a strong, rising current that seemed to have no upward limits.

He fixed its location carefully in his mind and then began to circle down toward the coven. Soon he was close enough to make out individual forms sitting silently around their little fires.

"Hey, Bull Pup," he yelled at the top of his lungs.

A stocky figure jumped to its feet and looked wildly around for the source of the ghostly voice.

"Up here!"

Porgie reached in his pocket, pulled out a small pebble and chucked it down. It cracked against a shelf of rock four feet from Bull Pup. Porgie's cousin let out a howl of fear. The rest of the kids jumped up and reared back their heads at the night sky, their eyes blinded by firelight.

"I told you I could come to the coven if I wanted to," yelled Porgie, "but now I don't. I don't have any time for kid stuff; I'm going over the Wall!"

During his last pass over the plateau he wasn't more than thirty feet up. As he leaned over, his face was clearly visible in the firelight.

Placing one thumb to his nose, he waggled his fingers and chanted, "nyah, nyah, nyah, you can't catch me!"

His feet were almost scraping the ground as he glided over the drop-off. There was an anxious second of waiting and then he felt the sure, steady thrust of the up-current against his wings.

He looked back. The gang was milling around, trying to figure out what had happened. There was an angry shout of command from Bull Pup, and after a moment of confused hesitation they all made for their brooms and swooped up into the air.

Porgie mentally gauged his altitude and then relaxed. He was almost at their ceiling and would be above it before they reached him.

He flattened out his glide and yelled, "Come on up! Only little kids play that low!"

Bull Pup's stick wouldn't rise any higher. He circled impotently, shaking his fist at the machine that rode serenely above him.

"You just wait," he yelled. "You can't stay up there all night. You got to come down some time, and when you do, we'll be waiting for you."

"Nyah, nyah, nyah," chanted Porgie and mounted higher into the moonlit night.

When the updraft gave out, he wasn't as high as he wanted to be, but there wasn't anything he could do about it. He turned and started a flat glide across the level plain toward the box canyon. He wished now that he had left Bull Pup and the other kids alone. They were following along below him. If he dropped down to their level before the canyon winds caught him, he was in trouble.

He tried to flatten his glide still more, but instead of saving altitude, he went into a stall that dropped him a hundred feet before he was able to regain control. He saw now that he could never make it without dropping to Bull Pup's level.

Bull Pup saw it, too. and let out an exultant yell: "Just you wait! You're going to get it good!"

Porgie peered over the side into the darkness where his cousin rode, his pug face gleaming palely in the moonlight.

"Leave him alone, gang," Bull Pup shouted. "He's mine!"

The rest pulled back and circled slowly as the *Eagle* glided quietly down among them. Bull Pup darted in and rode right alongside Porgie.

He pointed savagely toward the ground: "Go down or I'll knock you down!"

Porgie kicked at him, almost upsetting his machine. He wasn't fast enough. Bull Pup dodged easily. He made a wide circle and came back, reaching out and grabbing the far end of the *Eagle*'s front wing. Slowly and maliciously, he began to jerk it up and down, twisting violently as he did so.

"Get down," he yelled, "or I'll break it off!"

Porgie almost lost his head as the wrenching threatened to throw him out of control.

"Let go!" he screamed, his voice cracking.

Bull Pup's face had a strange excited look on it as he gave the wing another jerk. The rest of the boys were becoming frightened as they saw what was happening.

"Quit it, Bull Pup!" somebody called. "Do you want to kill him?"

"Shut up or you'll get a dose of the same!"

Porgie fought to clear his head. His broomstick was tied to the frame of the *Eagle* so securely that he would never be able to free it in time to save himself. He stared into the darkness until he caught the picture of Bull Pup's broomstick sharply in his mind. He'd never tried to handle anything that big before, but it was that or nothing.

Tensing suddenly, he clamped his mind down on the picture and held it hard. He knew that words didn't help, but he uttered them anyway:

> *"Broomstick stop,*
> *Flip and flop!"*

There was a sharp tearing pain in his head. He gritted his teeth and held on, fighting desperately against the red haze that threatened to swallow him. Suddenly there was a half-startled, half-frightened squawk from his left wingtip, and Bull Pup's stick jerked to an abrupt halt, gyrating so madly that its rider could hardly hang on.

"All right, the rest of you," screamed Porgie. "Get going or I'll do the same thing to you!"

They got, arcing away in terrified disorder. Porgie watched as they formed a frightened semicircle around the blubbering Bull Pup. With a sigh of relief, he let go with his mind.

As he left them behind in the night, he turned his head back and yelled weakly, "Nyah, nyah, nyah, you can't catch me!"

He was only fifty feet off the ground when he glided into the far end of the box canyon and was suddenly caught by the strong updraft. As he soared in a tight spiral, he slumped down against the arm-rests, his whole body shaking in delayed reaction.

The lashings that held the front wing to the frame were dangerously loose from the manhandling they had received. One more tug and the whole wing might have twisted back, dumping him down on the sharp rocks below. Shudders ran through the *Eagle* as the supports shook in their loose bonds. He clamped both hands around the place where the rear wing spar crossed the frame and tried to steady it.

He felt his stick's lifting power give out at three hundred feet. The *Eagle* felt clumsy and heavy, but the current was still enough to carry him slowly upward. Foot by foot he rose toward the top of the Wall, losing a precious hundred feet once when he spiraled out of the updraft and had to circle to find it. A wisp of cloud curled down from the top of the Wall and he felt a moment of panic as he climbed into it.

Momentarily, there was no left or right or up or down. Only damp whiteness. He had the feeling that the *Eagle* was falling out of control; but he kept steady, relying on the feel for the air he had gotten during his many practice flights.

The lashings had loosened more. The full strength of his hands wasn't enough to keep the wing from shuddering and trembling. He struggled resolutely to maintain control of ship and self against the strong temptation to lean forward and throw the *Eagle* into a shallow dive that would take him back to normalcy and safety.

He was almost at the end of his resolution when with dramatic suddenness he glided out of the cloud into the clear moon-touched night. The up-current under him seemed to have lessened. He banked in a gentle arc, trying to find the center of it again.

As he turned, he became aware of something strange, something different, something almost frightening. For the first time in his life, there was no Wall to block his vision, no vast black line stretching through the night.

He was above it!

There was no time for looking. With a loud *ping*, one of the lashings parted and the leading edge of the front wing flapped violently. The glider began to pitch and yaw, threatening to nose over into a plummeting dive. He fought for mastery, swinging his legs like desperate pendulums as he tried to correct the erratic side swings that threatened to throw him out of control. As he fought, he headed for the Wall.

If he were to fall, it would be on the other side. At least he would cheat old Mr. Wickens and the Black Man.

Now he was directly over the Wall. It stretched like a wide road underneath him, its smooth top black and shining in the moonlight. Acting on quick impulse, he threw his body savagely forward and to the right. The ungainly machine dipped abruptly and dove toward the black surface beneath it.

Eighty feet, seventy, sixty, fifty—he had no room to maneuver, there would be no second chance—thirty, twenty—

He threw his weight back, jerking the nose of the *Eagle* suddenly up. For a precious second the wings held, there was a sharp breaking of his fall: then, with a loud, cracking noise, the front wing buckled back in his face. There was a moment of blind whirling fall and a splintering crash that threw him into darkness.

Slowly, groggily, Porgie pulled himself up out of the

broken wreckage. The *Eagle* had made her last flight. She perched precariously, so near the outside edge of the wall that part of her rear wing stretched out over nothingness.

Porgie crawled cautiously across the slippery wet surface of the top of the Wall until he reached the center. There he crouched down to wait for morning. He was exhausted, his body so drained of energy that in spite of himself he kept slipping into an uneasy sleep.

Each time he did, he'd struggle back to consciousness trying to escape the nightmare figures that scampered through his brain. He was falling, pursued by wheeling, batlike figures with pug faces. He was in a tiny room and the walls were inching in toward him and he could hear the voice of Bull Pup in the distance chanting, "You're going to get it." And then the room turned into a long, dark corridor and he was running. Mr. Wickens was close behind him, and he had long, sharp teeth and he kept yelling, "Porgie! Porgie!"

He shuddered back to wakefulness, crawled to the far edge of the Wall and, hanging his head over, tried to look down at the Outside World. The clouds had boiled up and there was nothing underneath him but gray blankness hiding the sheer thousand foot drop. He crawled back to his old spot and looked toward the east, praying for the first sign of dawn. There was only blackness there.

He started to doze off again and once more he heard the voice: "Porgie! Porgie!"

He opened his eyes and sat up. The voice was still calling, even though he was awake. It seemed to be coming from high up and far away.

It came closer, closer, and suddenly he saw it in the darkness—a black figure wheeling above the Wall like a giant crow. Down it came, nearer and nearer, a man in black with arms outstretched and long fingers hooked like talons!

Porgie scrambled to his feet and ran, his feet skidding on the slippery surface. He looked back over his shoulder. The black figure was almost on top of him. Porgie dodged desperately and slipped.

He felt himself shoot across the slippery surface toward the edge of the Wall. He clawed, scrabbling for purchase. He couldn't stop. One moment he felt wet coldness slipping away under him; the next, nothingness as he shot out into the dark and empty air.

He spun slowly as he fell. First the clouds were under him and then they tipped and the star-flecked sky took their places. He felt cradled, suspended in time. There was no terror. There was nothing.

Nothing—until suddenly the sky above him was blotted out by a plummeting black figure that swooped down on him, hawk-like and horrible.

Porgie kicked wildly. One foot slammed into something solid and for an instant he was free. Then strong arms circled him from behind and he was jerked out of the nothingness into a world of falling and fear.

There was a sudden strain on his chest and then he felt himself being lifted. He was set down gently on the top of the Wall.

He stood defiant, head erect, and faced the black figure.

"I won't go back. You can't make me go back."

"You don't have to go back, Porgie."

He couldn't see the hooded face, but the voice sounded strangely familiar.

"You've earned your right to see what's on the other side," it said. Then the figure laughed and threw back the hood that partially covered its face.

In the bright moonlight, Porgie saw Mr. Wickens!

The schoolmaster nodded cheerfully. "Yes, Porgie, I'm the Black Man. Bit of a shock, isn't it?"

Porgie sat down suddenly.

"I'm from the Outside," said Mr. Wickens, seating himself carefully on the slick black surface. "I guess you could call me a sort of observer."

Porgie's spinning mind couldn't catch up with the new ideas that were being thrown at him. "Observer?" he said uncomprehendingly. "Outside?"

"Outside. That's where you'll be spending your next few years. I don't think you'll find life better there, and I don't think you'll find it worse. It'll be different, though, I can guarantee that." He chuckled. "Do you remember what I said to you in my office that day—that Man can't follow two paths at once, that Mind and Nature are bound to conflict? That's true, but it's also false. You can have both, but it takes two worlds to do it.

"Outside, where you're going, is the world of the machines. It's a good world, too. But the men who live there saw a long time ago that they were paying a price for it; that control over Nature meant that the forces of the Mind were neglected, for the machine is a thing of logic and reason, but miracles aren't. Not yet. So they built the wall and they placed people within it and gave them such books and such laws as would insure development of the powers of the Mind. At least they hoped it would work that way—and it did."

"But—but why the Wall?" asked Porgie.

"Because their guess was right. There is magic." He pulled a bunch of keys from his pocket. "Lift it, Porgie."

Porgie stared at it until he had the picture in his mind and then let his mind take hold, pulling with invisible hands until the keys hung high in the air. Then he dropped them back into Mr. Wickens' hand.

"What was that for?"

"Outsiders can't do that," said the schoolmaster. "And they can't do conscious telepathy—what you call mind-talk—either. They can't because they really don't believe such things can be done. The people inside the Wall do, for they live in an atmosphere of magic. But once these things are worked out, and become simply a matter of training and method, then the ritual, the mumbo-jumbo, the deeply ingrained belief in the existence of supernatural forces will be no longer necessary.

"These phenomena will be only tools that anybody can be trained to use, and the crutches can be thrown away. Then the Wall will come tumbling down. But until then—"he stopped and frowned in mock severity—

"there will always be a Black Man around to see that the people inside don't split themselves up the middle trying to walk down two roads at once."

There was a lingering doubt in Porgie's eyes. "But you flew without a machine."

The Black Man opened his cloak and displayed a small, gleaming disk that was strapped to his chest. He tapped it. "A machine, Porgie. A machine, just like your glider, only of a different sort and much better. It's almost as good as levitation. Mind and Nature . . . magic and science . . . they'll get together eventually."

He wrapped his cloak about him again. "It's cold up here. Shall we go? Tomorrow is time enough to find out what is Outside the Wall that goes around the World."

"Can't we wait until the clouds lift?" asked Porgie wistfully. "I'd sort of like to see it for the first time from up here."

"We could," said Mr. Wickens, "but there is somebody you haven't seen for a long time waiting for you down there. If we stay up here, he'll be worried."

Porgie looked up blankly. "I don't know anybody Outside. I—" He stopped suddenly. He felt as if he were about to explode. "Not my father!"

"Who else? He came out the easy way. Come, now, let's go and show him what kind of man his son has grown up to be. Are you ready?"

"I'm ready," said Porgie.

"Then help me drag your contraption over to the other side of the Wall so we can drop it inside. When the folk find the wreckage in the morning, they'll know what the Black Man does to those who build machines instead of tending to their proper business. It should have a salutary effect on Bull Pup and the others."

He walked over to the wreckage of the *Eagle* and began to tug at it.

"Wait," said Porgie. "Let me." He stared at the broken glider until his eyes began to burn. Then he gripped and pulled.

Slowly, with an increasing consciousness of mastery, he lifted until the glider floated free and was rocking gently in the slight breeze that rippled across the top of the great Wall. Then, with a sudden shove, he swung it far out over the abyss and released it.

The two stood silently, side by side, watching the *Eagle* pitch downward on broken wings. When it was lost in the darkness below, Mr. Wickens took Porgie in his strong arms and stepped confidently to the edge of the Wall.

"Wait a second," said Porgie, remembering a day in the schoolmaster's study and a switch that had come floating obediently down through the air. "If you're from Outside, how come you can do lifting?"

Mr. Wickens grinned. "Oh, I was born Inside. I went over the Wall for the first time when I was just a little older than you are now."

"In a glider?" asked Porgie.

"No," said the Black Man, his face perfectly sober. "I went out and caught myself a half-dozen eagles."

THE MODEL OF A JUDGE

WILLIAM MORRISON (JOSEPH SAMACHSON: 1906–1982)
GALAXY SCIENCE FICTION, OCTOBER

Professional chemist Joseph Samachson returns to these pages (see "The Sack" in Vol. 12) with this wonderful story of imposed behavior modification, a tale that is sad and funny at the same time. It is quite typical of the kind of material Horace Gold was looking to acquire for Galaxy—serious social speculation with a light touch.

Although his more than fifty science fiction stories contain a high percentage of excellent work, "William Morrison" never had a collection, and now is all but forgotten, a situation we are doing our best to correct.

—MHG

Here's an idea I've got—

There is a substantial fraction of science fiction writers who have special training in one branch or another of science; some who even are, or have been, working professionals in one field or other. There are among us mathematicians, computer scientists, anthropologists, biochemists, physicians, and so on.

I would like to see figures on how science fiction writers are divided among these specialties, and then I would be curious to see how many of the stories each such writer turns out are in their own field of specialization. Would we find out that a writer rarely pro-

*duces a story in his own field? If so, would that be
because he knows too much to allow his creativity free
reign; does the freight of knowledge he carries hold
him down?*

*I have a gut feeling that there might be something to
this, if only because I am a professional biochemist and
write very few stories in my field.*

*However, even if it is so, I do occasionally deal with
chemistry, and I imagine that every specialist sometimes hits home. At least here we have a story by
someone with a chemical background, and the story,
too, has a chemical background. (And yet the great E.
E. Smith, Ph.D., whose Ph.D. was in food chemistry
never wrote a story in the field. I'm sure of that.)*

—IA

RONAR WAS REFORMED, if that was the right word, but
he could see that they didn't trust him. Uneasiness
spoke in their awkward hurried motions when they
came near him; fear looked out of their eyes. He had to
reassure himself that all this would pass. In time they'd
learn to regard him as one of themselves and cease to
recall what he had once been. For the time being,
however, they still remembered. And so did he.

Mrs. Claymore, of the Presiding Committee, was
babbling, "Oh, Mrs. Silver, it's so good of you to come.
Have you entered the contest?"

"Not really," said Mrs. Silver with a modest laugh.
"Of course I don't expect to win against so many fine
women who are taking part. But I just thought I'd enter
to—to keep things interesting."

"That was very kind of you. But don't talk about not
winning. I still remember some of the dishes you served
for dinner at your home that time George and I paid
you a visit. Mmmmm—they were really delicious."

Mrs. Silver uttered another little laugh. "Just ordinary recipes. I'm so glad you liked them, though."

"I certainly did. And I'm sure the judge will like your
cake, too."

"The judge? Don't you usually have a committee?"

*   *   *

He could hear every word. They had no idea how sharp his sense of hearing was, and he had no desire to disconcert them further by letting them know. He could hear every conversation taking place in ordinary tones in the large reception room. When he concentrated he could make out the whispers. At this point he had to concentrate, for Mrs. Claymore leaned over and breathed into her friend's attentive ear.

"My dear, haven't you heard? We've had such trouble with that committee—there were such charges of favoritism! It was really awful."

"Really? But how did you find a judge then?"

"Don't look now—no, I'll tell you what to do. Pretend I said something funny, and throw your head back and laugh. Take a quick glance at him while you do. He's sitting up there alone, on the platform."

Mrs. Silver laughed gracefully as directed, and her eyes swept the platform. She became so excited, she almost forgot to whisper.

"Why, he's—"

"Shhh. Lower your voice, my dear."

"Why—he isn't human!"

"He's supposed to be—now. But, of course, that's a matter of opinion!"

"But who on Earth thought of making him judge?"

"No one on Earth. Professor Halder, who lives over on that big asteroid the other side of yours, heard of the troubles we had, and came up with the suggestion. At first it seemed absurd—"

"It certainly seems absurd to me!" agreed Mrs. Silver.

"It was the only thing we could do. There was no one else we could trust."

"But what does he know about cakes?"

"My dear, he has the most exquisite sense of taste!"

"I still don't understand."

"It's superhuman. Before we adopted Professor Halder's suggestion, we gave him a few tests. The results simply left us gasping. We could mix all sorts of spices—the most delicate, most exotic herbs from Venus or

Mars, and the strongest, coarsest flavors from Earth or one of the plant-growing asteroids—and he could tell us everything we had added, and exactly how much."

"I find that hard to believe, Matilda."

"Isn't it? It's honestly incredible. If I hadn't seen him do it myself, I wouldn't have believed it."

"But he doesn't have human preferences. Wasn't he— wasn't he—"

"Carnivorous? Oh, yes. They say he was the most vicious creature imaginable. Let an animal come within a mile of him, and he'd scent it and be after it in a flash. He and the others of his kind made the moon he came from uninhabitable for any other kind of intelligent life. Come to think of it, it may have been the very moon we're on now!"

"Really?"

"Either this, or some other moon of Saturn's. We had to do something about it. We didn't want to kill them off, naturally; that would have been the easiest way, but so uncivilized! Finally, our scientists came up with the suggestion for psychological reforming. Professor Halder told us how difficult it all was, but it seems to have worked. In his case, at least."

Mrs. Silver stole another glance. "Did it? I don't notice any one going near him."

"Oh, we don't like to tempt fate, Clara. But, if there were really any danger, I'm sure the psychologists would never have let him out of their clutches."

"I hope not. But psychologists take the most reckless risks sometimes—with other people's lives!"

"Well, there's one psychologist who's risking his own life—and his own wife, too. You know Dr. Cabanis, don't you?"

"Only by sight. Isn't his wife that stuck-up thing?"

"That's the one. Dr. Cabanis is the man who had actual charge of reforming him. And he's going to be here. His wife is entering a cake."

"Don't tell me that she really expects to win!"

"She bakes well, my dear. Let's give the she-devil her due. How on Earth an intelligent man like Dr.

Cabanis can stand her, I don't know, but, after all, he's the psychologist, not I, and he could probably explain it better than I could."

Ronar disengaged his attention.

So Dr. Cabanis was here. He looked around, but the psychologist was not in sight. He would probably arrive later.

The thought stirred a strange mixture of emotions. Some of the most painful moments of his life were associated with the presence of Dr. Cabanis. His early life, the life of a predatory carnivore, had been an unthinkingly happy one. He supposed that he could call his present life a happy one too, if you weren't overly particular how you defined the term. But that period in between!

That had been, to say the least, painful. Those long sessions with Dr. Cabanis had stirred him to the depths of a soul he hadn't known he possessed. The electric shocks and the druggings he hadn't minded so much. But the gradual reshaping of his entire psyche, the period of basic instruction, in which he had been taught to hate his old life so greatly that he could no longer go back to it even if the way were open, and the conditioning for a new and useful life with human beings—that was torture of the purest kind.

If he had known what was ahead of him, he wouldn't have gone through it at all. He'd have fought until he dropped, as so many of the others like him did. Still, now that it was over, he supposed that the results were worth the pain. He had a position that was more important than it seemed at first glance. He exercised control over a good part of the food supply intended for the outer planets, and his word was trusted implicitly. Let him condemn an intended shipment, and cancellation followed automatically, without the formality of confirmation by laboratory tests. He was greatly admired. And feared.

They had other feelings about him too. He overheard one whisper that surprised him. "My dear, I think he's really handsome."

"But, Charlotte, how can you say that about someone who isn't even hunan!"

"He looks more human than many human beings do. And his clothes fit him beautifully. I wonder—does he have a tail?"

"Not that I know of."

"Oh." There was disappointment in the sound. "He looks like a pirate."

"He was a kind of wolf, they tell me. You'd never guess, to see him, that he ran on all fours, would you?"

"Of course not. He's so straight and dignified."

"It just shows you what psychology can do."

"Psychology, and a series of operations, dear ladies," he thought sarcastically. "Without them I wouldn't be able to stand so nice and straight with the help of all the psychologists in this pretty little solar system of ours."

From behind a potted Martian nut-cactus came two low voices—not whispers this time. And there was several octaves difference in pitch between them. One male, one female.

The man said, "Don't be worried, sweetheart. I'll match your cooking and baking against anybody's."

There was a curious sound, between a click and a hiss. What human beings called a kiss, he thought. Between the sexes, usually an indication of affection or passion. Sometimes, especially within the ranks of the female sex, a formality behind which warfare could be waged.

The girl said tremulously, "But these women have so much experience. They've cooked and baked for years."

"Haven't you, for your own family?"

"Yes, but that isn't the same thing. I had to learn from a cookbook. And I had no one with experience to stand over me and teach me."

"You've learned faster that way than you'd have done with some of these old hens standing at your elbow and giving you directions. You cook *too* well. I'll be fat in no time."

"Your mother doesn't think so. And your brother said something about a bride's biscuits—"

"The older the joke, the better Charles likes it. Don't let it worry you." He kissed her again. "Have confidence in yourself, dear. You're going to win."

"Oh, Gregory, it's awfully nice of you to say so, but really I feel so unsure of myself."

"If only the judge were human and took a look at you, nobody else would stand a chance. Have I told you within the last five minutes that you're beautiful?"

Ronar disengaged his attention again. He found human love-making as repulsive as most human food.

He picked up a few more whispers. And then Dr. Cabanis came in.

The good doctor looked around, smiled, greeted several ladies of his acquaintance as if he were witnessing a private strip-tease of their souls, and then came directly up to the platform. "How are you, Ronar?"

"Fine, Doctor. Are you here to keep an eye on me?"

"I hardly think that's necessary. I have an interest in the results of the judging. My wife has baked a cake."

"I had no idea that cake-baking was so popular a human avocation."

"Anything that requires skill is sure to become popular among us. By the way, Ronar, I hope you don't feel hurt."

"Hurt, Doctor? What do you mean?"

"Come now, you understand me well enough. These people still don't trust you. I can tell by the way they keep their distance."

"I take human frailty into account, Doctor. Frailty, and lack of opportunity. These men and women haven't had the opportunity for extensive psychological treatment that I've had. I don't expect too much of them."

"You've scored a point there, Ronar."

"Isn't there something that can be done for them, Doctor? Some treatment that it would be legal to give them?"

"It would have to be voluntary. You see, Ronar you were considered only an animal, and treatment was necessary to save your life. But these people are alone with their infirmities. Besides, none of them are seriously ill. They hurt no one."

For a second Ronar had a human temptation. It was on the tip of his tongue to say, "Your wife, too, Doctor? People wonder how you stand her." But he resisted it. He had resisted more serious temptations.

A gong sounded gently but pervasively. Dr. Cabanis said, "I hope you have no resentment against me at this stage of the game, Ronar. I'd hate to have my wife lose the prize because the judge was prejudiced."

"Have no fear, Doctor. I take professional pride in my work. I will choose only the best."

"Of course, the fact that the cakes are numbered and not signed with the names of their creators will make things simpler."

"That would matter with human judges. It does not affect me."

Another gong sounded, more loudly this time. Gradually the conversation stopped. A man in a full dress suit, with yellow stripes down the sides of his shorts, and tails hanging both front and rear, climbed up on the platform. His eyes shone with a greeting so warm that the fear was almost completely hidden. "How are you, Ronar? Glad to see you."

"I'm fine, Senator. And you?"

"Couldn't be better. Have a cigar."

"No, thank you. I don't smoke."

"That's right, you don't. Besides, I'd be wasting the cigar. You don't vote!" He laughed heartily.

"I understand that they're passing a special law to let—people—like me vote at the next election."

"I'm for it, Ronar, I'm for it. You can count on me."

The chairman came up on the platform, a stout and dignified woman who smiled at both Ronar and the Senator, and shook hands with both without showing signs of distaste for either. The assembled competitors and spectators took seats.

The chairman cleared her throat. "Ladies and gentlemen, let us open this meeting by singing the *Hymn of All Planets.*"

They all rose, Ronar with them. His voice wasn't too well adapted to singing, but neither, it seemed, were most of the human voices. And, at least, he knew all the words.

The chairman proceeded to greet the gathering formally, in the name of the Presiding Committee.

Then she introduced Senator Whitten. She referred archly to the fact that the Senator had long since reached the age of indiscretion and had so far escaped marriage. He was an enemy of the female sex, but they'd let him speak to them anyway.

Senator Whitten just as archly took up the challenge. He had escaped more by good luck—if you could call it good—than by good management. But he was sure that if he had ever had the fortune to encounter some of the beautiful ladies here this fine day, and to taste the products of their splendid cooking and baking, he would have been a lost man. He would long since have committed polygamy.

Senator Whitten then launched into a paean of praise for the ancient art of preparing food.

Ronar's attention wandered. So did that of a good part of the audience. His ears picked up another conversation, this time whispered between a man and a woman in the front row.

The man said, "I should have put your name on it, instead of mine."

"That would have been silly. All my friends know that I can't bake. And it would look so strange if I won."

"It'll look stranger if I win. I can imagine what the boys in the shop will say."

"Oh, the boys in the shop are stupid. What's so unmanly in being able to cook and bake?"

"I'm not anxious for the news to get around."

"Some of the best chefs have been men."

"I'm not a chef."

"Stop worrying." There was exasperation in the force of her whisper. "You won't win anyway."

"I don't know. Sheila—"

"What?"

"If I win, will you explain to everybody how manly I really am? Will you be my character witness?"

She repressed a giggle.

"If you won't help me, I'll have to go around giving proof myself."

"Shh, someone will hear you."

Senator Whitten went on and on.

Ronar thought back to the time when he had wandered over the surface of this, his native satellite. He no longer had the old desires, the old appetites. Only the faintest of ghosts still persisted, ghosts with no power to do harm. But he could remember the old feeling of pleasure, the delight of sinking his teeth into an animal he had brought down himself, the savage joy of gulping the tasty flesh. He didn't eat raw meat any more; he didn't eat meat at all. He had been conditioned against it. He was now half vegetarian, half synthetarian. His meals were nourishing, healthful, and a part of his life he would rather not think about.

He took no real pleasure in the tasting of the cakes and other delicacies that born human beings favored. His sense of taste had remained keen only to the advantage of others. To himself it was a tantalizing mockery.

Senator Whitten's voice came to a sudden stop. There was applause. The Senator sat down; the chairman stood up. The time for the judging had arrived.

They set out the cakes—more than a hundred of them, topped by icings of all colors and all flavors. The chairman introduced Ronar and lauded both his impartiality and the keenness of his sense of taste.

They had a judging card ready.

Slowly, Ronar began to go down the line.

They might just as well have signed each cake with its maker's name. As he lifted a portion of each to his mouth, he could hear the quick intake of breath from the woman who had baked it, could catch the whispered warning from her companion. There were few secrets they could keep from him.

At first they all watched intently. When he had reached the fifth cake, however, a hand went up in the audience. "Madam Chairman!"

"Please, ladies, let us not interrupt the judging."

"But I don't think the judging is right. Mr. Ronar tastes hardly more than a crumb of each!"

"A minimum of three crumbs," Ronar corrected her. "One from the body of the cake, one from the icing, and an additional crumb from each filling between layers."

"But you can't judge a cake that way! You have to eat it, take a whole mouthful—"

"Please, madam, permit me to explain. A crumb is all I need. I can analyze the contents of the cake sufficiently well from that. Let me take for instance Cake Number 4, made from an excellent recipe, well baked. Martian granis flour, goover eggs, tingan-flavored salt, a trace of Venusian orange spice, synthetic shortening of the best quality. The icing is excellent, made with rare dipentose sugars which give it a delightful flavor. Unfortunately, however, the cake will not win first prize."

An anguished cry rose from the audience. "Why?"

"Through no fault of your own, dear lady. The purberries used in making the filling were not freshly picked. They have the characteristic flavor of refrigeration."

"The manager of the store swore to me that they were fresh! Oh, I'll kill him, I'll murder him—"

She broke down in a flood of tears.

Ronar said to the lady who had protested, "I trust, madam, that you will now have slightly greater confidence in my judgment."

She blushed and subsided.

Ronar went on with the testing. Ninety per cent of the cakes he was able to discard at once, from some fault in the raw materials used or in the method of baking. Eleven cakes survived the first elimination contest.

He went over them again, more slowly this time. When he had completed the second round of tests, only three were left. Number 17 belonged to Mrs. Cabanis. Number 43 had been made by the man who argued with his wife. Number 64 was the product of the young bride, whom he had still not seen.

Ronar paused. "My sense of taste is somewhat fatigued. I shall have to ask for a short recess before proceeding further."

There was a sigh from the audience. The tension was not released, it was merely relaxed for a short interval.

Ronar said to the chairman, "I should like a few moments of fresh air. That will restore me. Do you mind?"

"Of course not, Mr. Ronar."

He went outside. Seen through the thin layer of air which surrounded the group of buildings, and the plastic bubble which kept the air from escaping into space, the stars were brilliant and peaceful. The Sun, far away, was like a father star who was too kind to obliterate his children. Strange, he thought, to recall that this was his native satellite. A few years ago it had been a different world. As for himself, he could live just as well outside the bubble as in it, as well in rarefied air as in dense. Suppose he were to tear a hole in the plastic—

Forbidden thoughts. He checked himself, and concentrated on the three cakes and the three contestants.

"You aren't supposed to let personal feelings interfere. You aren't even supposed to know who baked those cakes. But you know, all right. And you can't keep personal feelings from influencing your judgment.

Any one of the cakes is good enough to win. Choose whichever you please, and no one will have a right to criticize. To which are you going to award the prize?

"Number 17? Mrs. Cabanis is, as one of the other women has so aptly termed her, a bitch on wheels. If she wins, she'll be insufferable. And she'll probably make her husband suffer. Not that he doesn't deserve it. Still, he thought he was doing me a favor. Will I be doing him a favor if I have his wife win?

"Number 64, now, is insufferable in her own right. That loving conversation with her husband would probably disgust even human ears. On the other hand, there is this to be said for her winning, it will make the other women furious. To think that a young snip, just married, without real experience in home-making, should walk away with a prize of this kind!

"Ah, but if the idea is to burn them up, why not give the prize to Number 43? They'd be ready to drop dead with chagrin. To think that a mere man should beat them at their own specialty! They'd never be able to hold their heads up again. The man wouldn't feel too happy about it, either. Yes, if it's a matter of getting back at these humans for the things they've done to me, if it's a question of showing them what I really think of them, Number 43 should get it.

"On the other hand, I'm supposed to be a model of fairness. That's why I got the job in the first place. Remember, Ronar? Come on, let's go in and try tasting them again. Eat a mouthful of each cake, much as you hate the stuff. Choose the best on its merits."

They were babbling when he walked in, but the babbling stopped quickly. The chairman said, "Are we ready, Mr. Ronar?"

"All ready."

The three cakes were placed before him. Slowly he took a mouthful of Number 17. Slowly he chewed it and swallowed it. Number 43 followed, then Number 64.

After the third mouthful, he stood lost in thought. One was practically good as another. He could still choose which he pleased.

The assemblage had quieted down. Only the people most concerned whispered nervously.

Mrs. Cabanis, to her psychologist husband: "If I don't win, it'll be your fault. I'll pay you back for this."

The good doctor's fault? Yes, you could figure it that way if you wanted to. If not for Dr. Cabanis, Ronar wouldn't be the judge. If Ronar weren't the judge, Mrs. C. would win, she thought. Hence it was all her husband's fault. Q.E.D.

The male baker to his wife: "If he gives the prize to me, I'll brain him. I should never have entered this."

"It's too late to worry now."

"I could yell 'Fire'," he whispered hopefully. "I could

create a panic that would empty the hall. And then I'd destroy my cake."

"Don't be foolish. And stop whispering."

The young post-honeymooning husband: "You're going to win, dear; I can feel it in my bones."

"Oh, Greg, please don't try to fool me. I've resigned myself to losing."

"You won't lose."

"I'm afraid. Put your arm around me, Greg. Hold me tight. Will you still love me if I lose?"

"Mmmm." He kissed her shoulder. "You know, I didn't fall in love with you for your cooking, sweetheart. You don't have to bake any cakes for me. You're good enough to eat yourself."

"He's right," thought Ronar, as he stared at her. "The man's right. Not in the way he means, but he's right." And suddenly, for one second of decision, Ronar's entire past seemed to flash through his mind.

The young bride never knew why she won first prize.

HALL OF MIRRORS

FREDRIC BROWN (1906–1972)
GALAXY SCIENCE FICTION, DECEMBER

*We all have our favorite types of science fiction; one of
mine is the time paradox story wherein time travel
makes possible an alternate future, enables a person to
meet his or her parents before he or she was born (as in
the current hit movie* Back To The Future*), or involves
a fight in the past, the outcome of which will determine
the "present" (as in the film* The Terminator *or in Fritz
Leiber's "Change War" stories), among many variants.*

*When well executed, this type can be both intellectu-
ally stimulating and profound. The intellectual stimula-
tion derives in large part from the fact that these stories
involve puzzles—as Malcolm Edwards has pointed out,
they can be science fiction's equivalent of mystery fiction's locked-room stories.*

*"Hall of Mirrors" is an outstanding example of the
potential of the type when in the hands of a consum-
mate craftsman like the late Fredric Brown.*

—MHG

*Here's another case where one reads the title, reads
the story, then re-reads the title. In this case, Fred
Brown explains the title, but you might amuse yourself
by asking if it is necessary. Would you have caught the
significance if he had not explained it?*

You can test that if you have never read the story

before. Narrow your eyes so that you can't quite see the print and place a blank piece of paper over the last page of the story so that it hides the final paragraph. Then read to the end of the next to the last paragraph and consider the title. Then read the last paragraph.

I tell you that the properly chosen title is lots of fun. You might ask yourself what you would do.

You might also ask yourself what paradoxes might arise from the situation described by the story.

If you come up with some juicy ones, just remember that it's these paradoxes that are probably the best evidence against the possibility that travel at will, backward and forward in time while not leaving the surface of the Earth, is impossible, even in theory.

However, there are two impossibilities that I find impossible to banish from my own conception of good science fiction. One is time-travel and the other, of course, is faster-than-light travel.

—IA

FOR AN INSTANT you think it is temporary blindness, this sudden dark that comes in the middle of a bright afternoon.

It *must* be blindness, you think; could the sun that was tanning you have gone out instantaneously, leaving you in utter blackness?

Then the nerves of your body tell you that you are *standing*, whereas only a second ago you were sitting comfortably, almost reclining, in a canvas chair. In the patio of a friend's house in Beverly Hills. Talking to Barbara, your fiancée. Looking at Barbara—Barbara in a swimsuit—her skin golden tan in the brilliant sunshine, beautiful.

You wore swimming trunks. Now you do not feel them on you; the slight pressure of the elastic waistband is no longer there against your waist. You touch your hands to your hips. You are naked. And standing.

Whatever has happened to you is more than a change to sudden darkness or to sudden blindness.

You raise your hands gropingly before you. They

touch a plain smooth surface, a wall. You spread them apart and each hand reaches a corner. You pivot slowly. A second wall, then a third, then a door. You are in a closet about four feet square.

Your hand finds the knob of the door. It turns and you push the door open.

There is light now. The door has opened to a lighted room . . . a room that you have never seen before.

It is not large, but it is pleasantly furnished—although the furniture is of a style that is strange to you. Modesty makes you open the door cautiously the rest of the way. But the room is empty of people.

You step into the room, turning to look behind you into the closet, which is now illuminated by light from the room. The closet is and is not a closet; it is the size and shape of one, but it contains nothing, not a single hook, no rod for hanging clothes, no shelf. It is an empty, blank-walled, four-by-four foot space.

You close the door to it and stand looking around the room. It is about twelve by sixteen feet. There is one door, but it is closed. There are no windows. Five pieces of furniture. Four of them you recognize—more or less. One looks like a very functional desk. One is obviously a chair . . . a comfortable-looking one. There is a table, although its top is on several levels instead of only one. Another is a bed, or couch. Something shimmering is lying across it and you walk over and pick the shimmering something up and examine it. It is a garment.

You are naked, so you put it on. Slippers are part way under the bed (or couch) and you slide your feet into them. They fit, and they feel warm and comfortable as nothing you have ever worn on your feet has felt. Like lamb's wool, but softer.

You are dressed now. You look at the door—the only door of the room except that of the closet (closet?) from which you entered it. You walk to the door and before you try the knob, you see the small typewritten sign pasted just above it that reads:

This door has a time lock set to open in one hour.

For reasons you will soon understand, it is better that you do not leave this room before then. There is a letter for you on the desk. Please read it.

It is not signed. You look at the desk and see that there is an envelope lying on it.

You do not yet go to take that envelope from the desk and read the letter that must be in it.

Why not? Because you are frightened.

You see other things about the room. The lighting has no source that you can discover. It comes from nowhere. It is not indirect lighting; the ceiling and the walls are not reflecting it at all.

They didn't have lighting like that, back where you came from. What did you mean by *back where you came from?*

You close your eyes. You tell yourself: *I am Norman Hastings. I am an associate professor of mathematics at the University of Southern California. I am twenty-five years old, and this is the year nineteen hundred and fifty-four.*

You open your eyes and look again.

They didn't use that style of furniture in Los Angeles—or anywhere else that you know of—in 1954. That thing over in the corner—you can't even guess what it is. So might your grandfather, at your age, have looked at a television set.

You look down at yourself, at the shimmering garment that you found waiting for you. With thumb and forefinger you feel its texture.

It's like nothing you've ever touched before.

I am Norman Hastings. This is nineteen hundred and fifty-four.

Suddenly you must know, and at once.

You go to the desk and pick up the envelope that lies upon it. Your name is typed on the outside. *Norman Hastings.*

Your hands shake a little as you open it. Do you blame them?

There are several pages, typewritten. Dear Norman,

it starts. You turn quickly to the end to look for the signature. It is unsigned.

You turn back and start reading.

"Do not be afraid. There is nothing to fear, but much to explain. Much that you must understand before the time lock opens that door. Much that you must accept and—obey.

"You have already guessed that you are in the future—in what, to you, seems to be the future. The clothes and the room must have told you that. I planned it that way so the shock would not be too sudden, so you would realize it over the course of several minutes rather than read it here—and quite probably disbelieve what you read.

"The 'closet' from which you have just stepped is, as you have by now realized, a time machine. From it you stepped into the world of 2004. The date is April 7th, just fifty years from the time you last remember.

"You cannot return.

"I did this to you and you may hate me for it; I do not know. That is up to you to decide, but it does not matter. What does matter, and not to you alone, is another decision which you must make. I am incapable of making it.

"Who is writing this to you? I would rather not tell you just yet. By the time you have finished reading this, even though it is not signed (for I knew you would look first for a signature), I will not need to tell you who I am. You will know.

"I am seventy-five years of age. I have, in this year 2004, been studying 'time' for thirty of those years. I have completed the first time machine ever built—and thus far, its construction, even the fact that it has been constructed, is my own secret.

"You have just participated in the first major experiment. It will be your responsibility to decide whether there shall ever be any more experiments with it, whether it should be given to the world, or whether it should be destroyed and never used again."

End of the first page. You look up for a moment,

hesitating to turn the next page. Already you suspect what is coming.

You turn the page.

"I constructed the first time machine a week ago. My calculations had told me that it would work, but not how it would work. I had expected it to send an object back in time—it works backward in time only, not forward—physically unchanged and intact.

"My first experiment showed me my error. I placed a cube of metal in the machine—it was a miniature of the one you just walked out of—and set the machine to go backward ten years. I flicked the switch and opened the door, expecting to find the cube vanished. Instead I found it had crumbled to powder.

"I put in another cube and sent it two years back. The second cube came back unchanged, except that it was newer, shinier.

"That gave me the answer. I had been expecting the cubes to go back in time, and they had done so, but not in the sense I had expected them to. Those metal cubes had been fabricated about three years previously. I had sent the first one back years before it had existed in its fabricated form. Ten years ago it had been ore. The machine returned it to that state.

"Do you see how our previous theories of time travel have been wrong? We expected to be able to step into a time machine in, say, 2004, set it for fifty years back, and then step out in the year 1954 . . . but it does not work that way. The machine does not move in time. Only whatever is within the machine is affected, and then just with relation to itself and not to the rest of the Universe.

"I confirmed this with guinea pigs by sending one six weeks old five weeks back and it came out a baby.

"I need not outline all my experiments here. You will find a record of them in the desk and you can study it later.

"Do you understand now what has happened to you, Norman?"

You begin to understand. And you begin to sweat.

The *I* who wrote that letter you are now reading is *you*, yourself at the age of seventy-five, in the year of 2004. You are that seventy-five-year-old man, with your body returned to what it had been fifty years ago, with all the memories of fifty years of living wiped out.

You invented the time machine.

And before you used it on yourself, you made these arrangements to help you orient yourself. You wrote yourself the letter which you are now reading.

But if those fifty years are—to you—gone, what of all your friends, those you loved? What of your parents? What of the girl you are going—were going—to marry?

You read on:

"Yes, you will want to know what has happened. Mom died in 1963. Dad in 1968. You married Barbara in 1956. I am sorry to tell you that she died only three years later, in a plane crash. You have one son. He is still living: his name is Walter; he is now forty-six years old and is an accountant in Kansas City."

Tears come into your eyes and for a moment you can no longer read. Barbara dead—dead for forty-five years. And only minutes ago, in subjective time, you were sitting next to her, sitting in the bright sun in a Beverly Hills patio. . . .

You force yourself to read again.

"But back to the discovery. You begin to see some of its implications. You will need time to think to see all of them.

"It does not permit time travel as we have thought of time travel, but it gives us immortality of a sort. Immortality of the kind I have temporarily given us.

"*Is it good?* Is it worthwhile to lose the memory of fifty years of one's life in order to return one's body to relative youth? The only way I can find out is to try, as soon as I have finished writing this and made my other preparations.

"You will know the answer.

"But before you decide, remember that there is another problem, more important than the psychological one. I mean overpopulation.

"If our discovery is given to the world, if all who are old or dying can make themselves young again, the population will almost double every generation. Nor would the world—not even our own relatively enlightened country—be willing to accept compulsory birth control as a solution.

"Give this to the world, as the world is today in 2004, and within a generation there will be famine, suffering, war. Perhaps a complete collapse of civilization.

"Yes, we have reached other planets, but they are not suitable for colonizing. The stars may be our answer, but we are a long way from reaching them. When we do, someday, the billions of habitable planets that must be out there will be our answer . . . our living room. But until then, what is the answer?

"Destroy the machine? But think of the countless lives it can save, the suffering it can prevent. Think of what it would mean to a man dying of cancer. Think. . . ."

Think. You finish the letter and put it down.

You think of Barbara dead for forty-five years. And of the fact that you were married to her for three years and that those years are lost to you.

Fifty years lost. You damn the old man of seventy-five whom you became and who has done this to you . . . who has given you this decision to make.

Bitterly, you know what the decision must be. You think that *he* knew, too, and realize that he could safely leave it in your hands. Damn him, he *should* have known.

Too valuable to destroy, too dangerous to give.

The other answer is painfully obvious.

You must be custodian of this discovery and keep it secret until it is safe to give, until mankind has expanded to the stars and has new worlds to populate, or until, even without that, he has reached a state of civilization where he can avoid overpopulation by rationing births to the number of accidental—or voluntary—deaths.

If neither of those things has happened in another fifty years (and are they likely so soon?), then you, at seventy-five, will be writing another letter like this one. You will be undergoing another experience similar to the one you're going through now. And making the same decision, of course.

Why not? You'll be the same person again.

Time and again, to preserve this secret until Man is ready for it.

How often will you again sit at a desk like this one, thinking the thoughts you are thinking now, feeling the grief you now feel?

There is a click at the door and you know that the time lock has opened, that you are now free to leave this room, free to start a new life for yourself in place of the one you have already lived and lost.

But you are in no hurry now to walk directly through that door.

You sit there, staring straight ahead of you blindly, seeing in your mind's eye the vista of a set of facing mirrors, like those in an old-fashioned barber shop, reflecting the same thing over and over again, diminishing into far distance.

IT'S A GOOD LIFE

JEROME BIXBY (1923–   )
STAR SCIENCE FICTION STORIES 2

This series is dedicated to bringing you the very best (at least in our opinion) science fiction of the past. We don't care how many times a story has been reprinted, and we don't care how famous or unknown the writer may be—if it is truly excellent and has stood the test of time (and if we have room for it), we include it. "It's a Good Life" is one of the most heavily reprinted stories in science fiction, and the subject of a very good Twilight Zone episode—and it remains a wonderful, frightening story of the casualness and abuse of power. It was one of our easiest choices for the best of 1953.

Its author, Jerome Bixby, is a solid professional writer who has produced hundreds upon hundreds of stories, only a small fraction of them sf and fantasy. He also contributed to our field as an editor, working for several magazine chains, including Galaxy publications and Planet Stories. In addition, he has worked frequently in Hollywood as a screen and television writer. The best of his short science fiction can be found in Space By The Tale, *a book that richly deserves to be back in print.*

"It's a Good Life" first appeared in the second volume of Frederik Pohl's excellent Star *series of original sf stories.*

—MHG

*There are a number of science fiction writers who are
known very largely for a single story, even though they
may have written a number. I can well imagine that the
writer in question gets tired of hearing that one story
thrown at his head forever; and Jerry Bixby may well
have reached the point where he turns and snarls at
anyone who refers to "It's a Good Life."*

*I sympathize, Jerry, I sympathize—but you wrote
this story, and it's so far and away the best thing you've
ever done (well, in my opinion, anyway) that what can
any of us do?*

*It's too bad that some of you aren't approaching this
story for the first time. I can't help but think, you see,
that you've all read it, or seen its television version, and
you all know what it's about. If you hadn't read it, I
would be able to ask you to imagine what the most
frightening thing in the world might possibly be; what
situation would reduce you to complete and utter help-
lessness. Whatever you guess (provided you haven't
read the story) I'm sure Jerry will have gone you one
better.*

*And you'll realize the double meaning in the title,
and the importance of the underlining. (All right, so
I'm a nut on titles. If you studied them as carefully as I
have done, you'd be, too.)*

—IA

AUNT AMY WAS OUT on the front porch, rocking back and
forth in the highbacked chair and fanning herself, when
Bill Soames rode his bicycle up the road and stopped in
front of the house.

Perspiring under the afternoon "sun," Bill lifted the
box of groceries out of the big basket over the front
wheel of the bike, and came up the front walk.

Little Anthony was sitting on the lawn, playing with a
rat. He had caught the rat down in the basement—he
had made it think that it smelled cheese, the most
rich-smelling and crumbly-delicious cheese a rat had
ever thought it smelled, and it had come out of its hole,

and now Anthony had hold of it with his mind and was making it do tricks.

When the rat saw Bill Soames coming, it tried to run, but Anthony thought at it, and it turned a flip-flop on the grass, and lay trembling, its eyes gleaming in small black terror.

Bill Soames hurried past Anthony and reached the front steps, mumbling. He always mumbled when he came to the Fremont house, or passed by it, or even thought of it. Everybody did. They thought about silly things, things that didn't mean very much, like two-and-two-is-four-and-twice-is-eight and so on; they tried to jumble up their thoughts and keep them skipping back and forth, so Anthony couldn't read their minds. The mumbling helped. Because if Anthony got anything strong out of your thoughts, he might take a notion to do something about it—like curing your wife's sick headaches or your kid's mumps, or getting your old milk cow back on schedule, or fixing the privy. And while Anthony mightn't actually mean any harm, he couldn't be expected to have much notion of what was the right thing to do in such cases.

That was if he liked you. He might try to help you, in his way. And that could be pretty horrible.

If he didn't like you . . . well, that could be worse.

Bill Soames set the box of groceries on the porch railing, and stopped his mumbling long enough to say, "Everythin' you wanted, Miss Amy."

"Oh, fine, William," Amy Fremont said lightly. "My, ain't it terrible hot today?"

Bill Soames almost cringed. His eyes pleaded with her. He shook his head violently *no*, and then interrupted his mumbling again, though obviously he didn't want to: "Oh, don't say that, Miss Amy . . . it's fine, just fine. A real *good* day!"

Amy Fremont got up from the rocking chair, and came across the porch. She was a tall woman, thin, a smiling vacancy in her eyes. About a year ago, Anthony had gotten mad at her, because she'd told him he shouldn't have turned the cat into a cat-rug, and al-

though he had always obeyed her more than anyone
else, which was hardly at all, this time he'd snapped at
her. With his mind. And that had been the end of Amy
Fremont's bright eyes, and the end of Amy Fremont as
everyone had known her. And that was when word got
around in Peaksville (population: 46) that even the members of Anthony's own family weren't safe. After that,
everyone was twice as careful.

Someday Anthony might undo what he'd done to
Aunt Amy. Anthony's Mom and Pop hoped he would.
When he was older, and maybe sorry. If it was possible, that is. Because Aunt Amy had changed a lot, and
besides, now Anthony wouldn't obey anyone.

"Land alive, William," Aunt Amy said, "you don't
have to mumble like that. Anthony wouldn't hurt you.
My goodness, Anthony likes you!" She raised her voice
and called to Anthony, who had tired of the rat and was
making it eat itself. "Don't you, dear? Don't you like
Mr. Soames?"

Anthony looked across the lawn at the grocery man—a
bright, wet, purple gaze. He didn't say anything. Bill
Soames tried to smile at him. After a second Anthony
returned his attention to the rat. It had already devoured its tail, or at least chewed it off—for Anthony
had made it bite faster than it could swallow, and little
pink and red furry pieces lay around it on the green
grass. Now the rat was having trouble reaching its
hindquarters.

Mumbling silently, thinking of nothing in particular
as hard as he could, Bill Soames went stiff-legged down
the walk, mounted his bicycle and pedaled off.

"We'll see you tonight, William," Aunt Amy called
after him.

As Bill Soames pumped the pedals, he was wishing
deep down that he could pump twice as fast, to get
away from Anthony all the faster, and away from Aunt
Amy, who sometimes just forgot how *careful* you had to
be. And he shouldn't have thought that. Because Anthony caught it. He caught the desire to get away from
the Fremont house as if it was something *bad*, and his

purple gaze blinked, and he snapped a small, sulky thought after Bill Soames—just a small one, because he was in a good mood today, and besides, he liked Bill Soames, or at least didn't dislike him, at least today. Bill Soames wanted to go away—so, petulantly, Anthony helped him.

Pedaling with superhuman speed—or rather, appearing to, because in reality the bicycle was pedaling *him*— Bill Soames vanished down the road in a cloud of dust, his thin, terrified wail drifting back across the summer-like heat.

Anthony looked at the rat. It had devoured half its belly, and had died from pain. He thought it into a grave out deep in the cornfield—his father had once said, smiling, that he might as well do that with the things he killed—and went around the house, casting his odd shadow in the hot, brassy light from above.

In the kitchen, Aunt Amy was unpacking the groceries. She put the Mason-jarred goods on the shelves, and the meat and milk in the icebox, and the beet sugar and coarse flour in big cans under the sink. She put the cardboard box in the corner, by the door, for Mr. Soames to pick up next time he came. It was stained and battered and torn and worn fuzzy, but it was one of the few left in Peaksville. In faded red letters it said *Campbell's Soup*. The last cans of soup, or of anything else, had been eaten long ago, except for a small communal hoard which the villagers dipped into for special occasions—but the box lingered on, like a coffin, and when it and the other boxes were gone, the men would have to make some out of wood.

Aunt Amy went out in back, where Anthony's Mom— Aunt Amy's sister—sat in the shade of the house, shelling peas. The peas, every time Mom ran a finger along a pod, went *lollop-lollop-lollop* into the pan on her lap.

"William brought the groceries," Aunt Amy said. She sat down wearily in the straightbacked chair beside Mom, and began fanning herself again. She wasn't really old; but ever since Anthony had snapped at her with his mind, something had seemed to be wrong with her body as well as her mind, and she was tired all the time.

"Oh, good," said Mom. *Lollop* went the fat peas into the pan.

Everybody in Peaksville always said "Oh, fine," or "Good," or "Say, that's swell!" when almost anything happened or was mentioned—even unhappy things like accidents or even deaths. They'd always say "Good," because if they didn't try to cover up how they really felt, Anthony might overhear with his mind, and then nobody knew what might happen. Like the time Mrs. Kent's husband, Sam, had come walking back from the graveyard, because Anthony liked Mrs. Kent and had heard her mourning.

Lollop.

"Tonight's television night," said Aunt Amy. "I'm glad. I look forward to it so much every week. I wonder what we'll see tonight."

"Did Bill bring the meat?" asked Mom.

"Yes." Aunt Amy fanned herself, looking up at the featureless brassy glare of the sky. "Goodness, it's so hot! I wish Anthony would make it just a little cooler—"

"*Amy!*"

"Oh!" Mom's sharp tone had penetrated, where Bill Soames' agonized expression had failed. Aunt Amy put one thin hand to her mouth in exaggerated alarm. "Oh . . . I'm sorry, dear." Her pale blue eyes shuttled around, right and left, to see if Anthony was in sight. Not that it would make any difference if he was or wasn't—he didn't have to be near you to know what you were thinking. Usually, though, unless he had his attention on somebody, he would be occupied with thoughts of his own.

But some things attracted his attention—you could never be sure just what.

"This weather's just *fine*," Mom said.

Lollop.

"Oh, yes," Aunt Amy said. "It's a wonderful day. I wouldn't want it changed for the world!"

Lollop.

Lollop.

"What time is it?" Mom asked.

Aunt Amy was sitting where she could see through the kitchen window to the alarm clock on the shelf above the stove. "Four-thirty," she said.

Lollop.

"I want tonight to be something special," Mom said. "Did Bill bring a good lean roast?"

"Good and lean, dear. They butchered just today, you know, and sent us over the best piece."

"Dan Hollis will be *so* surprised when he finds out that tonight's television party is a birthday party for him too!"

"Oh *I* think he will! Are you sure nobody's told him?"

" Everybody swore they wouldn't."

"That'll be real nice," Aunt Amy nodded, looking off across the cornfield. "A birthday party."

"Well—" Mom put the pan of peas down beside her, stood up and brushed her apron. "I'd better get the roast on. Then we can set the table." She picked up the peas.

Anthony came around the corner of the house. He didn't look at them, but continued on down through the carefully kept garden—*all* the gardens in Peaksville were carefully kept, very carefully kept—and went past the rusting, useless hulk that had been the Fremont family car, and went smoothly over the fence and out into the cornfield.

"Isn't this a lovely day!" said Mom, a little loudly, as they went toward the back door.

Aunt Amy fanned herself. "A beautiful day, dear. Just *fine!*"

Out in the cornfield, Anthony walked between the tall, rustling rows of green stalks. He liked to smell the corn. The alive corn overhead, and the old dead corn underfoot. Rich Ohio earth, thick with weeds and brown, dry-rotting ears of corn, pressed between his bare toes with every step—he had made it rain last night so everything would smell and feel nice today.

He walked clear to the edge of the cornfield, and over to where a grove of shadowy green trees covered cool, moist, dark ground, and lots of leafy undergrowth, and jumbled moss-covered rocks, and a small spring that made a clear, clean pool. Here Anthony liked to rest and watch the birds and insects, and small animals that rustled and scampered and chirped about. He liked to lie on the cool ground and look up through the moving greenness overhead, and watch the insects flit in the hazy soft sunbeams that stood like slanting, glowing bars between ground and treetops. Somehow, he liked the thoughts of the little creatures in this place better than the thoughts outside; and while the thoughts he picked up here weren't very strong or very clear, he could get enough out of them to know what the little creatures liked and wanted, and he spent a lot of time making the grove more like what they wanted it to be. The spring hadn't always been here; but one time he had found thirst in one small furry mind, and had brought subterranean water to the surface in a clear cold flow, and had watched blinking as the creature drank, feeling its pleasure. Later he had made the pool, when he found a small urge to swim.

He had made rocks and trees and bushes and caves, and sunlight here and shadows there, because he had felt in all the tiny minds around him the desire—or the instinctive want—for this kind of resting place, and that kind of mating place, and this kind of place to play, and that kind of home.

And somehow the creatures from all the fields and pastures around the grove had seemed to know that this was a good place, for there were always more of them coming in—every time Anthony came out here there were more creatures than the last time, and more desires and needs to be tended to. Every time there would be some kind of creature he had never seen before, and he would find its mind, and see what it wanted, and then give it to it.

He liked to help them. He liked to feel their simple gratification.

Today, he rested beneath a thick elm, and lifted his purple gaze to a red and black bird that had just come to the grove. It twittered on a branch over his head, and hopped back and forth, and thought its tiny thoughts, and Anthony made a big, soft nest for it, and pretty soon it hopped in.

A long, brown, sleek-furred animal was drinking at the pool. Anthony found its mind next. The animal was thinking about a smaller creature that was scurrying along the ground on the other side of the pool, grubbing for insects. The little creature didn't know that it was in danger. The long, brown animal finished drinking and tensed its legs to leap, and Anthony thought it into a grave in the cornfield.

He didn't like those kinds of thoughts. They reminded him of the thoughts outside the grove. A long time ago some of the people outside had thought that way about *him*, and one night they'd hidden and waited for him to come back from the grove—and he'd just thought them all into the cornfield. Since then, the rest of the people hadn't thought that way—at least, very clearly. Now their thoughts were all mixed up and confusing whenever they thought about him or near him, so he didn't pay much attention.

He liked to help them, too, sometimes—but it wasn't simple, or very gratifying either. They never thought happy thoughts when he did—just the jumble. So he spent more time out here.

He watched all the birds and insects and furry creatures for a while, and played with a bird, making it soar and dip and streak madly around tree trunks until, accidentally, when another bird caught his attention for a moment, he ran it into a rock. Petulantly, he thought the rock into a grave in the cornfield; but he couldn't do anything more with the bird. Not because it was dead, though it was; but because it had a broken wing. So he went back to the house. He didn't feel like walking back through the cornfield, so he just *went* to the house, right down into the basement.

It was nice down here. Nice and dark and damp and

sort of fragrant, because once Mom had been making preserves in a rack along the far wall, and then she'd stopped coming down ever since Anthony had started spending time here, and the preserves had spoiled and leaked down and spread over the dirt floor, and Anthony liked the smell.

He caught another rat, making it smell cheese, and after he played with it, he thought it into a grave right beside the long animal he'd killed in the grove. Aunt Amy hated rats, and so he killed a lot of them, because he liked Aunt Amy most of all and sometimes did things that Aunt Amy wanted. Her mind was more like the little furry minds out in the grove. She hadn't thought anything bad at all about him for a long time.

After the rat, he played with a big black spider in the corner under the stairs, making it run back and forth until its web shook and shimmered in the light from the cellar window like a reflection in silvery water. Then he drove fruit flies into the web until the spider was frantic trying to wind them all up. The spider liked flies, and its thoughts were stronger than theirs, so he did it. There was something bad in the way it liked flies, but it wasn't clear—and besides, Aunt Amy hated flies too.

He heard footsteps overhead—Mom moving around in the kitchen. He blinked his purple gaze, and almost decided to make her hold still—but instead he *went* up to the attic, and, after looking out the circular window at the front end of the long V-roofed room for a while at the front lawn and the dusty road and Henderson's tip-waving wheatfield beyond, he curled into an unlikely shape and went partly to sleep.

Soon people would be coming for television, he heard Mom think.

He went more to sleep. He liked television night. Aunt Amy had always liked television a lot, so one time he had thought some for her, and a few other people had been there at the time, and Aunt Amy had felt disappointed when they wanted to leave. He'd done something to them for that—and now everybody came to television.

He liked all the attention he got when they did.

Anthony's father came home around six-thirty, look-ing tired and dirty and bloody. He'd been over in Dun's pasture with the other men, helping pick out the cow to be slaughtered this month and doing the job, and then butchering the meat and salting it away in Soames' icehouse. Not a job he cared for, but every man had his turn. Yesterday, he had helped scythe down old McIntyre's wheat. Tomorrow, they would start threshing. By hand. Everything in Peaksville had to be done by hand.

He kissed his wife on the cheek and sat down at the kitchen table. He smiled and said, "Where's Anthony?"

"Around someplace," Mom said.

Aunt Amy was over at the wood-burning stove, stir-ring the big pot of peas. Mom went back to the oven and opened it and basted the roast.

"Well, it's been a *good* day," Dad said. By rote. Then he looked at the mixing bowl and breadboard on the table. He sniffed at the dough. "M'm," he said. "I could eat a loaf all by myself, I'm so hungry."

"No one told Dan Hollis about its being a birthday party, did they?" his wife asked.

"Nope. We kept as quiet as mummies."

"We've fixed up such a lovely surprise!"

"Um? What?"

"Well . . . you know how much Dan likes music. Well, last week Thelma Dunn found a *record* in her attic!"

"No!"

"Yes! And we had Ethel sort of ask—you know, with-out really *asking*—if he had that one. And he said no. Isn't that a wonderful surprise?"

"Well, now, it sure is. A record, imagine! That's a real nice thing to find! What record is it?"

"Perry Como, singing *You Are My Sunshine*."

'Well, I'll be darned. I always liked that tune." Some raw carrots were lying on the table. Dad picked up a small one, scrubbed it on his chest, and took a bite. "How did Thelma happen to find it?"

"Oh, you know—just looking around for new things."

"M'm." Dad chewed the carrot. "Say, who has that picture we found a while back? I kind of liked it—that old clipper sailing along——"

"The Smiths. Next week the Sipichs get it, and they give the Smiths old McIntyre's music-box, and we give the Sipichs——" and she went down the tentative order of things that would exchange hands among the women at church this Sunday.

He nodded. "Looks like we can't have the picture for a while, I guess. Look, honey, you might try to get that detective book back from the Reillys. I was so busy the week we had it, I never got to finish all the stories——"

"I'll try," his wife said doubtfully. "But I hear the van Husens have a stereoscope they found in the cellar." Her voice was just a little accusing. "They had it two whole months before they told anybody about it——"

"Say," Dad said, looking interested. "That'd be nice, too. Lots of pictures?"

"I suppose so. I'll see on Sunday. I'd like to have it—but we still owe the van Husens for their canary. I don't know why that bird had to pick *our* house to die . . . it must have been sick when we got it. Now there's just no satisfying Betty van Husen—she even hinted she'd like our *piano* for a while!"

"Well, honey, you try for the stereoscope—or just anything you think we'll like." At last he swallowed the carrot. It had been a little young and tough. Anthony's whims about the weather made it so that people never knew what crops would come up, or what shape they'd be in if they did. All they could do was plant a lot; and always enough of something came up any one season to live on. Just once there had been a grain surplus; tons of it had been hauled to the edge of Peaksville and dumped off into the nothingness. Otherwise, nobody could have breathed, when it started to spoil.

"You know," Dad went on. "It's nice to have the new things around. It's nice to think that there's probably still a lot of stuff nobody's found yet, in cellars and attics and barns and down behind things. They help, some-how. As much as anything can help——"

"Sh-h!" Mom glanced nervously around.

"Oh," Dad said, smiling hastily. "It's all right! The new things are *good!* It's *nice* to be able to have some-thing around you've never seen before, and know that something you've given somebody else is making them happy . . . that's a real *good* thing."

"A good thing," his wife echoed.

"Pretty soon," Aunt Amy said, from the stove, "there won't be any more new things. We'll have found every-thing there is to find. Goodness, that'll be too bad——"

"*Amy!*"

"Well——" her pale eyes were shallow and fixed, a sign of her recurrent vagueness. "It will be kind of a shame—no new things——"

"Don't *talk* like that," Mom said, trembling. "Amy, be *quiet!*"

"It's *good,*" said Dad, in the loud, familiar, wanting-to-be-overheard tone of voice. "Such talk is *good.* It's okay, honey—don't you see? It's good for Amy to talk any way she wants. It's good for her to feel bad. Every-thing's good. Everything *has* to be good. . . ."

Anthony's mother was pale. And so was Aunt Amy—the peril of the moment had suddenly penetrated the clouds surrounding her mind. Sometimes it was diffi-cult to handle words so that they might not prove disastrous. You just never *knew.* There were so many things it was wise not to say, or even think—but re-monstration for saying or thinking them might be just as bad, if Anthony heard and decided to do anything about it. You could just never tell what Anthony was liable to do.

Everything had to be good. Had to be fine just as it was, even if it wasn't. Always. Because any change might be worse. So terribly much worse.

"Oh, my goodness, yes, of course it's good," Mom said. "You talk any way you want to, Amy, and it's just fine. Of course, you want to remember that some ways are *better* than others. . . ."

Aunt Amy stirred the peas, fright in her pale eyes.

"Oh, yes," she said. "But I don't feel like talking right now. It . . . it's *good* that I don't feel like talking."

Dad said tiredly, smiling, "I'm going out and wash up."

They started arriving around eight o'clock. By that time, Mom and Aunt Amy had the big table in the dining room set, and two more tables off to the side. The candles were burning, and the chairs situated, and Dad had a big fire going in the fireplace.

The first to arrive were the Sipichs, John and Mary. John wore his best suit, and was well-scrubbed and pink-faced after his day in McIntyre's pasture. The suit was neatly pressed, but getting threadbare at elbows and cuffs. Old McIntyre was working on a loom, designing it out of schoolbooks, but so far it was slow going. McIntyre was a capable man with wood and tools, but a loom was a big order when you couldn't get metal parts. McIntyre had been one of the ones who, at first, had wanted to try to get Anthony to make things the villagers needed, like clothes and canned goods and medical supplies and gasoline. Since then, he felt that what had happened to the whole Terrance family and Joe Kinney was his fault, and he worked hard trying to make it up to the rest of them. And since then, no one had tried to get Anthony to do anything.

Mary Sipich was a small, cheerful woman in a simple dress. She immediately set about helping Mom and Aunt Amy put the finishing touches on the dinner.

The next arrivals were the Smiths and the Dunns, who lived right next to each other down the road, only a few yards from the nothingness. They drove up in the Smiths' wagon, drawn by their old horse.

Then the Reillys showed up, from across the darkened wheatfield, and the evening really began. Pat Reilly sat down at the big upright in the front room, and began to play from the popular sheet music on the rack. He played softly, as expressively as he could—and nobody sang. Anthony liked piano playing a whole lot, but not singing; often he would come up from the basement, or down from the attic, or just *come*, and sit on top of the piano, nodding his head as Pat played *Lover* or *Boulevard of Broken Dreams* or *Night and Day*. He seemed to prefer ballads, sweet-sounding songs—but the one time somebody had started to sing, Anthony had looked over from the top of the piano and done something that made everybody afraid of singing from then on. Later, they'd decided that the piano was what Anthony had heard first, before anybody had ever tried to sing, and now anything else added to it didn't sound right and distracted him from his pleasure.

So, every television night, Pat would play the piano, and that was the beginning of the evening. Wherever Anthony was, the music would make him happy, and put him in a good mood, and he would know that they were gathering for television and waiting for him.

By eight-thirty everybody had shown up, except for the seventeen children and Mrs. Soames who was off watching them in the schoolhouse at the far end of town. The children of Peaksville were never, never allowed near the Fremont house—not since little Fred Smith had tried to play with Anthony on a dare. The younger children weren't even told about Anthony. The others had mostly forgotten about him, or were told that he was a nice, nice goblin but they must never go near him.

Dan and Ethel Hollis came late, and Dan walked in not suspecting a thing. Pat Reilly had played the piano until his hands ached—he'd worked pretty hard with them today—and now he got up, and everybody gathered around to wish Dan Hollis a happy birthday.

"Well, I'll be darned," Dan grinned. "This is swell. I wasn't expecting this at all . . . gosh, this is *swell!*"

They gave him his presents—mostly things they had made by hand, though some were things that people had possessed as their own and now gave him as his. John Sipich gave him a watch charm, hand-carved out of a piece of hickory wood. Dan's watch had broken down a year or so ago, and there was nobody in the village who knew how to fix it, but he still carried it around because it had been his grandfather's and was a fine old heavy thing of gold and silver. He attached the charm to the chain, while everybody laughed and said John had done a nice job of carving. Then Mary Sipich gave him a knitted necktie, which he put on, removing the one he'd worn.

The Reillys gave him a little box they had made, to keep things in. They didn't say what things, but Dan said he'd keep his personal jewelry in it. The Reillys had made it out of a cigar box, carefully peeled of its paper and lined on the inside with velvet. The outside had been polished, and carefully if not expertly carved by Pat—but his carving got complimented too. Dan Hollis received many other gifts—a pipe, a pair of shoelaces, a tie pin, a knit pair of socks, some fudge, a pair of garters made from old suspenders.

He unwrapped each gift with vast pleasure, and wore as many of them as he could right there, even the garters. He lit up the pipe, and said he'd never had a better smoke; which wasn't quite true, because the pipe wasn't broken in yet. Pete Manners had had it lying around ever since he'd received it as a gift four years ago from an out-of-town relative who hadn't known he'd stopped smoking.

Dan put the tobacco into the bowl very carefully. Tobacco was precious. It was only pure luck that Pat Reilly had decided to try to grow some in his backyard just before what had happened to Peaksville had happened. It didn't grow very well, and then they had to cure it and shred it and all, and it was just precious stuff. Everybody in town used wooden holders old McIntyre had made, to save on butts.

Last of all, Thelma Dunn gave Dan Hollis the record she had found.

Dan's eyes misted even before he opened the package. He knew it was a record.

"Gosh," he said softly. "What one is it? I'm almost afraid to look. . . ."

"You haven't got it, darling," Ethel Hollis smiled.

"Don't you remember, I asked about *You Are My Sunshine?*"

"Oh, gosh," Dan said again. Carefully he removed the wrapping and stood there fondling the record, running his big hands over the worn grooves with their tiny, dulling crosswise scratches. He looked around the room, eyes shining, and they all smiled back, knowing how delighted he was.

"Happy birthday, darling!" Ethel said, throwing her arms around him and kissing him.

He clutched the record in both hands, holding it off to one side as she pressed against him. "Hey," he laughed, pulling back his head. "Be careful . . . I'm holding a priceless object!" He looked around again, over his wife's arms, which were still around his neck. His eyes were hungry. "Look . . . do you think we could play it? Lord, what I'd give to hear some new music . . . just the first part, the orchestra part, before Como sings?"

Faces sobered. After a minute, John Sipich said, "I don't think we'd better, Dan. After all, we don't know just where the singer comes in—it'd be taking too much of a chance. Better wait till you get home."

Dan Hollis reluctantly put the record on the buffet with all his other presents. "It's *good*," he said automatically, but disappointedly, "that I can't play it here."

"Oh, yes," said Sipich. "It's good." To compensate for Dan's disappointed tone, he repeated, "It's *good*."

They ate dinner, the candles lighting their smiling faces, and ate it all right down to the last delicious drop of gravy. They complimented Mom and Aunt Amy on the roast beef, and the peas and carrots, and the tender corn on the cob. The corn hadn't come from the Fremont's cornfield, naturally—everybody knew what was out there; and the field was going to weeds.

Then they polished off the dessert—homemade ice cream and cookies. And then they sat back, in the flickering light of the candles, and chatted, waiting for television.

There never was a lot of mumbling on television

night—everybody came and had a good dinner at the Fremonts', and that was nice, and afterwards there was television, and nobody really thought much about that—it just had to be put up with. So it was a pleasant enough get-together, aside from your having to watch what you said just as carefully as you always did everyplace. If a dangerous thought came into your mind, you just started mumbling, even right in the middle of a sentence. When you did that, the others just ignored you until you felt happier again and stopped.

Anthony liked television night. He had done only two or three awful things on television night in the whole past year.

Mom had put a bottle of brandy on the table, and they each had a tiny glass of it. Liquor was even more precious than tobacco. The villagers could make wine, but the grapes weren't right, and certainly the techniques weren't, and it wasn't very good wine. There were only a few bottles of real liquor left in the village— four rye, three Scotch, three brandy, nine real wine and half a bottle of Drambuie belonging to old McIntyre (only for marriages)—and when those were gone, that was it.

Afterward, everybody wished that the brandy hadn't been brought out. Because Dan Hollis drank more of it than he should have, and mixed it with a lot of the homemade wine. Nobody thought anything about it at first, because he didn't show it much outside, and it was his birthday party and a happy party, and Anthony liked these get-togethers and shouldn't see any reason to do anything even if he was listening.

But Dan Hollis got high, and did a fool thing. If they'd seen it coming, they'd have taken him outside and walked him around.

The first thing they knew, Dan stopped laughing right in the middle of the story about how Thelma Dunn had found the Perry Como record and dropped it and it hadn't broken because she'd moved faster than she ever had before in her life and caught it. He was fondling the record again, and looking longingly at the

Fremonts' gramophone over in the corner, and suddenly he stopped laughing and his face got slack, and then it got ugly, and he said, "Oh, *Christ!*"

Immediately the room was still. So still they could hear the whirring movement of the grandfather's clock out in the hall. Pat Reilly had been playing the piano, softly. He stopped, his hands poised over the yellowed keys.

The candles on the dining-room table flickered in a cool breeze that blew through the lace curtains over the bay window.

"Keep playing, Pat," Anthony's father said softly.

Pat started again. He played *Night and Day*, but his eyes were sidewise on Dan Hollis, and he missed notes.

Dan stood in the middle of the room, holding the record. In his other hand he held a glass of brandy so hard his hand shook.

They were all looking at him.

"*Christ*," he said again, and he made it sound like a dirty word.

Reverend Younger, who had been talking with Mom and Aunt Amy by the dining-room door, said "Christ" too—but he was using it in a prayer. His hands were clasped, and his eyes were closed.

John Sipich moved forward. "Now, Dan . . . it's *good* for you to talk that way. But you don't want to talk too much, you know."

Dan shook off the hand Sipich put on his arm.

"Can't even play my record," he said loudly. He looked down at the record, and then around at their faces. "Oh, my *God*. . . ."

He threw the glassful of brandy against the wall. It splattered and ran down the wallpaper in streaks.

Some of the women gasped.

"Dan," Sipich said in a whisper. "Dan, cut it out——"

Pat Reilly was playing *Night and Day* louder, to cover up the sounds of the talk. It wouldn't do any good, though, if Anthony was listening.

Dan Hollis went over to the piano and stood by Pat's shoulder, swaying a little.

"Pat," he said. "Don't play *that*. Play *this*." And he began to sing. Softly, hoarsely, miserably: "Happy birthday to me . . . Happy birthday to me. . . ."

"*Dan!*" Ethel Hollis screamed. She tried to run across the room to him. Mary Sipich grabbed her arm and held her back. "Dan," Ethel screamed again. "Stop——"

"My God, be quiet!" hissed Mary Sipich, and pushed her toward one of the men, who put his hand over her mouth and held her still.

"——Happy birthday, dear Danny," Dan sang. "Happy birthday to me!" He stopped and looked down at Pat Reilly. "Play it, Pat. Play it, so I can sing right . . . you know I can't carry a tune unless somebody plays it!"

Pat Reilly put his hands on the keys and began *Lover*—in a slow waltz tempo, the way Anthony liked it. Pat's face was white. His hands fumbled.

Dan Hollis stared over at the dining-room door. At Anthony's mother, and at Anthony's father who had gone to join her.

"*You* had him," he said. Tears gleamed on his cheeks as the candlelight caught them. "*You* had to go and *have* him. . . ."

He closed his eyes, and the tears squeezed out. He sang loudly. "You are my sunshine . . . my only sunshine . . . you make me happy . . . when I am blue. . . ."

Anthony *came* into the room.

Pat stopped playing. He froze. Everybody froze. The breeze rippled the curtains. Ethel Hollis couldn't even try to scream—she had fainted.

"Please don't take my sunshine . . . away. . . ." Dan's voice faltered into silence. His eyes widened. He put both hands out in front of him, the empty glass in one, the record in the other. He hiccupped, and said, "*No*——"

"Bad man," Anthony said, and thought Dan Hollis into something like nothing anyone would have believed possible, and then he thought the thing into a grave deep, deep in the cornfield.

The glass and record thumped on the rug. Neither broke.

Anthony's purple gaze went around the room.

Some of the people began mumbling. They all tried to smile. The sound of mumbling filled the room like a far-off approval. Out of the murmuring came one or two clear voices:

"Oh, it's a very *good* thing," said John Sipich.

"A good thing," said Anthony's father, smiling. He'd had more practice in smiling than most of them. "A wonderful thing."

"It's swell . . . just swell," said Pat Reilly, tears leaking from eyes and nose, and he began to play the piano again, softly, his trembling hands feeling for *Night and Day*.

Anthony climbed up on top of the piano, and Pat played for two hours.

Afterward, they watched television. They all went into the front room, and lit just a few candles, and pulled up chairs around the set. It was a small-screen set, and they couldn't all sit close enough to it to see, but that didn't matter. They didn't even turn the set on. It wouldn't have worked anyway, there being no electricity in Peaksville.

They just sat silently, and watched the twisting, writhing shapes on the screen, and listened to the sounds that came out of the speaker, and none of them had any idea of what it was all about. They never did. It was always the same.

"It's real nice," Aunt Amy said once, her pale eyes on the meaningless flickers and shadows. "But I liked it a little better when there were cities outside and we could get real——"

"Why, Amy!" said Mom. "It's good for you to say such a thing. Very good. But how can you mean it? Why, this television is *much* better than anything we ever used to get!"

"Yes," chimed in John Sipich. "It's fine. It's the best show we've ever seen!"

He sat on the couch, with two other men, holding Ethel Hollis flat against the cushions, holding her arms and legs and putting their hands over her mouth, so she couldn't start screaming again.

"It's really *good!*" he said again.

Mom looked out of the front window, across the darkened road, across Henderson's darkened wheat field to the vast, endless, gray nothingness in which the little village of Peaksville floated like a soul—the huge nothingness that was most evident at night, when Anthony's brassy day had gone.

It did no good to wonder where they were . . . no good at all. Peaksville was just someplace. Someplace away from the world. It was wherever it had been since that day three years ago when Anthony had crept from her womb and old Doc Bates—God rest him—had screamed and dropped him and tried to kill him, and Anthony had whined and done the thing. Had taken the village someplace. Or had destroyed the world and left only the village, nobody knew which.

It did no good to wonder about it. Nothing at all did any good—except to live as they must live. Must always, always live, if Anthony would let them.

These thoughts were dangerous, she thought.

She began to mumble. The others started mumbling too. They had all been thinking, evidently.

The men on the couch whispered and whispered to Ethel Hollis, and when they took their hands away, she mumbled too.

While Anthony sat on top of the set and made television, they sat around and mumbled and watched the meaningless, flickering shapes far into the night.

Next day it snowed, and killed off half the crops—but it was a *good* day.